SEEKING
HIDDEN
TREASURES

"Hidden Treasures" indeed! This extraordinary collection of "curious tales and essays," is full of them. In a lively, refreshing, new voice, James Magner creates humorous, heartwarming stories and personal essays—with tantalizingly complex plots that would give Edgar Allan Poe pause. Steeped in science and math, Magner is a physician with a passionate interest in many fields: American history, the great philosophers (past and present), texts of the Old & New Testaments, world religion, puzzles, anagrams, and enigmas. He has won chess tournaments and has won big in poker at a major Las Vegas tournament. These fascinating "tales and essays" celebrate a love of learning and a passion for knowledge. If your reading tastes bend toward intellectual challenge, you will revel in Magner's mastery.

— Leonard Engel, Professor Emeritus of English, Quinnipiac Univ, edited *A Violent Conscience: Essays on the Fiction of James Lee Burke* (McFarland, 2010) and *New Essays on Clint Eastwood* (Univ of Utah, 2012)

ALSO BY JAMES MAGNER:

Chess Juggler: Balancing Career, Family and Chess in the Modern World (Russell Enterprises, Inc., Milford, CT, 2011)

Free to Decide: Building a Life in Science and Medicine (Russell Enterprises, Inc., Milford, CT, 2015)

SEEKING HIDDEN TREASURES

A Collection of Curious Tales and Essays

JAMES MAGNER, MD

ARCHWAY
PUBLISHING

Archway Publishing books may be ordered through booksellers or by contacting:

Archway Publishing
1663 Liberty Drive
Bloomington, IN 47403
www.archwaypublishing.com
1 (888) 242-5904

ISBN: 978-1-4808-9338-2 (sc)
ISBN: 978-1-4808-9337-5 (hc)
ISBN: 978-1-4808-9339-9 (e)

Library of Congress Control Number: 2020913300

Print information available on the last page.

Archway Publishing rev. date: 08/06/2020

To my wife, Glenda, who provided advice and encouragement. My daughters and sons-in-law, Erin and Mike and Carly and Russ, were supportive. My two young grandchildren, Beverly and Remington, provided inspiration.

In Memoriam: John Caputo (1951 – 2019)
A kind man, and a poker buddy of mine who frequently played at Foxwoods Casino

In Memoriam: Lewis E. Braverman, MD (1929 – 2019)
A giant in thyroid science who loved good stories

CONTENTS

PREFACE TO THE SECOND EDITION

Updating a previously published book is not merely an exercise in vanity, though there can be a few corrections needed. Chasing annoying typos should not be the main purpose, however. I'm a physician and scientist, so throughout my career I've seen that new data and novel thinking compel medical and scientific textbooks to go through many editions. But my work on these pages is not strictly science. I provide fiction that contains some scientific elements as well as opinion. Still, given the general concept of issuing a second edition, examples from the scientific world provide insights.

As a young teenager I frequently read science fiction, and a favorite author was Isaac Asimov, who was also a serious scientist. He once shared in an essay that he felt immense pride and satisfaction as a young academic in Boston in 1952, when his new textbook of biochemistry, co-authored with B. Walker and W. Boyd, finally was completed and released for use. This was quickly followed by shock and surprise when the next month his publisher, Williams & Wilkins, sent him a copy of his precious textbook that seemed to be more than twice as thick when he first hefted it in his hand. A cover letter explained to the deflated Dr. Asimov that it was now time to start the year-long task of writing the next edition. To help authors in this situation, the publisher was providing a copy of the book in which each printed page alternated with two blank pages on which to write corrections and other new text. It turned out, I believe, that

Asimov was so broadly engaged with new ideas and projects that he never wrote an updated edition. (His biochemistry text was his eighth published book, but he eventually went on to publish a total of 468 books.) His brilliant textbook was soon eclipsed by newer books prepared by others. Since my stories are more fiction than science, fortunately I was not under a severe threat of obsolescence.

Darwin was in an analogous but somewhat different position after publication of *On the Origin of Species* in 1859. By the way, the correct full title of this work as published by John Murray, Albemarle Street, London was *On the Origin of Species by Means of Natural Selection, or the Preservation of Favoured Races in the Struggle for Life.* The book was widely read and went through many printings. But through the years Darwin did not just authorize new printings. He also changed the text substantially to create new editions. Though even in the first edition he anticipated objections to his theory and rebutted them preemptively, in subsequent editions he added arguments, corrections, and clarifications. For example, in the sixth edition he added a new chapter of about forty pages entitled, "Miscellaneous Objections to the Theory of Natural Selection." He also found it necessary to alter some of his ideas. Of course, his key, brilliant insights have been borne out.

My little book certainly pales in comparison to *On the Origin of Species.* Yes, I did have the intent to inform readers about certain scientific concepts (such as genetically proven breeding between *Neandertals* and *Homo sapiens*) and actual events (such as the clever smuggling scheme used by a Jewish chemistry professor to sneak assets out of Nazi-occupied Vienna). I also included some Christian elements to stimulate reflection because I believe that our modern secular society in the West values too little the importance of a mature spiritual life. But my main goal, unlike Darwin's, was merely to provide thoughtful entertainment.

Perhaps the most heartwarming (and mildly humorous) example of the production of a second edition, or more precisely a second full and different book, is the case of the eminent philosopher, Mortimer J. Adler. Born in 1902, he published in 1977 his carefully constructed autobiography, *Philosopher at Large*. He had many accomplishments to discuss and ideas to communicate, but he had no suspicion that he would remain healthy and active for decades more. In 1992, he published another autobiography, *A Second Look in the Rearview Mirror: Further Autobiographical Reflections of a Philosopher at Large*, in which he commented that he had written his first autobiography prematurely. He died in 2001, at age 98. Not to be outdone by Adler, I also published a memoir in 2015, and my goal is to have the need of publishing additional memoirs!

I prepared this second edition because I had new ideas I wanted to share, and it seemed appropriate to put most of my fiction works and essays together in one convenient place. This Preface and five new chapters have been added. Even one of my personal heroes, the mathematician and philosopher Martin Gardner, found it advisable to correct typos, add comments, and provide clarifications in a second edition of his much discussed book, *The Whys of a Philosophical Scrivener*. He chose to make most updates by adding a 31-page Postscript at the end of the book in which he makes comments, many hilarious, about each chapter in turn. Readers who wish to pursue this book by Gardner should be certain to acquire the second edition published in 1999. Similarly, I hope that readers will enjoy my stories and essays in this improved second edition.

James Magner, MD
Woodbridge, CT
June, 2020

INTRODUCTION

For most of human history, people lived in small groups as hunter-gatherers. Anthropologists who have studied surviving hunter-gatherer cultures believe that for hundreds of thousands of years, it was predominantly the males who matched their wits against nature to hunt. They learned the ways of herds or of small animals, observed carefully clues left as tracks, broken twigs, or other fragile signs, made plans based on the terrain and wind direction, and then used tools and oftentimes teamwork to bring meat back to the camp. The animals were hidden treasures, but they could be found and taken. Analogously, it was predominantly the women who foraged for edible tubers, nuts, fruits, and plants. Clues to their whereabouts had to be observed and these hidden treasures located and taken. These were matters of life or death. Other hidden treasures included flint, ochre, and even sexual partners. Men and women have been seeking hidden treasures for a very long time. It is what humans do, and we are very good at it.

Stories about finding hidden treasures have been shared orally for millennia. Consider *The Odyssey*. In more recent centuries, this has also been a popular topic in literature. Formulas arose involving pirates and chests of gold, for example, and entertaining tales have been written featuring ragged-edged maps, obscure clues, and coded messages. Daniel Defoe's *Robinson Crusoe*, published in 1719, is more of a shipwreck survival story than a treasure search, but the book is thought to have greatly influenced Edgar Allan Poe. Poe also became interested in cryptography, an ancient art used long before the birth of Christ; a simple letter substitution cipher was used by the Roman army. While in Philadelphia in 1840, Poe wrote essays in a newspaper challenging readers to send him messages in code to see if he could read them. The influence of *Robinson Crusoe* as well as his cryptography hobby were thought to have inspired him to write *The Gold-Bug*, a short story published in 1843 that tells of a buried treasure found by managing to read a coded message. Poe won a hundred-dollar prize for this story, which may have been the most he earned for any story. *The Gold-Bug* was widely read and was later viewed as one of his most sophisticated stories. *The Gold-Bug*, in turn, influenced many authors, including Robert Louis Stevenson, who wrote *Treasure Island* (serialized 1881–1883, published as a book 1883).

The general theme of this collection of ten short stories, two story analyses, and five essays is seeking hidden treasures. (The second edition has a Preface and five chapters added, and it consists of fourteen short stories, two story analyses, and six essays). The first story, *Gold for the Taking*, is perhaps the twenty-first-century version of *The Gold-Bug*. (Please take a few minutes to find and read Poe's classic tale.) My story is modern in that a bright young woman takes the lead to decipher clues. She works in partnership with her likable and loving husband. In this story, the code is not based on a simple substitution of letters but is much more sophisticated. Her gradual unraveling of the problem, step by step, is portrayed in a comprehensible manner. Very importantly, although the clues seem to be obscure, an astute reader could pause midstory, reflect on the clues for an hour or two, and have all the information necessary to solve them. But most readers will not succeed. Yet, when the solution is revealed at the end, essentially every reader will admit that the puzzle was fully solvable at midstory and the given solution is obviously correct. This makes, I think, for a very satisfying reading experience.

Yes, the treasures in these stories might be gold or silver, but in several cases along the way, romance, perhaps a greater prize, is found as well. In some cases, clues are followed to catch a murderer or to steal cash from gangsters. A more abstract and poignant gain is achieved when a husband cleverly sends an important coded message to his grieving wife.

One story deserves special comment since it contains rather dark elements. I have been very concerned for decades about unchecked global human population growth and the damage to the earth's ecosystems, so I recently wrote this story (perhaps never to be submitted) to explore my own frustrations about the unfolding tragedy that will eventually engulf humanity. The main characters are a scientist and a priest. They actually reflect two aspects of my own mind. They debate a need for decisive, urgent action that might be cruel and unthinkable, versus taking a more sanguine philosophical or religious view as the lights slowly go out. Thus, "Ends and Means" contains accurate facts, but the characters are fictional and are holding a conversation. My mental model was Galileo's 1632 book *Dialogue Concerning the Two Chief World Systems*. Galileo had been forbidden to publish in support of the Copernican view, so instead he cleverly crafted a conversation among characters about the old Ptolemaic and new heliocentric Copernican systems and the supporting available evidence. Galileo got in trouble, however, because the character supporting the Ptolemaic view was made quite a simpleton. The pope thought Galileo was mocking him. Galileo was put on trial and ended up under house arrest.

The longest story in this book is actually a short novel. Set in Las Vegas in 2015, a thirty-six-year-old doctor who recently lost his wife to cancer comes to Las Vegas to unwind by playing in a big poker tournament. He falls in love with a woman he meets there. The romance and the mystery, which involves an international plot to poison players, are fiction. But I wanted to make the technical aspects of the poker authentic, so the detailed poker information recaptures day by day my real-life poker experience in this major international tournament that year. I had attended a writers' conference in New York in 2018, and a program organizer, the author Paula Munier (*A Borrowing of Bones: A Mystery*, 2018), advised that writing short stories is wonderful but that novels are more commercially successful. After hearing about some of my interests, she advised me to write a poker mystery, and she wanted it to be ninety thousand words long. Paula actually knows many things about poker and Las Vegas. I went home and produced this poker mystery, although it is only about half as long as she desired. Still, Paula likely will be quite surprised when she sees this. Regardless of what the commercial success may be, I enjoyed the opportunity to recount the biggest poker adventure in my life. Poker enthusiasts will appreciate the detail, but the novel is arranged such that nonplayers need only skim the poker chapters. This manuscript was also an opportunity to develop discussions between characters that may seem a bit didactic but that share more serious thoughts. Also of note, I had never written bedroom scenes before. I was amused when my loving wife of more than forty years, Glenda, reviewed a draft and then requested that I allow her to see what I was intending to include in those romantic interactions.

Though most of this book is fiction, in the essays in part II, I discuss a variety of topics. Three essays explore the necessary limits of science as a tool for understanding the meaning of our lives and the world. Two essays reflect on luck and offer hope that riches normally out of reach might be found at casinos at the green-felt poker tables. So the general theme of seeking hidden treasures has been developed in these stories and essays in quite diverse ways. These texts are primarily intended to be entertaining but also thought-provoking. Have fun!

PART I
CURIOUS TALES

GOLD FOR THE TAKING

"You shouldn't just have things handed to you! You need to earn them!"

There was fire in the old man's eyes, and he wheezed a bit as his breathing quickened. He was eighty-five and had seen better days.

The wayward son, dressed somewhat sloppily and unshaven, stood silent for a moment. His father was always difficult when he asked to borrow more money. His struggles with alcohol and drugs were continuing, but he thought he was starting to make some progress. Surely Dad would understand and give him another helping hand. It was not easy to be chronically unemployed at age sixty, and he had never recovered financially from the divorce settlement twenty years ago. Jason Simms looked down at the carpet and took a breath. Both men stood in the well-worn living room, where so many memories still lingered.

The elder Simms continued; his tone was now less explosive, but the pain in his voice was clear. "I have sold off the farm piece by piece to help you, and all that is left is this twelve-acre plot with the house and barn. And the little family graveyard. I can't sell that!"

"Dad, I haven't had a drink for a month. I just need about five thousand dollars to hold me over while I try to find a new job. I promise I will pay you back in six months." Jason paused hopefully, and he glanced at the old man's chess pieces set up on the corner table. The shelves on one wall were full of books, including a Bible and several books about the Old and New Testaments. There were books about farming, others about chess, and still others about mathematics, his father's college major decades ago. But after college, his dad returned home to help run the farm.

"You know that I have almost nothing in the bank. The house and barn are practically falling down. I just can't do it."

"But, Dad," Jason began, and then he paused. "What about your gold coins? This really is an emergency."

Silence filled the room.

The old man finally spoke, but he spoke softly and without anger. There was just sadness. "Let's sit together in the kitchen. I have to talk to you."

The elder Simms did not have good news for his son. He had changed his will, he explained. A small checking account, the remaining bit of land, and the buildings plus their sorry contents someday would be Jason's—except for the chess books, which would be given to the Plainfield Library. And regarding the coins, there was a special provision about them.

Matthew Simms was a saver. He had worked hard, and through the years, little by little, he had purchased US and Canadian gold coins. It was his hedge against the uncertainty of the world. The quantity of coins grew sizable, and he had never sold even one.

"A special provision for the coins?" Jason repeated. "What do you mean?"

Jason had been aware of the existence of the cigar box of coins in the bedroom closet since about age fifteen. It was a special family secret, and he was sworn to keep his lips sealed. His father once let him hold one of the impressive gold discs; it was astonishingly heavy for its size. He never saw his father handle

2

them, but he knew that one box had grown to two and then three. And that was years ago. When his mother died twenty years ago, his father had mentioned in passing that he still had his "shiny assets," but he had moved them to a place he thought was a bit safer. And he added that he was buying more from time to time. There should be even more boxes by now.

"Charity," the old man replied.

Jason's mind raced as the ramifications sank in. "Why, Dad?"

"Jason, Mom and I tried to raise you the best we knew. And you know how I helped you through the years." The old man paused to wipe his brow with a red handkerchief and then stuffed it back into his jeans pocket. "But I figure I don't have much time left. And maybe there are other people who could use some help too."

"Other people?"

"There are lots of good young people in this county. Think of Tony Smith, who lives next to the church. And that young Bill Miller boy who just got married this year to Alice Parsons. They live right across the highway from us, and I see him work hard every day from sunup to sundown."

"Bill Miller ..." Jason's voice trailed off. Jason knew him superficially as a neighbor's only grandson. He was always well behaved and a good student. He worked hard to help his family with the farm and attended church every Sunday. Jason smirked. "A real goody boy," he mumbled almost silently to himself. He recalled that Bill walked across the highway for a weekly chess game with his father. But he had never seen them play. This year, Bill inherited the farm and had just married his high school sweetheart.

"So are you just going to give the coins to a charity?"

"Well, eventually," Matthew began. "But first, there will be a little contest." In spite of the recent tension in the house, the old man smiled a little, and there was a twinkle in his eye.

"A contest?"

"Yes. The coins may very well in the end go to the regional hospital. But when the probate process is almost complete about ninety days after my death, the attorney will begin the contest with the coins as the prize. Every legal resident in the county—including you, Jason—will be eligible to participate. If no one wins them within thirty days, then the coins will be donated to the hospital."

"Why a contest?"

Matthew sighed. "I do love you, Jason. And I know that you are clever. You are a survivor. But I think someone should *earn* those riches. Then, if no one can win the coins, the money can provide a lot of good for our community. Good that should also benefit you."

Jason was stung by his father's words. And he was angry. But in his heart, he knew that he had no right to be too angry. "What sort of contest?"

"The coins are hidden. Whoever finds the coins will be the winner. But they only have thirty days to solve the clues. After that, the regional hospital will get the money."

⌘

Bill Miller stood facing south on the edge of the east-west highway. He looked carefully both ways before starting to cross the road. Trucks are unforgiving. There was already a little private memorial seventy-five yards down the road for Brad Kinsley, a twenty-one-year-old farmhand who had been out drinking with friends. As he was walking along the highway one dark night, he was struck by a car. It would not do for a young husband to be killed while crossing the road on the way to a burial.

The church service in town had been well attended, and now the hearse was delivering the body of Matthew Simms for burial in the private family cemetery on his farm. Since Alice was not feeling well and needed to lie down, Bill parked the truck in his driveway and was just going to walk across to the cemetery.

Mourners had parked along the south side of the highway and were gathering at the grave. A flat, rectangular stone was the marker for Catherine Simms, and now Matthew would be placed at her side. There were only a dozen gravestones, some more than a century old. Most were rectangular markers flat on the ground, but a few were vertical, flat slabs with the classic rounded top. A larger marker in the last row had a good-sized winged stone angel with a shield and sword, and Bill seemed to recall that was the traditional image of Michael, the archangel. One flat stone had Greek letters on it, possibly a short Bible verse in Greek. Brief prayers were said, and then the two dozen mourners bid one another farewell. Bill approached Jason to shake his hand, though Jason seemed distant and was slow to extend his hand, probably due to the death of his father, he thought.

During the next few weeks, as Bill was doing chores, he often saw Jason walking back and forth on the property. Bill thought it odd that Jason was walking in circles, and one afternoon, he seemed to be cleaning weeds and debris out from under the front porch. But Bill reasoned that Jason probably needed to go through his father's things, donate clothes to charity, and so on. One afternoon, Bill saw Jason by the cemetery with a long piece of laundry line spooled out on the ground. Oddly, Jason kept walking back and forth along the line; then he angled the line differently and walked that path. He seemed to be intently looking at the ground. It didn't really make any sense. But Bill was too busy with his chores to think much more about it.

⁘

The Iowa summer passed quickly, and the first cool night in late September provided a sharp contrast to the ninety-degree heat the previous afternoon. But what really got the community talking was not the change in the weather. It was the legal notice that appeared that day in the *Plainfield Register.*

Bill had not seen the paper that morning, but at noon, the mailman excitedly explained the situation and gave him a newspaper. By that time, a police car was already in the Simms' driveway, and people had appeared across the highway. The estate of Matthew Simms was announcing that there would be a sort of treasure hunt in fulfillment of the old man's will. Police would be present on the property as well as a refreshment vendor daily for the next month, and orderly behavior would be enforced. Only Cass County residents were eligible to search for and ultimately claim the treasure, and police would be checking driver's licenses for residency. Of note, the probate judge had ruled that a portion of the treasure, if found, would be used to pay for town expenses and police overtime, since facilitating the execution of the will inevitably had costs. People were to follow the clues published in the notice to attempt to find and recover one or more boxes of valuable coins. If the coins were not located in the next thirty calendar days, then at a future time whenever they might be found, the money was to pay for related town expenses and the remainder donated to the hospital.

Apparently, Matthew Simms had provided clues but had not given anyone the actual location of the coins.

Bill was still working in the north acres during the late afternoon, but Alice took a break from laundry to sit at the kitchen table. She slid her Sherlock Holmes anthology out of harm's way, poured a glass of iced tea, and puzzled over the clues yet again. She grabbed a red pencil out of the miscellaneous-things mug sitting at the center of the table. Maybe if she underlined some of the words in red, they would make more sense. The five clues were as follows:

1. Just as you read the book of Revelation.
2. Michael, Archangel! Take retribution in Xerxes!
3. 000001100000000011000000000110000001111111 000111111110000001100000000011000000000011100

000000011000000000011000000001111000000011111
1000011111110001111111100011111110001111111
1000111111110

4. 200 feet S
5. 75 feet E

Alice was a smart and imaginative young woman with a college degree in English literature. She loved Shakespeare as well as mystery stories. But these clues made little sense to her. Obviously, the fourth and fifth clues were lengths or distances, as well as directions. Vectors, she recalled. But distances from where? The first two clues had something to do with the Bible or history. But the third clue was pure gibberish. After a few minutes, she could draw with moderate certainty only one inference. If the last two clues were distances and directions along a path from some point, then it seemed likely that the first three clues described the starting point. And if one is pacing off distances from a point on a farm in Iowa, then most likely the treasure was buried. Yes, she was sure about that. The coins were in the ground.

After Bill had washed up and sat down for dinner, Alice shared her guesses about the meaning of the clues. Bill liked Alice's analysis and complimented her. She beamed, stood up, and gave him a kiss on the cheek.

Bill had an additional thought. He recalled seeing the statue of the winged angel in the cemetery, and that had to be Michael, the archangel. Clearly that statue could be the starting point. He wanted to take a measured length of rope and a shovel over to the Simms' first thing in the morning. Maybe they would be rich! They both laughed. They agreed that looking for buried treasure almost always was a fool's errand.

⟨≈⟩

Bill was up at five thirty, and as he was making coffee, he was a bit surprised to hear voices until he remembered that a crowd might already be gathering at the Simms'. A few minutes later when he stepped out on his front porch, he counted twenty-five cars parked along the highway, including two police cars, and there were at least fifty people milling about on the property. Bill cut a 210-foot length of rope and used a yard stick and red marker to indicate seventy-five feet, one hundred feet, and two hundred feet. It dawned on him that this must have been what Jason was doing with the laundry line in June, just a few days after the funeral. The public was not informed of the treasure hunt until September. A short flash of anger rose within him, but he quickly quenched it. He was a competitive person, but he had common sense. The whole thing was rather silly, and there was no sense getting worked up about it. He grabbed his Boy Scout compass, canteen, and a shovel and hopped down the front steps.

Officer Richards checked his license, a mere formality since they knew each other, and he joined the gaggle of hopeful souls already standing in the cemetery. He was only slightly taken aback when he saw three ropes already on the grass, stretching southward from the angel statue. He walked south and east where others had already marked off the distances that he had planned to investigate. At the point two hundred feet south and seventy-five feet east, there was already a huge hole, about fifteen feet across and ten feet deep. Two men were down in the hole making it deeper, and a group of men and women stood above and cheered them on. People seemed good-natured, but there was a hint of tension in the air. Perhaps this was why there were two police cars here today, whereas yesterday there had been only one.

Bill realized that men digging another hole about thirty feet away had measured out two hundred feet south and seventy-five feet east, starting at the gravestone with the Greek letters on it. Their hole was not yet as large but was just as nonproductive. They were sweating and digging with enthusiasm, however. But

Bill was now fairly certain that neither of those two gravestones was the correct starting point. Poor old Mr. Simms could never have dug a hole more than ten feet deep. He and Alice and everyone else clearly did not yet understand the clues. The logical next step was to do more work with one's brain rather than one's back.

⌒〜〜〜⌒

"Clue three certainly is not gibberish. We need to figure that out," stated Alice with conviction. Bill sat next to her at the kitchen table. They had just washed the dinner dishes, and it was time to relax.

Bill had been an excellent student in high school but had returned to the farm rather than attend college. He was naturally bright, but he had substantial respect for Alice's considerable intellect. She was again wielding her sharpened red pencil, and she pointed at the string of zeros and ones. She underlined the ones in red. The ones were clearly grouped. A pair of ones occurred three times. Then a string of eight ones occurred twice. Then pairs of ones occurred five more times, followed by strings with larger numbers of ones. This regularity must mean something.

Alice shared an observation: "Clue three contains 187 digits, and those digits are only one and zero. Why 187 digits? What could be special about 187?"

"Maybe there are 187 coins," Bill suggested.

"No," Alice responded with certainty. "The clues are not about the coins themselves. The clues are describing the location of the coins. I think that the odd number 187 must be very important for locating the coins."

Incredulous, Bill smiled and teased his wife a bit, "You are focused on that number like it is one of your old friends!"

"That reminds me of the famous mathematician, Srinivasa Ramanujan," she replied. She stood to grab an old green-covered spiral notebook from the shelf and showed Bill a dog-eared handout she had been given by a math teacher in college. "Professor

Kirk told us the most interesting stories about Ramanujan, who was a poor young man from India who showed remarkable math skills. He was invited to study at Cambridge in England just before World War I."

"He really traveled a distance for those days."

"Yes, and he had key insights." Alice pointed at a paragraph. "See, he once was told that a taxicab number was 1729 and immediately remarked that it was a very interesting number."

"Interesting number?"

"Yes. He could instantly see that 1729 could be expressed as the sum of the cubes of two positive integers in two different ways."

"Sum of cubes?"

Alice pointed again at the page. "See, Bill. The number 1729 = $1^3 + 12^3$. And 1729 = $9^3 + 10^3$."

Bill blinked, then smiled at Alice. "So what are the secrets in the number 187?"

"We are just going to have to keep thinking," she responded.

∞

They were almost out of time to understand the clues. For two weeks, large crowds had gathered daily to look for treasure, and the property was pockmarked with countless holes. By the third week, the numbers of searchers gradually declined. Now nearing the end of the fourth and final week of the search, only two or three people came each morning. Enthusiasm was greatly diminished when the police chief and mayor of Plainfield gave interviews for the *Register*, stating that hundreds of man-hours had been spent by residents, and several hundred holes had been dug, all to no avail. They were now concluding that the entire project was a hoax, and they would be glad to have the efforts shut down in a few days.

Jason Simms had also given two interviews to the *Register* recently. In the first one, he expressed annoyance that the community had been put through this "trauma," but between the lines, it was clear that he was most annoyed that he had not simply inherited the money. Then two days later, there was an astonishing turn of events. Jason won $100,000 in the state lottery. He then commented in the *Register* that he loved Iowa, but his property would soon be put up for sale, and he was immediately moving to California.

Bill and Alice briefly discussed the clues each evening during dinner, but tomorrow was the very last day that someone would be able to claim the coins.

Alice darkened the red underlining below the ones. Bill remained silent, lost in thought, but he really had no ideas. Absentmindedly, Alice began underlining parts of the other clues with red pencil. Suddenly, she sat up straight in her chair. She had underlined the first letters of the words in clue two. "Look, Bill," she gasped. "The letters spell *matrix*."

"Matrix?" Bill mumbled, a bit unsure of what she meant.

"A matrix is a rectangular array of objects, usually numbers. Like having a rectangular garden containing smaller squares of beets, then potatoes, then petunias, then daisies."

"Sort of like a rectangular TV screen made up of lines of dots?" Bill asked.

Alice suddenly clutched Bill's hands as another insight nearly swept her out of her chair. "I think I might have it! What if there was a rectangular matrix with 187 internal digits?"

"So we are back to your friend, the number 187?"

Alice gave Bill an exultant knowing look, but Bill remained a bit lost. "Just look at the number 187 and tell me what observations you can make."

"Well," Bill began. "It has three digits. And it is an odd number rather than an even number."

"And, and, and ..." coached Alice.

Bill feigned discomfort as he placed his palm on his forehead, "And, let's see. Well. If you add the first and third digits, you get the middle digit."

"Brilliant!" Alice exclaimed. "So you conclude what?"

"Um. I'm not sure what I conclude."

Alice laughed. "Didn't you ever learn the rule about how to quickly multiply by eleven?"

"Multiply by eleven?"

Alice handed Bill her pencil. "Please write down the results for 10 x 11, then 11 x 11, then 12 x 11, and so on."

Bill smiled and dutifully started his task:

10 x 11 = 110
11 x 11 = 121
12 x 11 = 132
13 x 11 = 143
14 x 11 = 154
15 x 11 = 165
16 x 11 = 176
17 x 11 = 187

Bill paused and looked up at Alice, who was smiling broadly.

"Bill, when you multiply a two digit number by eleven, you just add the two digits and make that the middle digit of the answer. And there is my good friend, 187."

Bill nodded.

"And," Alice continued with a flourish, "both eleven and seventeen are prime numbers."

"Prime numbers, like three, five, and seven?" asked Bill.

"Yes! Both eleven and seventeen are prime numbers, so if we need to make a matrix having 187 digits, it can only be eleven units across and seventeen units down, or else seventeen units across and eleven units down. There are no other possibilities."

"Sort of like when you want to print something. Portrait versus landscape. I think I follow you," Bill said. Then he furrowed his brow. "And look at clue one. 'Just as you read the book of Revelation.' Every Bible I have ever seen has pages that are taller than wide—portrait pages. But how do we put the digits into the matrix?"

Alice could barely contain her excitement. "We read the book of Revelation starting at the top left and read left to right. Then we read each line in turn from left to right. The string of digits in clue three just need to be entered that way into an eleven-by-seventeen matrix."

"But what good is making the matrix?" asked Bill.

"Let's make it and see what it might be good for!" Alice exclaimed as she grabbed a large envelope containing junk mail with a blank back side. "Please read me the first eleven digits in clue three, then the next eleven digits, and I'll construct the matrix line by line."

As she scribbled, Alice decided to replace each zero with a period and each one with an X to make the contrast between the two digit types more striking. Within five minutes, she had entered the 187 digits in sequence, eleven across in seventeen rows. They stared in silence at the result:

```
    XX
    XX
    XX
XXXXXXX
XXXXXXX
    XX
    XX
    XX
    XX
    XX
   XXXX
  XXXXXX
XXXXXXX
XXXXXXX
XXXXXXX
XXXXXXX
XXXXXXX
```

Of course, they both immediately recognized the object, but intuitively they remained silent to preserve this special moment.

Finally, Bill spoke. "It's the roadside memorial for Brad Kinsley."

⚭

It was a gorgeous October morning as Bill and Alice sauntered across the road to check in with Officer Richards. As no one else was there, he had been dozing in his squad car listening to the radio.

Within two minutes, they had used their rope to mark off distances from the roadside memorial, but it took a full hour to dig up the twelve heavy cigar boxes, each meticulously swaddled in at least four layers of plastic wrap. Officer Richards watched as Bill stood in the three-foot hole and lifted out the boxes onto the grass one by one. Alice sliced open the wrapping of one box and lifted the lid to reveal the neat stacks of gold discs. Bill climbed out of the hole and gave Alice a sustained kiss.

Bill walked home to retrieve their truck. After the short drive, he backed the sturdy vehicle to that spot, and they loaded the boxes into the bed. They knew that their lives were changed forever. Grinning widely, Officer Richards gave them a police escort with lights flashing as they drove to the Plainfield Bank, which had just opened. Bill and Alice inspected the coins briefly with the manager. It appeared that there were about $2 million in gold on the counter, representing a lifetime of work by Bill's favorite chess partner, Matthew Simms, and his wife. There was no doubt that in a few days the regional hospital would receive a substantial donation in the names of Matthew and Catherine. Bill would ask for a plaque honoring the Simms to be placed in the lobby. The treasure was all locked up in several safe deposit boxes within an hour. That task was just completed when a breathless reporter from the *Register* burst into the lobby of the bank.

JOE'S MYSTERIOUS TALENT

My brother Joe was dead.

I knew that it couldn't be good news when my doorbell rang at 11:15 p.m., and I saw a police officer standing on my front porch. I was still dressed but had been headed to bed.

The young officer was professional and brief. He ascertained that I was James Simpson. He was sorry to inform me that my brother, Joe, aged thirty-eight, was driving west on Texas Highway 186 about five miles west of Port Mansfield when he was struck head-on by a drunk driver going east at a high rate of speed. Both drivers likely had been killed instantly. The accident happened only three hours ago. Joe's wallet contained information that tied him to me. The body was being taken to the funeral home in Raymondville, and I could provide formal identification in the morning, claim his watch and wallet, and make arrangements. I confirmed that Joe was unmarried and had no living relatives other than myself and my ten-year-old daughter, Betsy. The police would keep me informed if there were any new developments, and the officer made a note of my cell number and email address.

After the squad car pulled away, I stood silently by the front door for several minutes, then sat in the living room in the dark for nearly an hour. Joe was gone. There was nothing more to be done tonight. Before I undressed for bed, I peeked into Betsy's room. She was sound asleep. I would give her the sad news in the morning but encourage her to catch the school bus as usual. The normal school-day activities would distract her. I would need to stop at the funeral home before opening up the grocery store.

Poor Joe. He didn't deserve this. My older brother and I grew up in Raymondville, Texas, and he had been an odd man but a good and honest one. He and I had helped our parents by doing chores in the little corner grocery that our family owned. Mom and Dad loved that store, but money was always tight, and there was a lot of work. Joe was a poor student and never finished high school. Looking back, I realize now that he had some kind of learning disability. In contrast, I was the star student with all the As. During our teenage years, Joe and I mopped the floor, helped unbox newly arrived canned goods, stocked the shelves, and did a million other small tasks. But Dad wisely never let Joe work at the cash register. Joe didn't mind, as he was well aware of his limitations, and he was joyful and helpful most of the time. He could read and write but perhaps never exceeded the eighth-grade level. It was funny, though. In many ways, Joe seemed very, very smart. For example, when Dad misplaced his car keys, Joe could quickly find them. Many times, Joe would notice small, important details about things that I overlooked, like a carton of milk that would soon pass the expiration date, so Joe would move that one to the front of the display. But his below-average reading skill was a substantial impairment.

Although Joe was older, I always watched out for him. We were not just brothers; we were best friends. As teenagers, we often explored the nearby sandy shorelines, and we loved to repeat tales of pirates and of Spanish treasure galleons that had sailed off nearby Padre Island. For years, he had taken his bicycle, and later his old beat-up truck, out Route 186 east of Raymondville toward Port Mansfield. He spent hours and hours out there, but I never knew what he was doing. He tried to explain to me that he experienced a special thrill every time he traveled on the road out to Port Mansfield. As he spoke, he would get a strange expression on his face, and he told me that someday he would tell me all about it. It didn't make any sense to me, but that was Joe.

Through the years, we spent several memorable summer weekends in Corpus Christi. We drank beer and flirted with girls. We also enjoyed the display of shipwreck items in the local museum. One unlucky salvage company in the late 1960s found a Spanish shipwreck with interesting artifacts, but the Texas legislature passed a law two years later and claimed the objects for the state, so those finds were displayed in the Corpus Christi museum. We both thought it was pretty unfair for the state to swoop in and deprive those searchers of their small treasures, but it was fun and also a special privilege for us to see some of the old coins, jewelry, and rusted guns in the glass cases. Still, this dispute between the salvage company and the state reminded us of the time that Mrs. Baker bought groceries at our store, and the colorful Big Bingo game ticket given to her with the grocery receipt turned out to have a winning number for a $1,000 prize. She was all smiles, and she needed the money. But the next day, the company in Dallas that was running that promotion told her that there had been an error in printing many of the reward tickets, so her ticket was invalid. Read the fine print, they said. So she didn't get the $1,000, but they did mail her a twenty-five-dollar consolation prize.

Joe had few friends. He lived with Mom and Dad until he was twenty-eight, and he was very helpful in the store. He also did yard work and odd jobs around town. When I got a small studio apartment in town, Joe often slept on my couch just so that we could watch TV together. He liked to meet the few girls I dated, but he was shy, and I don't believe he ever went out on a date. Joe was my best man when I married Susan. After Betsy was born, he was her baptismal godfather, and he is beaming in all the photos. Three years later, Joe was a pallbearer when we buried Susan after she died of meningitis. He sat with me when I cried, though I tried not to cry in front of Betsy. Joe loved Betsy. He was constantly on his hands and knees with her, down on the floor, and he always brought her a small gift on her birthday.

Three years ago, Mom died from rapidly progressive breast cancer. Throughout her short illness, Mom still loved to see us, and she laughed with us nearly every day until just before she died. Dad was pretty upset by it all, though. Then two months later, Dad was killed when he ran off a road at a high speed into a ditch. Joe and I suspected that Dad might have been drinking that night, but we never knew for sure. Betsy was seven then, in second grade, and she handled those tragedies well because she was probably a little too young to be severely affected by deaths of grandparents. But Joe was absolutely crushed by the deaths of our parents, and it took him days to recover. He slept on my couch for a week after Dad died. He just wanted to be around me and Betsy.

I took over running the grocery store, and Joe helped when he could.

A few weeks after Dad's funeral, Joe said that he wanted a change. He was thirty-five years old at that time, and he wanted some cash so that he could establish himself as an independent person. He and I agreed, of course, that we would split the estate fifty-fifty, as Mom and Dad would have wanted. It made sense for me to take 100 percent ownership of the store and the small family home along with a little cash, whereas Joe wanted the cash that had been in savings and a few stock funds. Joe had an idea for the use of that cash, he said, but I could not exactly follow his reasoning.

Within days, Joe bought a new pickup truck because, he said, his worn-out vehicle would not be able to do the local traveling that he had in mind. He also said that he wanted to talk to me about something important. I grabbed two Cokes, and we sat down together in the back room of the store. He wanted me to help him use his new wealth to buy two acres of land with a small two-room cabin west of Port Mansfield. He drove me out to the property to take a look. It wasn't much. The property was on a slight rise that stood incrementally higher than the surrounding flat land. The run-down cabin was surrounded by scrubby brush and a few trees. The indoor plumbing worked, but the water heater, refrigerator, and electric stove were old. A small propane heater could be used on cool nights, and there was a bedframe, a wooden table, and three wooden chairs. Joe said that this was surely the place that he had always been looking for, and he confided that he had chills every time he walked onto that property. I admitted that the place did have a kind of stark beauty. I privately considered that he could do odd jobs for neighbors in the area to make a small income, and he would be less than twenty miles from Betsy and me in Raymondville, so he could visit us frequently. I told him that he might tire of living there, so I counselled him that if he kept the property at least five years, he would probably be able to sell for a profit. His desire to live in this rather isolated place was a little bewildering, but it was clear that this was what he wanted, so I helped him with steps to purchase the property, and all seemed well.

⚭

My talk with Betsy at breakfast went well. Such a sweet little girl. She cried for Joe but understood that she should go to school. We bowed our heads and prayed for Joe, and also for Mommy, Grandma, and Grandpa. Poor little Betsy's heaven was already well populated. I put a peanut butter and jelly sandwich and an apple in her plastic lunch box, and I stood on the corner with her until the school bus came by. She wasn't crying anymore. She was a good student, and she was already focused on her day's activities.

I finished my coffee in the kitchen, then walked six blocks to the funeral home. The manager was very professional, and we agreed that we had seen each other a bit too often during the last few years. Joe's face was not traumatized, but I didn't look below his shoulders. The funeral director said there was trauma to his chest and lower body. I had no desire to see it. I made the necessary arrangements, then signed for his personal items: one inexpensive wristwatch, one wallet, a comb, a key ring with car key and house key, and an iPhone 6 that now had a cracked screen.

I carried the small plastic bag with Joe's things as I walked the three blocks to my corner store. I unlocked the front door and flipped the Closed sign to Open. Mrs. Higgins saw me enter and rapidly crossed the street to follow me into the store. She had been surprised a few minutes earlier when the store had not yet opened. I briefly told her about Joe, and she offered her condolences.

After five more customers had quickly come and gone, the early-morning rush seemed to be over, and I sat on the stool behind the counter thinking about Joe. Why had he been driving so much recently? Joe often stopped briefly to say hi as he was headed north or returning home. I wondered if he had gotten mixed up in some sort of illegal activity, perhaps transporting drugs. But that was not like Joe. He was a kind, honest man who would never get involved with drugs or gangsters. Joe seemed to be making frequent trips north to Houston, San Antonio, and even as far as Dallas. He would drive north, spend three or four nights along the way, and then drive home. During his brief visits in Raymondville, Joe was all smiles, seemed comfortable and untroubled, and he never talked about the purpose of his travels.

My thoughts were interrupted by Frank as he dropped off the mail. More bills. As he turned to go, I initiated our usual banter, telling him that the mail he brought me was always frankly depressing. He replied with his standard remark that he frankly didn't care. The utility, tax, and insurance bills were expected but still worrisome. In the past month, I had to pay for a new roof; the old one had been twenty-eight years old. And the refrigerated display case had finally given out and had to be replaced on short notice. Admittedly, that display case was decades old, but all of these bills were really piling up. How would I ever save for Betsy's college tuition? Forget about retirement.

My thoughts turned back to Joe, and since there were no customers in the store at the moment, I pulled out the bag of Joe's belongings. The iPhone still refused to power on. The wallet contained forty-two dollars in bills. There was Joe's driver's license, and that wallet pocket also contained a small square of white thin cardboard cut from a three-by-five card that had my name, address, and phone number on it. That was how the police knew to contact me. I turned over the cardboard and was surprised to see another name printed in pencil. The words were Padre Fray Juan Ferrer. It seemed strange that Joe would have carried the name of a priest in his wallet. Joe had never been very religious. After puzzling over this for another moment, I set it aside. There was a little change pocket, so I unsnapped the flap and dumped the coins out on the counter. There were two quarters, three dimes, one nickel, five pennies, and, what was this? There was a small, flat gold-colored item shaped like a tiny slice of pizza. And it was heavy for its size. I turned it over and looked at both sides. There seemed to be some letters stamped into the metal. After another moment, my suspicions grew. It likely was actually a piece of gold but in a very odd shape. Where had Joe gotten this?

I was interrupted to tend to the needs of three customers who each bought a large supply of groceries. As I gratefully put the money into the register, I felt slightly better about those bills that had come in the mail. I sat down, alone at the counter. I looked again at the name of the priest on the white card. The name Ferrer was unfamiliar, and I doubted that this could be someone in the very tiny fishing village of Port Mansfield. There also was no such man in Raymondville. Curious, I pulled out my own iPhone and queried Google to see if I could identify which South Texas parish might have a Father Ferrer. I skimmed down several lines of search results until I came to text with that priest's name published in a National Park Service brochure for the Padre Island National Seashore. Opening the brochure, I read in astonishment, "1554. The Wreck of Three Spanish Ships on Padre Island."

Of course, as children who had grown up in South Texas, Joe and I had heard stories of the many shipwrecks along the coast, including stories of lost treasure. As I scrolled on my phone, the brochure explained that an Indiana company, Platoro, Ltd., actually found the wreck of a Spanish ship, the *San Esteban,* in 1967. As coins and artifacts were recovered, the state of Texas decided to claim most of the wreck. The state legislature passed the Antiquities Bill in 1969 to set procedures in treasure-recovery attempts. Nearly all of the recovered artifacts then went to a museum in Corpus Christi.

I swallowed hard as I read that three Spanish galleons loaded with treasure and passengers, the *San Esteban, Santa Maria de Yciar,* and *Espiritu Santo,* had encountered a storm in April 1554 and had been separated from a group of ships that had left Veracruz headed back to Europe. Padre Juan Ferrer was among the 302 passengers on those three ships, which carried gold and silver coins, gold and silver bars, cow hides, sugar, and wool. The ships sank off Padre Island in fairly shallow water. About half of the passengers survived and came ashore, but in the next days, they were harassed by aggressive Indians. A group of these survivors, including Padre Ferrer, made their way southward on foot along the shore on an arduous trek back to Mexico. Acting immediately upon hearing the stories of the survivors, the Spanish authorities in Veracruz sent a salvage mission to recover the gold and silver, and supposedly about 6,200 pounds were recovered. But about 15,000 pounds had been put on board.

I looked up as Tommy walked into the store. He was my relatively new twenty-year-old stock boy and part-time helper. He worked four afternoons each week from 1:00 p.m. until 5:00 p.m. His arrival would give me a chance to drive down to Joe's place to retrieve his will and any valuables that might be lying about in the house. Perhaps I should unplug the TV and bring that back home with me today. When Mom died, Dad insisted that Joe and I should each spend a few bucks to have formal, brief wills drawn up, and that was easy enough to do.

At least the hot midafternoon sun was behind me as I drove east toward Port Mansfield. I pulled up at Joe's place, but there was no shade for the car. I paused on the shady front porch and noted that there were two shovels and a pickax tossed casually on one side. The front door key worked without any difficulty. The home was neat but relatively bare, a bachelor's domain. I sat down at a small desk that Joe had placed below a side window of the house. The top drawer had some pens and pencils, a wooden ruler, a cheap plastic calculator, and some paper clips. I slid open the deep left-side drawer and was surprised to find an inexpensive fireproof box that was not locked. It contained copies of 1040 income tax forms for the past three years. I looked closer and realized that the forms had been completed on a computer using software, and the returns obviously had been prepared for Joe by someone else. The second page of the return for 2015 showed the name of the commercial preparer in Harlingen below Joe's signature. But what I noticed next stopped my breath. Joe's reported income in 2015 was $2,115,345.

I stood up and walked toward the front door in a daze. What? After a moment, I retraced my steps and sat again at the desk. The other two 1040s reported Joe's income in 2014 as $1,932,434, while in 2016 it was $1,345,672. As I lifted out the last 1040, I saw that Joe's will was on the bottom of the box.

I pulled open the deep right-side drawer, and this contained another inexpensive fireproof box. In that box were Joe's checkbook, with a balance of $950, and paperwork from banks in San Antonio, Houston, Austin, and Dallas that had big numbers. A single bank in Harlingen had only a small amount on deposit. Joe's extensive cash holdings were deposited all over Texas. I stared at the large numbers but then noticed another important detail. All of the accounts were titled "Joseph Simpson, POD James Simpson." I was pretty sure that POD meant payable on death.

I spent the next hour looking in every nook and cranny in the small cabin in search of gold coins or silver bars, but there were none. I began to piece together what all of this meant. Joe had spent hours and hours for many years of his life wandering in this area, and he must have stumbled across a treasure hoard. I suspected that he thought it was safest to tell absolutely no one about this, not even me! And it occurred to me that Joe had been impressed years ago, as I had been, by the story of salvage workers who were required to turn over their prizes to the state. I well understood the need for unique historical artifacts to be preserved and studied, but it seemed to me that there might be less academic study required for items like plain gold bars. The searchers who tracked down the loot certainly deserved better compensation. Joe was a good and honest man, but clearly that story from the 1960s about the *San Esteban* had aggravated him. So Joe must have made scores of trips in Texas to visit pawnshops or other places where he could trade gold or silver for checks. He deposited the checks in big banks and dutifully paid his income taxes. Of course, I had no proof at all about what Joe might have found or what he might have done. But he must have been quite a busy man, traveling widely and probably making hundreds of small transactions. And whenever he stopped in to visit Betsy and me briefly as he was making a trip, he must have been laughing inside about how his secret plan was working flawlessly. What a rascal!

I loaded up the two fireproof boxes, his TV set, and a half dozen other items. The sun was in my eyes as I drove west toward Raymondville. But I was not blinded to the possibility that my daughter now would be able to attend Harvard or Yale. And I was certain that she was smart enough. Moreover, my new store employee, Tommy, was about to get a substantial raise. This turn of fortune had all been made possible by my dear brother Joe, a loving and caring man who could barely read and write but who clearly must have had a special sixth sense. He had a unique, sensitive mind coupled with a loving heart. He not only noticed important small details, but he found ways to make his perceptiveness work for him and for the ones he loved.

CRAZY AUNT RUTH'S LEGACY

(First published in *Triumph: Stories of Victories Great and Small* edited by Meredith Maslich Eaton, 2018)

The mid-June late afternoon was pleasant enough in Western Illinois. But Tim was tired of waiting in the car parked across the street from the small Catholic church. Molly always wanted to go to 4:00 pm Saturday Mass, which messed up the weekend a bit as far as he was concerned. Tim checked his phone for the time – 4:45, so the congregation should start exiting soon. He flipped the radio from the Rock station back to the Country station. Both had a lot of commercials, which made him even more impatient.

Finally, some action. A young mother and two small children burst out of the church door. She was clearly ready to depart as soon as it was respectable. Then several middle-aged people stepped out, followed by an old lady using a walker who detoured right to descend on the ramp. Come on, Molly!

There she was. Blue jeans and an attractive summer blouse. He liked the way her long dark hair fell around her shoulders. And the bounce of her breasts as step by step she descended the five stone stairs in front of the church door. She was a very good-looking girl, he had to admit. And the love of his life.

She was a year younger at twenty-three. And very Catholic. Luckily that didn't stop her from moving in with him. She said it was okay because they were truly in love and engaged. Tim, an unenthusiastic Protestant, had never been religious and had rarely attended services. If she wanted to be an active Catholic that was fine with him.

Tim was unconvinced about Divine Providence. During the four years that he studied at a small liberal arts college – he did get a business-related degree – first his father and then his mother died from cancer. And Molly's parents were also dead. Since neither had a sibling, they were finding their way in the world themselves and saw the many advantages of teaming up. They were truly in love, yes, but their genuine partnership had many practical advantages as well.

Molly climbed into the front seat and leaned over to give Tim a warm, wet kiss.

"So, did you pray for me?"

"Of course, even though we both know there's no hope for a guy who only thinks about sex!"

"What? I also work for a living!"

"And that is much appreciated. So, Mr. Moneyman. I'm starving. Let's grab a burger." They always had fast food somewhere along the strip after Mass.

Money was tight. Molly worked as an assistant in a hair salon, and she really enjoyed the interactions with her small-town customers. For the past year Tim was an account manager at an office supply company. He liked his boss. Tim made a point of always being at his desk early, and he avoided making any trouble. The paycheck was small, but he and Molly really needed the income.

"Anything interesting at Mass?"

"Well, the Old Testament reading was about Jericho."

Tim pulled away from the curb. "Who was Jericho?"

Molly laughed. "Silly! Jericho was a place. An old city with a big wall around it to keep out bad guys."

Tim gave Molly a quick, blank stare, but he had to keep looking forward for traffic.

"Yeah, Joshua led the Israelites toward Jericho, but they didn't know how to get inside the wall. So, Joshua had the people blow trumpets and shout, and the wall suddenly fell down. End of story. The Israelites took the city."

"Impressive. Must have been some pretty loud trumpets."

"It's a metaphor."

"What?"

"It's a story that has a deeper religious meaning."

"Meaning what?"

"Well, when you face an impossible challenge while trying to do something important you prepare and do your best, but you also trust in God, and if it is His will He can make unlikely things happen to help you."

⁓

The weekend routine was interrupted Sunday at 2 pm by the phone call from Bill Edwards. He lived a block south of downtown Quincy next to Great Aunt Ruth. He accepted small payments to cut her grass and shovel her snow. Bill went next door at noontime to say hi like he did every Sunday, and he found her dead in the easy chair in the living room, the TV still on. Poor Ruth. She had been apparently pretty healthy for 96, but she refused to see doctors and something obviously caught up with her. Bill called the police. The coroner came, and the body had just been taken to the funeral home on Broadway.

Tim had last seen her just two Sundays ago. He and Molly visited her about one Sunday afternoon each month. But they weren't close. Ruth was a very strong-willed and independent woman who appreciated that Tim did little chores for her from time to time. But she maintained her distance.

Only six mourners came to the funeral. Great Aunt Ruth had outlived nearly all of her relatives and friends. She was childless and Great Uncle Jack had died decades before. A skilled carpenter, he had earned a comfortable living doing construction, and he also made quality furniture and kitchen cabinets. So Jack and Ruth had been fairly well off for many decades. When Jack's short obituary appeared in the newspaper it drew little notice except by an unscrupulous Bible salesman who knocked on Ruth's front screen door three days later. He said he was there to deliver the gold-leaf, deluxe Bible that Jack had ordered the prior month, and for convenience he could collect the $82 cost while he was there. Without missing a beat, Ruth instantly responded that it was unlike Jack to order an expensive Bible, but he would be home from work at 5:30 pm and the salesman could discuss it with him at that time. The salesman made a hasty retreat and never came back, but that encounter became an oft-repeated piece of family folklore.

Tim frequently mentioned Ruth to Molly as "Crazy" Aunt Ruth because of her many idiosyncrasies, but that was mostly a term of endearment. She was a hardworking and thrifty woman who had been a child during the depression years of the 1930s. She was uneducated but naturally quite bright. She thought doctors were too expensive, and that banks could not be trusted. Her parents and grandparents lost their savings in 1931 despite being held by reputable banks, and that made a lasting impression on Ruth. It was understood that she kept cash at home, but this was little discussed. Tim recalled that Ruth had given him a shiny, 1901 silver dollar on his sixteenth birthday, but on other birthdays and holidays her small gifts were mundane. When Tim was twelve he was surprised and impressed when he learned that she liked spy programs, and apparently on occasion read a spy novel.

Now Ruth's only surviving relative was her great-nephew, Tim. A few days after Ruth's death, Tim was contacted to see her attorney, Mr. McCarthy, about her will. Tim was a little nervous because he had never before met with an attorney, but he feigned confidence as he took a chair across the desk from the bespectacled, greying professional. The will was simple and brief. Tim, the executor, inherited her tiny house, her belongings, and her two financial assets: a checking account with $2000, and a savings account with $6000. Tim wasn't surprised that he was the sole heir, but he was rather shocked by the small amounts in the accounts. How could she have been surviving with very little money? The fact that she lived near the center of the small town, and that there was a small grocery store, a bank, and a post office just a few steps from her front door apparently eased her ability to run simple errands on foot.

The attorney pointed out the one puzzling paragraph in the will, which was addressed to Tim personally. Tim was to do his best to remain a reverent Christian, and it was imperative that he allow Moses and Joshua to guide him to the land of milk and honey. The attorney actually didn't know Ruth that well, and he offered no interpretation, but he did advise that the small, somewhat dilapidated house should be sold "as is" as soon as possible since the taxes and ongoing expenses would cause substantial costs month by month. The funeral expenses could be paid from the bank accounts. The probate process would be easily completed within a few weeks at a cost of about $1000, and all would be well. Tim thanked Mr. McCarthy, shook his hand, stuck his photocopy of the will in his jeans pocket, and drove home to tell Molly all about it. She was smart and would have some opinions.

⌘

Molly was aghast.

"It sounds like we need to sell that old house pretty quick or it will bankrupt us!" She took a breath and motioned for Tim to sit beside her at the kitchen table. "But let's think about this. What are our options?"

"Well, it would cost a fortune to make the house livable for us, and we just can't put that kind of money into that place. But I worry about selling quickly."

"Why?"

Tim lowered his voice and locked gazes with Molly. "Some of us thought Ruth was hiding cash at home. We need time to look around before we just sell the place."

"Hiding cash....?" Molly took a few more seconds to process the idea, then smiled. "Well, it's 2 pm. Why not go look right now?"

⁂

The key turned easily in the front door, and Tim and Molly stepped into the small, well-worn living room. The rug was stained and ragged, and some of the stuffing was coming out of seams in the couch and the easy chair. They knew the small color TV worked, so they wouldn't have to test that – but they were reminded that the cable bill would be an ongoing expense, and they should cancel first thing tomorrow.

Ruth's large purse was on the TV tray next to the easy chair, and it contained $115 in a tattered wallet. This was a great start, but they wondered what else might be in the house.

They walked through the kitchen and opened each drawer and cabinet, but all seemed routine. The single bedroom had a small chest of drawers, and they emptied each drawer onto the bed. Just old clothes and some toiletries. A quick search of the bathroom was unproductive. Tim stood in the hall and pulled down the attic access door that included a small wooden ladder to be unfolded. The attic light worked, and Tim spent fifteen minutes carefully stepping this way and that to look for a box or suitcase, but the attic was empty. There was no basement, so they stepped outside and lifted the door to the single-car garage. Ruth didn't have a car, but along the walls of the garage were a dozen boxes of old household goods and an ancient gasoline-powered lawn mower that likely hadn't been started in twenty years. The garage was attached to the house and was set on a single concrete slab. There was a chest-high, standard window looking out to the side-yard and a quite small rectangular window high up on the back wall, presumably not to be opened but just to let in daylight.

A bit disheartened, Tim motioned for Molly to sit in the easy chair as he collapsed onto the living room couch. "What do you think, Molly?"

Molly gazed first at one piece of furniture then another. "There's not that much stuff in this house, but I would say that a 'preliminary search' is negative – as might have been expected. Ruth was smart enough that if she was hiding money here, it probably could not be found just by looking for one hour."

"So. What next?"

"Let's tip over every piece of furniture to look at the bottom, or at least use a flashlight and mirror to look at the bottoms of things. There could be an envelope taped onto the bottom of something."

Tim retrieved his powerful flashlight from the glove compartment, and they spent the next hour in that systematic search – to no avail.

Tired and flustered, they decided to go home and have dinner. As they departed they took a few items from the kitchen home with them.

☙❧

They felt better after having something to eat, but were worried. They had looked pretty thoroughly. Perhaps there actually was no hidden cash.

After dinner the TV remained off, and they continued discussing possibilities. Tim decided that he would speak with his boss in the morning and take one more day off from work – he wanted to focus on the search.

"You know," Molly began. "There was that odd paragraph in the will addressed to you about Moses."

Bill pulled the photocopy from his pants pocket and read the sentence. "…Remain a reverent Christian, and it is imperative to allow Moses and Joshua to guide you to the land of milk and honey."

"That might mean something," proposed Molly. "I think your Great Aunt didn't trust the lawyer, so she left an obscure message for you. We can at least hope that she meant something important by that."

Tim remained doubtful, but he appreciated Molly's attempt to help. His enthusiasm had waned, and he only responded to her with a nod.

"And remember, there was a large Bible on the dresser in the bedroom. We should take a look at that tomorrow, especially at the pages that say something about Moses."

⊛

June 28 promised to be hot and sunny. They had coffee and cereal, and Tim was cleared by his boss to take another day off.

The key turned easily in the front door again. Molly retrieved the Bible, and they sat side-by-side on the living room couch to take a look. There were no notes written on the inside front or back covers, and apparently no marginal notes on any page. Not very promising. Being more familiar with the book than was Tim, Molly slid the Bible onto her lap. She looked through the early sections where Moses was mentioned, followed by mention of Joshua. But nothing was marked or stood out.

Molly sat in silence. This had probably been a wild goose chase.

Tim also was rather flustered. He stood and stretched to relieve tension. As he stood in the center of the small room to face Molly, his eye caught the 8 x 10 framed picture hanging on the wall above the couch. It depicted a prominent, bearded man in a flowing robe, and other men presenting him with a wealth of produce – grapes and figs.

Tim lifted the picture off the hook on which it was hung, and turned it so Molly, who was still seated, could see. "So, Molly," he laughed. "Is one of these guys Moses?"

Molly held the framed picture in two hands and stared at it for what seemed a full minute before responding, "I'm not sure."

Tim stepped into the kitchen to grab a pliers and screw driver from a drawer. "Let's open it up and see if it contains a secret note!" He was joking, but he actually was hoping that there might be a letter inside.

Tim quickly bent the four metal prongs on the frame, lifted out the back cardboard, and then lifted out a white, thin spacer piece of cardboard just behind the print. He tossed that spacer to the side. He carefully lifted out the picture itself and read aloud two words printed along the bottom, apparently placed there by the manufacturer. The words were a name: Giovanni Lanfranco. Tim looked at Molly for any reaction. She looked puzzled, but was reaching for her phone. After a quick search of the name, she smiled and held up her phone so Tim could see.

"Lanfranco was the artist, and here is our painting. And here's the title: *Moses and the Messengers from Canaan.*"

Tim felt a weak flutter of hope. He and Molly inspected both sides of the picture carefully, and held it up to the window glass to look through the print. After ten minutes, their hopes began to fade. There was nothing on the print to tie it to Ruth or to the house. But it was Moses.

"Hand me the frame," ordered Molly. Tim handed it to her, and she turned it this way and that looking for any small words written along the edges, but there was nothing.

"And the back cardboard."

Molly again conducted a withering inspection, but there was nothing suspicious.

"Wasn't there also a piece of white cardboard?"

"The spacer," answered Tim. He retrieved that from the floor, and Molly turned it in her hands.

After a second Molly sat up straight. She looked with wide eyes at Tim.

"What is it?" he asked.

"There are words written with an ink pen here, and there are five small, rectangular holes cut into this cardboard."

"Let me see." Tim held the cardboard by the window and read the sentence. "...Give me a sure sign, [13] and save alive my father." Tim handed the cardboard back to Molly.

Molly mumbled, "There are four quite small, rectangular holes cut near the left top of the cardboard, and the words are written below those holes. And there is a larger rectangular hole cut on the right top part of the cardboard. The height of that cut is the same as the other holes, but it's much longer horizontally."

Tim's mind was racing. He had seen something like this somewhere before, maybe on TV. It was a show about the Civil War. Spies, that's it! Civil War spies. Tim smiled, "I think I know what this is. It's a mask."

"A mask?"

"Yes. You place this cardboard mask over a written document or page in a book, and certain letters and words show through revealing a secret message!"

"Progress!" Molly exclaimed. But after a moment she frowned. "But what document or book page should we place the mask on?"

"Do the words mean anything to you?"

Molly paused and furrowed her brow. "It's very odd to say this. But those words are vaguely familiar. I think I've heard something like this before. But I can't say when or where."

Tim crossed his fingers. "Please think, Molly."

After a moment she smiled. "Better than thinking, I can just search that word phrase placed in quotation marks. If the phrase is widely known the source will pop up." Molly grabbed her phone and entered the required text in quotation marks.

Molly read the search result to Tim. "It's the end of verse 12 and the beginning of verse 13 of Joshua chapter 2. And that explains what the little superscript 13 is doing in the text."

Tim sat by Molly's side and excitedly pointed at the Bible, which was still on her lap.

Molly opened to the correct page of the book of Joshua, and she placed the mask over the text. The four holes to the left side of the cardboard each allowed only one or two letters to be seen. That part of the message was derived from the **bold** letters in the text that follows: "...Give me a sure **sign**, [13] and save al**i**ve my fathe**r**." Tim quickly pointed out that the letters showing through spelled "silver." His pulse quickened.

Without delay, Molly read the words that appeared through the larger rectangular slit on the right side: "...The scarlet cord in the window..."

Then Molly added with a smile, "This is from the story of Joshua's siege of Jericho. That's where I heard the phrase! At Mass. The scarlet cord was the sign left in the window of the prostitute, Rahab, who helped the Israelite spies enter the walled city."

Tim was so excited he could hardly speak. "And I think I know where there's a scarlet cord. It's in the high, rectangular window in the back wall of the garage."

They rushed to the garage, and Tim slid several heavy boxes full of junk away from the back wall. The scarlet cord was thumbtacked to drape across the top of the window, and it hung down both sides as far as the sill. It looked like the sorry remnant of what once had been red curtains that had covered the window, but now only the cord remained. Tim carefully inspected the wall from the concrete floor up to head height, but there was no access panel. They briefly walked outside, but the exterior of the wall also had no obvious access. It was a quite solidly built, wooden wall that didn't jiggle at all, and it was firmly set on the concrete floor.

Back inside the garage, Molly pointed upward toward four small, horizontal, dark stripes on the back wall. Located about six feet above the floor, and just below the level of the high window sill, each stripe was about four inches long horizontally, and only a fraction of an inch high vertically. The four marks were spread at about three-foot intervals across the back wall. Tim reached up and easily felt the marks.

"They're not stripes," he reported. He turned and grabbed Molly's hands, and the moment was electric. "They're slits."

Tim grabbed a large hammer and crowbar from the junk pile in the corner, paused, and held up the tools as he locked gazes with Molly. His gesture was asking for Molly's approval to proceed with some demolition.

She nodded. Then she added with a grin, "Shall I blow a trumpet?"

The wall had been solidly built, but within minutes a two-foot hole was clawed out at the base. And out poured thousands – *no, tens of thousands* – of silver dollars.

COMMENTS ABOUT WRITING "CRAZY AUNT RUTH'S LEGACY"

My short story *Crazy Aunt Ruth's Legacy* finished favorably in a national competition run by Possibilities Publishing Company. My story was included in an anthology entitled *Triumph: Stories of Victories Great and Small*, edited by Meredith Maslich Eaton, which is being sold on-line. I now want to describe how I decided to write such a tale, and I'll explain my method for putting such a story together.

When deciding to write a piece, one first needs a very general idea about what type of manuscript will be produced: fiction versus nonfiction, approximate length, intended audience, genre. Vital is to consider what emotional or other effect one desires to achieve in the reader. For *Crazy Aunt Ruth's Legacy*, I began by deciding to write a short treasure hunt mystery with likable characters set in my hometown of Quincy, Illinois. I merely wanted the reader to have fun and enjoy the story. There would be no deep philosophy.

Nearly every story I write is driven by a plot. The characters are invented simply to carry the story. I want the characters to be interesting, but my primary focus is the quality of the plot. I decided in this case that the key to finding the treasure would be use of a mask. This ancient method of communicating secret messages is quite simple. The spy and his master each have identical thin pieces of cardboard about the size of a page in a standard book. The cardboard has perhaps twenty small rectangles cut into it such that if the cardboard were placed over a book page, only a few words would show through. If the spy wants to send a new message to his master, he simply lays the mask over a blank piece of paper and then writes words in the rectangular holes (which may be widely separated), such as "Meet, me, vine, and, church, streets, ten, at night, June, 20." The spy removes the mask revealing that the words are scattered on the previously blank page, although the words are in reading order. Then the spy connects the words with numerous sensible words to make a letter with meaningful sentences but that has benign content. The letter might start, "Dear Joe. I hope you can meet me at my back garden sometime next week. My cabbage and corn are doing well, and I have many squash on the vine. Tom and Mary say their garden in the church yard is growing well also. Other gardens along the streets are very green," and so on. When the master receives the letter, he merely lays his identical mask over the document, which blocks out all of the superfluous words, revealing the message.

For this story, I chose to have an elderly lady, Aunt Ruth, hide cash at home because she didn't trust banks. I actually had a real Aunt Ruth who was hardworking and thrifty, although she didn't hide her money in the house. The fictional Aunt Ruth dies but leaves clues in her will so that her young heir can find a mask hidden in her home. Then clues direct the heir to place the mask over the correct page in the correct book so that he can learn additional clues about the location of the hidden money.

I decided that the treasure seekers should be likable characters for whom the audience could have sympathy. Like in another story in this book, "Gold for the Taking," the seekers are a young couple truly in love, but in the current story, I cast them as unmarried, working hard while trying to make ends meet, and basically wholesome, ordinary people. I conceived a simple arc to the tale in which puzzles would be solved, the treasure found, and the couple would be able to live happily ever after. Hardly profound but entertaining. I saw no need for a villain or other complications in this very short manuscript. I'll admit that had this been a novel rather than a short story, various complications and (or) villains would have been needed to carry the story.

To add a little more literary weight to this short tale, I introduced elements at the start related to the Old Testament city of Jericho. The early Israelites took this formidable walled city by sending a couple of spies inside to visit a prostitute, who was unsympathetic to the city dwellers because the men there were abusing her, and their women hated her. The prostitute, a desperate woman, was merely trying to support herself and some relatives. Reading between the lines of the Old Testament account, this prostitute apparently allowed additional male spies who were actually soldiers to hide in her rooms, which were located within one of the massive brick walls and which had a small window facing outside. Communications between people in her rooms and Israelites outside could take place via the window, in some cases by hanging a scarlet cord in view. Bible scholars believe that one night, some hidden Israelites snuck from the prostitute's room and merely unlocked the city's main gate, allowing a substantial group of soldiers suddenly and silently to capture that gate, which allowed even more enemy troops suddenly to pour in and take the city. The massive walls of the city were overcome by a simple ruse. In the Bible text, the action of God to allow the taking of the city was poetically dramatized by saying that the Israelites blew trumpets that caused the walls suddenly to collapse. Men hiding with a prostitute and then unlatching the gate was a less flattering tale, although one could speculate that the tactic might have been inspired by the Almighty. In my story, there is a satisfying tie to the walls of Jericho also at the end, but I won't give away the ending.

THE COMBINATION

The aroma of honeysuckle wafted in the warm August air as I stood on the shady front porch of the big house. I pressed the doorbell once. After a moment, the heavy, ornate front door slowly swung inward, and there appeared the most beautiful young woman I had ever seen.

I had expected an elderly lady, so I stood stunned for a moment. My brief silence prompted the angel to speak. "May I help you?"

Her blond curls bounced at her shoulders as she leaned forward, and her inquisitive blue eyes squinted slightly because of the bright sunshine behind me. She wore blue jeans and flip-flops, with a tight-fitting, short-sleeve navy blue T-shirt with bright orange letters: "University of Illinois." She appeared to be about twenty-five years old, so I suspected that she had recently graduated from college.

I had been prepared just to hand over a photocopy of a book page to the elderly woman who I thought would answer the door. As a single young man aged thirty years, however, I was not about to squander this unexpected opportunity. I also had attended the University of Illinois, probably finishing about the year she started. I met few girls there, and currently I was not in any serious relationship. I had been an avid student and had gone to few parties during college, perhaps a bit overly focused on academics. But I had made it to medical school, completed a busy pathology residency, and had just returned to Quincy, Illinois, my hometown, to work as a young assistant pathologist at Blessing Hospital. During my busy schooling and training, I had never met the right girl.

"My name is Stan Baxter," I started. "I found something that belonged to Judge Walter Buss, and I learned that this was his address. Does he still live here?"

As soon as I said the sentence, I bit my lip. I had just read his obituary, so I knew that he no longer lived here! What a dopey thing to say. I smiled, though, because I realized what was happening to me. The surprise of suddenly being face-to-face with a very attractive young woman had momentarily scrambled my thoughts.

"I'm sorry to say that my grandfather died quite suddenly four years ago. But, um ..." She paused for a second, uncertain about how to continue. "Would you like to give me the item?"

I fingered the folded photocopy page in my pants pocket. My mind raced. I could just hand her the paper and leave, but I was angling for a little more time for conversation. "Well," I replied, and took a breath. "This may be a little complicated since it is a personal matter. A little discussion might be required. I would be happy to come back at a convenient time when I could take a few moments to explain."

She looked me straight in the eyes. She had intelligent, kind, trusting eyes, but there was just a tiny hint of suspicion. I knew immediately that she must have been alone, and she was uncertain about whether to let me into the house. As she thought for a few seconds, her gaze dropped to the brown-covered book that I carried in my left hand. "Oh, is that one of my grandfather's books?"

"Yes." I smiled and held it up. "A chess book from the public library."

She seemed to have collected her thoughts and appeared relieved that perhaps she now better understood what I might be talking about. "That book is not a problem at all. When Grandpa died, my grandma asked me to clean off several shelves in the study. Those items were mostly history and art books, but I think that there were a dozen chess books as well. I loaded up my car and donated them all to the public library. It looks like you have been reading one, but I don't need that book back."

"It turns out," I continued, "that there is something special about this book." I decided that I did not want to make her feel uncomfortable by asking to enter the house, but I had another idea. "Perhaps I should return this evening, and I could explain the situation to you and to your grandmother."

Her lips tightened, and she took a breath. "I'll tell you what," she said. "It's such a nice day, let's just sit in the porch swing, and we can talk."

I stepped back to let her pass in front of me. I followed her to the swing and could not help but notice that her jeans fit her petite form very nicely. She sat on the swing, and then I sat on her right. I made certain to leave at least eight inches of air between us. She held out her right hand, palm up. I opened the book to show the inside front cover and placed it in her hand. A paper oval with the words "Judge Walter Buss, Quincy, IL" had been pasted inside the cover.

She looked up at me. "Yes, this belonged to my grandpa. So what's so special?"

"I'm sure that your grandma would want to know about some notes made in this book."

She remained silent a moment. She looked into my eyes again, and I could tell that she had just made another decision about what additional incremental piece of information she was willing to reveal to me. "I'm sorry to say that my grandma is now also dead." She took a breath and added, "So anything you need to say about this book, you can say to me."

I knew then that it was time to show her the information and quickly depart. But my heart was clamoring that I should try to better establish our relationship before I just walked away. I really liked this girl. Maybe she could come to like me.

"Please don't think this is too weird," I said. "I came here today just to give some information to the judge's wife, so I was expecting to talk to an elderly lady, and instead I ran into you. And by coincidence, I also graduated from the University of Illinois. I am going to tell you about the book, of course, but first I want to say that I just moved back to Quincy six months ago for a new job, and I am alone here. If you are willing, I would like to know your name, and I would like to see you again some time, perhaps just for dinner or a movie. What do you say?"

She seemed momentarily taken aback by my directness. She looked again into my eyes, then smiled. "Or maybe a movie and a chess lesson?"

I couldn't help but laugh. "Most women don't play chess. Are you secretly an expert setting me up for a big loss?"

"Well, I'm sorry to say that I have never played chess." She smiled, but then she became serious. "My name is Mary Simmons, and I think I need to tell you something. Because of past relationships, I am a little fragile right now. So I need to go slow, but perhaps we could have dinner some time."

I nodded, and casting about for a way to continue, I asked, "So what was your major in college?"

"Math," she said, and she seemed to be watching me closely for my reaction.

"I studied biology, and I am quite impressed that you majored in math." I really was very impressed. And I think she could sense my genuine respect.

"Well, I majored in math, but I minored in heartbreak," she added. "During four years in Urbana, I met a dozen supposedly nice guys, but every single one of them turned out to be a creep.

That's twelve out of twelve. My policy was to allow a kiss on the second date, but I discovered that four of them stole a kiss from my roommate only the day after I had kissed them! The others did even worse things, and I was so shocked and disappointed. I hope you can understand that I have developed a bit of a bad attitude about men."

I perceived that she was genuinely perturbed, but I also could tell by her tone that she saw some humor in the situation. But she said nothing further. I realized that she was prolonging the silence to see what I would say.

"I was a very serious student in Urbana, and I only went out on three dates because I was very focused on my studies. I'm ready to meet more girls now, though." I paused and then added, "I know about the kind of guys you are talking about. You have no basis to judge, but please believe me that I am not a bad guy."

After a brief pause, I could see that she had decided to change the topic. She closed the book and held it in front of me. "So please show me what is so special about this book."

I took the book and opened it to page one hundred, which happened to be a mostly blank page at the end of a section. In the blank space, some words and numbers were penciled. "Look at this," I said.

She looked for a few seconds, then took the book from my hands to look more closely. She mumbled slightly as she read, "Turn right four times to eight, turn left two times to thirty, turn right to six, turn left until the dial stops, then open." She blinked and looked up at me but said nothing. I could tell she was extremely surprised.

"As you can plainly see, that appears to be a combination for a safe," I stated. "Did your grandpa have a safe?"

She raised her hand and whispered, "Let me sit quietly and think just for a moment, please. Okay?"

After about thirty seconds, she spoke. "I really appreciate

that you brought this to my attention. I am not aware that my grandfather had a safe, but I presume now that he probably did." She swallowed hard and seemed a little short of breath. "I find it extremely disturbing that this information was sitting on a shelf in the public library for several years."

I sat in silence because I could see that she was becoming quite upset.

"Please forgive me if this seems rude," she continued after another moment, "but I would like to ask you to please leave now. And please say nothing about this to anyone else."

I was disappointed by the quick brush-off, but I could tell that this conversation was a shock to her. "I understand that this is a private matter," I said, "but here is my business card. These cards are brand-new, by the way. If you would like my help in any way, I just want you to know that I would love to be able to help you."

She stood up rather abruptly, still clutching the book. "Please tell no one, as I don't want any unexpected visitors. I am alone here." She looked me right in the eyes again, seemingly wanting to trust me but clearly uncertain at the moment just what to do. "Thank you very much for this," she whispered, and she tried to smile, "but now, please just go."

So I mumbled goodbye, turned, and retreated down the broad front stairway out into the afternoon sunshine. When I reached the sidewalk, I looked back up to the porch, but she had already slipped inside, and the large front door was closing. I heard her set the bolt.

⁂

The next day was Monday, so I was back at work in the hospital. My duties included technical supervision regarding the large, automated serum chemistry machines and the associated paperwork. I also examined tissue histology and pathology specimens using a microscope. I dictated my reports to be typed, and then a couple of days later, I proofread those reports and signed them. The morning passed quietly, but I was both troubled and hopeful. I was troubled, of course, because Mary had seemed so upset—but also because she had my library book, which was due in four days. At least I had an excuse to knock on her door this evening to see about getting the book back. She likely would smile if I told her that I had not had a library fine since I was in fifth grade. It would be a thrill to see her again, and I hoped that she would be feeling better about things today.

After my usual salad for lunch, I returned to my office and put on my white lab coat. I sat down at the microscope to review slides from a recent surgical case. Just as I was bringing the first slide into focus, I heard a soft knock on my door, and I looked up to see Mary peeking in. She saw me, stepped inside, and closed the door behind her.

"Good afternoon, Dr. Baxter," she said quietly. "I came to apologize for being so abrupt yesterday. I know that you were only trying to help me."

"Please, have a seat," I said, motioning. She was nicely dressed in black slacks and a neat blouse, and as I looked at her clothing for perhaps a few seconds too long, I realized that she had noticed me looking at her. I probably blushed slightly, then added, "I suppose you just saw me looking you up and down, and I guess I should apologize for that, but I am very happy to see you." After a short pause, I asked, "So does that make me a creepy guy?"

She smiled. "I think that makes you a normal guy with an acceptable level of creepiness." Then she added, "I knew that you would need your library book back, so here it is." She set the book on my desk. "I felt compelled to remove one troublesome page, but I photocopied the chess material on that page. I taped the trimmed photocopy into place in the book. So I hope the library will overlook that. By the way, I compared the handwriting of the book notations to some personal letters, and I'm sure the book entry was made by my grandfather."

I thanked her for returning the book, then added, "If it will make you feel any better, chess books generally don't circulate much. It's likely that in the four years since the book was donated, I may have been the first customer to check it out."

She nodded, then looked me straight in the eyes. Whenever she did that, I could feel my heart skip a beat.

"I couldn't find it," she said.

"Where did you look?"

"I was up half the night. I removed paintings from walls, knocked on mantel pieces, looked in closets, checked the garage, and I looked in all the kitchen cabinets. I can't find it."

"It's a big, old house. What is the story of that house?"

"It was my grandfather's house, of course. It was built about 1910 along the row of big houses on Broadway. I think my grandfather must have purchased it thirty or forty years ago. The garage is in the back and is large because it formerly was a carriage house with stables for horses."

"Did you grow up in that house?"

"My parents had a small house on Jackson Street." She paused, obviously considering carefully what to say next. "They were killed in an auto accident on an icy road when I was a junior in college. When I settled their estate, I sold that house, and I returned to stay with my grandma in the big house during school breaks." She paused again. "Then Grandma died right after I graduated. I have no siblings, so I have been staying in the big house for the time being while I sort out what to do next."

"Sorry for your many losses," I said. "I lost my mom two years ago, but my dad is doing well down in Arizona. My parents moved south a few years ago."

I brought the conversation back to the safe. "Did you look in the attic or the basement?"

"No." She paused and looked at me with what appeared to

be a bit of a sheepish expression. "I thought that I should not climb around in an old attic or crawl into little spaces in the basement when I was there alone. I want someone else in the house with me when I do that." She smiled, and there was a long pause. "That means you."

We began our explorations by having spaghetti, meatballs, and red wine in her kitchen at five thirty. We sat side by side, and our knees touched several times under the table; she seemed to take no note of that, but I certainly noticed. She laughed at several of my jokes during the meal. She had run errands and had gotten organized during the afternoon, while I was still working at the hospital. At the far end of the kitchen table, she had positioned three flashlights with new batteries, a hammer, a heavy-duty crowbar, and a large screwdriver. We were optimistic about our planned search, and we were enjoying the wine.

"Since you didn't even suspect that your grandfather had a safe," I began, "I presume that you have no idea what might be in it."

"He was a prominent judge. So probably just paperwork. But I need to know," she replied.

Her face was attractively flushed, perhaps an effect of the wine. Her old T-shirt and jeans signaled that she was serious about getting on her hands and knees if necessary. I also was wearing old jeans, so I was ready to pitch in as required.

We decided to start in the basement. There were only a few overhead bulbs, which didn't provide much light, and the cobwebs showed that beyond the small area where the furnace and water heater were located near the stairs, no one had ventured into the far corners of the basement for quite a while. Flashlight in hand and with Mary close behind me, I brushed the gossamer aside at intervals as I slowly moved forward. I could feel Mary's hand softly pressing into the small of my back. I passed between two stacks of crates, and then I stepped around an old wooden trunk. Curious, I raised the dry, cracked, dusty lid, but the trunk was empty. In an area of the basement quite far from the stairs, a closet had been built into a corner. The door was locked. It was a small closet, about three feet by three feet, and about nine feet tall from the concrete floor to the ceiling rafters.

"Do you have the key to this closet door?" I asked.

"I have two key rings with three keys each. The keys are for the front and back doors of the house and the garage door. But let me see if any of these work in this door."

None of the keys worked. So I grabbed the crowbar and looked at Mary. She nodded. I forced open the closet door.

There before us was a six-foot-tall pillar of concrete that had been poured so as to anchor a twelve-inch-by-twelve-inch wall safe, which was set in the concrete at shoulder height. Mary gave me a small excited hug around my waist, and I felt her momentarily press her forehead into my back between my shoulder blades. It was a trivial matter to spin the dial to and fro to open the safe. We took the paperwork that was inside upstairs to the kitchen table.

Triumphantly, I poured more red wine for Mary and me. Then I sat quietly as Mary looked down at a sealed white business envelope and a one-inch-thick accounting notebook. She sliced open the envelope and read to herself a one-page handwritten note. Then she looked at me, and tears came to her eyes. She asked me please to reach over to the counter and hand her a box of tissues. She flipped through the accounting notebook briefly, then closed it and sighed. "My grandfather was a good and loving man," she said, "but it appears that he was also a bit of a crook."

"Do you want to tell me about it?"

"This letter is an apology from him and an explanation. He had been the chairman of a county-wide fundraising effort for the hospital thirty years ago, and he writes that in a moment of weakness, he embezzled $200,000 of the funds that had been raised. I can't believe it!"

"Wow," I whispered. "So do you think the money is hidden in the basement?"

"No. He says he invested the money in CDs in State Street Bank. In the next years, his legal career grew, and he was very successful. I guess he hadn't counted on that. So he never had to use the money he'd stolen."

"He stole money and put it in the bank," I repeated, mostly murmuring to myself. "So is the money still there?"

"Stan, he died with an estate of more than $8 million. But apparently he never could bring himself to return the money that he had embezzled years before. So he just kept it in those same accounts in State Street Bank. When he wrote this apology letter eight years ago, those funds were worth about $500,000. I can't believe my grandfather would have done such a thing. He didn't even need the money!" Mary held her head in her hands, her elbows on the table.

"Mary, it seems to me that he may have intended to return the money someday. Perhaps he was going to return it with interest. But fate interrupted, and he died before he could bring himself to act." I paused a moment, then continued. "I guess we each have our flaws. Your grandpa may have been worried about his young family at that time, and the temptation to set aside some resources was one that he just could not resist. I think the letter shows that he felt badly about it for years."

Mary cried for a while, then wiped her tears and took several swallows of wine. "I am going to the bank tomorrow, and I am going to have a check prepared to donate that money to the hospital." She wiped away another tear.

I leaned toward her and spoke softly. "I have a suggestion, Mary. When you speak with the hospital, be sure to name the donation in honor of your grandfather. After all, he did safeguard the money, and he invested it wisely." I gently took

Mary's hand and then added, "Our actions today provide a kind of closure. We can imagine that, through us, your grandfather found a way to act from the grave to get the money properly delivered."

Mary made a tearful smile, and she wiped her nose with a tissue.

Then I had another thought. "And consider this, Mary. Have the donation officially publicized as a Second-Chance Award. The news release should declare that no one is perfect, and every human being deserves a second chance. Of course, only you and I will know the secret of the long delay of this donation!"

She stood and pulled me up from my chair. She stepped forward, put her arms around me, and gently kissed my lips. She was trembling. I instinctively placed my hands on her waist. When she kissed me again, I slipped my hands upward just under the lower edge of her T-shirt, and I felt her soft skin on my palms and fingertips.

"One more thing, Mary," I opined. "Members of the male sex also deserve a second chance in your eyes, and I hope you will allow me to show you that a man can love you with his whole heart."

Mary trembled in my arms, then whispered, "Stan, you have a loving heart and warm hands." Then she let out a little giggle and added, "That really is an unbeatable combination."

EMERGING FROM THE GRAY TWILIGHT

"**R**odney, Mr. Peterson will see you right now." Loretta's tone was neutral, but the gray-haired, longtime administrative secretary delivered her line in a manner leaving no doubt that when the boss called for you, that meant you stood up immediately.

Rodney sat up straight in his chair, slightly disoriented. He had been only half-awake in his tiny, thin-walled cubicle, staring with heavy lids at a spreadsheet on his computer screen. It had been a slow, mid-July Thursday afternoon. After a second, his adrenaline started to pump. "Oh, Loretta. Uh, thanks. I'll head right upstairs." His mind raced as he sorted through several possibilities as to why the big boss would need to speak with him. He stood, straightened his necktie, took a quick swig of the cold coffee still in his mug, and excused himself as he carefully brushed past Loretta and headed to the elevator.

Not a college graduate, Rodney had counted himself lucky

to land a job as an assistant in the Marketing Department of the Helen of Troy Hair Products Company in Peoria, Illinois. He thought of himself as having above-average intelligence, but at the time he was hired, he had only just graduated from Peoria High School. Neither he nor his widowed mother had the resources for him to make a start at college. Instead, he thought he might try to get some practical experience in the working world while saving some money. Though he was now twenty-two, by living with his mother, he saved rent and had put a few dollars in the bank. Unfortunately, frequent repairs on his rattle-trap Ford Escort were constantly eating away his funds.

He had been a bit surprised at age eighteen that he had gotten the job, since he knew nothing about marketing and even less about women's hair products. He quickly realized that they had hired him because he was healthy, young, and fairly strong, and he could quickly understand directions and follow them. So he was the perfect helper to load and unload boxes of product samples, make photocopies, run errands, and do the million small tasks that would only be time-consuming distractions to the marketing personnel.

His cubicle was on the second floor of the small building, and he was about to ride up to the highest floor—six—where the grand business strategies were devised. He could not imagine why Mr. Peterson wanted to see him.

His adrenaline had returned at least partially to normal when the up arrow dinged and the steel elevator doors slid open. But his heart skipped beats again when there in the elevator stood Darla Smith. She had a friendly, small-town manner and long brunette curls. She was a twenty-two-year-old newly minted graduate of the University of Illinois at Urbana who only thirty days ago had started her first real job as a junior administrative assistant to a vice president of finance up on six. They had met at the Taco Bell next door at lunchtime last week, and they laughed when they realized that they both worked at "Helen's," as many employees called the company. They also had signed up for the small, informal, two-hour Employee Leadership Session that was to be held the next day, and Rodney strategically waited until two minutes before the start to enter the conference room so he might be able to select a seat near Darla. Chronically shy, Rodney had been on few dates in his life, but he was trying to find ways to get to know her better.

Only nine employees had signed up for the session, all low-level workers who each would earn five credits from the Personnel Department by volunteering to take this optional training. Ring binders with a few pages of handouts were passed out at the start, and the cheerful external speaker began immediately with a series of PowerPoint slides and then conducted an icebreaker so the few employees might get to know one another a little better. Each person had to make a brief statement about themselves revealing something that they believed no one else knew about them. Darla volunteered that she had won her fifth-grade class spelling bee. Rodney had stumbled a bit trying to decide what to say when his turn came. Seizing on an idea, he shared that when he was eight years old, his father had been a janitor at Midwest Soybeans, and had taken him on a three-day trip to teach him how to fish, though his dad then died of a heart attack at the end of that summer. The brief silence in the room that followed caused Rodney to worry that he had perhaps not selected a good item to share, but the coordinator quickly moved on to the next employee.

Darla broke the silence in the elevator. "I had Taco Bell again at noon. I like their crunchy tacos."

"Yeah," Rodney replied, but he had no idea what to say next. He knew that this was an unexpected opportunity, so after a brief hesitation, he began again. "I'm going fishing in my little rowboat on Saturday afternoon. Would you like to come with me for an hour and try to catch a catfish?" This conversation should have been easy and natural, but the inexperienced young man was definitely in uncharted waters.

Darla looked surprised. Then she smiled. "Maybe. Tomorrow is Friday, so let's talk then." Her noncommittal response was no surprise to Rodney. But she didn't say no. As the doors slid open, he began to feel hopeful. She seemed like such a nice girl; he could be comfortable with her.

"See ya," he said as he motioned for her to exit ahead of him. She stepped out and turned right. Rodney turned left and headed briskly toward Mr. Peterson's office.

⚬〰︎⚬

Mr. Peterson's door was open, and Rodney stood for a second in the doorway. The executive wore an impressive dark blue suit with matching necktie. Though he was on the phone, he motioned Rodney to move forward and take a chair in front of his large desk.

"Okay. Okay. I understand. Okay. Bye for now." Mr. Peterson hung up.

"Unusual situation here, Rodney."

Rodney nodded and maintained eye contact.

"Marsha, Stephanie, and their assistant, Tim, are in Seattle, and they were just involved in a car accident on their way to the airport. Injuries are moderate, but they're going to be okay—hospitalized for one day or maybe two. One has a broken leg, one has bruises and cuts, and the other has a broken arm. Thank goodness it's not worse."

"So sorry to hear that," Rodney mumbled.

"With our Marketing Department out of commission, we are going to have to make some special arrangements about the Lasting Curls conference at the Hilton in Chicago this Saturday. Important Chicago customers. So I need to ask you to work this weekend to help out. Michael Vincent and his assistant will fill in to give the presentations, but Tim won't be available to move

58

all the boxes. You will need to ride in the van to Chicago with Michael and Janice early Saturday morning to help set up the room for the conference, which starts with a luncheon at noon, and then help take things down and pack things up at 3:30 p.m."

Rodney's heart sank, but without hesitation, he said, "Of course. No problem."

There was a brief pause, and then Mr. Peterson continued, "So, Rodney, you've been here two years, right?"

Rodney shifted slightly in his chair but tried to look calm. "Actually about four years, sir."

"And how do you feel that things are going?"

"I've been learning by doing. There are many practical tasks that must be done. Marsha and Stephanie both talk to me now and then—to explain some marketing things. That's nice of them and very helpful to me as a beginner. I know how to work with their standard spreadsheets of customers, and I sometimes help them compose their monthly report."

"So you can write?"

"Well ..." Rodney squirmed a little again. "I do like to read—probably a book a month. And I guess I try to write correct English when I send emails or help Marsha proof her marketing materials."

"What books do you read?"

"I like American history. Civil War. Abraham Lincoln. Dwight Eisenhower. That sort of thing. And sometimes novels, like *Huckleberry Finn*."

Mr. Peterson nodded, but just then his phone rang. "Thanks, and that's all for now," Mr. Peterson said. He motioned for Rodney to rise and leave, so without further comment, out the door he went.

Loretta was back at her desk now, and as he stepped by, he noticed that there were two dollar bills on the floor behind her chair. Rodney reached down and handed the bills to her. "I guess these must have fallen out of your purse."

A little taken aback, Loretta thanked him. "Thank you! You are so honest!"

Rodney had always tried to be fair and honest, but lately it seemed that life was determined to be unfair to him. Poor pay, low-scale job, old car, poor prospects ever to attend college, no girlfriend—and now he even had to cancel his plans with Darla. He walked past the elevator and on toward Darla's desk.

She looked up as he approached. He did his best to smile, and after taking a breath, he mumbled that plans had changed for Saturday afternoon. He was able to frame his words a bit better once he had gotten started. "Looks like I need to work on Saturday to help with a conference in Chicago. Hope we can go fishing some other time."

"Sure," was her only response, and he was not certain if she looked relieved or disappointed. He quickly turned and retreated toward the elevator. Why was he such a dork?

Back in his cubicle, he felt himself relax. What a day! He was a dork, but he had tried to be more outgoing today. He assured himself that making social progress in small steps was better than going backward. He had faced Mr. Peterson without totally wilting, and he had talked to Darla twice.

After a moment, he pulled down the ring binder from last week's leadership course, opened to the page of quotations at the end, and skimmed once again the quote that had most impressed him that day. Who knows? Perhaps reflecting on that one quote was actually helping him to change his life. He certainly seemed to be a bit braver today. Before closing the binder, he read Teddy Roosevelt's words once more softly to himself: "Far better it is to dare mighty things, to win glorious triumphs even though checkered by failure, than to rank with those poor spirits who neither enjoy nor suffer much because they live in the gray twilight that knows neither victory nor defeat."

By five o'clock Saturday morning, Rodney was already on the company loading dock moving boxes into the big white van. Most of the boxes were eleven by eleven by eleven inches and contained catalogues to hand out at the conference. There were catalogues for hair dyes, for hair straighteners, for curlers, for grooming instruments, for shampoos and conditioners, for this and for that. And each box was quite heavy; one thing he had learned well at his job was how heavy stacks of paper can be. He could easily lift one box, but he was always careful not to twist as he was moving a box from here to there. And he always lifted mostly using his legs rather than his back.

He was happy to be needed, and he was doing useful, honest work. But he feared that he was not actually making a vital and intellectually satisfying contribution. Was he going to be doing this for the rest of his life? How could he advance without a college degree? In recent months, he had become determined that he must somehow find a way to afford to go back to school.

The VP, Michael Vincent, seemed like a reasonable guy. He had been friendly enough that morning, but he was not going to move any boxes, that was for sure. Rodney knew his place. He followed directions as Michael and Janice pointed, and soon they were ready to start the drive to Chicago.

The big Hilton was easy to find, and the staff guided them to where they could best park to unload. The supplies were taken upstairs in two trips, using a dolly on a back elevator. A large meeting space on the mezzanine level had been subdivided into three equal parts by temporary moving walls. Helen of Troy was assigned the center meeting area, while on the right side would be a retirement-planning seminar, and on the left side a meeting of some elementary school teachers. Each of the two mobile walls that trisected the space had a doorway that gave passage to the space next door, whereas wooden, permanent double doors at the front of each of the three meeting spaces allowed attendees to pass from the mezzanine lounge area into the meeting room of their choice. Helen of Troy had placed about one hundred chairs in ten rows of ten so that local salon owners from all over Chicago could be seated comfortably at one o'clock, once they had finished their complimentary luncheon downstairs in the main lobby of the hotel. There was a podium and screen up front. Five large rectangular banquet tables had been placed along a side wall of the Helen of Troy meeting space, to display the catalogues and product samples. The tables were draped with white linen tablecloths that hung all the way to the floor. Under each table were the twenty-five or more empty cardboard boxes from which catalogues and samples had been removed. Depending on customer interest, after the session, only about half of those boxes would be required to haul the remaining materials back to Peoria.

At 11:45 a.m., Michael, a little nervous, announced to Rodney that he and Janice would now need to head downstairs to help guide the salon owners into the luncheon area. Rodney was to change the way some of the catalogues were displayed, however: the six stacks on the second table should be moved back to the fourth table, while the six stacks on the fourth table should be moved up to the second table. Rodney smiled and responded, "No problem," although he was a little perturbed that they had not decided that arrangement in the first place. He was also mildly upset that no one mentioned whether or not he would be given a free lunch ticket. But as Michael and Janice rushed out of the room, he surmised that things were just disorganized enough that this slight had not been intentional.

It was a fifteen-minute task to switch the position of those catalogues. Then Rodney surveyed the layout. *Looks good*, he thought. But several empty cardboard boxes under the third table had toppled and were bulging the linen tablecloth forward. Those boxes would have to be better stacked underneath. So Rodney got down on his hands and knees and crawled under table three to pull back and restack those boxes. While under the table, he was surprised to hear a loud conversation between two men in the room. They seemed frightened and upset. A little alarmed, Rodney carefully peeked into the room using a narrow gap between two tablecloths.

Two men in their midthirties were wearing black suits with white shirts and black neckties. They were just inside the slightly ajar double door to this meeting space and were peeking out into the mezzanine lobby. With them, they had on a small dolly three large, brown, old-fashioned suitcases.

The taller of the two men was on a cell phone. "No, I can't see 'em, Eddie. No. We were about to come down the main elevator when you called. How many? What? Twenty? In the main lobby? Holy shit!"

"What?" whispered the shorter man.

"Twenty cops in the lobby," the tall man replied to his companion. Then he focused again on the phone conversation. "Okay. And more out back. Right. Yes, I understand. Okay. Will do. Stash the suitcases and then just walk out past the police. Got it. They'll check us, but we'll have nothing. Right. Okay. I got it, Eddie. Okay. Bye."

"This is crazy," volunteered the short man with a hint of panic in his voice. "We can't just leave these suitcases here!"

The tall man nodded and looked left and right. He blinked and smiled. "Look, Sammy. Let's slide 'em off the dolly and under that table with the white tablecloth. They should be okay there for two or three hours, just until the heat is off." Without further discussion, the pair rolled the dolly to table five, which was closest to the door. The bags must have been heavy because it took both of them to slide the three bags under the table and out of sight behind the white linen. They again peeked out of the double door, as it was slightly open.

"Change of plan, Sammy. You walk out past the police and then just stay at the house. Smile at 'em and say hi. They'll pat you down, but then they'll send you out. I'm going to sit in that big chair over there in this upstairs lobby and keep a close eye on this door. Those suitcases won't be going anywhere. If the police come by, I'll just talk real nice and keep readin' the newspaper. 'Just mindin' my own business, Officer.' They'll check my pockets, but I'm clean."

With that, they both disappeared out of the double door. The room fell deathly quiet. Rodney crawled out from under table three, stood, and looked at his watch: 12:05. He walked to table five and slowly lifted the white linen. He reached for the first suitcase but then stopped. After a couple of seconds, he walked up to table one, the hair dye display, and put on a pair of latex gloves. With very little further hesitation, he slid the three suitcases out into the room one by one and tipped the first one on its side. It was not locked. He quickly undid the latches and lifted the lid. Money. And lots of it.

Rodney felt chills as he let his gloved fingers stir the unwrapped loose bills that had simply been dumped into the suitcase. There were a few fives and tens, but nearly all of the bills were twenties and hundreds. It was a fortune. He glanced behind him at the double door and then back at the money. His brow furrowed. For the first time in his life—ever—he was facing a major moral dilemma.

He opened the other two suitcases. The contents were the same. Probably drug money, he thought. His stomach wound into a tight knot. He knew that this might be his one big chance—for college, for more financial stability, for a good start in life. He was certain that the suitcases belonged to crooks. They had no good intentions. Could he justify stealing this money? And what would happen if he got caught, especially if he got caught by the crooks?

Seconds passed, and his breathing quickened as he knew that he had little time. He had to make a decision. He knew in his heart that it was wrong to steal, but he also knew that this was a rare and unique opportunity. It made no sense to let the drug dealers walk out with the money. And he saw little value of letting a big pile of money sit in a police evidence room. Perhaps it was rationalizing, and it certainly was not what Teddy Roosevelt was talking about when he advocated daring mighty things, but on balance, he concluded that he could put the money to much better use than the gangsters.

"I'm going to do it," he mumbled to himself. "And I'm going to do it quick."

Working rapidly and systematically, he emptied the contents of the first suitcase into four cardboard boxes and placed them onto the dolly that the two men had conveniently left behind. In scant minutes, he had transferred the contents of the other two suitcases into eight additional cardboard boxes and stacked them on the dolly. *My golly!* Twelve boxes full of money.

Then he loaded a variety of catalogues, several from each of the many stacks, into the suitcases. But he didn't want to deplete his company's supply. He peaked next door using the door in the mobile wall. The room was empty, so he retrieved a couple of loads of handouts about elementary school lesson plans to add to the suitcases. And from the other empty neighboring room, he retrieved a couple loads of financial-planning handouts. When the suitcases were full, he closed them, tipped them upright, and slid them back under table five just exactly where they had been. After lowering the white linen to hide the suitcases, he tucked the latex gloves into his pocket. He quickly rolled the dolly through the mobile wall door into the teachers' meeting room and then out the other side to the back elevator. He still had the keys to the van in his pocket. Within minutes, he had loaded the twelve boxes of cash into the company van, still parked less than twenty yards from the hotel loading dock. After grabbing his banana from the van, he returned the dolly to the meeting room as quickly as he could, placing it carefully, exactly as he had found it. It seemed that no one had been in the room in the interval. He looked at his watch: 12:40. Within a minute, he was back out through the teachers' meeting room and down the elevator.

A bit breathless, he walked casually around the side of the hotel while eating his banana and entered the front door of the Hilton. *God, forgive me*, he thought. *Dear Lord, you know that I have good intentions. I had to decide in a hurry, so please forgive me if I made a bad choice under time pressure.* It was the most sincere prayer he ever sent heavenward in his life.

Just inside the lobby, he ran into Michael and Janice as they were returning to the mezzanine with some attendees to start getting settled for the presentations.

"Catalogues all set?" Michael asked.

"No problem," mumbled Rodney.

☙

Rodney sat in the second to last row and far from the display tables during the presentations. He had heard these talks at least six times before, so his mind was elsewhere. There were some unique occurrences during the session, however. At about one thirty, two uniformed policemen quietly entered the back of the room and just stood by the double doors for a moment. They looked left and right. After another minute, they quietly left. At two thirty, the tall man quietly entered the back of the room along with a uniformed hotel employee—a broad-shouldered bellman. The tall man tiptoed to table five and lifted the linen, and the bellman slid the three suitcases out from under the table and onto the dolly. The tall man gave the bellman some money, and the employee quietly exited with the loaded dolly. The tall man stuck a claim ticket in his coat pocket. Then the tall man sat in the last row for fifteen minutes, apparently engrossed with details about hair dye, before he also quietly left. Michael, who was speaking, took little note of these goings-on.

Michael was pleased that there seemed to be fewer than usual catalogues to pack up to return to Peoria. The presentations had gone well, and the company van was fully loaded by four fifteen. The drive back to Peoria was hindered by the usual traffic, but there were no surprises. Michael and Janice asked to be let out in the front parking lot so that they could just walk to their cars and drive home. Rodney was to unload the van and park it in its allotted place. Of course, after Michael and Janice had departed, Rodney made a quick trip home to load twelve boxes into his mother's garage. The locked paint storage cabinet, which was empty, made a convenient storehouse for his hoard, and the padlock would keep his mother from stumbling onto the loot. He was going to help her substantially financially, of course, but the less she knew about all of this, the better.

⚭

It was nine in the morning. The tall man and the short man entered the lobby of the Hilton and were quickly joined by a man in an expensive suit. The trio walked to the bellman's desk, which was just next to the main registration desk. The tall man presented his claim ticket, and the bellman disappeared into a back room and slid three heavy brown suitcases one by one out front.

"Are you certain that these three brown suitcases are yours, sir?" the bellman asked as he set the claim ticket on the counter.

"Yes, thanks," replied the tall man.

"But wait a second," the bellman replied in a rather loud voice. "A lot of suitcases look alike. Please check your claim ticket again, sir."

Now a bit annoyed, the tall man held his claim ticket an inch in front of the bellman's nose and brusquely responded, "See, you idiot! These are my suitcases. One more word and no tip for you, asshole!"

The bellman retreated to the far end of his counter, while at the same instant two uniformed policemen stepped forward from the back room to confront the three men.

67

Stunned, the three men stood motionless.

"Well, if these are your suitcases, I suppose we should check to see what's inside them," pronounced the policeman in charge. "I hereby present you with a court-ordered warrant, and we would like to open the suitcases now."

"Actually, Officer, I think that there has been some mistake. My suitcases were a darker color of brown, not these suitcases," protested the tall man. The blood had drained from his face, and his eyes were as wide as silver dollars.

The officer smiled. "Not likely." He turned to his partner and told him to open the cases.

Latches were unsnapped and lids flipped up, revealing catalogues for retirement planning, elementary school teaching, and hair dye. Jaws dropped all around, but it was not clear if the shady trio or the two policemen were the more surprised.

MIRACLE IN MONTANA

No coverage, not even one bar. The battery was dead anyway. It was still daytime, but it was overcast, and the sky had a perfectly even dullness, so there was no way to tell what time of day it was, much less which direction was north or south or anything else for that matter. A two-lane blacktop road snaked up into the distance and disappeared into some trees, or a forest if you wanted to get technical about it. It also snaked down toward some lumpy hills and disappeared there as well. What sounded like a two-stroke chainsaw could be heard in the distance, but it was impossible to tell whether it was up in the forest or down in the lumpy hills. This had been happening more often lately. Two different ways to go, with a dead battery and no bars, and nobody left to blame.

This sort of catastrophic breakdown of a new rental car with fewer than twelve thousand miles was unexpected and frustrating. Earlier that morning, the flights from Chicago to Great Falls had been unremarkable, and Michael had been excited to make his first visit to Montana. The polished blue Toyota provided a smooth and comfortable ride as he left the airport and headed southeast into the hills of the Lewis and Clark National Forest.

A few miles past the little town of Monarch, the red idiot

light first appeared on the dash, so he had pulled to the side of Highway 89 momentarily to consider options. That was when Michael realized that his phone had no battery left—quite careless of him and out of character. There had not been much in Monarch, and he judged that he could make it a few more miles south to his destination: Neihart, Montana. Then Uncle Jesse, a man familiar with this very rural area, likely could rescue him. He would get a charge on his phone and tell the rental company to come tow the car back to Great Falls.

But only a few miles later, the dire prophecy made by the red idiot light was fulfilled with a vengeance as the car suddenly lost power, radio, and clock. Michael glided well off the highway and sat for a moment in silence. Always even tempered, he calmly retrieved his bags from the trunk.

He stood forlornly by the side of the car. It must have been the alternator. Since he believed that he was still ten miles from Neihart, he decided just to wait with the car. He did have three water bottles, a hat, and some sunscreen, along with one carry-on bag and one heavy suitcase.

The chainsaw had stopped, and Michael stood in near silence. He could hear the wind intermittently rustle the pines, and for the first time, he took a moment to appreciate the fragrance of the trees. Large bumblebees buzzed in the roadside clover. Three black crows drifted down and landed on the other side of the road. They seemed to stare at him, their heads cocked a little as if they were curious.

His thoughts drifted to this week's unexpected phone call from Uncle Jesse. Michael was his only nephew. He had met his dad's lone sibling just once, when he was ten years old; Uncle Jesse had attended Michael's dad's funeral in Naperville, Illinois. He was too young then to maturely assess Jesse, but he recalled that he had hugged Jesse and spoke politely with him, and Jesse had smiled at him.

Even back then, he secretly held a bias that Uncle Jesse was an odd character. Michael didn't let it show when he hugged Uncle Jesse that day, but this bias had been created over several years by his father's accounts. Apparently, Jesse had always been unconventional. A mediocre student, he frequently was in trouble due to use of alcohol and pranks that were in poor taste. Right after high school, Jesse hitchhiked to Montana where, he said, a man could be free and could make his own way in life. Uncle Jesse then basically disappeared, though the family did receive an occasional Christmas card.

In contrast, Michael's father was a sensible man who worked two jobs to get through college, and he had married a kind and intelligent woman. But he was cut down by leukemia after just eleven years of marriage. As the only child, Michael did his best to avoid causing his mom any trouble, and she maintained the little house and doted on his small accomplishments as he made his way through high school and college. But she died too, just a year after his college graduation.

His first postcollege job as an account manager at a small company in Chicago was colorless and unfulfilling, but it paid the bills. He hoped to meet the right young woman, but that had just not happened yet. The mysterious call from Uncle Jesse actually provided a bit of relief from his routine. Michael had just gotten back to his small apartment last Tuesday evening when his cell phone rang. Jesse's voice was weak and breathless; clearly, he was not a well man. In spite of the fact that they hadn't spoken in fourteen years, Jesse insisted that Michael was the only one who could help him and that Michael must travel to Neihart immediately. He did have the presence of mind to clarify that he should fly into Great Falls, then drive southeast.

As the phone conversation continued, it became clear that Jesse's small cabin was actually a mile south of Neihart off Highway 89. Jesse said that Michael would meet his friend Bob in town and that Bob would direct him. He added that few other people in this remote area had been friendly to him and that he couldn't trust them. Jesse emphasized that the trip was important, and he would make it very much worth his while to come see him. Still off guard and a bit bewildered, Michael agreed to make arrangements with his boss for a few days off and suggested that he would fly the next Saturday morning. Jesse seemed very relieved, and without any further explanation, he said thank you and goodbye.

Shifting his stance as he stood by the roadside, Michael's thoughts wandered farther. If he had chosen the red Toyota instead of the blue Toyota that morning at the rental lot, by now he would already be talking to Bob in Neihart. If his father had not had a sibling, he would never be standing at this spot in Montana today. If his father had not contracted leukemia, he would still be alive. Life was full of contingency.

Michael's mind snapped back to the present as the crows across the road noisily took flight, and the rumble of an approaching pickup truck grew louder. He waved his arms and smiled. As expected, the driver slowed and stopped to talk to him, in spite of his uncle's rather bizarre warning that he should not trust the people around here. The passenger-side electric window lowered, and as Michael leaned into the truck to talk, his eyes met the most beautiful brown eyes he had ever seen. The dark-haired young woman remained silent as though she, too, was somewhat enchanted by their locked gaze. Then she asked if he needed assistance. Michael took a breath as his head spun. After his brief explanation, she told him to load his things into the truck bed, and he climbed into the passenger's seat.

Michael felt his heart skipping beats, but he cleared his throat and asked if she knew his uncle, Jesse Mason. She smiled. She did know him but only superficially, since he rarely came into town. A nice man who was very quiet, she summarized.

Then Michael and Sarah introduced themselves, and he asked if she knew his uncle's friend, Bob Smallridge. He was startled to learn that he was her father! He mused aloud for a moment about unlikely coincidences, but Sarah just laughed. She explained that only fifty-five people lived in and around Neihart, so everyone knew everyone in the area. She said she would drive him to her father's store, located right on the highway, since she had to relieve her father at the store counter now for two hours.

As Sarah looked straight ahead at the road, Michael stole another glance at her. She was petite and very pretty, dressed in jeans and a red plaid flannel shirt. Her abundant straight black hair was much longer than shoulder-length. He wanted to say something else but was not sure where to lead. He noticed the charms jangling on the silver bracelet on her right wrist, and a heart-shaped one turned toward him in plain view displayed the silhouette of a black crow on a red heart. He asked about it, and she said that she had collected charms for her bracelet over many years. The crow on the heart was given to her by her grandmother, who was a pure-blooded Crow Indian named Alsoomse, which was a name borrowed from the local Blackfoot that meant "independent." She went on to relate that the Crows are Northern Plains Indians, and they actually call themselves Apsaalooke: "Children of the Large-Beaked Bird," traditionally considered to be a crow or raven. Crows were often seen among the corn, and they were viewed as very wise servants of the Corn Mother. In the Crow language, such a blackbird was called *áalihte* and was respected for its intelligence and supernatural connections. Sarah paused to smile, then added that her grandmother, who supposedly also had a mysterious connection with the supernatural, gave her that charm with the explanation that it would someday help her find her true love. Michael swallowed hard but said nothing.

As the truck bounced over a bump, the charms jangled, and the crow charm rotated to flash briefly a red, blue, and white pattern on the back. Michael asked what the image was on the back, and Sarah held out her right hand to him so he could hold the charm in his fingers to examine it in detail. Michael suppressed a gasp as he saw that it was a small image of the flag of the city of Chicago, with two blue stripes and four red stars on a white background. He had seen it millions of times at home. Michael commented that he thought the image was related to the city of Chicago, and Sarah responded that her grandmother's brother had taken a trip to Chicago about thirty years ago, and he brought back that charm as a souvenir for his sister, and then because of the heart shape, her grandmother gave it to her when she turned eighteen.

Michael, for the moment, did not volunteer that he was from Chicago but asked if she had gone to school. He was quite impressed that she had majored in mathematics at the University of Montana at Missoula. But she wanted to return home for a while to help out her dad while she took time to consider what to do next, because a commitment to seek a PhD in math was quite a serious decision.

The nine-mile ride into Neihart passed quickly, and Sarah pulled into a parking lot below a large sign advertising Bob's Bar, Dining, and Motel. Michael unloaded his things and shuffled toward the lobby, his carry-on bag in one hand, while his suitcase rolled behind. As Sarah walked ahead, he could not help but notice how nice she looked in those jeans. Her father, a middle-aged man with a deeply tanned and wrinkled face framed by graying hair, was standing behind the reception desk, and Sarah kissed him on the cheek. Michael arranged to charge his phone while they talked. He explained that he was Michael Mason from Illinois, visiting his uncle Jesse, who had phoned him. Bob lifted the receiver from the phone at the desk and explained that Jesse had actually called using this very phone. He added that Jesse was a very private man, and he seemed to be sick in recent weeks. Bob lowered his voice and told Michael that they needed to talk privately in his office so that he could explain some other things. Bob ushered him into that room and closed the door.

Michael was a bit surprised that Bob first insisted that he confirm his identity by showing his driver's license. Then Bob related that Jesse had hung around this area for many years before purchasing four acres with a small cabin located south of town. Jesse also bought a used Cadillac but rarely came into town. Bob and Jesse had worked out a "secret arrangement" to be disclosed to no one else until a mutually agreed date in the future. Bob delivered groceries and supplies weekly to the cabin and sometimes pumped gas into Jesse's rusty El Dorado, agreeing to accept payment by an unusual method that only Jesse himself was allowed to explain.

With this portion of their conversation concluded, Bob stood and reached to grab a cardboard box from the corner. A practical man, Bob viewed this as an opportunity to make a delivery. He walked through the lobby to where he could load a few supplies for Jesse.

Michael thanked Sarah again for the ride. He was a bit surprised when she asked in rapid-fire several questions about his education and job—so it was no longer a secret that he lived in Chicago. They exchanged cell numbers, and she requested that they sit together to talk for a few more minutes while her father gathered the groceries. Sarah led him back into the office.

Michael was pleased that she wanted to sit with him but was uncertain about what exactly was happening. She seemed relaxed and curious about him and explained that several boyfriends in Missoula during the college years had proven to be unreliable and insincere. She wanted to be careful about starting any new relationships and asked what he thought about his attempts to meet new people.

As Michael looked her in the eyes, he explained that he had never had a serious girlfriend and had been raised by a father and mother who truly loved and trusted each other. They had provided a superb model for the type of relationship he ultimately was seeking.

Sarah asked how anchored he was to Chicago and emphasized that she wanted to remain geographically close to her father. Her roots were in Montana, and she loved the mountains and the seasons. Certainly for the next few years, close interaction with her father was important to her.

Michael's tone grew thoughtful, and he spoke softly. His parents were deceased, and his job was rather boring and nothing special. He felt that he might be able to make a much bigger contribution in some other arena, but he hadn't figured that out yet.

Sarah nodded and smiled. She said that she was not trying to make a federal case out of their chance meeting but that she appreciated getting a few more insights up front. She stood and led him to the office door, asking that he please not consider this to have been some type of grilling, but rather he should consider the conversation as a call for honesty and transparency as they got to know each other better.

Michael smiled. He could tell that Sarah felt much better after their brief talk, probably because of his lack of strong connection to Illinois. And he had to admit to himself that he felt better too. Sarah was clearly a unique woman who was intelligent, analytical, and cautious. After all, she was a mathematician. She was a sensible woman who was looking for the right kind of relationship, and she was going to be both systematic and sincere in her approach.

They stepped back out into the lobby behind the reception desk. Michael made a brief call to the rental car company. The agent was profusely apologetic and said he understood where to find the car keys in the back seat when they came to tow the vehicle.

Bob kissed Sarah on the cheek and motioned for Michael to walk out to the van. It was a practical white vehicle with the name of Bob's business in red letters on both sides. Michael loaded his bags and climbed into the passenger's seat, and the two of them headed to Jesse's cabin.

A mile south of town, they turned off of Highway 89 and drove a minute over a dirt driveway through the brush and pines. A small, dilapidated cabin appeared around a bend. It had a door and two windows with a stone chimney at one end. Jesse's old car was parked on the side.

Though shockingly Spartan, the little cabin was in a beautiful setting. It must have been lonely to live in this remote spot, but a certain type of person might thrive on the isolation. Michael had once read about Henry David Thoreau, who preferred to live in an isolated cabin at Walden Pond. Thoreau was thrilled to be surrounded by the serene woods and woodland creatures. But those nineteenth-century idyllic days were also fraught with risks, as somehow Thoreau contracted tuberculosis and began to cough blood and lose weight. A common ailment at the time, his diagnosis and grim prognosis were clear. When a concerned townswoman asked Thoreau if he had made his peace with God, Thoreau looked confused for a second and then earnestly responded that he was not aware that they had ever quarreled. Michael wondered if Jesse, the teenage rebel, had attained such a sense of peace as well.

As they walked to the cabin door, Bob carried the box of groceries as Michael toted his luggage, though he also carried a small gift in his shirt pocket. He had brought from home three old photos showing Jesse and Michael's father as young brothers growing up in Illinois.

Thin and pale, Jesse had aged decades since their last meeting, but he smiled broadly, and his kind blue eyes twinkled. He rose slowly and unsteadily from his chair with the help of a sturdy cane. He gave Michael a heartfelt hug, and Michael hugged him back.

Bob said little but placed the supplies on the table and shook hands with Jesse, at the same time accepting a small, folded square of white paper, which Bob quickly tucked into his jeans pocket. To Michael's surprise, Bob then reached to shake his hand and headed out the door. Michael looked at Jesse, who gestured for him to sit at the small table. Michael heard Bob start the van and the crunch of gravel as he drove away.

Michael handed Jesse the photos. Jesse stepped cautiously to hold them by the window to get a better look. Speechless for a moment, Jesse looked briefly at Michael, then back at the photos as he experienced a flood of memories. Jesse wiped away a tear.

Afternoon shadows were lengthening, and Jesse remarked that they now should start a fire as they talked. Jesse set the kindling, and Michael handed him several pieces of wood from the large pile next to the fireplace. Soon they each had a hot cup of coffee to sip.

Jesse took a deep breath, and after a brief pause, he confessed that he had been passing blood and had lost a lot of weight; he was sure that he was dying. He had loaded the trunk of the Cadillac with a number of important items and then had waited for Michael to arrive. Jesse wanted Michael to drive him to the Cascade County Courthouse in Great Falls on Monday morning so that he could sign over the deed to his property as well as the title to the car. And he had arranged for an attorney there to take care of his simple will.

Michael, a bit flabbergasted by this generosity, protested that perhaps already tomorrow, which was Sunday, he should take him to the hospital in Great Falls. Jesse replied that he would go to the hospital but not until Monday afternoon when all of the business had been concluded. He was adamant.

After Michael spoke about his college years, his job, and the death of his mother, Jesse asked if he had ever heard of Confederate Gulch. That was a new term to Michael, so as they set out two tin plates and opened a can of beef stew and vegetables to heat over the flame, Jesse began a story.

It was a tale of soldiers who had survived the early years of the Civil War and who made their way to Montana to prospect for gold. The young men who first searched the west slopes of the Big Belt Mountains in 1864 found rich veins of gold and silver in quartz deposits that had formed in cracks of the bedrock. The legend is that a flock of crows had guided the young men to where the gold nuggets were strewn in a creek bed. It was thought that the birds had been attracted by nuggets that sparkled in the sunlight. Jesse's thin and bruised hands waved in the air for emphasis, and his face glowed with excitement as he told the story.

Within a few years, a huge deposit of gold and silver was found, termed the Montana Bar. From 1866 to 1869, the gold production in the area surpassed all other mining camps in the Montana Territory. The little town of Confederate Gulch became the largest populated community in Montana. Then a new boomtown was founded nearby named Diamond City. The extensive use of hydraulic mining totally eroded the site of the new town, however, which was moved. But by 1870, there seemed to be no more gold, and the prospectors drifted elsewhere. These stories had captivated Jesse when he was in high school and precipitated his decision to hitchhike to Montana.

In subsequent years, many mines opened, including one in 1881 called the Queen of the Mountains that was rich in silver. The mines went through periods of boom and bust and were all closed now. But Jesse had been determined to search the area carefully for any additional ancient deposit of gold nuggets.

Jesse paused and smiled as he carefully watched Michael's face. Michael, a bit self-conscious now in view of his uncle's scrutiny, was sure that his expression was one of incredulity and hope—a strange blend reflecting his mix of strong emotions as he wanted to avoid appearing to be gullible while at the same time hoping that Jesse might be about to tell him that his search had succeeded. As the pause in the conversation became more prolonged, Jesse finally laughed out loud. Michael could tell that Jesse must have planned for days how he might tell him this story—as though he intended to hold that ten-year-old boy spellbound even though that boy had now grown into a man.

Jesse finally continued and explained that he had found an old stream bed with round, water-worn stones where gold nuggets had accumulated for eons, although the stream had been covered with two feet of dirt and dried up probably a thousand years ago, hiding its treasure. Jesse bought the property where the deposit was located and filed for the mining rights. For years, he had purchased food and occasionally gasoline from Bob, an honorable man and good friend, using gold dust or tiny gold nuggets, throwing in a bit larger nugget once in a while as a bonus to buy Bob's silence. But Jesse held back all of the valuable pieces.

Jesse lit a lantern and showed Michael his deed and claim paperwork. Then they walked out to the car. Jesse opened the trunk to show the many bags of large gold nuggets. Michael barely suppressed his urge to cheer out loud. Probably the sturdy car could not have safely carried a heavier load. It was a fortune! Jesse explained that he had already examined and weighed the material, and his experienced, trusted gold dealer would be waiting for them in Great Falls at three o'clock on Monday afternoon to provide a large check for the entire load. The plan was then to swing by the bank to deposit the check and finally get to the hospital.

Michael assured Jesse that he would help him get the best possible medical care, but Jesse seemed unconcerned, as if his life's work had been accomplished and he was ready to move on to the next world. On Sunday, he seemed much weaker, and Michael was anxious to drive him to Great Falls early on Monday.

Monday dawned clear and bright. Michael and Jesse arrived at Bob's Bar, Dining, and Motel at breakfast time and pulled in to buy gas. Bob came out to shake hands, and Sarah brought them cups of coffee. Michael and Jesse got out of the car to talk, and several diners who looked out the window, their curiosity piqued, also stepped outside by the gas pumps to join the conversation. Jesse was an odd recluse, so his appearance caused a small stir.

Bob understood that Jesse would not be coming back. Michael explained that Jesse was too weak to continue to live in a rustic cabin, and after getting needed medical attention, some sort of assisted-living arrangement would be needed, probably in Great Falls. Bob shook Jesse's hand and then gave him a hug. Michael tipped his hat to Sarah with the comment that he would be coming back to Neihart in a few days and hoped that she might have dinner with him. Sarah smiled and took hold of Michael's hand. After a few more minutes of conversation, Jesse and Michael stepped toward the car. It was time to go.

They made their way through the crowd and back to the El Dorado. And as they approached it, a crow flew directly over their heads and landed on the hood and then looked at them. They stood some distance away and watched the crow watching them. Another crow flew directly overhead and landed beside it. The first crow squawked, and then both flew away. They watched the crows disappear, looked at each other, and then got in the El Dorado. Only one way to go this time, with five bars and a full battery.

ENDS AND MEANS

He has set before you fire and water;
    to whichever you choose, stretch forth your hand.
Before man are life and death, good and evil,
    whichever he chooses shall be given him.
Immense is the wisdom of the Lord;
    he is mighty in power, and all-seeing.
The eyes of God are on those who trust him,
    he understands man's every deed.
No one does he command to act unjustly,
    to none does he give license to sin.
                    —Sirach 15:16–20

The May sunshine was pleasantly warm on the back of his neck and shoulders. The young Catholic priest's black shirt absorbed the afternoon rays as he strolled slowly on the sidewalk near the redbrick church. Father Tom's thoughts drifted to what his garden might look like this year. With a longstanding interest in biology and botany, he enjoyed tending his plants each summer. He had done research on the genetics and biochemistry of photosynthesis during three semesters in college, but then he had set biology aside when the seminary seemed the right path for him.

A breeze made the maple branches sway, and bright islands of sunlight danced on the green grass. The priest reached up to shake hands with a low-hanging branch, and he caressed a shiny leaf. The stems of the maple leaves grew from the twig opposite each other, whereas the stems of the lobed leaves of the neighboring sassafras tree grew from the twig in an alternating pattern. Many busy people are so engrossed with their problems at work or home that they never even notice that some trees have an opposite versus an alternate leaf pattern.

Father Tom smiled as he realized that most of his Saturday duties had already been completed. He would hear confessions for an hour, then say the 5:00 p.m. Mass. This morning, he had finished making breakfast for himself and Father Timothy, the elderly pastor, ahead of schedule. He had touched up the notes for his sermons this weekend, then completed home visits to sick members of St. Peter the Apostle parish. Fingers crossed, everyone seemed to be improving today, so perhaps there would be no funeral this week. Union Bridge, Maryland, was a friendly community that had welcomed him warmly two years ago, and he felt very comfortable here. Only thirty-five years old, he was happy to be of service to assist the pastor, now a little feeble at age seventy-two.

Father Tom's eyes took a second to adjust as he entered the dark, cool church. Two persons in the pews were waiting for him. Mr. Duncan likely had once again, in a moment of weakness, perused a pornographic magazine, while Mrs. Filbert probably had argued again with her adult daughter. He felt sure that he would help both penitents find the forgiveness they sought, and they likely would depart at peace and with the best of intentions for improved behavior.

The sixty-minute sacramental session was passing routinely enough, and Father Tom glanced at his watch. Ten more minutes to go, and then he needed to enter the sacristy to prepare for Mass. Just then, he heard footsteps, and the confessional door creaked open, then closed. One more customer.

"Bless me, Father. I want to confess," blurted an unfamiliar male voice. He seemed to be middle-aged or older.

"Bless you, and proceed," Father Tom replied.

"My last confession was six months ago. This is not my parish." He paused. "Well, I mostly want some advice, really."

"How can I help you?"

"Can this be guaranteed to be a totally confidential conversation? I think that was the case years ago, but I don't know all the church rules these days."

Father Tom took a breath. "Well, it can be a little complicated. In general, there is great sanctity and total confidentiality regarding confession as a sacrament. In very unusual situations, however, the church has a duty to protect innocent individuals, and that can complicate a priest's interactions with a penitent."

"How does that work?"

"If you told me that you were sexually abusing a small child, then I would pray with you and discuss things carefully with you. And I think you would agree that something would have to be done to protect the innocent party."

"It isn't anything like that, Father," the man replied. "But I need advice. I was running an errand in Union Bridge a few months ago, so it was convenient that day for me to attend Mass at St. Peter's. And I heard your sermon that day. I came back a couple more times. You seemed to be a pretty smart and personable priest. Someone I could discuss things with. So I need some advice."

"Do you want to confess a sin?" asked the priest.

"Well, I haven't committed the sin yet. But I am thinking I might just have to do it. It can't be helped."

"What are we talking about here?"

"Well." The man took a breath and paused. "I think I might have to kill some people."

The two men sat across from each other in the privacy of the living room of the small house in which Father Tom and Father Timothy lived. The mysterious penitent had agreed to walk from the church with Father Tom and sit down for a serious conversation face-to-face. This was still technically part of the sacrament of confession. Father Timothy had been roused from his paperwork and had agreed to say the 5:00 p.m. Mass in place of Father Tom so that the conversation could continue. Father Tom feared that the man might change his mind and just walk away without sharing more about his intentions. Perhaps tragedy could be prevented.

His name was Martin, but he wouldn't give his last name, at least not for now. The two men each took another sip of coffee, and they sat for a moment in silence. Father Tom noted that Martin was casually dressed, quite appropriate for a Saturday, and he was well groomed. Martin was Caucasian, about sixty-five years old, medium height and build, and he seemed more relaxed than when they had first walked out of the church together.

Martin broke the silence. "I had been worried that coming to talk to you would be a big mistake, but now I'm sure it was the right thing to do."

Father Tom smiled. "To avoid violence and find another solution."

Martin's brow furrowed. "Well, not exactly. I want to be reassured in my conviction that killing these people is the correct decision. I am not by nature a violent man, and this is very out of character for me."

Father Tom looked him straight in the eyes. "You don't seem to be a mental case, and you are very calm. But I don't understand. Some of your words sound like a crazy man speaking."

"I'm not crazy. In recent weeks, I have come to believe that I may be one of the most rational men on the earth. But I have concerns and doubts." Martin closed his eyes and leaned back in the cushioned chair.

"So help me understand. Is this a love story gone wrong?"

Martin opened his eyes and leaned forward, weighing the words just spoken. "No, not a conventional love story gone wrong. Not in the usual way." A slight smile came across his face. "But come to think of it, it is a kind of love story that has gone terribly wrong." He paused, then continued. "And the Catholic Church has played a role in this, so that is one reason I wanted to talk to a priest."

Perplexed, Father Tom swallowed hard. "Please explain."

"I am a scientist," Martin said, "so please let me speak for a few minutes about human evolution. You do believe in evolution, don't you, Father?"

"Well, yes," replied Father Tom. "I took quite a bit of biology and chemistry in college, and even a little astronomy. The modern Catholic view is that the processes of evolution are tools used by God for shaping the world. The Genesis creation stories are poetic verses that contain very important moral and religious insights, but those verses are not to be taken literally." Father Tom was a bit uneasy by the direction of the conversation, since the main goal in his mind was to interrupt the planning of murders rather than discuss evolution.

Martin took a deep breath and began his tale. "There is a remarkable anthropological site called Laetoli, in Tanzania. It was a warm, semitropical land 3.6 million years ago. In that long-gone era, on a day with intermittent, short rain showers, a volcano briefly belched a cloud of hot ash, which settled as a shallow layer on the surrounding flatlands. The ash became moist after a brief shower. Remarkably, two early human ancestors walked nearly side by side slowly through the wet ash. Their upright gait left seventy footprints in a trail eighty-eight feet long. Within minutes, the volcano belched more ash, and the footprints were covered and protected. Although the footprints look quite modern, potassium-argon dating of the ash confirms their great antiquity."

Martin paused a moment, but Father Tom remained silent, signaling that he should continue.

"In view of the 3.6-million-year date, we know from other data that the early human ancestors that made those footprints made no tools, did not make use of fire, and wore no clothes. They ate mostly a vegetarian diet and were barely surviving. Very few of these unusual animals were roving the landscape, so it was remarkable that these footprints were captured. Although these creatures had a fully upright stature, they were quite short and probably very apelike in appearance, with brains much smaller than that of a modern human. The African environment was a dangerous place for them, and they probably spent much of their time in hiding, trying to avoid many predators. The footprint makers likely were a type of animal similar to *Australopithecus afarensis*. A fossil skull of a child of this species has been found with leopard canine puncture marks suggesting that the child was snatched by a big cat."

Father Tom remained silent, but he studied Martin's expressionless face. Martin sighed, then continued.

"The first use of stone tools is dated to about 2.6 million years ago, and evidence of hearths and use of fire started about two million years ago. Note that use of tools and control of fire were not invented by our species, *Homo sapiens*. These were wonderful accomplishments of earlier species of *Homo*, notably *Homo habilis* and *Homo erectus*. The brain was getting gradually larger, perhaps helped by more meat in the diet, and driven by natural selection for more sophisticated social interactions."

Father Tom nodded, and Martin continued.

"By 1.2 million years ago, there were about 18,500 of these unusual hominids in Africa. This estimate was published in 2010 by Huff et al. from the University of Utah. The estimate was based on mathematical calculations related to mobile elements existing in genomes of different living humans, which gave a snapshot of the likely size of the breeding population in the ancient past. A population of 18,500 animals was larger than in previous millennia but was still a relatively small number; a series of unlucky events easily could have wiped out humanity. Hominids were barely making the natural selection cut. But brain size continued gradually to increase, and the dawn of our own species, *Homo sapiens*, in Africa is estimated to have occurred about two hundred thousand years ago, although recent finds may push this date back to three hundred thousand years ago. But our species was soon to be sorely tested."

Father Tom blinked. He knew a fair amount about evolution, but some of this was new to him.

"Genetic data suggest that there was a major reduction in the human population about 150,000 years ago. This population bottleneck left clear evidence in our genome, which is remarkably homogeneous for a species. If one compares the DNA sequences of two random living persons, about 999 out of one thousand DNA nucleotides are identical, whereas the genome of another species, the chimpanzee, is about seven to ten times more diverse. There may have been fewer than one thousand persons alive on the planet at one point, likely due to an extremely unfavorable cold and arid stretch from 193,000 to 123,000 years ago, termed the Marine Isotope Stage 6 period. This information is based on isotopic analyses of deep ice cores, which provide environmental information about the earth in ages past. During that challenging epoch, small groups of humans were able to survive in Africa in just a few favorable locations, one being along the South Africa coast where a bountiful supply of shellfish was reachable on the coastal rocks. Cave PP13B at Pinnacle Point sheltered small groups of humans for many thousands of years. Curtis Marean of Arizona State University has written about this remarkable place. It is actually possible that every living person today is a descendant of the few people who survived in that cave."

Father Tom could not help but be interested in this amazing

tale. It brought to mind the story of Noah's ark. But he began to think about how he could steer the conversation to his real concern, the potential murders. "You give amazingly clear explanations, Martin," Father Tom interjected. "But how does the evolution information relate to your desire for confession?"

Martin shifted in his chair. "I find the whole situation to be so frustrating," Martin started, his face reddening. "Whether it be by the hand of God, or by blind natural forces, over eons a very special animal has arisen on the earth. The animal is conscious, can imagine events in the past and the future, is aware of its mortality, and has a moral sense. This special, fragile species was nearly wiped out many times but managed to adapt and survive, and in time, humankind has populated all parts of the earth. This species has bent nature to its will, allowing for huge population growth. But in so doing, it has been enormously destructive, sending many species into extinction, consuming resources, and damaging ecosystems. Relentless burning of fossil fuels increases atmospheric carbon dioxide, and much of that dissolves in the sea, forming carbonic acid. The gradual acidification of the oceans, which is happening much more rapidly than fluctuations that had occurred naturally in the past, may disrupt diatoms and the key food chains in the oceans. This will endanger most life in the seas because the rapidity of the change is not allowing for life to adapt. Humans have become a threat to the planet. Most of the damage, I think, is simply a direct function of the huge population of humans. Like deer that are eating the forest bare in the absence of wolves that might limit their population, humans continue mindlessly to increase in number. Eventually, a catastrophic global collapse must occur!"

Martin was breathing fast now, and he looked intently at Father Tom for a reaction. But the priest remained silent, momentarily taken aback by the emotion in Martin's voice.

"The church has been of little help in this regard, I'm afraid to say, Father," Martin continued. "Prohibitions on contraception have undermined the work of the United Nations in many countries."

"But the church must defend the dignity of all human life," Father Tom protested softly, barely audible, and trying not to be confrontational.

"There clearly is a difference between contraception and abortion," Martin blurted, and he raised his hands palms up, as if the point was an obvious one.

"So, Martin, what does all of this have to do with your confession? Are you thinking of killing the pope?" Father Tom smiled to indicate quickly that his question was not a serious one.

Martin shook his head no and smiled in return, then spoke thoughtfully. "No one is really doing anything serious about human population growth. But it clearly is a dire threat. The human global population did not reach one billion persons until 1804, yet reached two billion by 1927. Subsequently, the population growth accelerated. There were three billion persons by 1960, four billion by 1974, five billion by 1987, six billion by 1999, and seven billion by 2011. United Nations estimates for the global population in 2050 vary from eight to ten billion, depending on assumptions. This population growth is making irreversible, harmful changes to the earth. Something must be done."

"What do you think can be done?" asked the priest.

Martin looked intently into the priest's eyes but kept silent. A long minute passed. Finally, Martin spoke. "I am not hearing voices or seeing visions. But after long reflection, I believe that I may have been given an opportunity by God to save humanity. But I tremble at this solemn responsibility. No committee, or government, or international organization would ever approve of what I am thinking of doing—because it is so unthinkable and shocking and, well, barbaric. Yet it is an action that I believe must be taken." Martin paused, sat upright, then leaned closer to the priest and lowered his voice. "I believe that for the long-term good of humankind, and to allow time for proper measures to be put in place by governments, I need to act now to kill some people."

"Kill some people?" murmured the priest.

"Yes," continued Martin. "I need to kill 3.5 billion people."

⟨⟩

The front doorknob rattled, and in walked Father Timothy. In the small house, one entered directly into the living room, and the pastor smiled at the two men seated in the cushioned chairs. "The Mass went well, but you owe me one, Tom," joked the older priest. "Have you guys been having a good discussion?"

"Yes," replied Father Tom. "This is Martin, who is from another parish but who came to confession today. Sorry that introductions were abbreviated when we entered and interrupted you an hour ago. Thanks for saying Mass."

"I am about to heat up some lasagna frozen dinners, and I could easily heat three dinners if our guest is interested. And we have some red wine." The older priest glanced at Martin.

"Thanks, Father, it would be my pleasure to have dinner with you," replied Martin.

After a few minutes in the kitchen, Father Timothy joined the two men in the living room, bringing the bottle of wine and three glasses. "I understand that I might be interrupting a confession, so please just tell me if you want some privacy for a few more minutes," said Father Timothy.

Martin reached out for a glass. "This is probably a good time for a break. Father Tom and I can continue later. I have so many sins, you know."

Father Timothy smiled and poured the wine.

"Let me say something," Martin offered. "I am in the middle of confession, but I mostly came today for advice. If I can get two opinions for the price of one, that would be fine. May I ask both of you a question now?"

"Fine," replied Father Tom as Father Timothy nodded.

Martin took a sip of wine and continued. "Father Timothy, I'm sure you have read in recent years about various ethical quizzes being proposed to research subjects. One quiz involves a trolley that is out of control and is about to run over five persons stuck on the track. The only way to avoid these deaths is for the research subject quickly to throw a switch and divert the trolley to a sidetrack, where, unfortunately, it will run over and kill one innocent person. Assuming that either throwing that switch or not throwing that switch is the only possible decision, do you think it would be ethical as well as rational to divert the trolley? This intentional action would kill one innocent person but save the lives of five."

The elderly priest waved his hand in the air. "What a terrible predicament. Pray that the merciful God would never put us to this test. Generally, one is not restricted to a single choice that so limits our actions. But if either throwing that switch or not was the only possible decision, then as horrible as it seems, I suppose it would be better to throw the switch so that only one person will be killed instead of five."

Martin smiled. "That is the way most people see it, according to the research data. But there is a follow-up question. The situation is slightly different. There is not a switch to be thrown to divert the trolley. Instead, the very limited only possible choice is presented differently. The trolley still is seconds away from crushing five persons, but in this scenario, the subject is standing next to a large, three-hundred-pound man who quickly could be pushed off an overhead platform onto the tracks. His bulk would slow and then stop the trolley, saving the five lives but at the cost of that man's life. Would it be ethical to shove that innocent man in front of the trolley?"

The two priests looked at each other but remained silent for a moment.

Martin spoke. "Let me interject that most people have

found this question to be much more problematic than the first. Although the fundamental alternative of five lives lost versus one life lost is the same in the two scenarios, psychologists have found that physically handling another person to harm them is more concerning to people than merely shifting an impersonal mechanical switch. Interesting."

Father Timothy frowned, then offered his view. "It is all well and good to be offered a crisp choice with perfect knowledge of the situation as part of a game. But the real world is extremely complex. No person can have perfect understanding of complex situations. We are not offered clear and crisp choices in the real world. One must remain humble and avoid the hubris of intentionally harming some people supposedly to help others if we are poor mortals with potentially a mistaken or incomplete understanding of the situation." The pastor reached for his wine glass.

Martin squirmed a bit in his seat. He glanced at Father Tom, who glanced back at him with a knowing look.

The lasagna was good, and the postdinner cleanup was quick and easy. Father Timothy retired upstairs.

"Shall we finish the confession?" proposed Father Tom, and Martin nodded.

⌖

The two men returned to their comfortable chairs in the living room.

"I think that Martin is probably not your real name, and that is okay," said Father Tom. "But I do believe that you are a scientist."

"You are right on both counts, Father. And I am deathly serious about potentially killing billions of people. Naturally, I want to conceal my name to be able to get that job well initiated before the police cars show up at my door," Martin admitted.

"But you are having second thoughts now?"

94

"I have always had concerns, which is why I am here. I remain undecided."

"I have also surmised," continued Father Tom, "that if you are a scientist who might have the technical means of killing billions of people, and you are sitting with me in Union Bridge, Maryland, then you probably work in an army biological laboratory at Fort Detrick a few miles from here. Am I right?" asked the priest.

"Of course you are right," said Martin. "I knew that you would quickly figure that out." Martin placed his hands somewhat self-consciously in his lap. "The virus that I have in hand, if inhaled, will attack the nervous system."

Father Tom shook his head. "You are a smart man, Martin, but it is sad that you have used your talents to invent such a terrible thing."

"I didn't invent it, really," protested Martin. "I just adapted a herpes encephalitis virus already present in nature. The virus binds to the olfactory nerves, which act as highways to enter the brain. This virus will be much more contagious and deadly than the natural virus, so it should spread widely and quickly. I have done no human experiments, of course, but I have studied the virus in humanized mice for more than a year. The mice have been genetically altered to carry one or the other of the two different human alleles for the nerve cell viral receptor. One type of receptor binds the virus and enhances infection, but the other type binds the virus poorly, protecting against infection. The experiments suggest that about half of humankind will be killed, while the other half will not be seriously impacted. That's why my estimate is 3.5 billion deaths."

"And I presume that you personally carry the nerve receptor type that will make you more resistant to viral infection?" asked Father Tom.

"I said earlier that this was a sort of love story playing out," responded Martin. "I love our species, and I want to save it! So I decided that I would not test myself to learn my receptor allelic status. My chance of survival will be like a flip of a coin, but my actions seem more ethical that way. I will share risk with everyone else." Martin looked up and caught the priest's eyes. "I am prepared to give my life to save humanity if that is what is required of me."

The priest said nothing, and Martin continued.

"I have two grown sons and three grandchildren. They also will be at risk and may be killed by the virus. The cause for which I act is more important than the lives of any few people. This is painful for me"—Martin's voice cracked—"but there is much at stake."

Father Tom spoke quietly. "But consider how complex the situation is and how many factors are unknown, Martin. What if your virus unexpectedly kills everyone? Or, alternatively, what if the virus weakens during person-to-person transmission and kills 'only' fifty million people? Those fifty million deaths would barely put a dent in the world's population growth from your perspective. That death toll would disrupt families and break the hearts of millions, yet it would actually be pointless in your scheme."

Doubts were rising in Martin's mind. He felt his stomach twist into a knot, and he was slightly short of breath.

"Moreover," the priest continued, "the responsible political leaders have been completely ineffective at stemming population growth up until now, so why are you so confident that they will be able to respond to this shock and implement policies successfully?"

Martin bit his lip.

Father Tom swallowed and began again. "I'm struggling here, but let me raise a scenario. What if a wild virus currently in nature mutates and starts to vigorously attack humans, threatening to kill nearly all of us? Let's say that the biology is such in this scenario that having eight billion people on the planet would be required to ensure that a thousand persons survive this natural calamity. If you prematurely reduce the human population using your encephalitis virus, Martin, then the human population might be too small to harbor the required number of resistant individuals. You would have unwittingly conspired to end our species."

Martin nodded but said nothing.

"Or rather than a natural virus that randomly mutates," continued Father Tom, "what about bioterrorism? Frankly, if terrorists were operating with slipshod safety practices, release of a biological agent might occur by accident rather than by intention, and the mortality could be massive."

Martin felt the knot in his stomach tighten. "I am still thinking that I should act. No one else seems capable of performing any meaningful intervention. Unchecked human population growth will be disastrous. There could be no greater tragedy than the destruction of earth's ecosystems and the total annihilation of every member of our species!"

Father Tom frowned and leaned forward in his chair. "Martin, do you really believe that there could be no greater tragedy than the destruction of earth's ecosystems and the total annihilation of every member of our species?"

Martin blinked. Then blinked again. "Well, I think that the destruction of the earth as well as every member of *Homo sapiens* really would be the ultimate disaster. How could it not be?"

Father Tom stood and walked silently to the front window. Shadows were lengthening on the green lawn. He turned back toward Martin and continued. "I presume that you know well that the earth is doomed to destruction. If some other tragedy does not occur in the intervening years, then in about six billion years, the dying sun will swell into a red giant star, boil away the earth's oceans, and then vaporize the planet."

"Yes, I have heard that. But billions of years is a very long time from now," Martin replied quickly. "In a small fraction of that time, our inventive species will have developed means to escape the earth and colonize other planets."

"I am sorry to propose limits to technology, but I think that in this case you might be overestimating the inventiveness of our species," replied Father Tom. "You likely are underestimating the enormous practical problems related to colonization of another planet several light-years distant. I have read that the necessary travel distances and travel times are staggeringly large. There was an article in the paper last week about the New Horizons Pluto mission. Even at the record velocity of the New Horizons spacecraft, the travel time to the nearest star would not be a century, nor would it be three centuries; it would be about eighty thousand years! The most realistic assumption is that humanity will never be able permanently to live away from our solar system. Like it or not, the poisoned and ravaged earth must remain our home base and only true refuge."

Father Tom's long interest in biology was beginning to help structure his arguments. "Also consider, Martin," added the priest, "that even under optimally low population stress and with perfect resources, gradual inevitable DNA base substitutions in the human genome will cause our species slowly to change into a different species, or possibly several different species if geography or other factors separate breeding groups. After five hundred thousand years or so, *Homo sapiens* as presently constituted will likely no longer exist. The species will have been transformed. Clearly your prior statement that the nonexistence of *Homo sapiens* would constitute the ultimate tragedy cannot really be true."

"I see what you mean," replied Martin. "But the future daughter species would be carrying the torch of life forward for *Homo sapiens*, so to speak."

"Agreed," said Father Tom. "But the individuals in a future daughter species will not be 'us,' just as a *Homo sapiens* is not an *Australopithecus afarensis*. We must realize that the species *Homo sapiens* must surely end at some time."

Martin closed his eyes and sat quietly.

Father Tom continued. "As intellectually honest persons, we seek ultimate truth. I agree that science is a superb system for finding truth in many areas of study. Science does not deal well with assigning ultimate meanings of things, however. Some quite intelligent scientists mistake the inability of science to discern ultimate meaning as a confirmation that there actually is no long-term meaning to our existence. But as religious persons, we have views about what the ultimate meanings of the world and of life actually are. We believe in an infinite God who operates on an infinite timescale. Let me emphasize that word—infinite! Science does not deal well with infinities; the infinite quantities mess up all of the equations. But the infinities are real. Martin, you value the supposedly huge timescale of six billion years for the future history of the earth, but placed on an infinite timescale, six billion years would pass in a tiny instant."

Martin exhaled and lowered his head. Then he sighed and queried, "So, Father, are you saying that humankind should just give up at this point and do nothing? Isn't is immoral to ignore the huge problems looming for humanity?"

Father Tom sat down again and leaned forward. "I don't have all the answers, Martin, and I do not advise giving up. But I am sure that releasing a germ next week that will kill 3.5 billion people is not the right answer. My approach sounds soft and ineffective, but I advise reflection, caution, discussion, and prayer. I think, Martin, that you may be feeling the sort of angst that Jesus felt in the garden the night before his crucifixion. He could see destruction looming and prayed that it might still be preventable, yet he knew that the flow of events could not be stopped."

"But Jesus believed that his death had meaning," Martin interjected. "What could possibly be the upside if one hundred years from now, the crush of human population destroys our planet's ecosystems and our resilient and very special species?

99

What meaning could be attached to this unspeakable tragedy borne of ignorance, poor planning, poor judgment, and the sad inertia of leaders?"

Father Tom closed his eyes a moment, then spoke softly. "Our biological lives as individuals on this planet, and even the life of our species, all will end at some point. Those physical things ultimately don't matter, because as religious persons, we believe that what does matter are the loving relationships that we develop and the moral decisions that we make. In the religious perspective, if you believe in God and if you believe that our lives have ultimate meaning, those loving relationships and moral choices define us in our brief present, and they define us for all time. Nothing that is physical actually lasts, not even the planet Earth."

Martin remained silent for several minutes. He knew that he did believe in God. But about many other things he now seemed less sure. He could not with high confidence believe that it was time to unleash his virus on humanity.

"Father," Martin began, "I have decided that there are far too many unknowns to release the virus. I cannot act."

"Martin, listen to me." Father Tom smiled. "Your concern for humanity and your despair at the present state of the world are commendable. But you are not God. You are an educated man who wants desperately to act to make things better, but you cannot carry the weight of the world on your shoulders."

Martin nodded, and he held his head in in hands. Looking back up at the priest, Martin asked, "Would it be possible for us to meet weekly for a while? Further discussion would be helpful to regain my equilibrium."

"I think that weekly visits would be great," replied the priest. "And I promise to brush up on my biology before you return."

Within minutes, Martin was on his way home.

Suddenly feeling very tired, Father Tom crept quietly up the stairs, relieved at least that his schedule would allow him to sleep until nine the next morning. As he turned on his bedroom light, he saw the note on his pillow. It read, "Feeling old and tired tonight. Since I took your Mass at five, I hope you could say the 8:00 a.m. Mass. Thanks, Timothy."

Father Tom brushed his teeth and set his alarm for 6:45 a.m.

THE BEST POLICY

(A short story in fewer than 150 words)

The red-haired seventeen-year-old sauntered homeward in the gathering dusk of a hot July evening. His eyes followed the cracks in the old sidewalk, but he thought about his friends. They had summer jobs and girlfriends. He was lonely and broke. His mind snapped to attention as his left shoe kicked a leather wallet. Stunned, he reached for it. Seven twenties—a fortune. He looked left and right. Another peek revealed the driver's license: "George Mason, born 1976." The address was the house where he stood. After a moment, he shuffled up the walk. Expecting a man, instead a petite brunette smiled at him from behind the screen door. Her eyes sparkled as she excitedly called to her father. The recovered wallet in hand, George beamed and slipped him three crisp twenties. Ann offered him iced tea, and they sat in the kitchen and talked.

THE MESSAGE

(First published in *2 Elizabeths*
Volume 1: Love & Romance
edited by Elise Holland, 2018)

The best thing that happened to me in college was meeting Olivia Ann Evans.

Those years prepared me well for my future career as a small-town high school chemistry and physics teacher. But more importantly, being on campus allowed me the opportunity to fall in love with a college classmate, Olivia, and we married two years after we graduated.

Olivia's black, curly hair and warm, brown eyes had drawn me to her as I walked into my freshman Latin class, and I took the empty seat next to her. I had chosen to take Latin because I thought it might help me later in science, whereas Olivia had taken two years of Latin in high school, so this language was a natural choice for her. It turned out that I was pretty terrible at Latin, but Olivia became a good friend. She studied with me and was a big help. So I passed.

I repaid Olivia for her language assistance by coaching her in analytic geometry. We had a running joke through the years. As she entered classrooms to sit for challenging math tests, I always sent her a brief text of encouragement, "Carpe diem."

Of course, this means "Seize the day." Afterwards, if she was certain that she had done well, she would text me back, "Omnes bene est"–"All is well."

Our friendship grew into love, and I proposed marriage during junior year with the idea that we would have the ceremony after we graduated. It turned out that those plans were delayed another year by the onset of my lymphoma. But after radiation to my chest together with other treatments, the doctors seemed satisfied that I was cured. Olivia and I had little money in our checking accounts, so to celebrate my medical recovery we kept it simple—we had steaks at a local restaurant where we exchanged humorous coffee mugs. The future seemed bright, and we shortly thereafter completed the wedding plans. She made clear, however, that she would keep Evans as her last name since she didn't really care for my last name, Debreceli. She was independent-minded, and I liked her for that.

I took a job as a science teacher at an academically strong but financially struggling Catholic high school, and Olivia became an account manager at a local company.

In December I received an invitation to a science teachers' retreat. The meeting was to be held in mid-March on the campus of my alma mater. I showed the invitation to Olivia, and I was excited that I likely would see some of my former classmates and learn how they were doing with their new teaching careers. Olivia was happy for me to go, but she had to work.

The retreat was valuable, and I also enjoyed strolling around the campus because Olivia and I had made so many memories there. After the retreat, I spent a vacation day with one of my good friends from school who was still living in town. I had dinner at his house with his young family, then started my 180-mile drive back home that evening.

My Chevy Cruze was comfortable to drive, and there was little traffic at midnight on the two-lane highway in this region of farm fields. It was dark, but the road was dry – good conditions for mid-March. Soon I would be crawling into a warm bed with Olivia. I was adjusting the radio when I saw a blur come at me from my left.

Wham! Suddenly I was dead.

Of course, I didn't realize it at first. It took several minutes for the notion to crystalize.

I had felt no pain. The lights came back on a second later, and I found myself floating about thirty feet directly above two mangled, smoking, entangled cars. Of course, I was pretty freaked out for the first couple of minutes to find myself floating there suspended by, it seemed, an invisible cable attached to my back. I touched my face, chest, and abdomen, and all seemed normal. My skin was warm, and I had no trauma. I was wearing the same flannel shirt and old blue jeans I had put on that morning. How could I just float in the air above these wrecked cars? After about two minutes I realized that I must either be dreaming or dead, and the second option seemed more likely because I clearly had just been driving. I waved my arms and kicked my legs without effect, and I looked down at the sandals and socks on my feet.

Olivia always told me not to wear socks with sandals. "That makes you look like an old man," she had complained.

But my sandals were my most comfortable shoes. And in the cool March weather I insisted on wearing socks with my sandals. Just logical to me.

"I wouldn't be caught dead wearing sandals and socks," she had said.

Well, I had been!

I realized that I was still thinking clearly, and after the initial shock had worn off, I was even finding some humor in the situation. I remained a bit nervous, but I was more optimistic that perhaps death might work out well for me after all. Besides, there was nothing that I could do about it. I was just hung in the air as if I were on a hook.

I looked to the left and right. No cars were yet coming along this lonely highway. The night air was cool on my face, and I could smell the earth. Stars twinkled overhead, and the familiar constellations were a comfort.

I placed my fingertips on a shirt sleeve to experience again the soft sensation of the flannel, but I noticed that the cloth now felt altered. I looked down and found that I was wearing blue and white striped pajamas. This unexpected change in my clothing was disconcerting, but within seconds I had calmed myself. The pajamas seemed familiar. Yes! These were the very same striped pajamas that Grandma Phelps had given me for my eighteenth birthday. I had loved these pajamas, and had worn them through my college years until they had gotten so worn and ragged that I had to throw them out. I concluded, still scrambling to think clearly, that my clothes, and probably my body, did not exist any longer as fixed physical entities. Yet, they felt normal to me.

It was only a little disconcerting when I looked at my sleeves five minutes later, and I found myself back in my flannel shirt and old blue jeans. For some reason, this shape-shifting did not bother me because I knew that I was in the grips of something far beyond my understanding. I would remain calm, I decided, as long as I had no pain and could think clearly.

I looked straight down and scanned the wreckage again. A car had crashed at high speed into the driver's side of my car, nearly cutting my car in half. As I looked left and right I could see that the car must have approached on a small paved road, and the driver had failed to stop at a stop sign. The idiot! The impact had caused the twisted, merged autos to slide sideways and forward off the highway, through a wire fence, and about thirty yards into the field, leaving marks in the stubble and black dirt along the trajectory. It must have been a tremendous collision.

My thoughts turned to Olivia. She would be devastated. I

wondered if there were some way I could communicate to her that I was still sentient and comfortable in the next life, but that seemed highly improbable. We were Catholics, but she had been less religious. I hoped her faith would comfort her. We had no children, of course, so my next thoughts were about my students and workmates. We would miss each other. My thoughts drifted further. I wondered if I might see my parents and others who were already populating heaven.

It may seem bizarre, but I next thought about how this was March 16, and my federal and state income taxes were due on April 15. I had assembled all of the 1099 forms and statements on my desk in the living room, and I had purchased the software package, but I had not yet begun completing the forms. I hoped that Olivia would easily find the statements on my desk. I felt a little guilty, but I also was happy that I would not have to struggle through that April exercise. In fact, it began to sink in that I would never again fill out income tax forms! I laughed out loud when it struck me that the topic of taxes was running through my spiritual mind twenty minutes after my death. Death and taxes, indeed.

Suddenly, I saw a small flash of light to my right. The invisible cable holding me in the air started to move me toward that light, which became gradually brighter. As it grew still brighter I had to shut my eyes, and I even covered them with my hands. When I next peeked out between my fingers I realized that the light intensity again was normal, and I was sitting in a chair in a small, ordinary-appearing office. At a desk in front of me was an elderly man dressed in a grey, pin-striped, three-piece suit, complete with white bow tie. He was typing on the key board of his laptop. After a moment he looked up at me.

"Mr. Stuart Debreceli, welcome to your entrance interview," he announced.

I sat in stunned silence, so he continued, "I'm Saint Peter and this is, as you would say, the pearly gate. Hardly a gate, though, as you can see."

"So this is heaven?" I murmured, still a bit disoriented.

"It's just the entrance, but before you enter there are a few things to clear up," he replied as he scanned his computer screen.

As I composed myself, I looked again at his immaculate, three-piece suit. "I thought that you would be wearing a white robe."

He smiled at me, and lifted his right index finger three inches from the keyboard. Instantly the three-piece suit changed to a flowing, white robe. He smiled a bit more broadly as he observed my startled expression. Then he briefly lifted his finger again, and the robe changed back to a three-piece suit. "The clothes and this little office are just manifestations to make you feel more comfortable as you enter your new life."

"And you use computers in heaven?"

"Of course not!" he replied. "Centuries ago I sat here with a scroll and quill pen, then for more centuries I sat here with a thick, leather-bound book. But the new fad is to use a laptop. The truth is, those things are only props, and all the information is right up here." He smiled and pointed with one finger to his head.

"So," I began tentatively. "Have I been approved to enter heaven?" My mouth was dry, and my hands were trembling. I swallowed hard as I realized what a momentous question this was.

"Of course you have been approved! You were a loving man with acceptably strong faith and hope. So you may now stand up and take a few steps through that door. You'll be there for all eternity, and you'll find it to be superb. Congratulations, and well deserved!"

I'm sure that my relief was plainly visible. I gathered a bit more courage

"That is truly wonderful," I replied. "But may I ask a question?"

"How can I help you?"

"My young wife, Olivia Evans, will be very upset by my death. Could I briefly appear to her to tell her not to worry about me—could I tell her that I'm in heaven?"

He looked me in the eyes for a few seconds, then responded. "No appearances or anything like that. In present times communications from the grave are strictly forbidden. All of that hocus pocus about mediums and ghosts is a bunch of hogwash." He paused, then added, "People on Earth must find their way to the truth without such help. It's all part of a larger plan, you see."

I was still worried about Olivia. I was afraid that she might become despondent, and perhaps even bitter. She was a strong woman, and I didn't want her to react to my death by starting an argument with God. She might come to view God as unfair and ugly. How could she respect a God who had snuffed out the young life of her good-hearted husband? After another moment I tried another approach with my host.

"If ghostly appearances aren't allowed, could I perhaps leave a short letter for her to find among my things? Please understand that I'm desperate to find some way to comfort and reassure her."

Saint Peter smiled knowingly at me. "No appearances, no phone calls, no vivid dreams, no letters."

My mind was racing. I had a feeling that once I walked through the door into heaven proper I might find myself with no opportunity ever to try to send a message to Olivia. Perhaps my mind might be elevated or changed in some way that I would no longer even have that concern about trying to console her. I suspected that I had to act fast.

"What if Olivia should find a little reminder of me that might console her? It would be a very general sort of thing without any concrete, specific message. Could that be allowed?"

Saint Peter sighed and shrugged.

"Allowing a loved one to find or experience a remembrance

can, in fact, be permitted. Your desire to console and reassure your loved one is not unique. I've had this conversation millions of times. I even have some suggestions for you. Presently the number one requested sign is to have a rainbow appear briefly after the burial. The number two request is to have a special song coincidentally play on the radio as a spouse is traveling to the funeral. Those are both acceptable signs. Of course, they are general occurrences that could be due entirely to chance, and they do not clearly communicate anything about your status in the afterlife. But either of those signs would be allowable if you would like to choose one. I can put in the order on this non-existent laptop right now if you like."

In a flash I had an idea. My heart was racing, though, because I thought that my request might not fully meet the restrictive communication criteria, and I might precipitate a scolding.

"Saint Peter, a few years ago I recovered from lymphoma. Then Olivia and I were able to start planning our wedding. To celebrate my cure, Olivia and I exchanged coffee mugs during a steak dinner. The coffee mug that I gave her that night is sitting with her sewing stuff in the corner of the bedroom, and that cup now holds a pair of scissors and several emery boards. Would it be possible to remove the stuff from the mug, then move the mug to the center of her desk on the other side of the bedroom? She writes letters and pays bills at the desk, so she'll quickly find the mug."

"A coffee mug?"

"Yes, it was a special gift from me and we had a running joke about it."

Saint Peter was amenable, but he remained a bit suspicious. "But are there slogans written on that mug? There can be no clear, concrete communication."

"No words," I replied. "Just initials." Then I continued, "And finally, it would be great to have my unopened box of income tax software placed next to that mug on her desk. She would see it as a sign that she could drink coffee and think about me as she completes our taxes."

"Just initials on the mug," Saint Peter mumbled. "Her name is Olivia Evans. Hmmm."

"Yes, there are just three letters on the mug. But she will certainly think of me when she finds it."

After a moment Saint Peter winked at me, but I was uncertain what he meant. "I actually think I'm being hoodwinked here," he said. "You had better take care if you try to play tricks on beings with infinite wisdom."

I swallowed and looked down at my socks and sandals.

I looked up again, and I was relieved that he was smiling. His smile, however, seemed to indicate that he knew more than he was about to say.

"Well, I will allow it in this case," Saint Peter responded with a definitive air. "You're a good man, Stuart." His fingers flew over his non-existent keyboard. Then he stood and reached out his hand. I stood and shook his hand, and then he guided me briskly through the door into heaven.

Heaven is gorgeous, but in spite of the many distractions I persisted with keeping a watch on my house. The next morning's phone call from the police with news of the accident was unbearably painful for Olivia. After she hung up the phone she sobbed in bed for an hour. She had coffee and showered, then curled up in bed to sob for another hour.

Finally she got dressed and sat for a moment at her little desk. I smiled as I saw her notice the mug and tax software. After a glance at the unopened software package, she set that aside. But she weighed the mug in her hand. She looked toward her sewing table then back at the mug. She walked across the room and picked up the scissors and emery boards, and after a few seconds she set them down again and returned to her desk. She looked at the mug for a full minute, seemingly without breathing.

Although my heart was already full of joy in heaven, my elation was further increased as I watched my true love murmur the initials on the mug.

"OBE," she whispered. "Omnes bene est."

Her eyes filled with tears of joy, and she fell to her knees on the carpet as she clutched the mug to her chest.

COMMENTS ABOUT WRITING "THE MESSAGE"

I was pleased that my short story *The Message* won second place in 2 Elizabeths Love & Romance contest in late 2017. This story was published in early 2018 in *2 Elizabeths Volume 1: Love & Romance*, edited by Elise Holland, and is being sold on-line. Let me now explain the multistep process that I used as I created this story. I've used this same general process as I have written other stories as well.

Note that few writers address a blank page by scribbling out a nearly perfect first draft. I think that a writer starts with a general idea about what they want to produce (nature, topic, approximate length, tone, etc.), and, very importantly, the writer must have clearly in mind what emotional response or other effect they intend to produce in the reader. Do they want the reader to laugh or weep? Shall the reader be intrigued, horrified, inspired, or perhaps induced to take some action or change some behavior?

I wanted to create a short story about a young married couple separated by death, yet their love and hope survive this catastrophe by an unusual and heartwarming turn of events.

Note that not just their love survives but also their hope. In recent years, I have been impressed by how the atheistic tendencies in our modern society have seemed to erode hope. I am a physician and scientist, and many of my colleagues seem not to value a reflective spiritual life very highly. I wonder if this materialistic world view is contributing to depression, poor marriages, alcoholism, drug use, or other ills. I wanted my story to be an entertaining yet benign vehicle that might cause a reader to think further about life-and-death questions and the ultimate purposes of our lives.

I also wanted there to be humor in the story. The tale should be lighthearted and fun to read. In spite of a tragic event, the story could illustrate aspects of the great mystery of human suffering and death and provide an imaginative glimpse of the afterlife. People of all cultures have wondered about such things, so why shouldn't I give my notions? I am a Christian, and I sometimes write essays for a local Catholic newspaper. Several of those essays are reproduced in this book, and you should read those before you read *The Message*. Those newspaper essays are intended to be thoughtfully written nonfiction pieces that contain insightful quotes and useful facts, whereas *The Message* would be a fictional story that illustrates how one could imagine an afterlife.

It is also important to mention that I intended to write a clever mystery, not actually a love story. In my work, having interesting and compelling characters is important, but I have always been more driven by plot than by characters. In my mind, a clever plot idea must come first, and then characters are invented to flesh out the storyline that is desired. In almost all of my stories, the main characters are quite likable. I want my reader to care about what happens to my main characters. Perhaps someday I will experiment and have a hateful main character but not soon. Thus, it is important to realize that my concept of *The Message* began with a plot idea of a solvable mystery, and the character details came later to make the plot work.

With the above general notions in mind, I explored the scenario of a young husband who dies suddenly, but he discovers that he is, in fact, not actually dead but remains sentient. His body, though, is clearly no longer a physical body made of ordinary matter. He wants to send a message back to his grieving wife that his existence continues in an afterlife. But he quickly finds out that the rules of his new heavenly life do not permit such a clear and unambiguous message to be sent back to earth. I tried to imagine clever ways that he might be able to sneak a message back to his wife. The message would have to be benign in appearance so that the heavenly authorities might not recognize that he was actually telling his wife that he was alive and well in heaven.

Because Latin was associated for centuries with the Roman Catholic Church, the idea came to me that if the husband somehow found a way to send to his wife the Latin phrase *omnes bene est*, which means "all is well," and if it also was very clear to her that this was a message from him, then perhaps his wife would realize that he had found this way to communicate to her not to despair.

To make the phrase *omnes bene est* significant to the wife and to make clear its potential vital meaning related to beating death, the story needed to contain some episode from earlier in their relationship in which the phrase had an analogous meaning to both of them. So I introduced early in the story the fact that the husband years before had a deadly lymphoma that fortunately was cured by chemotherapy and radiation treatments, and during the subsequent celebration of the cure, the phrase *omnes bene est* became a significant little inside remark between them. Many loving couples have such short phrases that carry a special meaning—sometimes bawdy, often humorous, but always with a special intimate meaning for them.

My next problem was that if heavenly authorities were forbidding any revelation that an afterlife exists, then they would never permit the husband to send his wife the phrase *omnes bene est*, as that would be too obvious. That message would have to be delivered disguised in some way. I hit upon disguising it as the initials OBE, which might be found on a leather wallet or briefcase. But the initials must clearly be seen by the wife not to be the initials of a person, yet their link to the phrase *omnes bene est* must be absolutely certain in the mind of the young wife. After a little additional thought, I came upon the scheme that the wife's name would be Olivia Evans, and she would have the middle initial A. This fact would be introduced in the very first sentence of the story, before the reader would have any notion that the initials of the wife, OAE, might be of importance later in the story. Then I introduced into the tale the fact that during the celebration for the husband's cure from lymphoma, he presented his then-girlfriend with a coffee mug with the initials OBE, which actually was celebrating "all is well" in terms of his medical condition. The young couple then move ahead to plan their wedding, and the initials OBE became unambiguously tied to the phrase *omnes bene est* in the mind of the young woman. But the coffee mug was forgotten and languished on the sewing machine as a container for scissors and emery boards.

Heavenly residents are sending little signs to their families, like rainbows or the coincidental playing of a favorite song on the radio. These are pleasant reminders of the deceased for the families, but they carry no concrete message. The husband asks St. Peter to physically move the coffee mug a few yards across the room to his wife's small desk where she will easily find it. When she awakens, the mug will be a nice reminder of him. Of course, the husband is counting on not merely providing a simple reminder but clearly communicating his status.

The last problem was how to pull off such a scheme of

sending the message OBE, standing for *omnes bene est*, if the heavenly authorities are all-knowing and likely would easily see through this ruse. As mentioned, I wanted some humor in the story, so I made St. Peter, who is the traditional gatekeeper to heaven, a rather idiosyncratic and likable character. When the husband asks to have his wife, Olivia Evans, rediscover the old coffee mug that has three letters on it, the all-knowing St. Peter quickly discerns that those letters are not Olivia's correct initials, but he just winks at the husband and allows her to find the coffee mug anyway, breaching the tight secrecy about an afterlife. St. Peter does this as an act of kindness and presumably has made a gracious exception in this case. The wife's reaction when she finds the mug is memorable. When my wife first read this story, she actually cried.

A few other details then were filled in. The young couple had actually first met during college in a Latin class. And the phrase *omnes bene est* once had more benign uses during their dating years. A few additional endearing personal details were added, such as the young man's preference for comfort rather than style, since he often chooses to wear socks with sandals in cool weather. Olivia tells him that she would never be caught dead wearing socks with sandals. Yet it happens that when the husband has his fatal auto accident, he is wearing socks with his sandals, so that is how he enters eternal life. Since the old saying about death and taxes is so well known, I also added some humor around that topic. Yet, while fun, I think that this story carries a very significant message.

HOMICIDE IN HARTFORD: NICE GUYS SOMETIMES WIN

Arthur Simmons was feeling a little more awake as he took another sip of hot coffee. It was early on a Tuesday morning in April, and he was at his gate at Bradley Airport a few miles north of Hartford. Arthur glanced at his watch: 5:55 a.m. His 6:35 United flight to Chicago should start boarding any time now. From the looks of it, the flight promised to be pretty full. He suspected that most passengers were taking advantage of the less expensive fare for such an early flight, but he had a different reason for his crack-of-dawn adventure. As a forty-year-old associate professor of criminal justice at the University of Hartford, he had been invited to give a noon lecture at Loyola University in Chicago about long-term trends in violent crime. He was happy to accept the invitation from a prestigious school. Because he had to teach classes on Monday, including an evening seminar, he couldn't fly on Monday. Not that he really had to teach yesterday, but he hated to cancel any classes; cancelling was not really fair to the students.

Long-term changes in the rates of crime had long interested him. It was a complex topic. The accuracy and quality of data had to be carefully assessed. Was there any methodological bias in the way that numbers were collected? Statistical analyses could be surprisingly complicated. Although as a student he had first been interested in how rates of crimes changed over ten or twenty years, he soon expanded his interests to really long-term periods—centuries. For his master of arts degree in criminal justice, he had focused on long-term crime statistics in England, supplemented by comparison with records from elsewhere in Western Europe.

Although time was short, he walked back to a shop to get a doughnut to have with his coffee. Good—only three people in line ahead of him. He smiled as he thought about the joke he told the clerk last June as he stood in this same line. As he ordered that day, the young man had proudly informed him that he could also choose one free doughnut in honor of National Doughnut Day. The server was serious. So Arthur had smiled and quipped that if the profit-driven business thought that it would be a good idea to give a free doughnut to each customer, there might actually be a hole in their logic! The clerk seemed to miss the pun, so his joke fell flat, unfortunately. Still, Arthur thought it was pretty funny.

Suddenly, a large, athletic man, about thirty-five with long reddish-brown hair, pushed ahead of him in line without looking back or saying anything. Very rude. The man was a head higher, and he had red and blue rock music tattoos on his muscled arms. The interloper stood as straight and tall as a giant redwood, seemingly proud of his stature and daring anyone to say anything to him. Arthur briefly considered tapping on his shoulder to complain, but he decided that he still would have time to get his doughnut and walk thirty yards back to his gate—so no need to make a big deal out of it. Some people had just not been raised right, he thought. Or perhaps the guy had just been jilted by his girlfriend yesterday or lost his job. Arthur decided just to give him the benefit of the doubt and not make a big issue out of his cut into the line.

Humorously, two minutes later, the big man blushed slightly as he fumbled for his wallet; it was in his carry-on bag with his wife at some gate down the hallway. He looked helplessly left and right, and his slumped shoulders indicated rising embarrassment. Counting the miscellaneous change salvaged from all of his jeans pockets, the big guy was still eighty-two cents short. Feeling that karma had punished the rude stranger enough already, Arthur reached forward and handed the red-faced man a dollar. The muscle man mumbled thanks, grabbed his food, and quickly walked away. No eye contact. Arthur smiled. Apparently the universe can exert its own brand of justice. This episode had cost Arthur a dollar, but it was priceless.

This incident caused Arthur to reflect on records from thirteenth-century London about minor slights that led to arguments and even murder. The eyre was a panel of royal justices who met at widely spaced intervals—sometimes several years between sessions. They were required to inquire about all homicides that had occurred in the district since the last eyre. A quarrel commonly arose after drinking or over a woman, and violence sometimes escalated immediately to murder, which was rarely premeditated. According to a review of data by expert Manual Eisner, in the eyre rolls of 1278, for example, two of the 145 homicides that were recorded resulted from a quarrel after a game of chess. The population of London at this time was about forty thousand, and it appears that in 1278, the homicide rate was about fifteen per one hundred thousand per year. The murder rate in London was fifteen to twenty per one hundred thousand for three hundred years (between 1200 and 1500), then gradually declined to fewer than five per one hundred thousand in 1700. In the first years of the twenty-first century, the homicide rates in England, Germany, and Switzerland were each 1.0 to 1.5 per one hundred thousand. Most people today simply don't realize that in spite of all the current violence and crime, murder was far more common in prior centuries.

Arthur's doughnut was half-eaten by the time he made it back to his gate. They had just started boarding Group 2, and he would soon board in Group 3. There was a minor kerfuffle when a young man and in his wife seemed to insist that they be the first to board in Group 3 instead of standing four persons farther back. A few stern instructions from the flight attendant settled things such that the additional delay of twenty seconds for the couple to enter the airplane was smoothed over. Arthur was near the end of Group 3 since he had been a little late returning with his doughnut. But all was well.

Settling into a coveted aisle seat, 14C, Arthur noted that there was a passenger by the window in 14A. About aged thirty-five, he wore jeans and a T-shirt and gave no greeting. He was engrossed in his paperback book, which seemed to be a western novel since it had a cowboy and an attractive young Indian princess on the cover. Broad shouldered and serious looking, this man also had muscular arms but no tattoos. Arthur considered that maybe it was time for him to join a gym. In the last couple of years, his most strenuous activity was occasionally walking up the four flights of stairs to his office in Hillyer Hall, though he likely raised his blood pressure a bit (was that good or bad?) when he struggled to change the ink cartridge in his printer.

Unexpectedly, an elderly, white-haired lady in 14D just across the aisle from Arthur looked at him, smiled, and asked a question.

"So do you live in Connecticut or Illinois?"

He explained that he taught at the University of Hartford and lived in the city, but then the safety instructions began, which ended the conversation.

The flight was uneventful, and the plane taxied to the gate at O'Hare. At the first allowed instant, most people in aisle seats stood up, but when seated about halfway toward the back, Arthur always preferred just to relax seated for a few minutes until most of the rows ahead of him had exited.

Arthur was just about to stand when he noticed the elderly woman across the aisle start to rise, so Arthur paused and remained seated. The man to his left must have been annoyed by Arthur's courtesy because, with some irritation, he voiced his first words of the trip.

"Come on, man! I'm in a hurry."

Arthur glanced quickly at him, then looked away. "Just waiting a second for the lady here."

After the fragile, stooped woman made one step forward down the aisle, Arthur promptly rose and took a step backward to allow the man in the window seat to brush past him, which he did with perhaps a bit too much enthusiasm. Arthur then sat down again to collect his small carry-on bag from under the seat in front of him. That's when he noticed that the window passenger had left his western novel in the seat pocket. Arthur grabbed the book and exited.

I'll catch the guy at the luggage carousel, he thought.

Arthur had a ticket for the 8:00 p.m. return flight to Connecticut, so he had not checked a bag. But he stood among the group picking up their suitcases with an eye out for the young man who had sat in seat 14A. Arthur would have been happy to return his book, but he was nowhere to be seen. The man must have had only a small carry-on bag as well. Arthur tucked the novel into his carry-on bag and stepped outside to catch a taxi to Loyola.

⁂

Arthur's lecture went well, and he enjoyed meeting with students and discussing several more topics in a small group before having a quick dinner near Loyola with his host. His filet was delicious, one of the perks of an academic position.

The flight home was unremarkable, but Arthur was tired as he let himself into the house at about eleven thirty that night. His wife was in bed but still awake. He told Sue that he had a good day, and she relayed a few details about her chores and minor accomplishments while teaching middle school. Arthur couldn't imagine how she routinely controlled the classroom and actually managed to teach anything to the squirmy, irreverent thirteen-year-olds. They were the future of America, but he knew well that middle school was not a place for the fainthearted. He was more comfortable sticking with straightforward major misbehavior—like murder.

He gave his wife a quick kiss and then hopped into bed while asking a final question: "Was there any news today?"

"Big crash on 91 just south of Hartford this morning at about seven. Six cars with three people injured seriously."

"Too bad. They drive too fast and change lanes too quickly," he pontificated.

"And that rich British lady, Martha Samuels, was murdered in a parking garage in Hartford last evening."

Stunned, Arthur took a few seconds to process. Then he responded softly, "Wow. I hadn't heard."

"Yes," replied his wife.

"She had lived in Hartford ten years," Arthur mumbled mostly to himself. Then he continued addressing his wife. "You've often seen her photo in the paper. As a good British lady, she always carried an umbrella! She was a character. Terrible, terrible. How did it happen?"

"It was after nine o'clock at night. She left a restaurant and walked to get into her car in the Fifth Street Garage. Apparently someone jumped her and robbed her and shot her twice. She was dead at the scene."

"Just terrible. She was a multimillionaire, but I'll bet she had less than $200 in her purse."

"Her husband gave an interview on TV this morning, asking

for privacy and thanking the community for their thoughts and prayers. What's his name?"

"Barnes. Clayton Barnes."

"He's still good-looking." She smiled as she said it.

"Well, he was an actor. And he was smart! He married an older woman who inherited an industrial empire." There was a pause. "But, of course, I'm quite happy with the girl I married."

"You better be ..."

"Student debts and all," he added.

"You're so silly!"

⁂

The next morning, Arthur was back in his office. He had brought along his small carry-on bag to unpack his lecture notes and other school items. As he reached inside for the last things, he pulled out the western novel. He had totally forgotten about it.

Just then his administrative assistant walked in through the open door with a handful of yesterday's mail for him. She eyed the novel.

"Researching criminal justice procedures in Dodge City?"

"Oh, good morning, Claudine. A guy left his book on the plane, and I tried to catch him to give it back, but he was too fast for me."

Arthur stepped down the hall a moment to make himself a cup of coffee. The local newspaper was on the counter in a little disarray after multiple readers. The main headline was bold and clear: "No Suspects in Samuels Murder."

As he sat down at his desk, he looked inside the front cover of the paperback to see if the seat 14A man might have written his name there, but no luck. He next glanced at the inside of the back cover. Bingo. There was a name and a phone number: Clayton 860-278-1820.

Pleased with his detective work, he set the book aside to

start up his computer, but then he suddenly sat straight up in his chair. Clayton? He picked up the book and slowly mumbled the name to himself once again: "Clayton."

He set down the book and dialed his good buddy at Hartford Police Headquarters.

"Tommy, can you talk? A strange thing has happened."

"I know you," replied Tommy. "You think it's fun when strange things happen."

"Tommy, are you guys any closer to a suspect in the Samuels murder?"

"Well ... we're not supposed to talk about that very much. Only limited information is being released."

"So tell me what you are allowed to say."

Tommy laid out what had been on TV. She probably had been approached from behind and may have been grabbed. She turned, and the shooter fired once with a small handgun, striking her in the left shoulder. She struck out at the shooter with her umbrella, and then the shooter fired a second shot—fatal—into the center of her chest. The shooter took her purse and ran.

"It sounds like someone actually saw it the way you have described it. Is that true?"

"Well ..." Tommy paused again. "It won't be announced until noon today at a news conference, but there was a distant surveillance camera, and there are useable images that we are still looking at. Even though the camera was thirty yards away, the basic movements were about as I have described them. We're getting enlargements made now."

"Male assailant?"

"Yes, with a hat and mask."

"Fingerprints?"

"Nope. The shooter grabbed her purse, but that's gone. We basically have very little." Tommy wanted to say more, it seemed, but he stopped.

"Tommy, were you about to say something else?"

Tommy took a breath. "I can't say more. The chief would kill me."

After an uncomfortable pause, Arthur decided to explain a little about why he had called. "Tommy, you can't tell me more right now, fine. But information can flow the other way. I think I may have a vital tip for you."

"A tip?"

"Yeah. But first, does Clayton Barnes have a personal cell phone?"

"Of course. I think most people in Timbuktu have a personal cell phone."

"What's his cell number?"

Tommy hesitated. "Arthur, we have his number here in the record, but it is private, and I can't tell you that."

Arthur took a breath. "Is it 860-278-1820?"

Dumbfounded silence.

"Tommy, are you there?"

"Arthur, I just cannot even imagine how you do these things!"

"I'm coming to the station right now, and I want the chief and the lead investigator—and you—to hear something directly from me in person."

 formed

It was ten in the morning, and the chief was sitting with the small group, hoping that this was not going to waste his time. He glanced at his watch.

Arthur started. "Thanks for your time. Martha Samuels was shot at 9:15 on Monday evening. At 6:35 a.m. Tuesday, I was taking off from Bradley to Chicago on a United flight, and I may have been sitting next to someone related to this case—possibly even the shooter."

The chief blinked. "Go on."

"In seat 14A, there was a well-built young man, Caucasian,

about thirty-five. I was in 14C. He accidentally left his book behind on the plane, so I tried to chase him to return it but missed him. This is it." Arthur pointed to the novel, now in a plastic bag. "I looked for a name in the book. There was one on the inside of the back cover. It said 'Clayton.' And it had Clayton Barnes's cell phone number written there."

"Amazing."

"United Airlines will have this passenger's name and address, at least what are given officially on his government ID. And his fingerprints are on this book." Arthur paused. "Unfortunately, my fingerprints are also on this book, so please be aware of that."

Tommy smiled. "This is extremely valuable. You may have cracked our case."

Arthur's brow furrowed. "But maybe he was just one of Clayton Barnes's business partners and had nothing to do with the shooting. How can you tie him to the victim?"

Tommy looked at the Chief, who nodded. Tommy continued, "What I couldn't tell you until now is that although we don't have fingerprints, we do have some of the shooter's blood."

"His blood. How is that possible?"

Now the chief spoke. "Martha Samuels did not just carry an umbrella everywhere because she was British. In fact, as a wealthy woman, she was a little paranoid. Her umbrella was specially made with a steel shaft. And if you pressed the umbrella tip against someone, the spring-loaded end would slide toward the handle, unsheathing a three-inch spikelike end of the shaft. It was a nasty defensive weapon. And she apparently stuck or grazed the shooter once with that tip because there is blood on it, and so far we know that those bits of blood are not Martha's."

"Fantastic!" Arthur was elated that chance events had come together potentially to solve this case. "Sadly, though, the handsome Clayton Barnes may be implicated in his wife's murder."

The lead investigator and the chief stepped toward the door to start the process of finding the man in Chicago. That should be easy, they said. And after sampling him, the blood comparison testing should be definitive within a couple of weeks.

Arthur and Tommy walked out together. Arthur was reflecting on the fact that because he had been polite when exiting an aircraft and was delayed leaving his seat, this allowed him to notice the forgotten book. What a fortunate turn of events. Karma again?

"I have something else to tell you," began Tommy.

Arthur nodded.

"This morning at eight o'clock, the children of Martha Samuels posted a $250,000 reward for anyone who provides the key information that leads to the arrest and conviction of the killer or killers. A little time will tell, but I think you just earned the money."

FOOLING THE DEVIL

The two young German soldiers were well groomed, but the Nazi insignia on their crisp uniforms left no doubt that they worked diligently with a purpose that sent a chill up the worried husband's spine. Herman Mark stood at the roadside with one arm around his wife's waist, while their two young sons sat nearby on a bench. The search of belongings in their car was speedy yet thorough. Dozens of shirts, pants, dresses, and several coats had been hung on metal hangers using a wooden rod suspended over the back seat. The two boys barely had room to squeeze in at one side of the seat. But now the soldiers placed fingers in every pocket, and they carefully felt for suspicious lumps that might reveal an item sewn into a lining. After thirty minutes, the soldiers seemed satisfied; nothing had been found. The suitcases also had no contraband. Stern but polite, the young soldiers made sure the clothes were again hung in a reasonable manner on the rod, and they waved the family back toward their car. Herman tried not to look excessively relieved and managed a nonchalant smile as he climbed back into the driver's seat. The horizontal checkpoint barrier was raised, and Herman started the car and shifted into drive. They had made it to Switzerland.

Events months earlier had culminated in this high-risk but potentially lifesaving trip. As the two-lane highway wound its way through low hills, Herman allowed the memory of that first business meeting to replay in his mind, almost as if it were a movie that he was watching.

The distinguished Austrian professor shook hands with the Canadian businessman, and they sat in comfortable chairs facing each other in a small lounge adjacent to the hotel lobby. Dr. Herman Francis Mark quickly glanced left and right and then once again toward the open door; they were alone for the moment, and this was a relatively private venue.

"I'm pleased that we could meet for a few minutes, Professor," beamed Mr. C. B. Thorne. "You have many skills that could be of great use to us at Canadian International Pulp and Paper." Thorne was wearing an immaculate three-piece suit with sharply creased trousers, and the shine of his black shoes was impressive.

Dr. Mark nodded politely. His suit was rather more worn and rumpled than Thorne's.

"Let me start by saying," Mr. Thorne continued, "that I have heard privately in recent weeks from several of your colleagues that you may be feeling more uncertain about the political situation in Austria. If there is any way that I could entice you to leave the University of Vienna and come to work for us in Hawkesbury, Ontario, the company would arrange for you to have superior research equipment." Thorne smiled and lit a cigarette.

Dr. Mark declined a cigarette with the wave of his hand. The sight of so many Nazi flags in Dresden had been disquieting, and he felt fortunate that his trip to the scientific conference had gone well so far, although there were a number of disturbing conversations in the hallways. Jews in Germany were being harassed, and Jews in Austria were becoming increasingly worried. Now in September 1937, there was talk that Germany intended to annex Austria within a year.

It was widely known that Dr. Mark's father, a prominent physician, had been born a Jew, although his father had converted to Christianity for his marriage. Dr. Mark feared that if the anti-Semitic program spread to Austria, he likely would lose his university appointment as professor of physical chemistry. He might even be arrested because of his well-known friendship with Chancellor Dollfus, who had been outspoken in his views that Austria should remain independent. But Dollfus was murdered by ten Nazi conspirators who had burst into the Chancellery building during an attempted coup in July 1934.

After a deep breath, Dr. Mark spoke quietly. "I think that this Canadian opportunity would be very good for me and my family, but there are many hurdles. I have a wife and two young sons. It is illegal to transport significant amounts of currency or any valuables out of the country, so we would be paupers on arrival in Canada. We have lived a comfortable life, so that state of extreme poverty would be disconcerting to us. Soldiers would search us carefully at borders, and there would be severe punishment if we were caught with currency or gold coins."

"Well, you know well the ways of soldiers, having been so decorated as a young man in the Great War."

Dr. Mark sighed again. "At age eighteen, in 1913, I enlisted in the Austrian army to perform my mandatory one year of military service, and I intended thereafter to enter college. The onset of the war in 1914 caused my twelve-month enlistment to be prolonged to five years."

"And a remarkable military career it was," commented Thorne. "You were wounded and came to be known as the hero of the Battle of Mount Ortigara. Impressive."

"Thank you for mentioning that," replied Dr. Mark. "But these days I am much more interested in the macromolecular structure of polymers than in military matters."

"Well, polymer chemistry is the topic that interests us the most," said Thorne. "Your x-ray crystallographic studies of cellulose are particularly noteworthy." Thorne pulled a paper from his coat pocket to recheck some of Dr. Mark's career details.

"Born in 1895 in Vienna, doctorate in chemistry in 1921 from the University of Vienna, worked for a year with Professor Schlenk at University of Berlin, invited by Fritz Haber to join the Kaiser Wilhelm Institute in 1922, where you devised groundbreaking x-ray crystallographic methods for polymers, became an assistant director at a laboratory at IG Farben in 1926 to work on new polymers ..." Thorne paused and looked up at Mark. "Due to political changes in Germany, you moved to the University of Vienna in 1932, where you now serve with distinction."

Dr. Mark nodded but said nothing.

Thorne continued, "If you can find a way to move to Canada, we would love to have you help us improve methods to make cellulose acetate, cellophane, and rayon from Canadian trees."

Both men stood and shook hands.

"Thank you for the offer. I will talk to Mimi. But if I accept the offer, we may arrive each carrying only a small suitcase. It would be a bit of a shock for us."

༄

It was cool and wet in Vienna on January 1, 1938. Herman Mark and his wife stood in their bedroom looking at the lining of a coat.

"But, sweetheart," Herman protested, "if you try to sew currency into a coat lining, you will get us caught. It is an obvious ploy."

A tear appeared in Mimi's eye. She feared for their future and for their two sons. She set the coat down on the bed, took a step forward, and embraced her husband. "Please think, Herman," she sobbed. "You must find a way for us to get some money out of Austria."

As she looked up, she saw a slight smile on her husband's face. She wiped away a tear and smiled back at him. "I believe that you may already have been thinking. Now, tell me."

"You must be willing to take a risk with me," replied Herman. "I have an idea."

Mimi clasped both of his hands, and they sat together on the side of the bed.

"Two weeks ago, I needed to buy more platinum wire to use as a catalyst in the laboratory. Mueller & Sons sells me some every few months, so it is fairly routine. I am thinking that I should use the cash that we have hidden here in the house to buy much more platinum wire in the next three months. I can say that it will be for several large chemical reaction vessels."

"But, Herman," Mimi blinked. "If we have large coils of platinum wire in our suitcases that will surely be viewed as highly unusual."

"Of course, that certainly would be suspicious. But this is my idea. I can cut the wire into lengths and bend each piece exactly into the form of a coat hanger. Then we will hang shirts and dresses on the hangers. The soldiers will look carefully in every pocket of the clothing, but they most likely will not examine the hangers very carefully."

Mimi smiled. "It should work! And I have an additional idea. I will sew cloth covers for the hangers so that the shiny metal won't show very prominently."

Herman nodded. The plan was set.

⁂

On March 12, 1938, truckloads of German troops entered Austria, and the Anschluss was celebrated in the streets. But Jews did not celebrate. Within a few days, Herman Mark was arrested, his university professorship was cancelled, and he was held in a Gestapo jail. Herman was allowed to send a message to a former classmate who now was a junior Nazi official. They had been friends, but he would only help if paid a substantial bribe. Herman paid, and within a day, he was released from jail, and his passport was returned. But Herman knew that he and his family should depart Austria immediately.

Without delay, Herman affixed a Nazi flag to the radiator

of his car and tied ski equipment to the roof. Mimi settled the boys in the back seat, along with clothing on hangers. On their way to Zurich, their belongings were searched several times carefully, but their ruse using the coat hangers went undetected.

Postscript:

1. Herman Mark and his family traveled through France and eventually to England. In September 1938, Dr. Mark took a ship to Montreal, and his family joined him in Canada a few weeks later. Herman worked at Canadian International Pulp and Paper, then moved his family to the United States when he accepted a position at the Polytechnic Institute of Brooklyn, where he had a long, productive scientific career. Herman remained active and healthy into his late nineties.

2. One of the small boys in the back seat, Peter, became a professor of electrical engineering and computer science at Princeton University.

3. The other boy in the back seat, Hans, became a world-famous aeronautical engineer who helped develop the Osprey aircraft, supervised the Pioneer spacecraft missions to the outer solar system, served as deputy administrator of NASA where he supervised the first fourteen space shuttle missions, and was appointed secretary of the United States Air Force by President Carter in 1979. Hans then served as the chancellor of the University of Texas, and Herman loved to visit him in Austin.

4. George Herbert (1593–1633) famously said, "Living well is the best revenge." The odyssey of the Mark family is a sterling example of this principle.

BAMBOOZLE: A POKER MYSTERY

A Surprise Encounter

"No! I won't go with you!"

I was surprised to hear a female voice as I stepped off the hotel elevator on the eighth floor. It was three o'clock in the morning, so I had not expected anyone to be in the hallway—but this was Las Vegas. I could tell that she was upset, perhaps a little panicky. I took a few more steps away from the elevator and tried to walk calmly toward where I thought she might be standing around a corner. I turned right into the main hallway, my hands still in my pants pockets. As I stepped around the corner, I saw a petite young woman some ten yards away, perhaps about thirty, wearing a short, tight skirt, facing a large football linebacker sort of man. Faded jeans, white T-shirt, muscled arms, tattooed right upper arm, crew cut. He was leaning with his hands flat against the hallway wall, his arms slightly bent, the woman trapped between them.

I continued walking slowly and exclaimed in a loud voice, not really appropriate for a hotel hallway in the middle of the night, "Sweetheart! There you are! The whole gang is waiting in the lobby!"

Both of their heads swiveled to look at me. Her eyes were wide. He looked me up and down but said nothing, and he kept his palms planted on the wall.

My mind raced as I took several more steps toward them. I quickly fixed on a plan.

"Sugar, you said fifteen minutes. Hey, buddy! This must be your lucky day!"

The giant scowled at me a bit, but he seemed to be bleary-eyed. He was probably drunk. I took several more steps.

"You almost walked away from the hundred-dollar bill you dropped!"

Now standing just next to him, I removed my right hand from my pocket, having scrunched up the hundred I had placed there earlier in the evening before my poker cash game. Unfortunately, the bill's three companions were now absent from my person due to some bad luck at the table. I stooped down and reached to the floor behind his left shoe. As I straightened up, I waved the wrinkled bill for him to see.

"Is this yours?" I smiled and looked innocent.

He blinked and looked at the bill, then at me, then back at the bill. He blinked again but still said nothing. I knew now for sure that he was quite drunk. Very slow processing. I was calculating as to whether he was drunk enough that I might be able to push him hard and knock him over so that I could run away with the young woman. Not the best plan, though. The elevator generally took at least a minute to arrive, so we would have to make a perilous run for it down a stairwell.

Finally, he spoke as he removed his hands from the wall and turned to face me directly. "A hundred dollars." He reached out and took the bill with a somewhat dazed expression as I extended my left hand to the woman.

"We have to go right now, sweetie. Everyone is waiting."

She instantly took my hand—boy, did she have a grip—and we walked quickly toward the elevator. Hurriedly turning the corner, I pushed the down button. We stood there in silence, but she looked me up and down with wide eyes, and I could see the pulse pounding on both sides of her neck. Poker players never miss that.

Mercifully, the elevator came in less than ten seconds, probably because it was three in the morning. I hit the lobby button, conveniently labeled in large letters "Casino." The doors closed, and we started to descend.

Her stance relaxed, and she looked at the floor as she repeated, "Oh, my God!" about five times. Then she looked at me. "I was just walking back to my room, and that guy grabbed me! He said he had a room down the hall, and he wanted to have a drink with me." I tried to look suave, but I was ten times more relieved than she was.

"Lucky I came along."

We walked out into the lobby amid the beeping of slot machines and loud music. Plenty of revelers still going strong.

She stopped, but I suggested, "We should get away from this bank of elevators. Let's head off that way."

We walked side by side, but we didn't speak further as we weaved around clumps of people. After turning left and right for about five minutes, I stopped in front of a restaurant that seemed to have only half the seats filled.

"My room is on the eighth floor," I began, "so I'm going to kill some time in here before I go back upstairs." I extended my right hand and smiled. This was goodbye.

She smiled. I could tell that she was completely relaxed now.

"Thank you so much! I'm not going to let you sit in there by yourself. I'll buy you something. And I think I owe you a hundred dollars."

We found a booth in the back, and the ambient noise dropped ten levels, much more conducive for conversation. We looked at menus and made our choices.

"My name is Susan, and I'm from Austin. I went to college there and just stayed on. I'm originally from New Hampshire— got tired of the cold winters."

"Connecticut. But born in a small town in Illinois. I'm Jim Miller, and I'm getting tired of the New England winters, but my job is there." As I spoke, I saw her glance down at my wedding ring, then look up again, her expression unchanged. She had no ring. Her long black hair fell just below her shoulders to attractively frame her face.

"What do you do?" she asked.

"I'm a ..." I started. I hesitated briefly, then continued. "Sort of a biologist and researcher. I work at a pharmaceutical company doing clinical studies." I had decided after Sheila died last year that I wouldn't introduce myself to women as a medical doctor. I feared that some women might not be serious but only liked the panache of dating a doctor. After all, I only saw patients as an endocrinologist on Friday mornings. The rest of the week, I was a medical researcher writing protocols and evaluating scientific papers.

She smiled. "After college, I got an introductory office job in the Texas state government. Mostly paperwork. I stayed because they liked me and I got promoted several times. So I run a branch now in the State Agriculture Department. Still mostly paperwork and handling personnel issues."

She took a sip of water and looked toward the door. "How long do you think we have to sit here?"

"He was drunk. A half-hour should do it. He's probably already in his bed asleep."

She took another sip of water, looked at me, and then took another sip of water. Poker players notice these things.

"So are you here with your wife?"

"Sheila died last year. Ovarian cancer. Her disease was aggressive, and she only lasted a year. We had been married ten years." I paused to take a sip of water, then continued.

"I'm on this first trip after her death to regain my equilibrium. I play poker, and this is the place to be." I paused, but Susan made no response, so I continued. "I still wear the ring to remember her. She's only been gone ten months. I also thought that wearing the ring could save me some issues in Las Vegas. I'm just here to relax a few days and play poker in the big tournament."

"I'm here to rethink things a bit too," Susan responded softly. "I had a great boyfriend during my senior year of college. But then Randy was killed in an auto accident in Austin. Drunk driver ran a light." Our gazes met. The sadness of the moment was palpable. "I just started working and kept working, but ..." She didn't finish her sentence.

The burgers were good, but we both left the fries on the plate. I was thirty-six, and I noticed that my metabolism was slowing down. I was still lean, but I didn't want to gain weight. Susan actually was thirty, as I had originally guessed, and I presumed she kept her admirable figure by watching the calories as well.

It was time to go. Susan paid as she had promised, and as she put her card away, she pulled out a crisp hundred-dollar bill and her business card on which she wrote her personal email and hotel room number. She motioned for me to take it. "It's the least I can do. We should stay in touch." After a brief pause, she continued. "Besides, you're probably going to lose all your money playing poker."

I laughed. "It looks like the ink on this bill is still wet." I took it and thanked her and handed her my business card as well.

"I actually did just get some hundreds from the bank yesterday," she said. "I never carry hundreds, but I knew I should have some cash if I was flying to Las Vegas."

"I have to quickly tell you my hundred-dollar bill joke."

"Okay."

I pointed to the portrait of Benjamin Franklin and then stashed the bill in my pocket. "Last Christmas, a wealthy man wanted to decorate his house in part using his favorite thing—money. So he took some of the pine cones off the evergreen wreath he was to hang over his fireplace, and he taped on several hundred-dollar bills. Do you know what he called it?"

"What?"

"Aretha Franklins."

She smiled, which was about all I could have expected from that joke.

An Enlightening Day

The next day, the cash poker tables were more crowded because players were arriving in Las Vegas from all over the world to play in the big tournament later that week, the World Series of Poker Main Event. But before the big one, players liked to warm up and perhaps make a little money by testing their skills at smaller games for a day or two. The rules of the cash games were similar to those for the big tournament, but players could start and stop playing when they wished, could always purchase more chips, and the stakes were much lower in the cash games. You could play cash for $200, but the big tournament's entry fee was $10,000.

I enjoyed sitting with players from Germany, France, Canada, Argentina, Brazil, Japan, South Korea—from everywhere. Although I believe there was likely no one from North Korea. The young man sitting next to me wore dark sunglasses, as is popular with some players. He was from Uruguay and had stacked his plastic chips in front of him in a ten-inch-tall, spiraling double helix. Amazing. I suspected that he might not want to enter a pot just now because he would have to take chips away from his sculpture. But I quickly found out otherwise when I made a bet with a weak hand and he promptly raised me, so I had to fold, and I lost those chips.

This player from South America built a double helix of chips.

I was licking my wounds and glancing around the room when I noticed that Susan had entered the poker room, which was quite large, and she was walking here and there among the many tables. She turned and saw me looking at her, and she gave me a smile and a little wave. I waved back. As she walked toward me, I stood up and took a few steps toward her.

"I don't want to disturb your game. I thought I'd play the slot machines in Vegas, but as long as I'm here, there's no harm learning a little more about poker. How are you doing?"

"I've been playing for two hours, and I have just about the same chips as when I started."

"Don't you have to stay in your seat?"

"No. This is a cash game, so you can walk away for a few minutes and then pay a small penalty when you come back. A part of poker etiquette, though, is that many people at a table are not supposed to depart at the same time. That affects the play."

Susan followed me a few steps to my seat, and I noticed

that the man from Uruguay had picked up his chips and exited. An older gentleman was now sitting in his seat on my left. He looked vaguely familiar.

"Hi, I'm Stuart," he said as I sat down.

"I'm Jim from Connecticut. You look familiar. Have we met before?"

He smiled. "I'm Stuart Davies. You've probably seen me playing on TV."

Of course. I recognized him then. It was not good news for me to have a strong professional player immediately on my left. In nearly every hand, I would have to make some decision or take some action before Stuart. So he would better know what I was thinking about my cards before I would know what he was thinking about his cards. Poker is a game of information and decision-making. Information is key. And the position of players around the table makes a difference.

Susan watched a few minutes. She had learned a little about Texas Hold'em poker from her older brother, but she had not played since high school days. We agreed to have dinner together at Patterson's at six o'clock. She would walk by and make the reservation while I was still playing. As we were setting up these plans, Stuart volunteered that the meat loaf and creamed corn there were great. I asked Stuart if he would like to join us there at six, and he agreed. I told him I wanted to hear some good casino stories.

The next two hours passed quickly, and I was disappointed as my chips dwindled. At ten minutes before six, only about 10 percent of my chips remained, so I decided to play my hole cards, eight of spades and nine of spades, by making a good-sized early bet preflop. I was not happy to be raised by Stuart. The other players folded. The flop, the first three cards placed faceup at center table by the dealer, were deuce of clubs, seven of hearts, ten of diamonds. Just my luck. Not even one spade. But I had straight possibilities, which would be completed by either a six or a jack. The probability calculation of success was fairly easy. To my knowledge at this point, four sixes and four jacks potentially remained in the deck, with two cards yet to be dealt onto the shared board by the dealer. There were eight outs that would make my straight. With two cards to come, one can use a convenient rule of thumb and simply multiply the number of outs by four, which gives thirty-two, meaning that by the end of the hand, I would have a 32 percent chance of success. Not great, but I had few chips left, and I was about to end my day by going to dinner. So I moved all of my remaining chips into the center, hoping that Stuart would fold. Instead, he called and turned over two queens. The dealer dealt the next two cards, and, as expected statistically, I missed my straight and lost my chips to Stuart.

I waited by the cashier's cage as Stuart cashed his chips to lock in a nice profit for the afternoon. As we walked toward Patterson's, he said he wanted to give me some important poker advice.

Stuart spoke a little louder as we meandered through the noisy crowd in the hallway. "It's okay to play suited connectors aggressively, but you were betting them when you were the first to bet around the table. That is the worst possible position. You have no idea if someone else might have a strong pocket pair, like tens or jacks or queens or kings or aces. There are many possible strong opposing hands. In general, depending on the exact situation, you probably should fold suited connectors if you likely will be playing out of position. These same cards play much better if you have position on your opponent. If while in position you recognize that someone seems to have a strong hand, then you can just fold the suited connectors and wait for a better spot. Or you can see that a player appears to have a weak hand. Then you can top his small bet with a big bluff, which could win the pot for you even if at that moment you mathematically have a low chance of winning based just on the cards. There is usually no rush to bet your life when out of position with only a 32 percent chance of success."

"Thanks. I learn something every time I play. I have one more day to practice before I start in the big tournament. Think I can learn all of the remaining poker lessons in about five hours?"

He knew I was kidding, and he smiled. "You know what they say. It only takes an hour to learn how to play, but it takes a lifetime to perfect."

Stuart was seventy and had the wrinkles to prove it. I would say that his tanned face was handsomely wrinkled, and it contrasted satisfyingly with his short white hair and brilliant blue eyes. He had been perfecting his game for many years. I knew that he was from Oklahoma, but I hoped to learn more about him during dinner. And more about Susan.

It turned out that we took Stuart's advice. We all had the meat loaf. Stuart ordered a beer, while Susan and I had red wine.

"I never drink alcohol when I play poker," Stuart commented.

"I don't either," I responded. "The long hours playing in a tournament tire me out, so the alcohol would only make that worse."

"Playing many hours a day is tiring." Stuart nodded. "My little house is only fifteen miles from this hotel. But I don't like to take the time to drive back and forth during the Main Event. I splurge a bit and just stay in the hotel. Much more convenient."

I looked at Susan and asked, "What did you study in college?"

"Major in business and minor in math."

"I studied biology and chemistry."

Stuart winked at us. "I never went to college, but I learned a lot from my first job in a slaughterhouse. Then I worked on a ranch for a decade and saved up some money before I moved to Vegas to try my luck as a gambler. During the next ten years, I only lived here part-time and often returned for many months to the ranch. But I started winning more in Vegas, so I have been a professional gambler ever since."

"But there can be so many ups and downs, right?" Susan replied. "How can you live with that kind of uncertainty?"

"Everything is uncertain in life," he pronounced. "You might not wake up tomorrow. Some people fall in love and have a nearly perfect marriage, while other people get hit by a train or come down with cancer. So much of life is luck. You might as well learn more about odds and how chance works and try to make chance work for you."

Susan had glanced at me, and I could tell that she saw me blink when Stuart mentioned cancer.

"So help me understand, Stuart," Susan started. "If so much is chance, how can a professional gambler count on winning more than other gamblers, like in poker? Won't he eventually just go bankrupt?"

"Well," Stuart began, and he appropriated a sly countenance. "Not everything is chance, both in life and in poker. You have to know the rules, know people, and become experienced and skilled at whatever you are doing, whether it's running a bakery or playing poker. Both in life and in poker you have to be sensible and play smart. You have to prepare and show up ready to perform. And you must be comfortable taking risks, whether it is taking a new job, making a new financial investment, or sitting down in Vegas at a poker table. Intelligent and appropriate risks—educated bets—will lose the minimum and gain the maximum."

As he spoke, Stuart pulled out a deck of cards secured by a rubber band from his shirt pocket, and he set them before us in the center of the table. He removed the rubber band.

"Hey, can't you get in trouble in Vegas if you have cards in your pocket?" I asked, although I was smiling.

"The backs of these cards say Atlantic City plain as day,

so there's little risk of being accused of anything here," he explained. "Jim, watch as I cut the cards three times to assure you that they are properly mixed." His hands moved effortlessly to cut the deck several times.

"Now I'm going to lay out the top sixteen cards facedown in a four-by-four square," Stuart continued, and each card snapped sharply on the table top as he set it out. "So there are four aces somewhere, either still in the deck or here with these sixteen cards, right?"

"Yes," I said, "and probably just one or two of the aces will be among the sixteen cards in the square."

"In poker, it's important to find aces," Stuart continued with a serious tone. "So let's turn over a few cards to look for an ace the old-fashioned way." One by one, he turned over four of the sixteen cards, seemingly at random, but none was an ace.

Feigning disappointment, Stuart commented, "It's hard to find an ace the old-fashioned way. So instead let's use magic!"

Susan laughed. I smiled, but I was carefully watching Stuart's hands.

"Now, Susan, you tell me which edge of the square of cards you want me to fold inward onto the top of the neighboring row."

Susan pointed, and Stuart folded, then directed her to make additional folds of edges as she wished until all sixteen cards were in a single stack, although within the stack, some cards might be faceup now.

"It's magic!" Stuart announced with a flourish as he spread the sixteen cards out on the table.

Susan and I gasped as we saw twelve cards facedown and the four aces faceup.

After a moment, Stuart winked at us. "I cheated. But it was only for fun."

Amazed, I complimented him and told him that I didn't see how he did it.

"So I'll tell you part of the secret. It's a nice trick. Everyone loves aces, and people always gasp when just the four aces are turned faceup at the end."

"What's the secret?"

"Obviously, I had stacked the deck at the start before I even took off the rubber band. The four aces were on top, so I could place them in the square of sixteen cards anywhere I wanted. So I put them on the diagonal from upper left to lower right."

"But, Stuart," I protested. "You cut the cards three times before you made that square."

Stuart smiled. "I performed three false cuts that look like real cuts, but the order of cards in the stack actually doesn't change. It happens so fast it's hard to see. Let me do it now slowly so you can see." He showed us, and at slow speed, we could see how it worked. "It's a very elementary sleight of hand and very easy to do."

I understood the false cuts, but I still had questions. "But Susan directed you multiple times how to fold the edges of the square inward. It seems impossible that all four aces would turn out facing the same direction."

"You are correct to raise that issue, Jim, but it's a matter of very simple geometry, and I can't reveal everything about my trick. This trick is published in books, though, so you could probably look it up."

I nodded and promised that I would try to look it up.

"The most important thing for you to learn is that I cheated; the whole thing was rigged from the beginning," Stuart cautioned. "And life can be like that too. You will get swindled by companies that charge hidden fees, for example. So in life and in poker, you need to stay alert and pay attention. Try to maintain a positive and joyful attitude even though you must be constantly on the alert because someone might try to stab you in the back."

"Sounds pretty grim, Stuart," I responded.

"Don't be depressed by it. It's really just common sense. Reagan used to say 'Trust but verify.'"

I nodded.

"Importantly, you don't need to cheat at poker to win. You need to have a very thorough understanding of the game, only play in games that likely have honest dealing, always watch everything carefully, know people and their emotions, know the key tactics and strategies, show up well rested and sober, never play if you are under financial or emotional stress, and get plenty of experience so that you can instantly read boards correctly and quickly assess the nuances of situations."

"Is that all?" Susan laughed.

"No, it also really helps to be lucky!"

Competitors on the Horizon

As we left the restaurant, Stuart pointed out two German poker players who were talking in the lobby near the hotel reception desk. "Watch out for those guys," Stuart whispered. "They're really strong players. And they bluff a lot, sometimes with huge bets."

"An opportunity," I quipped. "If one of them makes a big bluff against me, I could just call and win a bunch of chips."

"It sounds easy," Stuart responded, although he was addressing Susan. "You can't take a player's chips unless he voluntarily puts them out in the middle. But if you need to call a huge bet and your entire $10,000 is on the line, it can be nerve-racking. A big apparent bluff actually might not be a bluff. In the Main Event, you can't just keep playing by buying new chips. Once you're out, you're out."

Susan nodded.

"I know," I murmured. "Just hope one of those Germans isn't sitting on my left."

"And those two Swedes by the ATM are also strong," Stuart added. "If you only have a middle pair and haven't hit your set, you should quickly fold to them. Don't try to bluff with a missed set, a missed straight, or a missed flush. They will likely call and take your chips."

"I try not to bluff much."

"Well, everyone needs to bluff sometimes," Stuart opined. "You have to steal lightly contested pots to stay alive." Stuart turned to Susan and added, "Unlike the cheating I just performed for you, a good player *must* steal chips in poker by betting when he has nothing or only a good draw. That's not cheating. Stealing is a skill in poker."

"And lying is also a skill in poker," I added with a chuckle as I turned to Susan.

"Lying?"

"Just part of the game. Talking may not be allowed during some parts of the betting, but at other times, it can be very useful during a long game," I added.

"I've only known you for one day, but it's hard for me to believe that you are a good liar!" Susan declared.

"I don't lie in other contexts, but it's useful at the poker table. After I win a pot with a bluff, I sometimes say softly to the man who folded, as though my comment is intended only for him, 'I had a set.' Of course, I really had nothing. But he might feel at least for a few minutes that he is playing correctly and he made a good move."

"I see," Susan murmured.

"One time I was visiting Las Vegas briefly for a business meeting," I added. "I only had a couple of hours to play cash poker that evening. So I just kept on my nice shirt and necktie and took a seat at a cash table where all the other players—all men, which is not unusual—were dressed very casually. During the first hour, I told them truthfully about my business meeting that day and that I had to fly home in the morning. Then

I invented a bit, saying that I had seen poker on TV but had never played, and I hoped to learn the basics. Several times, I intentionally put out the wrong amounts for the blinds and looked confused and ill-informed. Twice I intentionally bet out of turn and then apologized for my mistakes, but I didn't want to be too disruptive, so I didn't continue that. In my mind, this was just an entertaining experiment to see what would happen. It was not really lying; it was strategy. Buyer beware. In the second hour, I waited for good hands and then made confusing-looking bets because several of these experienced players seemed anxious to get involved with me. I won several small pots and three big ones, scooped up my winnings, and thanked them all for their advice and help as I walked out the door with their money."

Susan seemed quite surprised by my confession. "So you didn't get shot?"

"All people who sit at a poker table are trying to take the other guys' money. Deception is a very important part of the game. I never play at private games, by the way. Just at casinos. I just finish playing, walk with my chips to the cashier's cage, and they hand me my money."

Susan seemed more interested. "So what is the best deceptive play you ever made?"

I laughed. "Stuart would have many more stories than I do! But an incident late in a big tournament at Foxwoods, in Connecticut, is one of my favorites. Only a few players remained in the tournament, maybe fifteen out of the more than ninety that had started. But only about twelve cash prizes would be awarded. I had an above-average number of chips, but I needed more to try to win a larger prize. I sat in the big blind, so I would be the last to bet on the first round."

As I continued, I could tell that I had piqued Stuart's interest. "By very good luck, my two hole cards were aces."

Susan smiled. "Dangerous."

"The first man to bet made a moderately big bet. I suspected that he might have pocket jacks, but I had no idea. After some hesitation, the man to his left called. There were lots of chips in the pot now. As I sat there waiting my turn, I noticed out of the corner of my eye that the player three seats to my right was looking at me, and he seemed alert and excited. I didn't look at him, but I changed the way I was holding my two aces. Instead of leaving them flat on the felt, I picked them up and raised them an inch above the felt; I held the cards between my right thumb and index finger with my wrist cocked as though I was just waiting my turn to toss the cards away. As the bidding moved around the table, several players folded, and then the excited man to my right hesitated and pondered whether to bet. As he hesitated, I set my cards flat on the felt again and looked down at my lap, as though I was hoping that he hadn't noticed that I'd been holding the cards as though I would soon discard them. He moved all his chips forward. His stack was about 90 percent of what I had. The next two players folded, then I went all in. The face of the excited player showed a rush of confusion, and all the other players who had bet folded."

"With just two of us in contention for the pot, we turned over our cards. He had ace-jack unsuited, so he was clearly posturing with his big bet. He was stunned to see my aces.

"He grimaced and commented, 'I thought you were going to discard your hand.'

"I responded very quietly, 'I guess it looked like that.'

"He stood up, and I also stood and extended my right hand across the edge of the table. We shook hands, and then he walked quickly away. I added a mountain of chips to my stack, which allowed me later to win a substantial prize."

"All part of the game, I see," commented Susan.

"I heard recently that some software engineers created a

computer program that can play excellent poker. That may be true from a mathematical, bet sizing as well as table position and relative chip-stack sizes perspective. But there is much more to poker than just technical elements. My deception of holding my aces as though I was about to discard them could not have been performed by a computer. Understanding well what people see, what people fear, what people hope, what people are thinking just at that moment are also very important."

Stuart changed the subject. They were near the front entrance of one of the many bars and he had glanced in. He saw something that deserved comment.

"Let's go in and have some drinks," Stuart proposed. "And I want to point out some people to you." He found a side table so they could sit with their backs to the wall. That gave a good view of the noisy crowd inside. The waitress appeared surprisingly quickly and took their orders.

"The three Chinese men at that third table are relatively new to Las Vegas," Stuart explained. "They first came last year, and the best player, the biggest guy in the middle, is from Macau. I understand that he gambles a lot there year-round. He seemed to have a lot of money to play with last year during his two-week visit for the Main Event, though he got knocked out of the tournament just before the pay line."

"They seem to be enjoying themselves," I commented.

"Last year, those three players came to Vegas with a male Chinese assistant," Stuart added. "I know that for this year's tournament, they arrived two days ago with about five male assistants. That seemed like an unusually big group to me. They're all in adjoining rooms on the ninth floor."

"Isn't nine viewed as the luckiest number by Chinese?" Susan asked.

"You're right," Stuart confirmed, "either eight or nine. I sometimes play poker in California, and the Chinese there love nine and hate four."

"Pretty superstitious," I observed. "How could that tradition have started?"

"Well," Stuart answered, "they told me that nine traditionally stands for completeness or eternity. The pronunciation of the number nine, Jiu, is the same sound as the word for 'everlasting.' But the number four is unlucky because it sounds like the word 'death.'"

"But wait a minute," Susan interjected. "Why would three poker players need five assistants? Those plastic chips aren't that heavy."

"Good question," replied Stuart. "My suspicion is that last year the Chinese players were attracted because the prize pool was well over $60 million. I think they scouted things out. The number of people they brought this year suggests that they are very serious about this tournament, which may have an even larger prize pool. But I can't imagine why they would need five assistants.

"And don't overlook that there are two tables of Russians over in that corner," he added. "I count ten guys and know four of them are definitely Russian. They have been coming for at least five years. I'm presuming that the other six fellows are also Russian since they are all yacking it up together."

"Could a couple of Russian players at the same poker table communicate in their language to help each other?" Susan asked. "I guess 'collude' is the popular word now."

Stuart responded quickly. "Collusion can happen, and that's the reason for some special house rules. Only English is allowed at the table. Table seats are assigned randomly by a computer, so two friends cannot just choose to sit together at the same table. And if two players are all in, both hands must be turned faceup as the board is run out. That helps prevent a player from losing on purpose just to give his chips to his more capable partner. It would be seen that someone made a big bet with a nothing hand, which anyone can do legally at any time, of course, but the management would watch for any ongoing suspicious transfers of chips."

"But what if those guys keep speaking Russian anyway?"

"Then the floor manager is called to the table by the dealer, and that manager usually just gives a warning for the first infraction. But if a violation happens again, the manager may require that a player or players need to step away from the table for a set number of hands, usually three to ten hands depending on the severity of the issue. When you stand away from the table, you still lose your blinds and antes, so late in a tournament that can be a severe penalty. If violations continue, a player could be required to forfeit his chips and is disqualified."

We walked toward the bank of elevators. As Stuart got off on the fourth floor, I said good night and offered my condolences that he was staying on the death floor. Susan and I continued up to eight. We got off the elevator together and took a few steps, but we stopped at the main hall where I would turn left and she would turn right.

"Thanks again for saving me," she said. "This trip has been more interesting than I had expected."

"Glad I could help. This has been fun."

After a second of inaction, she stepped forward and planted a quick kiss on my lips, then stepped back.

Pleasantly stunned and flattered, I stood silent for a couple of seconds. Then I smiled.

"Wow. That was nice," I said softly.

Then I stepped forward, put my arms around her, and kissed her on the lips. She was a great kisser. After a few seconds, my left hand slid down to her backside, and I gave her right butt cheek a little squeeze, then I stepped back.

"And that was nice too. Good night, Susan."

"Good night, Jim."

Breakfast

I had set no alarm, but I woke up a little before nine. I stared at the ceiling for a minute or two and said a little prayer of gratitude that I had awakened. Most people take this for granted. During my college days at University of Illinois at Urbana, one of my classmates there seemed perfectly healthy, but he went to bed one night and died in his sleep. I didn't know him well, but I heard from someone a few days later that his death was due to unexpected sudden bleeding in his brain. A few years later, a young man who had been one of the smartest students in my medical school class at Pritzker School of Medicine unexpectedly died in his sleep, and the autopsy confirmed that an unsuspected brain aneurysm had burst. Every day is a gift. We should not waste our time.

Maybe it's a sign of being overly obsessive if one dwells on such morbid thoughts. But I believe it's fitting to count one's blessings and constantly assess how one is living one's life. I appreciated that I had been born in a stable and prosperous nation, had loving parents, and had access to education, good health care, and real opportunities. I had fallen in love with a kind and intelligent woman—a truly special person. Her death at a young age was tragic, but life is fleeting for all of us, and it was a privilege to have shared her life. We were truly in love. We worked hard and provided numerous benefits to each other, to our neighbors, to our communities. Sheila provided knowledge of reading and mathematics to her countless elementary students, practical knowledge that will serve them for a lifetime. I helped thousands of patients directly as their physician, and now I'm potentially aiding hundreds of thousands of patients globally by developing new medications in a pharmaceutical company. How better to live?

My wandering mind snapped back to the present as several young men walked past my door speaking loudly in some

Eastern European language. I suddenly realized that I was hungry. I wanted scrambled eggs, sausage, toast, and hot coffee. I got cleaned up and quickly headed downstairs to my favorite breakfast place.

Relatively few people were in the main lobby when I first stepped out of the elevator, in sharp contrast to the hubbub last night. Three elderly, thin, white-haired ladies, each with a green oxygen cylinder on wheels and a nasal plastic tube, sat at adjoining slot machines while talking and laughing. Good for them. I made my way past closed bars and a couple of open ones. Just ahead was the restaurant, which had a Midwest USA 1940's agricultural theme with old farm photos on the walls and a big 1920's era metal tractor at the entrance. There was a line of about twenty people waiting for a table.

The third person from the end was Susan. She wore jeans and a sweatshirt: casual, neat, and, I must say, cute.

I caught her eye and said good morning as I walked about four steps past her and stood at the very end of the line. She immediately stepped out of her place and moved back in the queue a little to stand with me.

"I didn't want to wake you, but I'm glad we had the same idea," she said, "and at the same time."

"Weren't you up at six to play the slots?" I joked.

Within ten minutes, we were at the front. The hostess grabbed two menus and called us to follow her. Susan walked briskly after her, and I trailed. We wound among the tables left and right, and I could see that we were headed for a small table next to a rail that separated the eating area from the main hallway where there was a steady flow of people just outside a large, open window. Suddenly, Susan stopped cold. I stopped. The hostess kept walking. Susan turned to me and whispered, "There he is on the left, up ahead."

It took me a couple of seconds to find her harasser seated by himself, remnants of his breakfast before him on two large plates. He was sipping coffee and looking at his phone, apparently waiting for the check. He wore a red T-shirt with white lettering "Born to be Bad," and I could see now that he also had tattoos on his left upper arm.

"Just keep walking," I advised in a whisper.

Within a few more seconds, we were seated across from each other at a table for two, perhaps fifteen yards beyond where the big guy was seated; his back was to us.

"I can't believe it!" Susan began. She was tense. "He looked up from his phone, and I think he glanced straight at me, but then he just went back to his phone."

"Not surprising," I replied.

"Not surprising?" she queried.

"His mind is on something else, you are wearing different clothes, and he was drunk then but sober now. So he simply didn't recognize you. This was actually a fortunate occurrence this morning. It proves to you that you can likely forget about him and the hallway incident. He can't even remember who you are."

Susan nodded. "But it's weird, isn't it? For something like that to happen, but we do nothing about it?"

"I agree that in a just world, a man who seriously frightens and threatens a woman should face some consequences. I don't condone his bad behavior. I agree that he definitely scared you, but he didn't actually cause you any permanent harm."

Susan exhibited a confused expression but said nothing, so I continued.

"The world is full of problems. You have to choose your battles. I think it's much more important that you're able to put the episode behind you and just go on with life. He'll likely face his own serious problems soon enough."

"What do you mean?" she replied, seemingly a little indignant but mostly curious.

"Some people call it karma. I'm not superstitious. But bad

things happen so frequently to everyone that he will certainly get his share, ranging from minor annoyances to major crises. Flat tires. Spilled coffee. Bad luck in a casino. Strep throat. Infected tooth. Broken arm. And eventually even worse. Heart attack. Brain tumor."

"So I should just forgive him for scaring me out of my mind?"

The waitress brought two cups of coffee, and I reached for the creamer. "The short answer is yes."

She processed this for a moment and then responded, "And what is the long answer?"

"All I can do is give you my opinion. The short version of the long answer is that forgiveness, although it may be difficult and take a little time, is always the right choice. Forgiveness can still be given even if a just punishment is enforced. Compensation for a wrong is appropriate. But then we need to recognize that people can make bad choices. Mistakes. Misjudgments."

"You sound like Jesus."

The waitress was back to take our orders, which were simple. Then I continued.

"I am Christian, but I'm certainly not Jesus. I have made my share of mistakes. Receiving forgiveness is not just a good thing for the offender. Giving forgiveness is also very beneficial to the person harmed."

"How?"

"The short version of the answer to that question has been summed up in a little proverb: "Hate (or a grudge) corrodes the container in which it is carried.'"

Susan blinked but said nothing.

After a few minutes, she said in a friendly tone but with some determination, "I need to ask you a serious question. But it sounds unusual or even funny."

"You can ask me anything. If you ask about a few very personal things, then I might have to tell you that I can't answer that question right now, but I hope to tell you later. I'm sure you have some extremely personal items as well that you might not be ready to share just yet."

"Well, let me ask you this. I do believe in forgiveness, but the way you talk ... Well ... Are you a hyper-religious person? Basically what I'm asking is, Are you a fanatic?"

I finished my sip of coffee, set my cup down slowly, looked at her, and took a breath. "I was born and remain an active Catholic. I go to church each week, I help in my parish by reading the scriptures publicly at some services, and I have read widely about ethics and religion. I try to be a good person. I think the correct answer is, 'No, I'm not a fanatic.'" I picked up my cup again to let that answer sink in.

"And let me add," I continued, "that as a Christlike action, this morning I bought your attacker breakfast." A shadow of incomprehension passed over Susan's face, so I quickly added, "He probably paid using my hundred-dollar bill." We both laughed.

Then she smiled more broadly and stated a novel conclusion. "Since I reimbursed you, it seems that I actually paid for his breakfast!" We laughed again.

"But why ..." she started, then paused. "Why didn't you introduce yourself as an MD?"

"Just my policy about how I can best start to interact with new people. I only see patients on Friday mornings. The rest of the week, I'm sitting in front of a computer, going to meetings, reading, making phone calls, or doing paperwork. Those aren't what most people would think of as predominant activities for an MD. Too many doctors on TV."

"Agreed," she responded.

"After we talked awhile that night, I didn't make an effort to hide my degree. After dinner, I handed you my business card; you likely were going to see it there." I smiled. "I like to meet people on my own terms. I believe in the importance of first impressions. I meant no deception."

The food was great. The waitress brought the check, and I picked it up, announcing, "You bought dinner the other night. My turn." There were more empty seats in the restaurant now, so I didn't feel any need to give up our table just yet. The big guy who had threatened Susan was gone.

"Susan, can I ask you something?"

"Of course."

"Are you able to tell me why you decided to come to Las Vegas by yourself? That seems just a little unusual."

She was amused by my question, then responded, "That probably does look odd. I went to high school in New Hampshire, and my best friend from senior year agreed to fly to meet me here, a girl trip thing. We bought cheap plane tickets, and everything was set. But her dad had a heart attack and was in the intensive care unit, so she had to cancel. As of today, he's improving, thank goodness. My ticket was nonrefundable, and I had arranged my vacation time from work, so I just went ahead with the trip."

"I'm glad you did."

Mother Teresa?

I paid the bill; Susan and I walked out of the restaurant. I said that I wanted to complete my registration for the Main Event tournament. She was welcome to accompany me for a few minutes, and I could explain how that process works.

"So is this when you reach into your backpack and pull out a big stack of hundreds—$10,000?"

"No, no," I responded. "I don't like to carry around that amount of cash. I already preregistered for day one of the tournament, and I used a bank wire last month to pay. That guaranteed a seat on the particular day one I wanted. There will be so many players that there will be three independent day one groups. I had to nail down a specific day one so that I could make my travel plans and hotel reservation."

"Three starting days," Susan mumbled as she gazed straight ahead while we walked.

"As players get knocked out," I continued, "by the start of day three, the tournament director will be able to pool all the remaining players into one large group of survivors. The initial six thousand entrants will by that time be reduced to about two thousand."

"Six thousand entrants paying ten grand each. That does make $60 million," she observed.

"Of course, the casino takes out money from that pool for operational expenses before the prize pool is set, and a rank list of prizes is published by the end of day two. If more than 6,300 players enter, as expected, then the prize pool will easily reach $60 million.

"Even though I preregistered, I need to complete my registration by showing proper government ID. And I need to show my plastic player's card that I obtained when I first checked into the hotel. I previously had opened a player account to get a player ID number to be able to send the wire payment. A consent form for photography is mandatory since I might get caught on the edge of a scene among the thousands of players. I will receive a paper ticket with my randomly assigned table number and seat number, which I will need to hand to the dealer when I first sit down. And I'll get a receipt showing my payment made, table, and seat to keep in my pocket."

About twenty preregistered players were ahead of us at the counter, but with six clerks at work, I soon was able to take my turn, confirm my payment, sign the paperwork, and get my seat assignment. All was set for me to take my seat the next day at noon.

"It's past noon now. I'm going to play in a cash game for a couple of hours, probably $2-$4-No Limit. You can head out to challenge the slots if you want."

Susan responded, "So that means the small and big blinds will be two dollars and four dollars, right?"

"Yep."

"Well, let me just see where they seat you so I can find you when I walk by later."

I showed my plastic player's card and bought $400 in chips from the central cashier. I noted that there were only eight more hundred-dollar bills in my wallet. I had better start winning some money, or my recreational fund would run dry. We strolled to the reception desk for the cash tables. There was no waiting list, so the manager told us to walk toward the overhead sign for table twelve and I would be seated. The assistant standing near the table, walkie-talkie held near his ear, saw us approaching, my plastic rack of chips in hand. He waved us forward and pointed at seat six. The other nine player seats were filled. Still ten yards out, Susan grabbed my arm, and we both abruptly stopped.

Once again, Susan's eyes were quicker than mine. "There he is, right next to you in seat five!" We were approaching the table from behind him, but the red T-shirt, tattooed upper arms, muscular build, and hairstyle were fairly distinctive. Susan stayed planted ten yards back, but I walked forward and stood quietly behind my seat as the red T-shirt man and another player were finishing a big hand. The players had just seen the river card turned over by the dealer. A gray-haired, distinguished-looking man was in seat one and was the first to bet. He pushed all of his chips forward as he declared, "All in." Mr. Red T-shirt immediately called, and he had just a few more chips than his opponent. The players turned over their cards, and it was, horrifically, set over set, with the victory going to Mr. Red T-shirt. This is a one-in-a hundred poker confrontation. Mr. Red T-shirt doubled his chips to a new total of about $2,000, whereas the older man in seat one was left to shake his head and slowly walk away, likely considering whether or not to purchase more chips.

The action over, I slid into my seat and unloaded my chips onto the felt. The button would now be in seat eight. I didn't look left or right, and I said nothing. I was betting that if Mr. Red T-shirt hadn't recognized Susan, then he wouldn't recognize me. He probably was focusing on her the other night ten times more than on me. She's better looking.

During the next two hours, I was pretty lucky. I won four big hands with three sets and a flush. My chips increased five-fold to $2,100, which is a remarkable run in two hours. Mr. Red T-shirt gave no indication that he had ever seen me before. During that time, he seemed to grow progressively more frustrated as he won a hand, and lost a hand, and folded most hands. He was fairly tight, apparently, and his chip stack remained level at about $2,000. I looked over my shoulder a couple of times, and, yes, Susan was still standing a few yards away behind us. When I was looking once, she gestured by raising her eyebrows and opening her mouth. I could tell that she couldn't believe that this situation had arisen.

About ninety minutes later, I was on the button and would be the last to bet in all but the first round. Excellent position. The young man in seat three was the first to bet: twenty-five dollars. That was a pretty hefty bet when the big blind was four dollars. An elderly man in seat four was neatly dressed and had rarely played a hand, but he raised to $200. I was convinced that this old guy must have a very strong hand, maybe even pocket aces or pocket kings. Mr. Red T-shirt in seat five hesitated, then said, "I need more time," although he hadn't used very much time yet. He took a breath and called the $200. It struck me that he could have a reasonably strong hand also, like pocket queens, but in view of his not winning much during recent hours, he might just be gambling, or perhaps was angling to make a big bet later to try to steal the pot. I peeked at my cards: eight of spades and nine of spades. I had lost with this hand the other day to Stuart. But now I was in position.

I just called the $200. After my bet, I perceived that Mr. Red T-shirt seemed to smile and nod a little, as if he were happy that I had entered the pot. The $200 was only 10 percent of my chips. And suited connectors potentially could play very well against big pairs if the cards fell right. If I had instead raised, then the worrisome players in seats four and five would have another chance to bet. If following my raise someone went all in, then I would probably have to fold my cards without a glimpse of a flop. By just calling, I likely would close the betting. If the remaining players to my left as well as the guy who had bet twenty-five dollars folded, then I was guaranteed to see the flop. That is what happened; we three remaining gamblers, each in for $200, were ready to see the flop.

The dealer spread out the critical three cards: seven of hearts, ten of clubs, ace of hearts. Just my luck that there were no spades. But I had an open-ended straight draw.

The old man in seat four sat more erect in his chair. I figured he must have connected with something, probably the ace. He immediately bet $300. Mr. Red T-shirt had not changed his posture after the flop. He sat silently for thirty seconds. Then he called the $300.

After a few seconds, I also called the $300, which closed the betting. I now had a quarter of my chips in the pot. It was a big proportion of my chips, but I could survive a loss. Nothing ventured, nothing gained. I had eight outs to make my straight. The two hearts on the board worried me, though. One of those guys might need just one more heart for a flush. And somebody could already have two pair if they were holding ace-ten.

The dealer set down the fourth (turn) card: six of diamonds. I didn't even blink as I hit my beautiful straight. And I had dodged a heart. I tried just to breathe at a normal, steady rate and sat quietly. After a brief hesitation, the elderly man in seat four went all in with about $1,100. He had all $1,600 of his chips in the pot. That was a surprise. I thought he had connected with the ace, but maybe he had ace-ten.

Mr. Red T-shirt quickly went all in as well, so he now had $2,000 of his chips in the pot. Of course, I also went all in, and I just threw in a single chip as I verbalized my bet. I was hoping that the river card would not be a heart. Everyone turned over their cards, and I could see that I had other cards to dodge.

The man in seat four held pocket tens and had hit a set. Mr. Red T-shirt held pocket aces, and he held a bigger set. But my straight was winning at the moment. If the river card was a ten or ace, I would lose to quads, but there was only one ten and one ace left in the deck. If the board paired, then Mr. Red T-shirt's full house would beat me. The dealer turned over the last card, the king of spades. My straight held up. The old man rose silently, but Mr. Red T-shirt cursed under his breath as he rose and then walked slowly away. I remained motionless and said nothing. The dealer pushed me a huge pile of chips. I looked back at Susan, and she was beaming.

I played for fifteen more minutes, but I folded every hand; my hole cards ranged from two-seven to three-nine. Susan had walked briefly to a vendor to buy a bottle of water, but she had returned to stand in that same spot. Tired of playing for the moment, I stood to retrieve five plastic empty chip racks from a nearby table, loaded up my chips, and bid my colleagues good-bye as I gave the dealer a nice final tip. As I shuffled slowly away from the table carrying my racks of chips carefully with two hands, Susan walked briskly up to me, smiled, and exclaimed, "Oh, my God!" And she gave me a little kiss on the cheek while trying not to disturb the balancing of my load.

"That's what I call karma," I said softly so that only she could hear. "Walk with me to the cashier, and I'll cash these in."

Within minutes, I was puzzling over how best to carry fifty-six additional one-hundred-dollar bills. The stack was too fat to fold into my wallet. So I put two of the bills in to join the eight already there. I slipped fifty-four bills into my front left pants pocket next to my wallet, and I made a mental note that I would have to take care when I withdrew items from that pocket.

"So tell me," she began. "With so many variables at work, how can a player focus that sort of devastating poker power against a despised opponent?"

My bemused expression alerted Susan that we were not thinking along the same lines.

"I didn't focus my devastating poker power against a despised person. I just made technically appropriate decisions to maximize potential gains and minimize potential losses. Recall that I took that old man's chips too, and I certainly didn't despise him. A favorable sequence of cards was coupled with how my opponents chose to bet; Mr. Red T-shirt made a huge error by choosing to slow-play his pocket aces, which did turn into a set of aces on the flop. But his continuing slow-play let me hit my straight. My ability to close off the betting while in position also helped to give me a big victory."

Susan seemed a bit incredulous. "So you didn't take all of that big guy's chips to get revenge and show him his place?"

"I'm happy that I took all his chips. But from a technical point of view, I would have played it exactly the same way if he were, well, Mother Teresa."

"Mother Teresa?"

I sensed my face blush a little, and I wondered why I had said that. "Well, if I had taken chips from Mother Teresa, I would have given a big portion back to her as she left the table. But in view of our history, I certainly was not going to give back any chips to that guy—Mr. Born to be Bad!"

"That's the spirit!" Susan crowed. "It's almost four o'clock. Let's go have some champagne."

Getting to Know You, Getting to Know All about You

We were enjoying our libations in a small bar that wasn't too noisy.

"I just got a text," Susan reported. "Kathy's father was moved out of intensive care today to a regular hospital room. That's progress."

"Good."

"So tell me, Jim. Your parents must be approaching sixty. Do they know that you like to play poker? Or is that a secret?"

"They know. They also hear tales from my chess tournaments. And they understand that a poker hobby costs more than chess. But they don't pry."

"Nice."

I winked at Susan. "I told them that I would be playing in Las Vegas for a few days, but I didn't disclose that I was spending $10,000 to enter a tournament. They understood that the trip would be expensive with the hotel and all, but this was my vacation. I didn't want to worry them. They just said, 'Good luck and have fun.'"

"Great."

"Yeah, they know that poker is popular now. I read that twenty-three million Americans play, which is about 10 percent of the adult population."

"Are your parents still in Illinois?"

"My dad's big employer moved him to a new factory in a small town near San Antonio. You probably have heard of Seguin. They like the warmer weather and have adjusted well."

"San Antonio is a nice place to visit. I've spent several weekends there with friends. Not far from Austin."

"I did my medical internship and residency there. Three years. But I was way too busy during that period to see much of the city."

"Do you have siblings?" Susan continued.

"One brother. He's married and lives in Michigan."

"They get some snow there for sure."

"So what about your family?"

"My parents are still in New Hampshire. I try to visit them when I can, and they have come to Austin several times. My dad is a pharmacist at a corner drugstore, and he loves that role. My mom has worked as a bookkeeper for many years but is starting to cut back her workload now. My brother is older. He's married and lives in New Mexico."

As Susan took another sip of champagne, I noticed that her face looked especially bright and happy. She set down her glass and smiled at me. Her eyes sparkled, and she seemed to be completely content. She was beautiful.

My phone dinged. A text from my boss. He apologized for bothering me during my trip, but an issue had come up with the drug registration project in Japan. The regulators had three additional medical questions. They wanted brief answers ASAP. Could I please check the full email on my laptop and send him my medical responses? Our Regulatory Department would then format that document and forward the answers to the Japanese regulators tomorrow. I texted back, "Message seen about needed responses to Japan. I will send you information in a few hours."

"Susan, I have to use my laptop to answer some medical questions at work now. It's about five. Would you like to meet for dinner at seven?"

"Wow, it's eight at night in Connecticut. You guys work around the clock."

"We're a global business. So there's always something happening somewhere."

"Let me suggest this," Susan said. "You head upstairs now to do your laptop work. I'll walk down the hall to that fancy steak house and make a reservation for us for 7:15. I think we should get dressed up in nice clothes tonight and have filet mignon. You get your work done, and I'll knock on your door a little before seven, and then we can head downstairs together."

"Sounds like a plan."

It took only an hour to get the straightforward responses written for the Japanese, and I sent the email to my boss at 6:20. That gave me time to get cleaned up and shave again. I had several pairs of jeans and old shirts, but I brought only one nice shirt and one nice pair of pants. So my choices were limited to dress up a little for Susan. I was catching a few minutes of CNN when Susan knocked on my door at 6:55.

I swung open my door and had to catch my breath. Susan was stunning. She wore a beautiful ivory and black blouse. Her dark, tight skirt came to midthigh and showed off her gorgeous legs. I guess she had on some fancy makeup because her face and hair were right out of a magazine. I thought to myself, *How lucky to be going to dinner with this woman.*

"You are beautiful!" I exclaimed.

"Well, thank you. I learned a few tricks from my mom and friends. It's fun to get dressed up sometimes."

"I'm ready, except I need to put on my shoes."

I had the desk chair pulled out into an open area to better watch TV. I sat down and bent forward to start putting on my left shoe, and Susan walked forward and stood right in front of me. She took hold of my shirt collar with both hands, one on each side of my neck, and gently began smoothing it where it had been folded over while packed. Her knees were right at my face. I had one shoe on, but I was mesmerized by the beautiful dimples on her knees. "You have cute knees," I volunteered, and I kissed her right knee.

I presume that Susan was looking down at the top of my head as she responded, "Thanks. That's the first-ever compliment for my knees."

I sat up straighter in the chair and looked up at her. I winked and put the palm of my right hand on her inner right thigh just below her hemline. "And you have nice legs." She smiled down at me. I gently rubbed her thigh just above her knee with my palm for a few more seconds. I was not sure what was coming over me.

"That feels good," she volunteered. "I guess that you haven't slept with a woman for a long time."

A little taken aback by her statement, I swallowed hard and simply responded, "It's been about a year."

"Intimacy is very special, and I think our relationship might be headed that way." She paused a moment, I presumed to see if I made a response. I was a little stunned and stayed silent, so she continued. "I think we could have some sexually tender moments together, but we are miles away from a bond that would justify intercourse. We can't rush to that," she whispered. "Agreed?"

"I agree. We don't want to rush that." I swallowed, then looked up at her. She winked at me.

"We don't want things to go too far, but I do believe that you could slide your hand up a little higher. If you want to."

I maintained gentle contact with her thigh and slid my right palm upward under her skirt, to above midthigh. Her skin was very smooth. I felt my heart skip a beat. *Epinephrine*, I thought.

"That's nice," she murmured. I sensed her shift her weight a little first to the right and then to the left. She had replanted her feet wider apart as she still faced me, her hands in my hair. She dropped her right hand and touched my hand under the edge of her skirt. She slowly guided my hand with a gentle firmness upward along her thigh.

My right fingertips gently stroked the crotch of her cotton panties, though I couldn't see them. I stroked forward and back, forward and back. I felt her warmth below the cotton.

She bent forward and gently rested her upper arms on my shoulders. As she leaned over me, her lips touched my right ear. Her breath was hot there. "Please touch me a little harder."

174

I complied. In another minute, her sensitive tissues grew even warmer, and then my fingertips felt the moisture accumulating. Her breathing was a little hurricane in my ear.

I was quite aroused. I whispered to her, "I think I'd better stop now." I dropped my hands to my knees.

She slowly stood up straight and smiled at me. Then she took one step to the side and leaned over so that she could give me an impressive kiss on the lips.

"You are absolutely fabulous," I confirmed. "Too bad we have to stop, but I think it's for the best."

"Of course, you're right."

"And now I have some problems. I only have on one shoe, and I won't be able to stand up for a few more minutes."

She laughed.

Soon we were walking hand in hand toward the elevator. It was time for dinner.

High Times

White tablecloths, filet mignon, red wine, and a gorgeous, intelligent woman who was romantically attracted to me: these were high times. The restaurant had every seat filled, although it didn't seem overly crowded. The waiters scurried here and there with high efficiency. The ambient sound was a steady buzz of pleasant conversation rather than the raucous noise found in the nearby eateries and bars. Civilized. And the place perfectly fit what we wanted that evening.

Susan and I sat face-to-face at a small table near the back wall.

"Based on what you said this morning, you sound like a very active Catholic," Susan commented. "I was born and raised Catholic. Went to Catholic elementary school and four years of Catholic high school. I still go to church a few times a year, but in college, I got distracted and had other priorities."

"That's understandable. That happens to a lot of Catholic kids."

"But you sound like more than just a routine Catholic. You seem to be a true believer—committed."

"I had loving parents, though you did as well, but my parents were a particularly good role model regarding church attendance. They are genuinely good people and committed Catholics, so it made sense for me to stay in the flock." I took another bite of filet and then swallowed it with a sip of cabernet. "Besides, I trained intensively in science, and that brought me closer to religion."

Susan looked astonished. "Brought you closer to religion? I thought that many scientists are atheists."

"I saw the workings of God in nature. The universe is a beautiful and astonishing place."

Susan took a sip of wine and looked at me closely. "But there's Darwin and evolution. I loved my science courses too, though I was a business major. But science seemed to contradict many things in religion, and I just kind of gave up on Catholicism. You're a highly educated, sensible, and data-driven guy as far as I can tell. I hope that there is a God. But how can you believe in God if there are no data to support his existence?"

"Not all puzzles in life can be solved by a purely rational process."

Susan's brow furrowed. "I'm not sure what you mean by that."

"After your mother had known your father for a while, she came to believe that he loved her. So she married him. She didn't use a purely rational process to decide that he loved her. Just because he did helpful things for her, and gave her gifts, and was kind to her, that didn't actually prove that he loved her. There is no rational process that would support such a conclusion. It is a matter of trust and faith."

"That's true."

"If you're building a rocket to the moon, you had better be highly rational. But there are some things in life—very important things—that you can come to believe without evidence." I paused for emphasis. "But this sort of leap of faith, as one great philosopher called it, can only be justifiable under certain limited conditions."

"I know that was Kierkegaard's term," Susan commented, then grinned widely. "See? I've had a solid liberal arts education. But I don't know what conditions allow such a leap of faith to be made."

"Well, this is my understanding, based in part on the famous American philosopher William James. Several years ago, I read a book by Martin Gardner who summarized James's argument a bit more clearly."

"Wait," Susan interrupted. "I was a math minor, remember? Martin Gardner was the famous author of all of those *Scientific American* columns with mathematical puzzles. I've read a bunch of those."

"Yes, he was a multifaceted genius. And he believed in God. His book, *The Whys of a Philosophical Scrivener*, generated lots of discussion, pro and con. He wrote that the first condition that allows a belief based on faith alone is that the two alternatives—God exists or does not—must both be reasonable and possible in light of everything else that is known. Gardner used the clarifying example that you couldn't claim to believe that the earth was flat based on faith alone because the option of a flat earth has already been definitely ruled out.

"That makes sense."

"The second condition is that the choice must be forced."

"Forced?"

"Yes, you can't ignore the issue, and you must make a decision. Though you must choose, you lack definitive data, and there is no rational process that will allow you to come to a proven conclusion. Like when your dad proposed to your mom.

She had to say either yes or no. The alternative paths were very different, but she couldn't avoid making a decision for year after year."

"That makes sense too."

"The third condition is quite easy to understand based on what we've already talked about. The choice has to be highly consequential, not trivial. An unimportant choice doesn't merit agonizing reflection to come to a decision without data. You could just postpone the decision and wait for data to turn up."

"I see. Very enlightening." But then Susan frowned. "I'm still not sure I grasp this concept well enough to bet the farm on it. I'm a modern, educated person. It worries me that people are willing to make leaps of faith too willingly. I guess I need more examples, and I need to give this more thought."

I carefully slid my wallet out of my pocket, trying not to litter the restaurant floor with loose hundred-dollar bills. "I should read a quote to you. It was used by William James, and I copied it from Gardner's book. I actually liked it so much that I carry it around with me. The situation described by the English author Fitzjames Stephen is a metaphor for needing to make a choice for or against a belief in God. He wrote, 'We stand on a mountain pass in the midst of whirling snow and blinding mist, through which we get glimpses now and then of paths which may be deceptive. If we stand still we shall be frozen to death. If we take the wrong road we shall be dashed to pieces. We do not certainly know whether there is any right one. What must we do? Be strong and of a good courage. Act for the best, hope for the best, and take what comes ... If death ends all, we cannot meet death better.'"

Susan looked at me, her eyes sparkling. "That's wonderful."

We finished eating and were still sipping wine, and we decided that dessert was unnecessary. We opted for more wine instead.

After the waiter refilled our glasses, I smiled at Susan. "I'm not intending to push, but maybe you should try attending a Catholic service again now and then, when the mood is right. I find religion to be an important part of my life."

"I have nothing against Catholicism, really, but"—she paused to gather her words—"I think the culture of Catholicism left a mark on me that was perhaps not entirely to my benefit."

"How so?"

"During my Catholic school years, I was a very good girl. What I mean ... about sexual things."

"Oh," I acknowledged. I folded my hands in front of me and looked into her eyes. There was a brief silence. She knew that I was waiting with some interest about what she might say next.

"Well, in high school, I kissed a couple of boys. But I never did anything." She smiled, and I smiled back. She pouted a little as she recognized that I was slightly amused. "I mean I never did anything! Anything!"

"That's good!" I exclaimed. "Neither did I."

"Well, it may have been good," she continued, "but it was also perhaps a bit extreme and juvenile." She paused again. "It didn't really prepare me for college."

I nodded but said nothing. I smiled slightly. She knew that I was waiting for more.

"During my first two years in Austin, I met several very nice boys. They were smart and good-looking."

I nodded.

"So for these boys ... well, I did want to meet boys. I would meet one, and we would grab a burger or something, and after another date or two, he would want to cuddle. It was nice. But then they always wanted me to take off my pants."

"Shocking."

Susan looked a little indignant but smiled. "Now stop teasing me. I'm trying to tell you something important."

"I'm listening," I insisted. Then I smiled and added, "I'm actually glued to every word."

"Well, you may think it's funny, but it was very disturbing to me at the time. This happened with five boys in a row. I stopped seeing all of them."

"I've been smiling a little, but I hear what you're saying. You were a totally innocent young woman, and you were in a new and unsettling environment. I can understand how you felt."

"Now this next part is not so funny, and I want your opinion about this."

"I understand."

"I met boy number six. He was very clean-cut, a good student. And he was even nicer than all the others."

"Good."

"We got to the cuddling stage. It was okay. Nice actually. Then he asked me to take off my pants, and I told him I wasn't ready for that yet. He seemed to change in an instant. He was angry. It was scary. He sat on me and held me down, unbuttoned and unzipped my jeans, and pulled them down to my ankles." Susan's eyes teared. "But the pants wouldn't come off over my shoes."

I frowned and reached out my right hand, and Susan grasped it. "I'm so sorry that happened to you." Her eyes told me that she realized that I was sincere. The time for teasing her was over.

"We were outside at dusk near some bushes between two buildings. A low-traffic area. I became frightened. I screamed and told him to get off. That startled him, and he moved, so I managed to stand, pulled up my jeans, and I started yelling and running."

"Did he chase you?"

"No. I looked back, and he was just standing there. I think he was so surprised by events that he just froze."

"That was a terrible experience," I said in a soft voice.

Susan reached into her purse for a tissue. "I get upset every time I think about that."

"I'm sure you do. So sorry."

"Well, my Catholic upbringing and that traumatic experience seemed to deeply affect me."

"In what way?"

"I never saw that boy again, and my life seemed to go back to normal. But I didn't date during my third year in Austin. Then just before Christmas break in my senior year, I met Randy." She sniffled and grabbed another tissue. "We went out a few times when we were back on campus in January. He was really a special guy. By March, I was sure that he was the guy for me."

"It's great that you met."

"After seven or eight dates, he still never tried to get into my pants, though when we kissed, his hands were squeezing me in all the right places. You know, he was a normal guy. He was so sweet. I just knew he wanted to move on to that next stage."

"I'm sure you were right."

"As we were ending our next date, we were in his dorm room. I decided to be brave. I kissed him again and told him that I thought we had reached the stage when we could ditch our blue jeans, but I didn't want things to go too far."

"And?"

"His face lit up. I could tell that he was so excited. He was out of his jeans in two seconds. I stood up, unbuttoned and unzipped my jeans, and then, well. And then I just froze."

"Oh," I responded.

"He reclined on his bed, watching me, waiting. I felt a little weird. I knew that this was not normal. How could this be happening to me?"

I remained silent.

"I just stood there. Finally, I said that I was shy. I told him he had to look the other way when I pulled down my jeans. He rolled over and faced the wall. For several minutes, I still couldn't move. I felt dizzy, but I finally slipped off the jeans and crawled up beside him on the bed. We cuddled and kissed a few minutes. Then we got dressed, and I said good night." She paused. "So. I'm serious. Is there something wrong with me?"

I reached out and took her hand again. "That's very touching. You clearly were recovering after the trauma of boy number six. And Randy was going to help you through it." I paused and smiled. "I really don't mean to pry, but I want to ask you something important. Were you much more comfortable the next time with Randy?"

"There was no next time. He was killed three days later."

I sat dumbfounded. Horrified. I could tell that Susan read my shock. A moment passed, and we remained silent. I was processing what Susan had just revealed, while she was processing my facial expression.

Finally, I spoke. "Sad story." I paused. "So tell me. You're thirty. Have you had any serious relationships with men since college? I guess that would be about eight years."

"I'm a little embarrassed to tell you, but I actually want to put all my cards on the table. I need your advice. I've had a dozen dates for just an evening. But there's been nothing serious." She paused. "I just work."

"So," I began and lowered my voice. "Never had intercourse?"

"Never. I want to mention something else, but I don't want to talk about it. So after I say this, please just drop it." She took a deep breath. "I've never had intercourse with a person. But a girl has other methods, and every girl has her needs. So I think all of my biology works, but that's all I want to say about it."

I sat silent. There was a clatter of dishes in the background.

"It's a remarkable story. And you were very brave to tell me."

Susan remained silent, but she continued to look at me. It appeared that she was experiencing great relief. Her face brightened, and she smiled. It was as though a great weight had been lifted from her. Then she spoke. "You're a very special guy. I had to tell you." She paused and smiled at me again. "When you kissed my knee tonight, I decided that this was the right time for me to stretch my wings a bit more. I want to be very brave and make myself a little vulnerable. I want to connect with you in a special way." She lowered her voice and whispered, "I loved every minute. It was a healing experience."

Back in my Room

The bill paid, we strolled hand in hand back to the elevator bank. It was not very late. Susan knew that my starting time in the big tournament tomorrow was at noon. As we stepped off the elevator on the eighth floor, Susan said that she had thought of something else she wanted to tell me but that we shouldn't talk in the hallway.

"Follow me," I volunteered, and we swung around the corner to the left toward my room.

Once inside, we sat side by side on the small couch. I waited for her to begin since she obviously had something else to say.

"These recent days have been, well, a surreal experience for me," she said.

"For me too."

"Do you agree that we barely know each other, yet we can tell that there is real potential in this relationship?"

"Yes."

"Of all the tens of thousands of visitors in Vegas this week, we have found a special resonance." She paused and looked at me with soft eyes. "We are two mature adults, each with special problems in our lives right now. And we seem to ..." She paused to search for the right word. "We seem to exactly complement each other."

I nodded but said nothing. I did feel a special connection with Susan, but I wasn't sure that I could properly express my feelings just then. I thought that perhaps Sheila's death was still too fresh in my mind.

"Jim, earlier this evening, you felt compelled to kiss my knee. And then you put your hand on my thigh."

"Yes."

"Although we don't know each other well, I could tell that this action was quite out of character for you." She paused. "But you felt a strong need to do that."

I swallowed. "Yes. I very much wanted to touch you."

"Your hand was trembling."

"I'm sure it was. I've never done anything like that with a woman I barely knew."

"I think I'm seeing things clearly now," she started. "You're a highly competent and good person, married for a decade, but you recently lost your wife. You feel pressures, desires. You are a healthy, red-blooded man."

I nodded.

"And I have my own odd sexual situation going on. A weird one. I think I desperately need a mature and caring person, a truly gentle man, to help me." She looked directly at me. "And you desperately—and I mean desperately—need someone to help you. That person needs to be your type: educated, middle class, responsible, kind, good sense of humor. And—dare I say this? She needs to be very sexually attractive."

"You're probably right." I smiled.

"I believe fate has thrown us together," she said. "And I want to say right now that I will be your willing partner if you want to continue to strengthen our relationship."

"I agree that we need to get to know each other much better. And we have the perfect opportunity this week to do that."

"But, Jim," she added. "Although I'm thirty, you need to be supportive and patient and treat me like ..."—she took a breath and shook her head as though apologizing for something—"like an extremely sexually inexperienced high school girl."

"Like a freshman," I joked.

"Well ..." She paused and smiled. "A first-year Catholic

high school girl is generally about fourteen. And some of the activities I'm thinking of would get a man arrested if he pursued them with a fourteen-year-old."

Again, I smiled.

"So please think of me as a mature, kind, thirty-year-old woman who is sort of an eighteen-year-old Catholic high school girl with the sexual experience of a fourteen-year-old."

I laughed, then responded, "I'm preparing all of my forbidden fantasies right now." I stood and extended my right hand. "Let me walk you to your room. We'll get to know each other much better during the next few days."

"Please kiss me," she said as she stood. And I did. "You may have thought our conversation tonight drifted into odd places." She paused to gauge my reaction.

I smiled. "It was unique in my experience." After a short pause, I continued. "But I hope our talking helped. You did suffer real trauma in college. But you seem to be working your way through things. And I clearly recognize that I am needy too."

She pulled my hand and took a step. "Please cuddle with me on the bed."

She lay flat on her back, and I was beside her on one elbow. She raised her lips to mine.

I was a little surprised when she spoke. "I have a request."

"Please ask."

"Perhaps I've had a little too much red wine tonight, but here's what I'm thinking: I want us to be naked together. No intercourse, you remember. But naked."

I swallowed hard but then found my words. "Well, I think that would be very nice. And you know that I will be very respectful of you."

"I have not the slightest worry about you. I want to see if I can do this. I want to see if your attention and kindness have helped me."

I laughed. "Maybe I'm a miracle doctor."

Then she added, "And I think it will be extremely good for you. I believe you may not realize how tightly you're wound. That's not healthy."

With that, she gently pushed me off the bed, though not really off the bed to the floor. I just rolled slowly to the edge and stood up. Then I got my marching order.

"You sit there on the little couch. I'm going to stand in front of you and undress."

"Yes, boss," I responded and I took my seat. I admit that I was rather excited by this turn of events. And I tried to assuage my conscience—did I really have anything to regret?—by considering that this exercise might be therapeutic for Susan.

She hopped out of bed, kicked off her shoes, and stood at mock attention before me. She was barefooted since she had not worn hose, as I could well attest. She smoothed her dark skirt in front and straightened her ivory and black-trimmed top.

She winked at me and then undid the uppermost button of her blouse. Then the next. And then the next and the last. She slipped her lovely arms out of the blouse, carefully folded it, and took five steps to carefully lay it in the big easy chair by the wall. Her ample breasts filled the snow-white bra and bounced slightly as she stepped back to stand at attention in front of me.

She smiled again, and then using two hands, she slowly lifted the front edge of her black, midthigh skirt. Her progress was agonizingly slow. Fantastic! She wasn't taking her skirt off but just raising the front edge to tease me. She *was* getting more confidant. More and more of her lovely thighs gradually came into view. I shifted position and unzipped my pants the rest of the way to make a little more room, but my eyes never left the edge of her skirt. It rose ever more slowly. It was glacial. I was tempted to step over to assist her, but I held my place. After a seeming eternity, a tiny bit of intensely white panty crotch began to show.

"Hooray!" I gave her an encouraging cheer. "I couldn't see

your panties before dinner. I had imagined that they were white, so my hunch was correct."

"You're a regular Sherlock Holmes."

After another minute, the entire front edge of her skirt was above her dainty waist. Her panties were now entirely visible from the crotch to the top edge.

"I like this," I encouraged her.

She let the skirt fall into place again but quickly reached behind her to unbutton and unzip her skirt, then slid it down her legs and stepped out of it. She folded it and placed it neatly on the large chair at the side with her top.

She was smiling broadly now. "I thought the skirt was going to be the hard part, but it was easy. I hate to say it, but it was even fun. I wish you could have seen your face."

"Nicely done," I complimented her.

The smile disappeared, and her face grew serious. Her hands disappeared behind her back as she reached to undo the bra strap. It should have taken only a second, but she stood perfectly still for some time.

"This is a little harder," she admitted.

After another ten seconds, the statue spoke. "Jim, please step forward and get on your knees, and please kiss my knees."

I am excellent at following directions, and I kissed first the right and then the left and retook my seat.

She unhooked the bra, quickly slipped her arms out, and dangled it in one hand. She smiled at me. "I was mostly just teasing you about kissing my knees, but it did give me a little push." She stepped to the side chair and dropped the bra on the pile.

She assumed a stern countenance as she again stood before me and announced, "I guess this actually will be the hardest piece." She slowly placed her left thumb inside the top edge of her panties, her elbow bent with the backs of her fingers on her left hip. Then she very slowly and deliberately placed her right thumb inside the top edge of her panties at her right side with the backs of her right fingers on her right hip. She froze for a full thirty seconds. It was a stance that Wonder Woman might have taken.

Another thirty seconds passed. She remained motionless.

"Well, this is a bit agonizing. Do you need more help?" I asked.

She laughed. "It's wonderful. I actually feel perfectly comfortable. But I'm just trying to add a little drama to my performance."

I was still waiting after another fifteen seconds. "You're absolutely beautiful, and I'm really anxious for this part to proceed."

Her lips tightened, and a slight frown appeared. "I'm thinking about changing my mind. Maybe this wasn't a good idea."

I'm sure she saw my eyes widen as my mind raced to interpret if she might actually be serious.

"Scared ya, didn't I?" She laughed. And with lightning speed, she bent forward as she pushed her panties down and stepped out of them. She tossed them at me, and they hit me right in the face. In an instant, she turned toward the bed and wiggled briefly in a seductive way as she pulled the cover sheet and light blanket down to the foot of bed. She crawled hands and knees-style onto the end of the bed, turned, and lay looking at me while on her side, propped up on her right elbow. "Your turn," she prompted with a surprisingly devilish smile.

Perhaps overwhelmed for the moment by these activities, I said nothing and remained seated as I unbuttoned and removed my shirt, then my white T-shirt, then my shoes and socks. I stood while using my left hand to hold up my unzipped pants so that they wouldn't fall to my ankles. I stepped toward the side of the bed, and she straightened herself and lay flat on her back, her head on a pillow and her feet near the foot of the bed, her ankles and knees together. As my left hand held my pants up, I reached forward with my right and lay my palm flat on her smooth abdomen. She smiled. I rotated my right hand and ran my fingertips through her small, dark triangle. She flexed her back a little and then raised her knees, still held tightly together.

"Let me just say that you gave a magnificent performance. Very brave. And very sexy."

"I'm surprised you're a good poker player. As I was undressing, your facial expressions were totally transparent—sheer joy." She smiled. "I'm proud to be able to make you feel that way. I think you really needed it."

I took a step to the right and grabbed the edge of the top sheet that was at her feet. My left hand was still anchored to my pants. "I was extremely happy. And grateful. You really are gorgeous." I pulled the cover sheet up over her knees and then as high as her shoulders. She immediately exhibited a perplexed expression. "But I want to reserve the right in our relationship to express an opinion." I paused, and she remained silent. "My opinion is that we might be moving just a little too fast."

Still flat on her back, she extracted her hands from under the sheet, placed them quietly over her abdomen, and interlaced her fingers. She dropped her knees to straighten her legs, ankles together.

"My opinion is so far, so good," she responded. "I'm not aiming at intercourse right now, as you well know."

"When I put my palm on your abdomen just now I could tell that you were very happy to have my hand there, but you were nervous. Very nervous, actually."

"Well, what girl wouldn't be nervous in this situation?"

I smiled. "Of course, you're right. But don't you think we should take a little break until tomorrow?"

"Well," she started, "this entire day has been a wonderful benefit to me. I feel that my life has new purpose." Then she grew serious and continued, "But I think there's a problem. A serious problem."

"Go on."

"Our intimacy today has greatly helped me. I'm happier and more confident than I've ever been in my life. But the problem is you. Watching me get naked certainly made you happy—for the moment. But you need to listen to me. You have extreme tension inside. Pressure. It's not healthy." She paused a second. "And I'm determined ... I'm sure the correct word is determined. I am absolutely determined that just as you helped me today, I am going to help you. And I mean help you today. Right now. You need it."

I said nothing, but I knew at that moment that she was right. Since Sheila's death, I had tried at times to release my sexual energy by myself. But it was a bit strange and even embarrassing after having been married ten years. Those efforts were an odd return to adolescence.

I took several steps to walk around to the foot of the bed. Susan's eyes followed me silently. She knew that I was thinking, considering, planning. But her expression was not tense. She was curious, and she was determined to be still and wait for me to make up my mind. I could see it in her eyes. She was determined that she was going to help me, perhaps in spite of myself.

I stood at the foot of the bed looking at her face, and her eyes drifted down to my open fly. "My memory may be failing, but a few minutes ago, I thought that we agreed that we would be naked together." She smiled. "I did my part."

I smiled and let go of my pants, which slid to my knees. In a series of rapid automatic motions, I stepped out of them as well as my shorts. Then I stood motionless, looking at her eyes.

Now she was the one with surprise and joy on her face. She recovered enough after a few seconds to say, "My God! You should be careful swinging that thing around. You could conk someone in the head."

"Let me assure you that mine is about normal size. You just haven't seen very many, I presume." With two hands, I gently reached out for the top sheet, and I began to slowly pull it toward her feet. She raised her hands off her abdomen so that as the sheet was pulled, her two nipples popped out, then her dainty belly button, then the mysterious dark triangle, then her muscular, gorgeous thighs, then her beautifully dimpled knees, and finally her skyward-pointing toes. Her ankles touched, so I gently tried to push one foot to the side, but her knees and ankles remained firmly pressed together, and they could not be tenderly separated. Her legs had turned, for the moment, to bronze. "I think I may need a little cooperation here."

Surprisingly, she didn't move or respond. More seconds passed. "Now I'm the weird one again," she volunteered. "With you standing down there, I'm not sure that I can spread my legs."

I smiled and took hold of one of her big toes with a thumb and forefinger, while taking hold of her other big toe with my other thumb and forefinger. "The ancient Greeks had a special method to help girls spread their knees, but it was lost for centuries until just recently."

"Really?" she feigned curiosity. "Was that Aristotle?"

"The ancients recommended gently bending the right large toe forward and back, like this," I said as I demonstrated. "Then do the same with the left toe, like this. Then the right again. Then I should put the palms of my hands over the tops of each of your feet and hold them tight." She smiled. "Now the girl needs to focus; she must completely relax both of her legs so that my hands can rock her feet easily up and then down, up and then down." At first it was hard to swivel her feet about the ankle joints because her leg muscles were tensed, but as she focused to relax her leg muscles, her feet became flexible on her ankles. Then with one sudden, steady push, I extended my arms to slide her heels apart, and I quickly climbed up into the bed to crouch on my hands and knees between her thighs. It all happened so fast that she let out a little gasp.

"Well, that was a little sneaky," she complained. "But I agree that I needed a polite push."

I winked at her and observed, "When I registered for this hotel room, it was described as 'city view,' but it turns out that the view is much, much better than advertised."

"You silly guy."

I kissed her right thigh just above her knee, then her left thigh just above that knee. I moved back and forth, kissing first one thigh and then the other as I slowly moved higher up her legs.

"This is so nice," she whispered.

"Do you really know what I'm about to do?"

"Well, I lack experience, but I don't lack imagination. I think I know very well what you're about to do."

But I just kept kissing one thigh, then the other, then commented, "I'm just checking my watch," although I was not wearing a watch.

"Checking your watch?" she repeated, with a tone of moderate exasperation.

"Yes," I replied. "I need to draw this out for the same number of seconds that you stood like a statue with your thumbs in the waistband of your panties."

"Well, let me tell you ..." she started, but she didn't finish, because at that instant I fulfilled her request. I'm a man who delivers what is needed. Her ecstasy during the next several minutes was immensely gratifying. She may have used a vibrator in the past, but I was pretty sure that I achieved a new personal high for her.

After she recovered, she expressed the desire to be coached as to what she could do for me. She was a fast learner and an enthusiastic one. And determined. She seemed intent on doing the best possible job. After a few minutes, my body exploded in rapture, and then I lay limp on the bed, my sexual tension as completely dissipated as a morning mist at midday.

Day One, World Series of Poker Main Event
Start-of-day chips: thirty thousand

We must have fallen asleep together because she gently nudged me, and my glance at the clock revealed 7:30. She kissed me, then stood and started getting dressed.

"That was memorable," I volunteered.

"You are without a doubt a truly sweet guy."

She was dressed but climbed into bed again to kneel next to me. She bent down and kissed me. "Got to run now. I'll see you at breakfast at ten." And out the door she went.

You can be assured that we had our coffee and fuel for the day. And our conversation was spirited and informative. We traded a lot more information about our families, our jobs, our likes and dislikes.

Our late breakfast ended at eleven thirty. I paid the bill, and we walked together toward where I was about to take my seat for the first day of the big tournament. The computer had assigned me seat two at table thirty-three in the Brasilia room, silver section. Seat one is the first player seat to the left of the dealer. I preferred to play from seats four, five, or six because I can see the board better from those more centrally located posts, but seat two would be fine. The mostly male crowd of players stood in the hallway outside the room because the managers intended to keep the entry doors closed until 11:45. Various networks were filming the excited crowd, and reporters were doing some interviews on camera. It was a circus atmosphere. Shortly after we arrived at the edge of the crowd, the entry doors swung open, and the crowd surged forward. People were anxious to take their seats and get settled. The adrenaline in the air was palpable.

Susan saw me to my seat, gave me a little kiss on the cheek for good luck, then waved goodbye as she walked away. There was little for her to watch since, without knowing who held what cards, the various bets had obscure meanings. When broadcast on TV using a specially designed table, the electronic chip detectors or seat cameras could display each player's cards for the audience, and that actually turned poker into a viable spectator sport that advertisers would support.

I didn't know any of the players at my table. All were male. We each sat nervously fingering our starting stack of thirty thousand chips. Few players spoke. Although I usually introduce myself to the players on either side of me, on this day I just sat quietly waiting for dealing to start. Each player had $10,000 at stake, and the competition should prove to be keen.

There was a rumor that in future years the management might give each player fifty thousand chips to start, but the scheduled mandatory blind bets at each timed level of play then would accelerate faster, cancelling out most of the advantage of starting with more chips. We heard that the idea of starting with more chips in future years was just to allow more flexibility in bet sizing in the first few levels of play. I was happy with my starting stack of thirty thousand in the two-hour-long level-one environment during which the small blind would be fifty and the big blind one hundred. Players each had a huge excess of chips relative to the blinds, so there was no need to go crazy with big bets during the first few levels of play. The potential problem could be that competing players might make very large and rather inappropriate bets just to steal pots. The only way to stop that was to answer a big bet with a big bet, creating big risks.

A nice touch was playing the famous instrumental theme ("Titoli") by Ennio Morricone from the movie *The Good, the Bad, and the Ugly* over the loudspeakers as players were in the final minutes of finding their seats. It was the perfect choice for music. After several other announcements, the call came to "Shuffle up and deal!"

I was pretty relaxed because I had already decided to lie

low during this first two-hour level. I would avoid risk and just gauge how my nine opponents were playing. I was determined not to be knocked out in minutes at a cost of $10,000. I likely could play for a day or two without getting bounced out if I was careful. If I could make it into day three, I might even cash with a minimum prize of $15,000, which would give me minor bragging rights back home, while the $5,000 profit would more than pay for my hotel and travel costs. But just making it to the pay line would be challenging. You could lose all your chips in a single hand, or more likely in a short series of disastrous hands. Trouble tends to cascade at a poker table.

Players were given a twenty-minute break every two hours and were scheduled that day to have five levels of play (each lasting 120 minutes), along with three twenty-minute breaks and one ninety-minute dinner break after level three. So, in total, the day of play would end sometime after midnight, when survivors would bag their chips: place their plastic chips in a tightly sealed, heavy-duty plastic bag on which the player's name and ID number were written. This bag would be held by the casino overnight and opened at the start of play on day two. Chip numbers were also reported on cards at the end of the day, which allowed clerks during the early hours of the morning to enter onto a website the names and chip counts of surviving players. The system was pretty well designed since the paper cards distributed to survivors also served the function of giving each survivor his assigned table and seat for the next day of play.

After two hours of play, my chip count was down about 20 percent. Not a big success, but I was paying to remain safe and to have time to learn how my specific tablemates handled difficult situations: did someone readily slide all of his chips forward and risk everything? Or were some people ready to fold if confronted. At least for these first two hours, I was rather timid and tended to fold to pressure.

During level two, I started taking a few more risks, such

as paying to try to flop a set when holding middle pairs. This so-called set-mining can be costly, however, since a player hits his set on a flop only about 10 percent of the time. If you miss your set, you find yourself sitting there holding two small cards with little hope of eventually winning the pot, unless you are prepared to gamble with a big bluff. By good fortune, I played pocket jacks pretty aggressively against several players who were betting big, and a jack came on the flop making my set. I also hit a different set, so by the end of level two, I had doubled my chips to about sixty thousand, which was a remarkable turnaround for me. During the next two hours of play, level three, I managed just to keep my chip stack level at about sixty-one thousand.

During the quite short twenty-minute breaks, the main goal was to get into and out of the men's room. More than a thousand guys all trying to pee at the same time caused big bottlenecks, but there were several large men's rooms in different directions. I preferred to take a longer walk within the hotel to stretch my legs. After level three, there was time to buy a sandwich and drink from a vendor, and I excitedly shared my battle stories with Susan, who sat with me in a quieter hallway where we could talk and eat. Those ninety minutes went by in a hurry, though, and I had to get right back to my seat as level four was starting.

My chips gradually dwindled back to about forty thousand as I tried to avoid risks and as I missed hitting sets, straights, or flushes. Level four had an ante of twenty-five and blinds of 150 and three hundred. As cards were being dealt each time, there were already seven hundred chips in the center of the table. I decided that I needed to gamble more. I needed to steal some of those valuable chips, or I would likely end the day with fewer chips than when I started.

With stealing in mind while in middle position, I saw that my next hole cards were ace of hearts, eight of hearts. A weak suited ace. Gamblers have lost tons of money trying to push hard with a weak suited ace, but I decided to give it a try. I was the first to bet. I made a three–big blind bet of nine hundred, hoping that everyone else would fold. The older man on my immediate left had been pretty quiet most of the afternoon, so I was not pleased when he called my nine hundred. Then another man called the nine hundred, but everyone else folded. There were now 3,400 chips in the pot preflop, so this was going to be a big hand. The flop came queen of hearts, nine of spades, five of hearts. I was very happy to see the two hearts, and I felt that I needed to play aggressively and try to just win this pot; with nine outs to make my flush, I had a 36 percent chance of making my hand by the time the last two cards had come. First to bet, and unfortunately out of position against two players, I made a sizable bet of 3,200, just a little below pot size. The old man next to me called me—bad news, but the other player folded. I figured that my remaining opponent perhaps was holding ace-queen. Or he might have had pocket queens (now giving him a set) or even pocket kings. The turn card was the six of clubs, which likely didn't help my opponent but it really didn't help me at all. I just had ace high. With 9,800 chips sitting out in the center of the table, I still had thirty-six thousand chips sitting in front of me. My elderly opponent had fewer chips, about twenty thousand, so I was hoping that if I made a big bet, he might get cold feet and fold. I bet fifteen thousand so my opponent would have to commit the majority of his chips to call. He hesitated, then called, which left him with just five thousand chips. Basically, my semibluff had failed, and since his call likely meant that he had a made hand, I was probably about to lose a big hand. I would be left with less than starting chips. I had taken a big risk and was losing. The dealer turned over a deuce of hearts as the last card, a miracle card since at that point I had only an 18 percent chance of hitting a heart. A massive wave of relief washed over me, but I was careful not to let it show. I bet five thousand, which would put my opponent all in if he chose to call. He was visibly upset, but there were so many chips in the pot he felt that he had to call, so he did. I quickly turned up my ace-high flush, made by the lucky fall of a heart. He mucked his hand without showing, murmuring a little to himself. Although I wasn't sure, I think he did have the set of queens.

We shook hands as he stood up, and then he slowly walked away. I gambled and won, and that is just part of the game. This risky hand ensured that I would easily survive to play in day two as long as I didn't screw up during the rest of the session. During the remainder of day one, I lost quite a few chips set-mining, but in one hand, I played pocket tens aggressively and was astonished that by the end of that hand, I had quad tens, a rare turn of events.

As the final seconds ticked down on level five, the last level of play that day, I was pleased that I had avoided being eliminated by being timid most of the time, won several nice hands by being clever, and won a big hand by being extremely lucky. With seventy-four thousand chips at the end of the day, I had more than doubled my starting stack. It was not until the next morning that I was able to look at WSOP.com to find out that of the 1,716 players who began at noon in this Tournament 68 group B, 1,154 players survived to play in day two. I ranked in 165th place in this group. I was very satisfied, as this was my first time playing in the World Series of Poker Main Event.

It was about one in the morning, and there was time for a quick congratulatory kiss from Susan, but then I collapsed into bed. We would have time to talk more at breakfast.

Miracles?

Susan and I rendezvoused for our morning caffeine and conversation. The waitress had just brought our omelets, and she returned to our table briefly to top up our coffees. I had slept well. We were in no rush to finish eating since I had a free day, because day one for starting group C would be underway at all the tables today. My main emotion was still relief. I had feared that I might spend $10,000 only to be knocked out of the tournament after one or two hours. Embarrassing. Now sitting pretty waiting for my day two, I explained to Susan that if I could manage to last until day three, I would have outlasted the great majority of the entrants. Though I was certain to be eliminated at some point, I was hoping to survive until late day three when the payouts would begin.

"You should be so proud of yourself. You played with great skill," she said encouragingly.

"I was skillful by folding most of the time." I laughed. "I was very selective so that I rarely was exposed to a big risk." I took a gulp of hot coffee. "It was so sad. I saw one pretty good player who was betting more and more with ace-king, and he ended up all in against the other aggressive bettor, who in the end showed pocket aces. The poor guy who went crazy with ace-king lost all of his chips—and that wasn't even a necessary confrontation on day one."

"I see. You were ducking and weaving," she replied.

"I got in trouble with that ace-eight, though. I got way ahead of myself. I should have realized that the old man on my left who was betting big must have had a very strong hand. I should have lost more than half of my chips to him. But instead I was saved by a miracle card, a heart, at the end. It was a miracle."

Susan bit her lower lip. "I guess I don't know you well enough yet, but are you speaking metaphorically or are you being serious?"

I blinked and caught my breath. What had I just said? Then it clicked. "I see," I replied. "Miracle."

"Yes. Miracle. You seem to be a pretty serious Catholic, although I know you're intelligently liberal regarding some aspects of behavior between mature, consenting adults." She paused to smile at me, then continued. "But do you believe that the appearance of a fortunate card at the poker table could be a true miracle?"

I shook my head. "It was certainly not a miracle in the biblical sense. I believe that most of the time God is probably too busy to worry about who wins a poker hand. Or a football game or some other sports event."

Susan sat silently pondering the question. "But ..." She paused. "Do you believe that God hears prayers? Can he actually help people? Or is that just old-fashioned superstition? I noticed that you provided a caveat that *most of the time* God is probably too busy to worry about poker."

I delayed my response to find the right words. I'm a religious person, but I'm not a fanatic. "Well," I started, "I think it's a complex question that cannot be answered briefly." I knew, however, that my response wouldn't satisfy her.

"Why not a brief and clear yes or no?" she countered. "Although we don't know the answer, surely the answer should be for starters a simple yes or no, with caveats to follow."

"You're right." I nodded. "So, answering as a lifelong Catholic, I feel certain in my heart that the simple answer is yes, God does hear prayers, and he can help people. But having said that, it's clear that there must be many caveats. Many, many of them."

"Such as?" She sat up a little straighter.

"Why do little children suffer from terrible diseases? Why does one person recover from cancer, but another person dies? These are age-old questions. Recall the trials of Job. There certainly was not a very satisfying answer for him."

Susan leaned forward. "I haven't thought about Job since high school." Her brow furrowed. "But I can't remember. When the good man Job had all his unearned sufferings, what was the explanation that God gave him?"

"God took the form of a whirlwind and reprimanded Job for seeking too much understanding."

"How can seeking understanding ever be bad?"

"That does sound odd," I replied. "But remember that we live in an age of humanism. There is widespread belief today that the brilliance of the human mind will be able to understand the world, solve problems, and make life better. Such attitudes were not engrained thousands of years ago when the author of Job was contemplating the mystery of human suffering."

"But that's progress, right? People do get smarter, and they will solve problems. Humanism has replaced old superstitions."

"I see what you're saying," I began, "but intelligent people centuries ago were not ignorant. They cried when they buried their children. They loved their families. They had deep insights into human relationships and sophisticated thoughts about the meaning of life. Their wisdom should not be ignored. We can still learn from them today."

"What can we learn? We're so much more advanced now."

"Be careful, my sweet." I smiled at Susan. "We can easily make international phone calls or fly across continents. But is technical knowledge actually wisdom? Modern proponents of humanism can be rather arrogant. I'm a scientist and physician, so I certainly believe in the value of technical knowledge and progress. But we still struggle today with the deep mysteries of our existence."

Susan remained silent. Her eyes widened, and she took on a sincere expression. "So do you pray for things? Do you believe in the efficacy of prayer?"

"Yes," I replied, and took a breath. "I say brief prayers that deal with important things, but I recognize that the world is complex and perhaps what I'm seeking might not be for the best. I've prayed for patients who were suffering, for families that were troubled." I paused and smiled at Susan. "After Sheila's death, I prayed that God would help me meet another special woman. I even tried to make a little argument that it would be very good both for me and for the woman and for the broader world. So please, God, why not let this happen?"

"Did you hear any answers?" She smiled.

"No words from on high." I laughed. "But a few nights ago, I turned a corner in a hotel hallway and ran into a huge man who had a pretty woman pinned to the wall. Somehow that situation worked out well."

"It did work out well," she agreed.

We finished our coffee, but we weren't in a hurry to go anywhere.

"I'm still curious," Susan confessed. "So you pray for important things. For mature and reasonable things. But haven't you ever prayed for help to get over an earache, or for good luck at the poker table? Isn't it very human to have those sorts of concerns as well?"

"You've hit on an important point. Humans do have focused and often overly self-interested concerns. That is the way human beings are; that is the way they think. I believe that God is personal. He is, astonishingly, truly concerned about human beings, about their desires, about their foibles. The ancient analogy of God being a caring father has great attraction for me."

"But how can God be concerned about your earache while children are dying of starvation in some poverty-stricken backwater?"

"All I can say is that it is a mystery. The alternative is that you simply acknowledge that the world is totally absurd. Our short, insignificant lives are enriched by local and transient circumstances that give them fleeting meaning, but in actuality, there is no lasting or ultimate meaning. We are born and die with no purpose and then are dead forever."

"That is rather harsh."

"I want to read one of my favorite quotes from the famous mathematician, philosopher, and atheist Bertrand Russell." I reached for my wallet, again being careful not to spill loose hundred-dollar bills. "He wrote, 'That man is the product of causes which had no provision of the end they were achieving; that his origins, his growth, his hopes, his fears, his loves and beliefs are but the outcome of accidental collocations of atoms; that no fire, no heroism, no intensity of thought and feeling, can preserve an individual life beyond the grave; that all the labors of the ages, all the devotion, ... all the noonday brightness of human genius are destined to extinction ... all these things, if not quite beyond dispute, are yet so nearly certain, that no philosophy which rejects them can hope to stand. Only within the scaffolding of these truths, only on the firm foundation of unyielding despair, can the soul's habitation henceforth be safely built.'"

"Wow," Susan observed. "Quite harsh, indeed."

"I am a humanist. But I'm more than a humanist. Unbounded, blind, and unapologetic humanism can lend little comfort when one stares with agony into the abyss."

Then Susan smiled. "Allow me to make this observation. When you reach into your wallet, you dig out a beautiful or thought-provoking quotation. Every other guy in the building is reaching for either a credit card, cash, or a condom."

"I guess that's a compliment, so I'll say thank you."

"But let's come back to poker. Do you ever pray for success at poker?"

I smiled at her and shifted my position slightly. "That's an uncomfortable question, since you now view me as basically a levelheaded and rational guy. But let me just say, yes, every time I start to play, I say a little prayer."

"What do you pray?" she asked, a little amused.

"First, let me explain that poker is a zero-sum game. When someone wins chips, someone else loses them. So I briefly pray that God please recognize that this activity is important to me, and I hope that he will prosper the work of my hands. Someone has to win, so why not me? But I am never making a bargain with God or trying to put God to the test. Not for poker and not for any other desire. I just want to play my best and get a little lucky once in a while. And I'm resigned to live with however the game comes out."

"That seems very reasonable."

"I don't think of it as being superstitious. Rather, I think of it as including God in my activities." Then I recalled an anecdote. "There is a story that Niels Bohr, the famous physicist, had a good-luck horseshoe nailed on the wall of his office right behind his desk chair. A visitor once expressed surprise that a scientist would have a lucky charm displayed so prominently, and he asked Bohr, 'Do you really believe that a horseshoe on your wall can bring you good luck?' Bohr replied, 'No, of course not!' But after a brief pause, Bohr continued, 'But the friend who gave the horseshoe to me told me that it would bring me good luck whether I believed it or not.'"

"That is hilarious. But coming back to poker, do you think that if God has so many other tragedies and crises to observe, he would bother to have a favorable card show up for you?"

"It may sound silly, but I think of it this way. God is not just a million times smarter and more powerful than I am. Nor a billion times more. Nor a billion, billion times more. He is *infinitely* smarter and more powerful. In other words, it is a very mysterious world, and God has huge capabilities—a lot of bandwidth. So he certainly has the ability to help me a little if he so chooses."

"But if there are starving children, why would he choose to help you win a poker hand?"

"That seems like a sensible question, but the world is quite mysterious. I don't know the answer. Nor did Job. Suffering in the world, as cruel as it may seem, must have some purpose—unless our existence is totally absurd." I paused, not very satisfied with this discussion of the troubling and puzzling human condition. Then I looked at Susan and smiled a little. "One thought I've had as a partial explanation is that God is, at times, whimsical."

"Whimsical?"

"It sounds sacrilegious, but I think it may be true. Because of the vastness of the universe, there is also room for whimsy. A well-rounded human being has room for humor, for whimsy. If the Almighty is a personal God, I see no reason why he might not have those characteristics as well."

Susan seemed to be astonished. "But is there whimsy in the Bible? Did Jesus ever tell jokes?"

"Sure he did. Remember when he met with the Pharisees and started his parable, 'Three apostles walked into a bar …'"

"He did not!"

"Okay, I was teasing you. Humor is rarely found in the Bible, which has always seemed strange to me. Humor is so important to people. I think that the men who were writing the texts and then copying and recopying them were pretty serious guys, and they were trying to write about serious topics. Any bits of humor were for the most part left on the cutting room floor, so to speak." I paused. "But I think a few bits that reflect God's whimsy remained."

"Really? I can't think of any."

"One instance that struck me as whimsical was the episode when Mary, Jesus, and some friends were attending a wedding at Cana. Remember? The hosts ran out of wine, a very embarrassing development."

"Yes."

"Mary, perhaps displaying the ages-old ability of a mother

to press a son into action, asked Jesus if he could please do something about the problem. Jesus, perhaps displaying the ages-old tendency of grown sons to be rather resistant to suggestions from their mothers in social settings, replied that his time had not yet come, so it was none of his business. I suspect that he might have been engaged in discussions or thinking about a future sermon or something, and helping the kitchen staff didn't seem to be appropriate."

"I remember that."

"I have a mental image of Mary glaring at Jesus and placing her hands on her hips in a determined fashion. Jesus quickly found out that Mary was serious. She was not going to allow the wedding hosts to be embarrassed. I think that Mary knew that Jesus could solve the problem, but she had no idea how he was going to do it. So she didn't tell Jesus precisely what to do. She just grabbed some of the kitchen staff by their collars and basically told them, 'This is going to be a disaster unless you get on top of this. See that guy? He's my son. Listen up fast. You do whatever he tells you.'"

"Yes," Susan recalled. "Jesus instructed them to fill up several large stone water jars, and the water was miraculously changed to wine."

"Various religious interpretations have been proposed over the centuries, but while there are likely religious themes at work, the story is rather whimsical."

Susan smiled.

"Another instance of possible humor is Jesus's story of the corrupt judge. A poor widow can't get the crooked judge to give her a just ruling because, as is repeated several times for emphasis, he neither feared God nor cared about men. She kept pestering the judge. I imagine the widow as being a physically large and worldly, honest woman who has been in many arguments and scrapes during her life. I imagine the judge to be an elderly, scholarly, small man who is very clever about making money and pursuing his interests but who avoids fistfights. He refused several times to help her but finally was worn out by her persistence and ruled in her favor."

"I had never thought of it as a story with a humorous tone."

"Even the Old Testament has some humor, I think."

"What?"

"Some of the text in Genesis is written just like a late-night comedy sketch."

"I don't believe it!"

"Well, the texts have serious religious messages. But one text comes to mind that involves bargaining back and forth as might occur in a dusty street market. Abraham is trying to press God for a better price, so to speak. This could have been written in different ways, but the conversation as portrayed seems a little humorous to me. Here is a mortal man trying to barter with and outwit the Almighty."

"I have no idea what you're talking about."

"Let me pull up the text on my phone, and I'll read it to you. The text is written as a conversation, and it's striking that way, I think. The author is trying to engage his audience in a special way, as if he is telling a story within a story." I fiddled with my phone, cleared my throat, and got ready to read. "This is the interchange between Abraham and God after God told him that he was going to totally destroy the city of Sodom because of the evil deeds of its citizens. Abraham wanted to avoid the destruction. It's Genesis 18:23–33 in the Oxford Annotated Bible."

> Then Abraham drew near, and said, 'Wilt thou indeed destroy the righteous with the wicked? Suppose there are fifty righteous within the city; wilt thou then destroy the place and not spare it for the fifty righteous who are in it? Far be it from thee to do such a thing, to slay the righteous with the wicked, so that the righteous fare as

the wicked! Far be that from thee! Shalt not the Judge of all the earth do right?'

And the Lord said, 'If I find at Sodom fifty righteous in the city, I will spare the whole place for their sake.'

Abraham answered, 'Behold, I have taken upon myself to speak to the Lord, I who am but dust and ashes. Suppose five of the fifty righteous are lacking? Wilt thou destroy the whole city for the lack of five?'

And he said, 'I will not destroy it if I find forty-five there.'

Again he spoke to him, and said, 'Suppose forty are found there.'

He answered, 'For the sake of forty I will not do it.'

Then he said, 'Oh let not the Lord be angry, and I will speak. Suppose thirty are found there.'

He answered, 'I will not do it, if I find thirty there.'

He said, 'Behold, I have taken upon myself to speak to the Lord. Suppose twenty are found there.'

He answered, 'For the sake of twenty I will not destroy it,'

Then he said, 'Oh let not the Lord be angry, and I will speak again but this once. Suppose ten are found there.'

He answered, 'For the sake of ten I will not destroy it.'

And the Lord went his way, when he had finished speaking to Abraham; and Abraham returned to his place.

I looked up from my phone and smiled at Susan.

"That is a remarkable text." She shook her head. After a brief pause, she continued, "But I think Sodom got destroyed, right?"

"Right. This is the Old Testament, after all. I guess that part's not very funny."

"So what about praying for success in poker?" Susan brought the conversation back to what we had been discussing.

"Remember, I mostly play poker because I enjoy the challenge of the game. I'm not trying to make a financial killing. I just want to play well, meet interesting people, and make at least some small profits to pay my expenses. I don't need to fret about getting the Almighty involved in my little games." I paused and smiled. "But I'm basically a good person, a person deserving to win as much as anyone else. So if God wants to send me some help, I'm certainly ready to accept it."

Day Two, World Series of Poker Main Event
Start-of-day chips: seventy-four thousand

The next morning, Susan and I met for breakfast at ten. I opted for the French toast and sausage; she ordered pancakes. Coffee, of course, was mandatory. We were pleased to run into Stuart Davies, so we all sat together. Stuart had played well in group B along with me, but the crowd was so large that I hadn't even seen him that day. He ended day one with eighty thousand chips, so he was also in pretty good shape to start day two at noon.

As we sat together, we could look at WSOP.com to see the outcomes of day one for groups A, B, and C. Group A had 750 entries, and there were 470 survivors, while group B had 1,716 entries, and there were 1,154 survivors. The survivors of these two starting groups would play their day two today. Group

C survivors would play their day two tomorrow. Survivors of day two from all three groups would be combined to play on day three. Counting all three starting groups, there were 6,420 entrants, and after overhead was removed, the prize pool had been set at $60.3 million.

Stuart was excited. He had played in this Main Event tournament eleven times and had cashed three times, so he was a very accomplished player. But that statistic was revealing. It was difficult even for an expert player to cash reliably in this big tournament. There was a lot of competition, and chance was always a confounding factor.

The WSOP.com site also had a feature to allow you to look up the names and chip counts of people seated at tables, so you could get some feel as to whether you might have a favorable or unfavorable seat assignment. I didn't recognize the names of any of my competitors at table eighty-five in the Brasilia room. I would start in seat three. To my immediate left was a player with 63,250 chips, comparable to my stack, while the player in seat eight had 63,575 chips. The most worrisome opponent at table eighty-five was apparently a German in seat nine who would start today with 128,725 chips. His name was Dominic, but I wasn't familiar with him. I knew that I would have to tread very lightly around him. He could take all my chips in one hand.

After breakfast, Susan headed off on a bus to tour the huge dam outside of town. She took a big hat because the sun would be brutal. Stuart and I retired to our rooms to rest a few more minutes before taking our seats before noon.

The Brasilia room buzzed with excitement. Stuart had disappeared to the far end of the room. My table was along one edge of the room along the wall. The advantage of that was the proximity to an exit; at break times, I might be able to quickly make my way to the men's room. Within a minute during a break, the lines for the toilets already were long.

The casino management had placed our bagged chips at

our individual seats, a process that probably took hours during the night and morning. We had to show our ID to the dealer, then we each tore open our bags and restacked our chips. Ten minutes until start. The German in seat nine was young, lean, and tall and sat with a confident air. Two photographers came to our table and began snapping dozens of photos of him; they asked him a few questions about how he felt and about his strategy for the day. I had already identified him as a threat at breakfast during my online review, but now I became even more guarded. He was clearly a globally famous player. But I also began to formulate a plan. I would try to avoid him, but I would be suspicious if he made a big bet to scare me out of a pot. He struck me as just the kind of player who would be willing to make big bluffs to chase away less experienced players. I might lose all my chips, but if he was bluffing, I could make a big gain. If the photographers had not paid so much attention to him, I probably would not have formulated that tentative plan.

After a few announcements, the traditional call to "Shuffle up and deal" set the cards in motion. In this first two-hour level, level six, the blinds would be 250 and five hundred with a fifty ante. We would play five levels and again finish after midnight.

After a few minutes, I was dealt pocket jacks, and luckily a jack came on the flop, so I made a nice profit on that hand. An hour later, I made a set of kings. You can play poker for ten hours and never make even one set; I had made two sets in ninety minutes and boosted my chips to about 110,000. This was a superb start, and I decided to fold even fairly good cards for the next hour or two. You can lose a lot of chips with moderately good cards, so I thought my best plan was to lie low. I especially folded every time the German was in a hand. After several hours, I had played just a few additional hands, and my chip stack had slowly drifted downward again to about seventy-five thousand chips. I was surviving and taking few risks but making no upward progress.

Susan and I met to have sandwiches at the dinner break. I was so exhausted I could hardly converse. She enjoyed seeing the big dam and turbines. She knew I was tired and still had to play, so she let me rest in my room thirty minutes before I headed back downstairs.

I knew that it would happen eventually. I ended up head-to-head in a big hand against the German late on day two. He had about 160,000 chips, while I had only seventy thousand. With blinds of five hundred and a thousand with a hundred ante, he was first to bet and made a four–big blind bet from early position, and I called this substantial bet with pocket tens. I hoped to hit another set. I had to play some hands, or my chips would have dwindled further, and pocket tens is a fair hand when in position. The flop came queen, jack, nine of three different suits. I had a feeling that the German might be holding ace-king, but he also could have many other good starting hands: aces, kings, ace-queen, ace-jack, and many others. I waited patiently for him to bet and tried not to look too nervous. Of course, I had an open-ended straight draw, so unless he did something crazy, I definitely wanted to pay to see another card.

The German stared at me and still took more time to think. I knew he was well aware that I was an amateur, and he had many more chips. Finally, he moved a large stack of chips forward. There were already about ten thousand chips in the center, and he bet twenty-five thousand. I swallowed but tried to maintain my poker face. I really wanted to see another card to possibly make my straight. He seemed confident and sat quietly. I suspected that he had hit either the queen or jack, and my tens were potentially beaten. But I wanted to take the risk to get the straight, so I called his oversized bet. There were now about sixty thousand chips in the pot, and I had only about forty thousand chips remaining in front of me. The dealer set out the turn card; it was the meaningless deuce of clubs.

The German looked at me, looked at his chips, and then

announced a bet of thirty thousand. It seemed to me not to be an entirely appropriate bet. If he was holding a clearly winning hand, why would he bet me off the action rather than enticing me to stay in for one more round of betting? There were many hands that were beating me right now, but I just had the feeling that he was bluffing. I called with most of my remaining chips. The dealer set out the river card; it was the meaningless four of diamonds. I had not made my straight.

The German tilted his head from side to side as he counted my few remaining neatly stacked chips and then bet exactly that amount. Everyone at the table looked at me. There were a dozen ways that I was already defeated, but I had decided previously that even at the risk of losing, I was not going to be bluffed out of a pot by this player. So I said, "Call," and immediately turned over my pocket tens. The German sat like a statue, staring. He was now supposed to turn over his hand. A few more seconds passed. Then, amazingly, he mucked his hand without showing, stood up, and walked away from the table. The dealer pushed the big pile of chips to me. I actually couldn't believe for a few seconds that I had just won. I had more than doubled my chips from about seventy thousand to about 143,000 in that hand, and we only had another hour to play for the day. I glanced at the computerized screen and saw that of the 1,716 players who had started in this group A and B, day two, only about 910 players remained.

It had been nerve-racking, but I took a gamble that his big bets were bluffs. Sometimes a challenge can end up being a huge opportunity. The player I feared the most had given me a big stack of chips.

In retrospect, based on the way he bet during the hand, I suspected that the German made the preflop raise holding ace-king, and on subsequent rounds of betting, he was semibluffing, hoping to hit an ace, king, or ten for the straight. But I held two tens, blocking some of his outs, and he just couldn't hit, so he made a big bluff. This was a hugely fortunate turn of events for me.

During the next hour, I cautiously played four hands but couldn't hit the board, so my stack declined more than twenty thousand. When it was time to bag chips at the end of day two, I held 122,500.

It was one in the morning, and I sent texts to Susan and Stuart with my status. Susan replied with a big smiley face, a good night wish (she was half-asleep in her bed), and suggested a plan to meet for breakfast at nine thirty. Stuart had just bagged his 130,000 chips and said he would join us at nine thirty. I then made a quick call to Southwest to move my 8:00 a.m. departure back two days; I had hoped I might need to do this, so I had chosen Southwest to avoid change fees. I stopped at the registration desk to alert the hotel, and they were happy to have me stay a little longer. Within minutes, I collapsed into bed.

In Pursuit of a BMW

It was a short night, and I sat on the edge on my bed at eight thirty in the morning, still rather tired. But excited. I had a real chance to cash in the Main Event. I answered several work emails about committee reports and Japanese project issues, and received clearance from my boss for two more days of vacation. He was confident that I would stay up-to-date by email. My workmates actually knew very little about my interest in poker, so I said nothing about that to them.

I sent emails to my parents and brother to let them know my status. My family members responded that they were happy that I might win a prize. They would try to follow WSOP.com online to watch for developments. I got cleaned up quickly and was walking down to the breakfast place by nine twenty. I could take a nap this afternoon since I had the day off; group C survivors were to play their day two today.

Susan and Stuart were already standing in the hallway near where the line for breakfast was forming, so I joined them, and we took our place in line. I was quite impressed by the appearance of my friends. Susan was bright-eyed and seemed well rested in her tight jeans and classy-looking Las Vegas T-shirt. Stuart, who I considered to be an old man, was beaming and looked fit as a fiddle. I felt tired, and I hoped I looked better than I felt. "I really need some coffee," I offered.

We were shown to seats, and we ordered our food. Stuart was looking at his phone and pointed out some players on the survivor list. "The tough but mysterious new Chinese player is this guy," he reported as he turned his phone so I could see. "He is Hsi Tseng Lee from Macau, and he now has 135,000 chips after playing in day two yesterday with us." Stuart swiped several more times on his phone, then commented, "And the toughest Russian guy, Vladimir Komarov, also survived day two and now has 128,000 chips."

Susan was excited for us. She said she heard yesterday afternoon that a lot of the very famous players are in group C and would be playing their day two today.

"They'll be playing while I take a nap this afternoon," I replied. "I thought I was in pretty good shape, but the continuous mental tension of playing hour after hour seems to be wearing me down. I don't mean to be antisocial, but I think I need more rest."

Stuart and I traded war stories from our day-two experience. He had gotten a lot of good cards, which made his day fairly easy. He was astonished that I put my last chips into the middle holding just pocket tens while a jack and queen showed on the board. He shook his head. "That was really gutsy." He made it sound positive, but I could tell what he was thinking: it was a little crazy.

"I felt certain that the German had been bluffing a lot already. Then, in that hand, his bet sizing made it seem like he was bluffing again. So I just made up my mind that I would play my tens to the end, come what may. It was a big risk, but I decided to go with my gut."

"Pretty strong gut. They term that a crying call. Turned out you were right. And I agree that he probably did miss while holding ace-king." Stuart lowered his voice and leaned toward me. "But there were a dozen other hands that would have beaten you."

"I know."

As we finished our meal, Susan announced that she had a ticket to fly back to Austin tomorrow but that she thought she would extend her vacation a couple of days. She had gotten the approval from her boss.

"That's really nice, and now let me tell you something funny," I replied. "When I set up this trip, I estimated that I would be knocked out on day two, so I had a return flight reserved to New England scheduled for this morning at eight. So I already had to move that flight back."

"So you moved it back ten days?" Stuart smiled.

I laughed and replied, "I'm not quite that confident. Moved it just forty-eight hours. My plan is to fold often to survive to cash on day three, and after that make some big bets to try desperately to add chips after I'm in the money. And since my attempt to chip-up likely will fail, I'll just fly home with my $15,000 the next morning. But I'll be satisfied with that."

"Makes sense." Stuart nodded. "It's the classic BMW strategy."

Susan looked puzzled. "BMW? You mean the car?"

Stuart smiled. "Not the car. In big multiday poker tournaments, no one wins a prize after the first day. The main goal is to survive to bag your chips so you can play again the next day. B is for *bag*. Then when you reach the day when money will start to be awarded, you need to be very cautious. Don't get eliminated right before the money. But veterans take advantage of cautious players; they can use the overly timid play of opponents to add chips to their stacks. But whatever you do, you must survive to make the money. The M stands for *money*. After you're in the money, you can take the gloves off, play to win first prize. But it's risky. You could go out quick and take home just a minimum prize. So the W is for *win*. You see? BMW."

After breakfast, Stuart went to play in a cash game. He would just relax and not think too hard, he assured us.

Susan and I decided to walk outside to the pool deck. The July air was already quite warm at eleven o'clock, but there were a couple of shadowed places where we could talk in the shade. The swaying palm trees provided a nice ambiance. We decided that in Las Vegas it was not too early for margaritas, so we placed the orders, and they quickly appeared. We settled into comfortable chairs.

"This is the life," Susan observed.

"So how did you do yesterday wrestling with the slot machines?"

"I met some interesting people and took lots of breaks. But I didn't hit one jackpot."

"You need to practice more," I advised.

"Well, according to Stuart, you were pretty lucky to pick off that guy's bluff yesterday."

"I was lucky, but it's strange." I paused and watched three thirteen-year-olds playing with a large beach ball in the shallow end.

"Strange?"

"I just knew. I knew almost for certain. I knew he was bluffing."

"How could you know?"

"I couldn't really know. But somehow I did."

Susan smiled. "Was it a poker miracle?"

"Odd that you should say that. I was just thinking about that."

"Spooky."

"I'm not sure that spooky is the right term."

"How about creepy?" Susan suggested with a slight chuckle.

"Too negative. It was a positive experience. I think that uncanny describes it better."

"Hmm."

"It was akin to when George Washington decided to gamble the outcome of the Revolutionary War by making an unexpected, rapid march from north of New York City all the way south to Yorktown to try to trap Cornwallis and his Southern Army. Washington and Rochambeau juggled a nightmare of logistical challenges to move thousands of American and French troops and their heavy equipment many hundreds of miles quickly. The roads were poor, and feeding the large group required a lot of creativity. The army was strung out for miles and was vulnerable to ambush. Washington was counting on the French fleet to show up along the Virginia coast at the same time he did, a vague plan that had been discussed weeks ago. But there were poor communications and many potential pitfalls. It was a desperate long shot, but Washington knew that it might prove decisive if it worked." I paused. "And Washington captured an entire British army."

"I think you must know American history better than I."

"Washington actually had several terrible predicaments during the war, and somehow fate intervened to bail him out each time."

"Predicaments?"

"In the defense of New York City early in the war, Washington occupied Brooklyn Heights on Long Island with most of his army. But within days, that entire army was nearly surrounded and faced certain defeat. Only one thing saved him." I paused and smiled at Susan but said nothing further.

"C'mon. Tell me. What was the one thing that saved him?"

"Fog."

"Fog?" Susan was incredulous.

"On a late afternoon in August 1776, Washington decided that he had to evacuate his troops on Brooklyn Heights back to Manhattan using rowboats. During the night, those few boats would need to make many trips back and forth to carry the men and weapons, while a few men kept fires burning and made noise to give the illusion that the army was still camped for the night. It seemed that the massive transfer of personnel and equipment would take many hours and would easily be detected. But a thick fog appeared. A man could not be seen at ten yards. The air was so thick that it also dulled the noise of the oars, although the vulnerable troops waiting patiently in line for boats kept such order and discipline that they barely made any sound. The fog persisted the next morning, allowing the last of the colonials to escape. When the fog lifted in the late morning, the highly expert British general, William Howe, looked out across the field and was astonished."

"Astonished?"

"Yes. The entire, quite large Colonial Army and all of their weapons had simply vanished."

"Ha! I'll bet he was surprised. But is that story really true?" Susan seemed incredulous.

"David McCullough, the famous historian, elegantly wrote of this unlikely episode in his famous essay, 'What the Fog Wrought.' You can read that online."

"It seems impossible," she replied.

"And then there was the time that Washington found all the fish."

"The fish?"

"Washington's army was cold and on the edge of starvation during a long winter at Valley Forge. In very early spring, all of the supplies had nearly run out. Desperate, Washington ordered boats to drop fishing nets into the small river there to see if a few fish might be caught." I smiled.

"So. Were there fish?"

I laughed. "The nets came back full to nearly bursting. The type of local fish was called shad. The townspeople said that they had never seen anything like it before." I paused, as Susan seemed suspicious. She raised one brow. "I'm not joking," I assured her. "Pulitzer Prize–winning author John McPhee researched this event and wrote a book about it. There are some uncertainties about details. He humorously entitled his book *The Founding Fish* because the well-fed army went on to maneuver and fight well and eventually won the war."

"I guess I believe you." She smiled as she leaned back in her chair and took another sip of her drink. "But those are truly remarkable stories." She sat forward again, looked at me, and asked in a serious tone, "Do you believe those events actually were miracles? Seriously?"

I smiled, leaned forward, and held out my drink so that we could click our glasses together. "I have no idea if those events were miracles are not," I confessed. "But they were strange, eerie, mysterious—almost as eerie as having an unlikely card turn up on day one of a huge poker tournament, or having a sense of near certainty that an opponent was bluffing on day two."

"Almost as uncanny as meeting a very special person by chance in a strange city," she pondered, and leaned back in her chair again.

"Almost as mysterious as the way a woman can perceive loneliness and need in a man's touch," I added.

"You were easy to read. And you were desperately in need," Susan assured me with a wink. She sat forward in her chair and looked at me intently. "And now I need to reveal something to you."

I shifted in my seat, not quite sure where the conversation was about to go. "Okay."

"I need just to say this out loud." She paused. "I am now certain—positive—that I am thoroughly and unreservedly in love with you."

Smiling, I responded immediately, "And I think you can tell that I am totally in love with you." I was a little surprised by how easy this was for me to say, but I knew it was true.

Tears appeared in Susan's eyes. "I always dreamed that something like this would happen to me. And now it has." She sniffed, then continued. "I know that my heart and my life will never be the same."

Now I had a tear in my eye as I responded, "And I know that my heart and my life will never be the same."

We sat in silence for a few minutes, finishing our drinks. We both knew that this sort of very special moment happens only once or twice in a lifetime. Many people, perhaps, never experience such a moment.

"Could I ask you ..." I began but then paused. "When we finish our drinks, could you please join me in my room? I want to be close to you again."

She smiled at me. "And I want to be close to you again too."

Within minutes, we made our way upstairs. She joined me for another very intimate session, after which I presume that she tiptoed out of my room, as I had fallen sound asleep.

A Quiet Evening

I rolled over, momentarily confused. Bright sunlight penetrated tiny gaps around my curtains, but the room was fairly dark, and the bedside clock said 5:05. Then I remembered. Susan. I sat up in bed, but it appeared that she was gone. I must have fallen asleep. And it was late afternoon.

I stretched. I felt much more rested. I glanced at my phone and saw a text from Susan received about an hour ago: "Come by my room at 6:30 if you want to have a light dinner. I'm thinking I just need a salad tonight."

I texted back: "Just woke up. Having very sweet dreams. I'll come by 6:30." I actually knocked on Susan's door at 6:29.

There was a little café we had seen down one hall north of the hotel lobby, so we stopped in there to get garden salads, although I threatened Susan that I might have ice cream for dessert.

"I go to the gym almost every morning but just for forty minutes," she explained. "So a salad is right for me tonight."

"I admire you. I walk a lot. And I often walk up a couple of flights if I have the option. But I get into a pool or gym less than once a month."

"I was pretty athletic in high school," she replied. "I ran track and loved tennis and basketball. But I did much less activity in college. Nowadays, I belong to a gym near home, and I try to go about five times a week."

"Tell me, Susan. What was the most important thing you ever did in your life?"

"Wow," she responded. "You move pretty fast. From gym attendance to probing for profound insights?"

"Well, maybe that transition was a little abrupt. But I'm curious. How would you answer?"

"It's a hard question to answer." She paused. "It's hard because I've done a million important things."

"You've done a million important things?" I asked as though I still couldn't grasp her comment.

"Well, it depends on how you count. I've probably done an important thing every day. At least I try to do so daily."

"That is the last answer I expected from you. Can you explain?"

She grew serious. "Now listen to me. Life is short. I try to do important things all the time."

"Like what?"

"When I called my parents to tell them I was going to fly to Las Vegas a few days, I told my mom I loved her. That's one. And that was very important."

"Hmm."

"And then my dad got on the phone for a minute, and I told him I loved him."

"I see."

"And when I was four, I used crayons to make my mom a happy birthday card. She loved it."

"Yep, I see where you're going with this conversation ..."

"And that year I made her a Thanksgiving card and a Christmas card. And my dad too."

"What a sweet way of looking at things." I grinned.

"It's true. Each of those acts was very important. And there have been tens of thousands of others over decades."

"Of course, you're completely right."

"I knew how much my parents loved me, so I made big efforts to avoid causing them any headaches when I was in high school. I studied hard, got good grades, and never stayed out past my allowed time. So I guess I did one hundred thousand important things just during the four years of high school."

"I follow you."

"I was a careful driver. I was very responsible in college. I tutored several classmates who really needed help with math, and all of them passed and eventually graduated. I graduated with honors, got a job, and earned income. Paid back my educational loans. Paid my taxes. Registered to vote and acted as a good citizen. Attended church. Delivered hot meals to elderly parishioners. Donated to charities. The list goes on."

"I surrender. I believe you," I responded and smiled, my palms raised. "You actually have done a million important things."

Then she leaned closer to me and began to whisper, "And I kissed you. Multiple times, actually."

"Very sweet."

"And this is very important." She feigned a wise expression as if she were about to tell me a big secret. "I did a lot more—a *lot more*—than just kiss you." She nodded and winked.

I couldn't help but give her an enthusiastic, heartfelt kiss right there in the little café.

After dinner, we walked the long corridors from one end of the casino to the other just for the exercise. We enjoyed seeing the people—all kinds, shapes, and sizes. After a few minutes, we walked through one of the several large rooms where group C, day-two contestants were still playing; we hoped to see some famous players. Daniel Negreanu is one of my favorites from TV, and it appeared that he had about one hundred thousand chips and was likely to build that higher. I recognized several other prominent players, but they had experienced some misfortune and had few chips. The slings and arrows of a big poker tournament could wound even the best players.

Day Three, World Series of Poker Main Event
Start-of-day chips: 122,500

As we three waited in the breakfast line, Stuart brought up the WSOP.com site on his phone and read us the details. Of the 6,420 entering players, 4,371 had survived day one and had started day two, but now only 1,796 players were survivors to start day three. With 122,500 chips, I was above the average of 107,238 chips, so my rank was 615th out of the 1,796 survivors. Stuart was ranked a little higher than me. We both should have an excellent chance to cash, he assured me, and he thought the pay line might be reached by about six or eight that night. The management had decided that exactly one thousand players this year would be given a prize.

As we finished breakfast and were enjoying our refilled

coffee cups, we noted other interesting details on the website. Daniel Negreanu would start day three with 123,600 chips, almost the same as me. Another famous player, Phil Hellmuth, the so-called poker brat because he sometimes has a temper, had 88,800.

Stuart and I assessed the cost of playing in level eleven, the first level of play in day three. Blinds would be eight hundred and sixteen hundred with a two hundred ante. This gave me a stack equivalent to seventy-six big blinds to start the day, a healthy stack. One need only worry if one fell below twenty big blinds, and one would need to start sweating a lot at ten big blinds. That was the time to go all in with any two hole cards.

In level eleven, each round of nine hands at the table, which might require twenty minutes to complete, will cost each player $800 + 1600 + (9 \times 200) = 4,200$ chips. This cost per round provides a way to calculate another poker statistic that can guide a player as to how much risk he appropriately should take in that round. If one divides a player's current chip stack by the cost in chips of one round of play, the result is a player's so-called M-value. An M-value of four or less means the player is in trouble and will need to play aggressively with medium-strength hands, like ace-ten off suit. Stuart and I had quite generous M-values, mine being $122,500 / 4,200 = 29.1$, so I could still afford to fold marginal hands and wait for better cards or a better table situation. I was pretty relaxed at the start of day three, knowing that for the first several levels I could wait for opportunities. That low-activity behavior might then allow me to win a hand even with bad cards if I just looked out of character by making a big bet. I could win a hand uncontested at reduced risk.

We were getting ready to pay the bill, so I asked Susan what she planned to do this afternoon while Stuart and I were playing.

"You're both going to think I'm a nerd," she replied.

"I guess that rules out the local strip clubs," Stuart joked.

"Are you going to tell us?" I asked.

"I'm going to start by taking an Uber pretty far north on Las Vegas Boulevard, way up to 900 North, to the Las Vegas Natural History Museum."

"That should be great," I encouraged her. "As a biologist, I would love to see that sometime."

"I'm a little tired of casinos," she confessed. "And please remember that I had already planned to be back home by now. But the museum sounds interesting. On the way back, I hope to stop at the famous big pawnshop in town. They have lots of weird things in there. When I return here by about five o'clock, I'll send you guys texts so I can stop by your tables and see if you are still surviving. I guess the real exciting time of hitting the pay line will be some time after five."

We bid Susan goodbye as she started out on her adventure. Stuart wanted to play cash for an hour before sitting in the day-three play at noon. Since the restaurant wasn't busy, I decided just to keep my seat while I looked at WSOP.com to check out the details of my next opponents at my table in the Brasilia room.

I would have seat four, with favorable table visibility, so I was happy about that. It was worrisome that in both seats five and seven there were fellows with substantial chip stacks of more than 145,000. But since I already knew that I could afford to fold many hands, I thought I could stay out of trouble from them. The biggest stack at the table was in seat two where a guy named Andrew from Indiana would start the day with 248,000 chips. The Hendon Mob database listed him as having already won hundreds of thousands of dollars in tournaments. And the photo of him on that website showed him to be a lean, good-looking, and very serious guy. I didn't want to tangle with him unless I was sure I had the better hand. At least he was on my right side. So I actually was pretty confident that I might survive to make the money if I played carefully.

After resting upstairs a few minutes, I went to Brasilia and found my table. Cards were in play right at noon. I was excited and pretty confident that I could do this. I was prepared to allow my chip stack to dwindle a bit so long as I had a reasonable number of chips remaining when we hit the pay line that evening. The large TV screens around the room helped me keep track of the number of remaining players, each elimination bringing me closer to my goal. I actually had some good cards and played some hands aggressively against players who had smaller chip stacks. But I folded fairly early in hands when the bigger stacks were playing.

The young man two seats to my left, maybe thirty years old, looked very nervous. He started the afternoon with 47,300 chips. He folded many hands, and after every fold, which was about every two minutes, he stood up and walked away from the table for a minute. He just could not sit still. I was happy just to take quiet breaths and relax, but he was like a jack-in-the-box. I guessed that it was his technique for dealing with stress. And with fewer than fifty thousand chips, he was right to be somewhat nervous.

At two o'clock, it was time for our first twenty-minute break. My chips had climbed to 146,200, and I was a little astonished at my good fortune. Of the 1,796 who started at noon, only 1,512 remained. I was anxious for another 512 players to be eliminated to reach the pay line of one thousand.

The next two levels were also favorable for me. I stayed away from confrontations with the big stacks, but I tangled with smaller stacks using semibluffs several times to scare them out of a pot that they might have won. My chip stack climbed to 222,500 at the end of three levels of play, which was the start of our ninety-minute dinner break. There were only 1,060 players remaining, and I was exultant and now nearly certain that I would win a minimum prize. Susan had texted me sometime before, and she walked around and found me. As players were eliminated, I had been moved to a table in the Amazon room, so we walked out together to get a sandwich. She was so happy for me. There was almost no way that I could screw this up now. Although the hour was late, I had a strong cup of coffee to help me through the remaining four hours of play.

After dinner, Susan went upstairs to rest and await developments. I sent an email to alert my family of the situation. They had fingers crossed.

Then came the period of hands when we intermittently waited five minutes as the floor managers kept careful count of the remaining players. There were 1,010 remaining players. Then 1,007. Then 1,003. Finally we reached the so-called bubble. There were exactly 1,001 players remaining, and the next player to be eliminated would be the unfortunate "bubble boy." Normally, he won no money, but at this point, the management announced that the bubble boy would be given a free entry ticket worth $10,000 for this same tournament next year. That was nice. So we played hand-for-hand; each table completed one hand and then waited for all the other tables to finish one hand as well. This method prevented a player with only a few remaining chips from just stalling to allow some other player to be eliminated first.

A bright young man at my table was all smiles even though he had only 2,500 chips remaining. Hope springs eternal. We were playing a level in which each hand required an ante of five hundred. Fortunately for this hopeful player, he was not due soon to submit a blind, but he could only play five more hands—five more antes—and then he would be eliminated. Playing hand-for-hand, he first paid one ante then folded. And the next hand, he paid another ante and then folded. Then he paid a third and a fourth ante, folding each time. Magically, the bubble burst on that hand. The young player, all smiles, sat triumphantly holding up his single remaining five-hundred-value chip. Several of us took his photo. Astonishingly, he had survived by the slimmest of margins and would claim a $15,000 prize. The dealer reached under his chair to bring out a bag with nine lucky baseball hats, each decorated by a four-leaf clover, and every remaining player received a little remembrance of the moment to take home.

After the bubble burst, players were aggressive with their small stacks, so eliminations occurred at a brisk pace. Although that sort of postbubble aggression had been my intent earlier in the day, I felt that I had a large enough chip stack to be more selective. I was not just going to throw away my chips in desperate efforts. When play ended and I bagged my chips, I had 214,500, and there were 661 players still in contention. I had somewhat below-average chips, but this was not worrisome. We had dropped from one thousand players to only 661 players in a relative flash, and that was very good news for me. As players were eliminated, the prize value for each place climbed.

At 1:05 a.m., I sent Susan a gleeful text. Susan responded from her bed, I presume: "Congrats. Get some sleep. Zzzzz. Breakfast at 10:00."

Stuart had cashed and had 195,000 chips. So there was good news on all fronts.

I sent a short email to my sleeping family members, who would see it in the morning. And I phoned Southwest to move my morning flight back another twenty-four hours. I would have to speak with my boss in the morning. I almost had to pinch myself to believe that this was happening.

Day Four, World Series of Poker Main Event
Start-of-day chips: 214,500

I woke up spontaneously at eight forty-five and shut off the alarm, which was about to go off. The shower was delightfully warm, and I wondered how many people in the USA reflected on what a luxury it is to step behind a curtain and just turn a knob to get hot water. I had at least fifteen important work emails, but most only required three-sentence responses. I sent an email to my boss explaining that I needed to stay in Vegas another day and fly back tomorrow, and not to worry: I'm not sick. But I thought it best not to tell him that I was in a big poker tournament. He would know that I had a good reason to stay, and that was enough. My parents and brother had seen my late-night email even before I had awakened, and they wished me good luck. They had found my name on WSOP.com in the list of survivors and saw that I was ranked 372 out of the remaining 661 players, with a chip stack substantially below the average of 291,376. And they noted that the next prizes would be about $17,000 per player, so they hoped I could survive even longer.

It was only nine thirty, so I had time to study my competitors at table 367 in the Amazon room, where I would have seat seven. I made a list of the players, assigned seats, and approximate chip counts to keep in my shirt pocket. I could quickly check online the poker earnings history of each player, which gave me an indication of their experience.

Seat	Player	Chips in Thousands	Comments
1	George W.	167	
2	Adam F.	536	Experienced
3	Tim S.	251	
4	John M.	305	Very experienced
5	Stephen N.	101	
6	Hans H.	298	Very experienced
7	Me	214	
8	Albert M.	173	Amateur
9	Daniel F.	498	Experienced

These would be my critical opponents today, and to win a substantial prize, I would have to beat most of them. I felt fortunate to have a man with fewer chips on my left, and his online record seemed to show little poker experience. That positioning was fortunate for me. But just one more seat to my left was an apparently experienced player with a lot of chips. He would cramp my activities, most likely. Caution was called for. The players in seats two, four, and six also looked pretty tough. So what should be my strategy?

I next made a list of the upcoming step-ups in prize money as shown on WSOP.com. Players eliminated in places 648 to 550 would all get the same prize of $17,282, and I was pretty confident that I could fold for an hour and make it into that group. Players eliminated in places 549–478 would get $19,500. Players eliminated in places 477–415 would get $21,786. With those three payout ranges in mind, I decided that I would fold almost every hand in the first two hours, which would allow me to observe the playing style of my tablemates and likely let me fold my way into the $19,500 payout group. That was pretty good money. Then I might get more aggressive in the next two-hour level, taking the risk of getting knocked out. Even if that happened, I could cheerfully fly home tomorrow. Seemed sensible.

It was nine fifty, so I shut down my laptop and headed downstairs to meet Susan.

Susan walked toward me as she saw me approaching her. She put her arms around me and kissed me on the cheek. "Congratulations! I know how much it means to you to cash in this tournament. It's a big deal."

During breakfast, Susan wished me luck with my strategy for very conservative play this afternoon and assured me that she was arranging to stay in Vegas a little longer. "I want to celebrate with you after you get knocked out, because I'm sure it'll be a bittersweet moment for you. You want to finish higher,

I know. But you can be really proud if you can have fun playing poker and then fly out of Las Vegas with a check in your pocket for about $20,000. Not many people can do that."

I was at my seat ten minutes early. I texted Stuart good luck, and he responded that he also was already in his seat.

The young man to my left looked pretty nervous, but all the other players seemed stoic—good poker faces. I had to be careful of nervous Albert. He had 173,000 chips, so if I made a three–big blind bet of fifteen thousand, he might go all in, causing me likely to fold and lose my precious chips. So the conservative play of folding every hand right now seemed best.

I watched and waited. After forty minutes, George in seat one got involved in a big hand, and soon all of his chips were in the pot against two other players. George was eliminated in place 609, and within minutes, the floor manager brought a different player to sit in that seat. That player had only about sixty thousand chips, so that seemed to be a potential future opportunity for me.

With blinds of twenty-five hundred and five thousand and ante five hundred, each round was costly, and my chips were dwindling. I nearly always had poor hole cards, so it was not very difficult to maintain discipline and just fold them. After a few more minutes, nervous Albert next to me got into a big hand and was eliminated in place 583, so he would get a check for $17,282. For the moment, that seat remained unfilled. I continued to wait out the group. I would let more people get knocked out. At the end of the level, after two hours of play, we were ready for our first twenty-minute break. The big TV screen near us reported that 531 players remained, so elimination now would earn a prize of $19,500. The relentless blinds and antes had lowered my stack from about 214,000 to 160,000, but I thought I could still wait about thirty more minutes of play before gambling more.

The second level of the afternoon, level seventeen, with

blinds of three thousand and six thousand and ante one thousand, started with me getting pretty favorable hole cards of pocket tens. I had to play those. I entered a moderately expensive pot, and I hit my set of tens. I couldn't believe that I was so lucky. The board had both straight and flush possibilities, so I thought I had better bet. I made a moderate bet on the flop, and my opponent folded, but I went ahead and turned over my pocket tens to show the table that I had hit my set. "Good hand," several voices volunteered. They actually didn't need much convincing that I had good cards because they had seen me fold every hand during the two hours of the first level. As I picked up on their view of me as being a very tight player, I was struck with the urge to bluff preflop with very little but fold if raised.

Two hands later, I was in late position with hole cards ace-deuce unsuited. Players folded to Hans on my right, who made a three–big blind raise. Although my ace-deuce was extremely weak, only the blinds were left to bet behind me. So I sat up straight in my chair, tried to look a little excited, and raised to six big blinds. The players to my left folded, and the decision came back to Hans, who I knew from my morning homework was a very experienced player. I hoped that he would be experienced enough to clearly recognize this interruption in my usual style of play. He seemed unhappy, and after ten seconds, he folded, giving me a nice pot. My chips were back up to about 210,000.

As I was raking in my new chips, a manager brought a new player to sit in the empty seat on my left. The player was young but quite well groomed in a suit with necktie. He had about three hundred thousand chips, so caution lights were flashing in my mind. After a few minutes, a film crew came with their big camera and stood a few steps toward my right as they took video of the mysterious new player, so I knew he was someone special. I was certain that I was in the video, since I was sitting immediately next to the player. The reporter asked the stranger how he was feeling and if he had been lucky. "I'm hoping for the best," he responded with a smile. He seemed to be a pleasant fellow.

The camera people departed, so I turned to the new player. "I'm Jim, from Connecticut."

"I'm Max."

"You look sharp in the suit."

"I wear it because it helps me play better. When I get dressed up, I feel like I'm trying to do something important. It helps my game."

"Makes sense. I want to look up who you are. What's your last name?"

"Steinberg."

"Thanks. I'm Jim Miller. I've had poor cards today, but things have been a little better in the last few minutes. I'm being very patient."

"Good strategy."

A few minutes later, I was in the big blind holding seven of clubs, eight of clubs. I thought I might try to play these suited connectors, although I would be out of position. Stuart might not approve, but I was prepared just to fold if the pot got too expensive. My new neighbor, Max, was the first to bet, and he raised to two and a half big blinds. The other players folded in turn to me. I sat for a few seconds and did nothing, then raised to five big blinds. Max looked at me, then back at his cards. He was thinking. After thirty seconds, he shook his head and tossed away his cards. I was extremely fortunate to have successfully made that raise to win the pot. My chips were now up to 254,000. I continued to take some chances with two or three hands during the next forty-five minutes, and my stack rose to 308,000. This was going much better than I had expected. I looked up at the large TV screen nearby and saw that only 477 players remained. My guaranteed prize was now $21,786. The next payout jump occurred at elimination 414, and I was pretty sure that I could survive until that payout increase.

During the next hour, I folded most hands, pacing myself, but I got lucky and hit a set of sixes. My stack rose to 330,000 with 441 players remaining. We took our second break of the afternoon, with four hours of play completed.

I sent some texts. Stuart was still in the game. Susan was excited that I had achieved my $21,000 prize target. She said, "Keep going." I decided that for the next two hours, level eighteen, I would gamble more and see if I could get lucky. I had won money, so why not try to hit a big hand?

Level eighteen had blinds of four thousand and eight thousand with an ante of one thousand. I played several hands with pocket pairs, hoping to hit another set, but my expensive investments didn't pay off. My chips were dwindling again. Adam, who had started in seat two today with 536,000 chips, got involved in a huge hand and lost all of his chips. I was astonished. At noon, I had been envious of his large stack of chips, but now he was caput. He finished in place 387, and his prize was $24,622. As the level ended and we prepared for the ninety-minute dinner break, I had 270,000 chips; 360 players remained.

Susan and I rendezvoused for quick sandwiches, but Stuart offered his best wishes as he walked past us headed to a Mexican restaurant. I took a thirty-minute rest in the room. As I walked back to my table, I knew that something good had to happen soon, or I would be gone that night. I only had about half the average chip stack at that time. But I would have twenty-nine big blinds to start level nineteen, which had blinds of five thousand and ten thousand with an ante of one thousand. The next payout jump was at elimination 351, just nine eliminations away. So I decided to lie low to make that increased prize, which was $29,329, and then I would increase the risks I was willing to take.

My family had figured out how to follow some real-time graphics on WSOP.com. Chip counts were updated for all players every few minutes. It was very late for them, but they would be able to watch the roller-coaster rise and fall of my chips during this next level. And, I strongly suspected, they would see the graphic as I crashed to earth. But I would have a nice prize.

Not long after we resumed play, the man in seat four, John, was eliminated at place 325. Mentally, I rolled up my sleeves. I had 250,000 chips, and since the big blind was twelve thousand, I had twenty big blinds. It was time to live or die.

My quiet table image helped me. I made two big bluffs, and that boosted my chips to 320,000. Then in short order, I played pocket pairs twice and hit two sets, an amazing run. My stack rose to 420,000, which was still somewhat below average but was a huge improvement in my status. I wondered if I should slow down again. Certainly I should rest a little bit. Be selective. I now had thirty-seven big blinds, a very comfortable stack. I was astonished at my success.

At about nine o'clock that night, I was in the big blind and was dealt nine of diamonds, ten of diamonds. I was determined to see what I could make of these cards. In the first round of betting, the strong player in seat nine, Daniel, was in early position and made a three–big blind bet. The player on the button called, and I made a speculative call. The flop was great for me, showing deuce of spades, nine of hearts, nine of spades. Hitting trips on a flop occurs only about 2 percent of the time. I was the first to bet on this round, and I disguised the strength of my hand by checking. The player to my left also checked. But the man on the button made a moderately large bet. I was thrilled that he was betting, but I concealed my excitement, and after a short pause, I just called. Surprisingly, the man to my left then executed a check-raise, making a substantial bet of about half of his chips. I suspected that he had a good pocket pair, such as two queens, and this was a wonderful development for me, since for the moment my trips had him beat. The man on the button folded. I hesitated a bit and then just called that large bet, using about three-quarters of my remaining chips. The pile of chips in the center was massive.

The dealer set down the next card (the fourth card on the board), the jack of hearts. If my opponent had pocket jacks, I was now heavily favored to lose, since only making quad nines could save me. But he might still be holding aces, kings, or queens. I paused, took a breath, and stared at my hole cards, waving them slightly, and I did *not* look back at the shared cards.

"I have a pretty good hand here, and I'm not sure that I can lay this down," I said, and I looked intently at my hole cards. I was implying that I likely held two excellent hole cards but had not connected with the board.

"Then play your hand," Daniel replied curtly.

After another brief pause, I went all in, which would require him either to call with about half of his remaining chips or else give up the substantial number of chips in the pot. He squirmed a little while thinking.

"Can you beat kings?" he asked. "Have a flush draw?"

I remained silent and looked down at my shoes. After thirty seconds, he pushed his chips into the pot, and we both turned over our pocket cards. He did have the pair of kings, while I had trip nines. Only the very unlikely appearance of a king as the last card (river card) could save him, but that card was the two of diamonds. I had more than doubled my chip stack to about 950,000.

Very relieved but ecstatic, I was amused that friends or family watching the near-real-time chip counts online might think that there was a bug in the system. In only an hour, I had increased my chips from 250,000 to 950,000. I stepped away from the table to send them a brief text to confirm what their eyes might be seeing: "Won several huge hands. Went from 250,000 chips to 950,000 chips."

It had been a draining session of poker, and I was tired. I was content to slow down. A player in seat three, Tim, who had started with me at noon, was knocked out in place 263, earning him $34,157. Then near the close of the evening, poor Daniel in seat nine, who had run into my trip nines, was eliminated in place 238, for which the prize was also $34,157. Shortly thereafter, the 237 survivors of day four bagged their chips. My 936,000 chips were slightly above the group average of 812,658, and I ranked in seventy-eighth place in the tournament for the moment. When I considered that 6,420 players had started, it was an arresting realization. I exchanged texts with Stuart, who had eight hundred thousand chips and was already riding up the elevator, and Susan, who told me to knock on her door when I came upstairs.

Her door opened a crack, and I identified myself. She closed the door, unchained the lock, and opened the door wide. She jumped out at me and put both arms around my neck. "I can't believe it. You should be so proud." She smiled. "This outcome is so wonderful that I'm running around the hallway in my pajamas!"

"Just don't let the door close behind you," I joked. We kissed. "Now go back to sleep, and we can talk at ten in the morning. I'm absolutely exhausted."

"I'll bet you are tired." She grew silent as she took a step backward into her room. "You go to bed. I'm going to say a special little prayer now."

"A prayer?"

"I'm not sure. But I think this really is a miracle."

"I'm going to say a prayer too. But it will be short because I'm going right to sleep. We can decide at breakfast if this is really a miracle."

"Good night."

"Good night, sweetheart."

I made my call to Southwest airlines to delay my return flight reservation, said a short prayer, and was in bed almost immediately. I knew I had to rest, and I actually went right to sleep.

Licking Wounds and Taking Stock

Stuart knew that Susan and I would likely be at the breakfast place at ten o'clock, so he ran into us as we were joining the line for a table. Stuart and I joyfully shook hands. We were both so happy to be playing in day five.

The crowd for breakfast was smaller than past mornings, likely because so many players were at the airport on their way home, so we were quickly seated. Stuart was working his phone.

"So we're at different tables again today," Stuart noted. "Just as well since I would hate to take all of your chips."

I smiled, but I was quite relieved that we were at different tables. Confrontations between us would have been awkward.

I had lost two big hands during the day, so I went over those with Stuart. He pointed out that my bet sizing was way off, and at one point I should have closed out the bidding by just calling. So, I certainly was trying to learn from my mistakes. I would try not to make those mistakes again today.

Stuart confessed that he lost a big hand by slow-playing kings. He probably would have had a million chips now if he had just played those kings more aggressively. I certainly wasn't going to criticize him. It can really pay big to slow-play a major pair. But it also can come back to bite you.

Stuart started looking at the WSOP website again. "Adam Churchill leads the pack, with about three million chips, followed by Sammy Darwin. He has 2.8 million. By the way, I saw Sammy at the restaurant last night, and he seemed not to be feeling well. Hope he's better today."

"Pretty sad if you get sick during a big tournament. Do you see Negreanu's chip count?" I asked.

"Yep. He has 1,335,000. He's going to do well in this tournament."

"We'll catch up to him, I'm sure," I added, smiling.

"The Russians and Chinese are doing well too," Stuart

added. "Vladimir Komarov is in third place with 2.7 million, and Hsi Tseng Lee is in fourth place with 2.5 million."

"That's well and good, but with 936,000 chips, how should I play at the start today?"

"Level twenty-one will have blinds of eight thousand and sixteen thousand with a two thousand ante. So you have fifty-eight big blinds," Stuart pointed out. "I know you like to play pots, but you did so well restoring your stack during day four that you certainly don't want to throw chips away in a few hands this afternoon. I think you should fold a lot during the first hour or two and just see how things go. I only have 810,000, so that's what I'm going to do."

"Stuart, you have average chips. The average is 812,658. So we're both fine. At least for the first hour."

We spent the next few minutes analyzing the competitors at our tables. I didn't recognize most of the names, but based on the earnings history, my opponents were going to be pretty tough. Folding most of my hands in the first hour sounded better to me.

Susan was off on another bus tour today, so she bid us farewell with the promise to watch for texts. She would see us later. Stuart and I retired to our rooms for a brief rest before starting play.

Day Five, World Series of Poker Main Event
Start-of-day chips: 936,000

I was at my seat in the Amazon room ten minutes early as usual. I had seat eight. All of the men at my table were strangers. They sat pensively fingering their chips. The biggest stacks were in seats four and five, which was fine with me. On my left sat an older gentleman who had about the same-sized stack as mine. Then came the call: "Shuffle up and deal."

Fold, fold, fold. I had bad hole cards anyway. So the folding caused me little pain.

I saw the famous TV poker broadcaster, Norman Chad, sitting twenty yards away at an empty table making notes on papers. I decided to miss a few hands, and I walked up to him and said hello. I remarked that I enjoyed his broadcasts. He was friendly and was surprisingly much taller than I had expected. And he was smart and not goofy at all. His naïve and offbeat persona for the broadcasts was clearly an act, and an entertaining one. I gave him my business card and told him that I was a physician back in Connecticut. He asked how my family was enjoying Las Vegas, and he was quite surprised that I had come by myself for this tournament. I asked him to please briefly mention my name and to give my best to my family. "I'm playing in day five, and I'm not sure how much longer I will last."

I scurried back to my table having missed only a few hands.

Thirty minutes into the level, there was some loud talking on the far side of the room. Then more loud talking. Then an announcement, "Stop the clock. Stop the clock." This was decidedly unusual. The many TV screens in the room showed the clock frozen. A small crowd had gathered where the loud talking had occurred. Then I heard the words make their way through the crowd, table to table. The message spread across the room like a wave. "Heart attack." "Ambulance."

Of course, as a physician, I wondered if I should try to do something. So I rose from my seat and strode quickly between the tables toward the commotion. At the outer edge of the crowd, I gently pushed between two people. "Excuse me, I'm a doctor. Perhaps I can help." As I took more steps forward, I repeated that a couple of times until I was close enough to see what was happening.

A gray-haired man was sitting on the floor, gasping for breath, one hand to his chest. He was alert and breathing, so I just stood where I was for a moment since a clean-cut young man, also a player, I suspected, was kneeling next to the distressed man. The young man was taking the pulse by the carotid artery. Since the event had been ongoing for about ten minutes already, I was not surprised to see a uniformed security guard push through the other side of the crowd with a small cart having several plastic boxes and a green oxygen cylinder. The security guard, who clearly had practiced this before, put the plastic oxygen mask on the elderly man, turned the nozzle on the green tank, put his hand near the mask to confirm the flow of gas, and told the young kneeling man that an ambulance would be there with a stretcher in less than five minutes. The young guard, needing no direction, then handed the kneeling man a blood pressure cuff. The cuff was quickly placed on an upper arm. "One hundred ninety over one hundred fifteen," the young man announced. "Just relax, sir. Your heart is strong and generating a very good pressure, too high just for now, of course. And your pulse of 115 is a little fast, so please just try to relax a minute."

"Can't ... catch ... my ... breath," the old man replied.

"Chest pain?"

"Only some," the man gasped. "Moderate. But I ... can't ... breathe."

The man was distressed, but it appeared that he would be fine for a few more minutes until the ambulance arrived. I just stood where I was, acting as a sort of backup. If the old man arrested and needed CPR, then I could certainly help with that.

Another minute passed, and the man looked a little more comfortable. The oxygen was probably helping. The young man inflated the cuff again. He was speaking to the guard, but I was listening carefully. "One hundred eighty over one hundred ten, pulse 110," he reported. The numbers were a little better. But I had fingers crossed that the ambulance guys would show up shortly.

"Ever had a heart attack? Heart disease?"

"No."

Allergic to anything?"

"No."

"Take medicines for anything?"

"Three different pills for … high blood pressure. And a … cholesterol pill at night."

"Do you know the names of your pills?"

"Cholesterol pill's in my room. Always leave … my pills in my room. But almost forgot my pressure pills … this morning. So I brought them in my pocket. Took them with … coffee here at the table … a few minutes ago." The patient reached into his jacket pocket and handed three small plastic bottles to the young man, who took a quick look and put them in his shirt pocket.

I thought about suggesting an aspirin tablet for anticoagulation, but just then two EMS technicians showed up with a stretcher. They worked efficiently to put the man on the stretcher with his back tilted up at forty-five degrees, they switched his oxygen supply to their tank, and they established an IV in his left arm within thirty seconds. The young man walked alongside the stretcher and was relaying the information he had obtained to the technicians. I saw him hand the three medication bottles to the taller technician. Then they were quickly out the door of the ballroom and out of sight. I walked slowly back to my chair. Less than fifteen minutes had passed.

"Too bad," I said to the man on my right. "He's probably having a heart attack."

"Start the clock," came the announcement. "Shuffle and deal." Cards were quickly in the air again. I smiled as I remembered some paragraphs from Doyle Brunson's autobiography. When he was a young player in Texas and poker was illegal, Brunson had many adventures in backroom private games. One time a player suddenly became ill, and within a minute he had dropped dead on the floor. Two customers took his body out to the street, and within five minutes, the poker game continued. "If there's nothin' you can do about it, don't worry about it."

We continued with several more hands, which I folded, but I began to hear more words crossing from table to table like a wave. "Adam Churchill. Heart attack."

I sat bolt upright in my chair. Adam Churchill? He was the chip leader of the tournament! I didn't know the man, so I hadn't recognized him. I stood and walked briskly to where Churchill had been seated. Yes, there were eight players at the table and one empty seat, and there was a huge pile of chips stacked in front of the empty seat. Adam Churchill! I knew that his chest pain would be worse if he could see that every two minutes he was losing another ante, and he was giving away a small blind and big blind every round. He was absent, so he would forfeit chips. I had seen this sort of chip loss at the start of play when someone had over-slept and was a few minutes late arriving. But I had never seen this situation in the setting of a serious illness. I returned to my seat.

I looked at my next hole cards: two of hearts, three of clubs. When the action was on me, I mucked my hand. Another wasted hand. Another wasted ante. But worse things could happen. That had just been reinforced for me quite dramatically.

During the first hour of play, I lost one small hand and won one big pot in another hand. My chips were up to 1,015,000, but an hour later at the time of the first break, I had bled down to 910,000.

I decided that I only needed to win a hand once in a while. During the next level, I won a big hand with four of hearts, six of hearts using a big bluff. I was over a million chips again.

During the third level, I won three big hands using bluffs. I had 1.6 million chips. But that gradually dwindled to 1.2 million when I became inactive again. A few minutes later, I was quite excited to be dealt pocket kings and was heads up in position against one player. An ace came on the flop, and the opponent made a big bet, so I had to fold. Very sad.

But luck can work in both directions. I was dealt ace-king unsuited in the small blind. Everyone folded to me, and I made a minimum raise. The remaining player in the big blind raised to 160,000. I called, and the flop came king, king, three in three different suits. After thinking for a minute, I checked. My opponent made a big bet. I pondered the situation for two minutes and then just called his bet. After a six of spades came on the turn, putting two spades on the board, I checked. He bet big, and after a pause, I called. The river was a deuce of spades, not a great card for me since a flush would beat me, but I bet big and tried to breathe normally. He folded. I then had 1.5 million chips and was headed out to dinner break.

Susan and I met for a snack, and we were both ecstatic that I had lasted this long. I rested in my room for a few minutes, and then play resumed.

Odd whisperings were passing from table to table after we returned from break. Another player had suffered chest pain during dinner in a restaurant yesterday evening. He had been taken to a hospital. I realized they might be talking about Sammy Darwin in light of what Stuart had told me. There is stress in these tournaments, but I had never heard of two medical emergencies in a poker tournament within twenty-four hours. Then the real shocker. As more gossip reached my table, I learned that the ill person hospitalized was Sammy Darwin. A chill went up my spine. At breakfast time, he was in the database as the second highest stack in the tournament. What a coincidence that the number one and two players were both disabled. It seemed to be too improbable to have occurred without cause, but what could this mean?

As I was still processing this odd situation, the announcement came that we were now down to just one hundred surviving players. But I thought to myself, *It's really only ninety-eight if two are sick.* The other exciting part was the pay jump at ninety-nine. Players ninety-nine to ninety-one would receive a prize of $55,649. We were really getting up there now.

During the next hour, I lost a hand and won two using bluffs. My stack had returned to 1.5 million chips. Gradually the number of players fell to eighty. The payout would now be $79,668. I made a big bluff with ten-six, and my chips rose to 1.8 million.

During the last hour of play, my chips dwindled again. I was tired and a little frustrated. You can't bluff too often, but I was not getting good cards. It was just about the last hand of the evening, and two players had made moderate bets. I had ace of diamonds, five of diamonds, and I moved all in with a few more than a million chips, a move I had not made before at the table the entire day. The other players could knock me out, but they would be crippled if they lost to me. After some reflection, both of my opponents folded, and I raked in enough chips so that I ended day five with 1.5 million chips to bag. I was grateful to have gotten this far even though the chip average was a substantial 2.79 million. But I was still alive and was among the sixty-nine surviving players out of 6,420 who had started. It was 1:10 a.m.

I texted Stuart and was happy to hear that he was also bagging about 1.5 million chips. I texted Susan that I was headed straight to bed but we could have breakfast at ten. She simply responded, "Okay. Zzzzzz."

I called Southwest to move back my departure, and I was asleep shortly thereafter.

The Mystery Deepens

Susan and Stuart sat with me during breakfast, our spirits high. Whichever player went out in sixty-ninth place would be compensated with a superb payout: $96,445. I had exceeded my wildest expectations for this tournament. But I knew that I was near the end of my rope. With only 1.5 million chips,

I was way below average, and I ranked fiftieth among the survivors. I would be out soon.

Stuart was also ecstatic, but he was more optimistic. At noon, we would start level twenty-six with blinds of twenty-five thousand and fifty thousand with an ante of five thousand. Stuart and I each had about thirty big blinds. "Plenty of room to maneuver," he assured me. I was struck by the fact that the amount of a single big blind was more than the total chips I had started with at the beginning of the tournament.

Federico B. (left) and the author. This skilled Italian player was seated on my left at the start of day six. He went on to survive as one of the final nine players. He is a wonderfully nice guy.

I was also worried by the competitors at our table. Interestingly, Stuart and I would be seated at the same table for the first time.

I would be in seat four, and on my left would be an experienced Italian player, Federico B., with 2.9 million chips. He could cause me a lot of trouble. Stuart would be in seat one, and he was extremely unfortunate to have the chip leader on his left; Hsi Tseng Li had 7.2 million chips and likely would try to strangle the table into submission. I expressed my concerns to Stuart.

He just smiled. "It'll be rough. But I'll try to be careful. We are both pretty short, so we have to play some hands."

"I know you're right, but the pay jumps are huge. If we could just make it to sixty-third place, the payout would be $113,000.

At fifty-fourth place, it rises to $137,000. That's big money just for lasting a few more hands. I think I'm going to fold a lot at the start."

"As you lose a few more chips by folding, it will be harder and harder for you to recover. But suit yourself."

"It's going to be weird. Churchill's empty chair will be at seat eight," I added.

"Free chips," Stuart counseled. "If we can win any pots."

"Too bad about Churchill," I mumbled.

"A little disturbing." Stuart nodded. "And don't forget that Darwin is sick too. I was one table away from him in the Mexican restaurant on the evening of day four when he got sick."

"What happened?" Susan asked.

"There was a small commotion when he called out to the waiter that he wasn't feeling well. I think he was with his wife. The manager called security. Within minutes, the ambulance guys came and took him away, and his wife went with him."

"So he was alert and talking?" I asked.

"Yes, but I could see that he was in pain and breathing hard. He looked pretty sick, so I'm glad the emergency crew came pretty fast. I heard them say that his blood pressure was high and that his finger-stick blood glucose also was high, but I couldn't hear much else."

"Wow. Two top players are sick," I mumbled.

"When I was playing yesterday afternoon, my buddy Tommy, a floor manager, pointed out to me a detective that came to snoop around a little to ask some questions," Stuart added. "But see over there, at the third table by the wall? Those are the same police guys right there, having breakfast."

I glanced over and noted that one young policeman was uniformed, and he sat with a middle-aged, serious-looking man who wore a jacket and necktie, probably a detective. My mind was troubled. It seemed very odd that the two top players had both gotten ill within a few hours. Quite a coincidence. But it could happen.

"I think I want to talk to them," I started.

"What?" Susan was rather taken aback.

"I was a witness when Churchill got sick, and I might have something to contribute."

"Well, if they make you do paperwork or something, you might miss the start of play," cautioned Stuart.

"That's not likely, I think," I opined. "They seem to be finished eating. I'm going to say hello to them right now." And with that, I excused myself as my colleagues sat in quiet consternation. But I felt I should say something. As I walked, I carefully extracted my wallet, which was still in the pocket with my loose hundred-dollar bills.

"Hi," I began as I walked up to their table. "I was a witness when Adam Churchill got sick yesterday. Can I talk to you for a minute?"

They both looked up at me and made no immediate response.

I held out my driver's license and my wallet medical license card and sat the two items in front of the detective. "I'm a poker player and a doctor from Connecticut. Do I need to fill out a form? I want to tell you a couple of things."

The older man said, "Well, thanks. We're just finishing our coffee. Please sit with us for a minute, and we can take your statement."

I sat down and related exactly what I had seen, which only took two minutes. The detective, Ralph Vuolo, slid his business card across the table to me.

They nodded as I spoke but wrote nothing down. Then the detective looked at my medical license card more closely, took out his pad, and wrote down my name and medical license number.

"And as I conclude, I want to speculate briefly. Just to give you a couple of thoughts. Just want to be helpful."

"Hmm," remarked the detective. As I started my next sentences, I saw him look at my driver's license again, and he wrote down my home address.

"Sorry to take your time, but I have some ideas. I suppose you know that those were very important players who were doing very well in the tournament. So it seems like quite a co-incidence that they would both get ill."

"A little odd," the detective commented. He was poker-faced. I wondered if he played.

"The man I saw get sick said he had just taken pills out of those three bottles that he had in his pocket. Did someone look carefully at those pills?"

"We can't comment on any information that we have," the young policeman chimed in. "I'm sure you understand."

The detective smiled. "We can't say much. But a tox screen for poisons is pending. Let me assure you, Doctor, since you have been so kind to come forward, that we did have the pharmacist at the hospital examine the pills, and they had the correct markings and colors. They were the correct prescribed pills. So don't worry about that, thank you."

"Thanks, but let me mention something. You might not have thought of it," I added. "A patient needs to take blood pressure medication every day, or his pressure will gradually rise over a couple of days. This man had serious high blood pressure issues in the past because he was prescribed three medications. If he missed his medications for a few days, his pressure likely would rise a lot, and recall that his pressure was 190/115 when first measured. Maybe he actually had missed his medications for a few days."

"Thanks, but he was taking his pills," the young policeman replied.

"But here is my thought," I said quickly. "You should have a lab examine the chemical composition of the three medications in those bottles. The pills may have had the correct markings, but perhaps they had been treated by heat or some other means to deactivate the medications. Or maybe the authentic pills had been substituted with dummy pills that just looked authentic. You should check for the actual chemical activity of those pills. That could easily be done by the manufacturers within a few days. I work for a pharmaceutical company, and we have assays that can quickly and accurately measure attributes of all the medications that we make."

Neither man replied, but they seemed to be thinking.

"And a tox screen will not detect a poison if a person was actually poisoned by eliminating a needed drug from his system. That would be, in effect, an undetectable poison—unless an investigator was very alert to check for what is missing."

"I see," was the detective's only response.

"The last thing I want to mention is that a Chinese player, Hsi Tseng Lee, is staying at this hotel accompanied by an unusually large number of Chinese assistants. I don't want to make any unsubstantiated allegations. But the Chinese seem to have a lot of manpower here, and my colleagues and I had noticed this the other day. It might be worth looking into what all those assistants have been doing during their stay."

The policemen said nothing, and I stood up. I felt I was finished. The detective handed me back my licenses and thanked me, and I returned to my table. I wasn't sure if they would take any note of what I had said. But I had given them my thoughts, and my conscience was clear. The coincidence of two top players getting ill was just too striking for me to accept as being due to chance alone.

"Well?" Susan remarked, expecting a recap.

"I told 'em what I saw and what I thought. Pretty quick. They took my name."

"Feel better? You are so responsible," she declared.

"At least now they have the information."

We were finishing our coffee. "I'm going to hang around the

tables today. There's big money at stake, and I want to see what happens," Susan volunteered.

"As you heard, Stuart and I are at the same table, so watching should be easy for you. And we have the tough Chinese guy with us. It might be a sad show today," I warned. "I'm going to stop upstairs for a few minutes, so I'll see you both in the Amazon room. Table 378."

"See you there."

Day Six, World Series of Poker Main Event
Start-of-day chips: 1,500,000

After twenty minutes of rest, I headed back downstairs. As I got closer to the Amazon room, I noticed that the hallway ahead was filled with people with cameras, some taking video. Much more media than prior days.

As I walked by one reporter, he looked at me. "Are you a player? What's your name?"

"I'm ranked fiftieth today, but I'll do my best."

"Name?"

"James Miller from Connecticut." The big camera with lights was in my face now. "Let me say hi to my family and friends. This is lots of fun." Then I kept walking. Not much of a message, but I guess it was what he wanted.

The managers had just opened the doors to the Amazon room, and I showed a security man there my ID because he was stopping people saying, "Players only at this time, please." I walked forward and quickly found my seat, and I was the first to arrive at my table. It was a good thing that I arrived early because at each seat there was a form and pen. The management wanted each player to give more information about themselves on this one page so that broadcasters would have a little more to say as they were reporting the action. I finished the form in five minutes, and just then Stuart and some others showed up to take their seats.

Norman Chad, the broadcaster, happened to be walking by, and I caught his eye with a wave. He stopped, smiled, and seemed rather surprised. "You're still playing. That's great." He walked past me, but a minute later, he returned and bent down next to me to ask a few questions about how long I had played poker, my favorite strategies, where I usually played, and so on. Then he briskly walked away as he wished me good luck. I was excited because I was pretty sure that I would get a brief mention on the tape, and my family would get a kick out of that when it appeared on TV in a few weeks.

The sixty-nine players were distributed to eight tables. One table was special, the high-tech TV table that was set in a small arena and had many large cameras around it for filming. The table had small seat cameras at felt level to be able to show each player's hole cards. There was an electronic detection system also, which could tell what hole cards a player held even when facedown. That technology worried me just a little bit, as there was at least the potential for misuse of important information. But it made the broadcast interesting to viewers. So the seat cameras, an older technology, were mostly for backup in case the electronic chip in a card could not be read by the detector under the felt. I was relieved that the computer had not assigned me to the TV table.

Two other tables did not have the special seat cameras but did have chip detectors to read hole cards, and they had extra lighting so that cameramen with large portable cameras could do some filming. I had been randomly assigned to one of the several ordinary tables with no special provisions for cameras.

As time for start of play neared, the security team allowed spectators into the room, and Susan arrived as promised. Unless I had a really big hand, I planned to fold a lot in the first hour, so she wouldn't have much to watch if she was focused on me.

I started in the big blind, so my little stack was down the five thousand ante and fifty thousand blind immediately, a modestly painful hit. Cards were dealt, and a player a few seats to my left made a small raise. Several players folded, then Stuart reraised. I looked at him carefully, but he just looked down at the table. Seconds went by. The Chinese expert on Stuart's left seemed to be deep in thought. After a few more seconds, he announced, "All in." Of course, his bet was more than seven million chips. Players to his left quickly folded, as did I. The player to my left who had opened also quickly folded. Stuart looked sick, but I knew he was trying not to show it. He had put 250,000 chips out for his reraise, and he would just have to forfeit those unless he put all the rest of his chips into the middle. After a few more seconds, Stuart mucked his cards. He had just given away one-sixth of his chips. I could see who was going to try to take control of this table. That is the power of an overwhelmingly big stack.

I looked forlornly at the pile of chips in front of Churchill's empty seat. During the many hours of play yesterday, his substantial pile had declined markedly, and it would gradually decrease today as well. I wasn't sure how long it would be until his last chip disappeared. I had no idea how he was doing in the hospital, and I had no authority even to request that information. I continued to suspect that he was the victim of some kind of plot. But I had no proof. It was not that I was rooting for his poker success. I would have gladly swindled him out of his chips with a big bluff. But I am an advocate of fair play. He should not be swindled out of his chips by being poisoned.

Another hour passed, and I had not played a single hand. But players were being eliminated, and my potential prize was increasing. There were forty-eight players remaining, so an elimination now would win $137,000. Stuart had also been sitting quietly, and his chip stack was slowly falling as well.

I was on the big blind again, and the men to the left of me

folded around to Stuart. He clearly was thinking about something and took a little time. He had a little less than a million chips left, whereas several players in the room had five to eight million. I guess he felt that this was the time to take a stab. He made a moderate raise to 250,000. That was more than 25 percent of his chips. The next player, Hsi Tseng Lee, took about thirty seconds to think and then went all in with 7.8 million. Players folded back to Stuart. His resigned expression told me what he was about to do. "Call," he responded, and he flipped over his cards: pocket jacks. Hsi immediately flipped over his cards: ace-queen. It was a classic poker race, with the jacks having a tiny edge. But it was basically a coin flip with all five cards of the board yet to come.

The dealer alerted the floor manager by calling out, "Two players all in," and the manager arrived at the table while waving the video crew into place. The casino wanted to capture such confrontations for later broadcast on TV. When the camera was ready, the manager indicated for the dealer to run out the board. The three shared cards were all low or medium sized and were safe for Stuart, as was the turn card, the nine of diamonds. But the queen on the river paired Hsi, and Stuart was out of the tournament. I immediately stood and walked around the table to shake Stuart's hand.

"Great job, Stuart. You took a shot. Now go get your money."

He smiled at me, but he was devastated to have just been knocked out. It is only later when you're putting the winnings in the bank that it becomes clear that such a turn of events is a victory and not a defeat.

Susan came over and hugged Stuart. "I'm proud of you," she said.

Stuart regained his equilibrium a bit. "I'm going now with the clerk to get my check, but I'll be back later to see how far you get, Jim."

Cards were about to be dealt for the next hand, so I quickly retook my seat. My hole cards continued to be poor, so I kept folding. My stack dipped below 970,000. I couldn't really bluff well with Hsi at the table. He could afford to call me with many hands and would barely feel a loss or two. I needed another miracle; should I use that term? And then it happened. Our table broke.

The floor manager appeared with a box full of plastic chip racks. "Hold up. Table breaking." He dealt a plastic seat card to each of the seven players remaining at our table and then slid two empty chip racks to each player. Hsi needed four racks, however. The manager would move Churchill's few remaining chips. The players were to be reseated throughout the room at all the other tables, one here and another there, at random. Those seats had become empty due to eliminations in the recent hours. It was better to play with eight or nine players at each table.

I was hoping that this redistribution of players might give me a favorable seat with no big stacks to my left; hopefully, there would be no dangerous, superbig stack at my table at all. Getting a favorable seat is a matter of luck, and it can be an important determinant of poker success. I was lucky. I was randomly tossed the plastic card for seat five at one of the two minor video tables, lighted for filming. I arrived at my new seat and looked around. There were more cameras, but they were not too distracting. The three players to my left had stacks only a little larger than mine. And no one player at this table had a dominating stack. This looked like an improvement in my environment.

As my stack approached 840,000 I tried to play more aggressively. My king of diamonds, two of diamonds was worth calling a three–big blind raise against a single player to get to see the flop. Hoping for diamonds, or perhaps two deuces, the flop came medium-sized cards with two diamonds. I was in position and called a bet to see the turn card, but no diamond, and also no diamond on the river. So I was below eight hundred thousand. Three hands later with ace of diamonds, three of diamonds, I made a call to see the flop, which luckily had two diamonds. And this time I hit a diamond on the turn. So I was back up to nine hundred thousand. But I was just treading water.

Susan and Stuart were standing ten feet behind me on the other side of a crowd control belt. I waved, and they waved back. Stuart then waved his big check in the air before stashing it back in his shirt pocket. He seemed in better spirits now.

We had begun level twenty-eight, the two-hour level just before dinner break. Blinds were forty thousand and eighty thousand with a ten thousand ante. Exactly forty-five players remained, an important detail because after forty-six was eliminated, the payout increased to more than $164,000. I had rarely played a hand during the day, as I was just trying to climb the payout ladder. My approximately nine hundred thousand chips were equivalent to eleven big blinds, and it was clear that I could wait no longer. I would leap at the first good opportunity and hope for the best.

Thirty minutes into the level, I was positioned just before the button and was dealt ace of hearts–king of hearts. I immediately suspected that this was likely to be my do-or-die hand. An experienced player on my immediate right, Mr. K., had more chips. He made a two–big blind raise to 160,000, and I called, risking 18 percent of my chips to see a flop. I have always believed that under most circumstances it is prudent to see a flop when holding ace-king, unless you are terribly desperate. At that point, you don't even have one pair. If he already had a pair, even two deuces, he would be a small statistical favorite preflop to win the hand. These odds changed when the three shared cards came jack of hearts, six of spades, ten of hearts. I had numerous outs: nine hearts, three nonheart queens, or three aces for a total of fifteen outs. Suddenly I was favored to win sixty to forty with two cards to come. I sat very still and made no expression. He was to bet first, and there were already 530,000 chips in the middle. He bet five hundred thousand, and I went all in, and then he quickly called the all in. The big camera started filming our death struggle. We turned over our cards, and clearly our betting was well justified. He had pocket kings, but my ace-king suited was ahead. The turn was the six of clubs, but the river was the eight of hearts, giving me the victory. I had more than doubled my chips to about two million, about twenty-five big blinds. Mr. K. was left with 835,000. I should note that the online WSOP commentary did not correctly report the series of bets, but that was of little practical importance.

Grinning widely, I walked the few steps back to my supporters in triumph. I could now last a little longer. Then I quickly returned to my seat. I folded about fifteen hands during the next thirty minutes, which gave time for multiple eliminations to occur. As dinner break approached, only thirty-six players remained, and the payout rose to $211,821. Now we were talking about real money. And just at dinner break, our table broke. The tall, middle-aged floor manager, who was wearing an immaculate suit and tie, tossed plastic seat cards to each player and then took a few steps to deliver the last plastic card in his hand to me. The seat card read table one, seat two. "Where is table one?" I asked.

"Hey, lucky guy. That's the TV table."

It didn't occur to me at the time, but I wondered a few days later if someone had deliberately arranged for me to get a seat on the TV table. I was a clean-cut amateur mixed with many professionals and other highly experienced players. That seat assignment was fine with me, and I guessed that might have been a special act of kindness in view of my expressed enthusiasm for the game. When broadcast weeks later, my family and friends could more fully enjoy my rather unique adventure.

Drowned in Blessings

In high spirits, Susan, Stuart, and I walked to the white-tablecloth steak house at 7:05 p.m. where Susan and I had eaten once before. She had made a 7:10 reservation for three.

We were quickly seated, but at first we said little while at the table.

"I'm sitting here in shock. I'm dumbfounded by my good fortune," I stated sincerely.

Stuart took his check for more than $137,000 out of his shirt pocket and spread it on his bread plate. "And I am dumbfounded by my good fortune."

Susan moved both her hands forward to grasp Stuart's right hand and my right hand, and she squeezed. "And I'm dumbfounded by my good fortune."

"If this were a movie," I observed, "right now the director would yell, 'Cut!' and call for a script rewrite. 'Too schmaltzy!'"

"Or he could give other descriptions of the moment," proposed Susan with a big smile. "Soppy, slushy, sobby, sugary, syrupy, soapy, touching, mawkish, mushy, dewy-eyed, saccharine, weepy. I could go on. But I love those moments in movies."

Stuart's jaw dropped. "Susan, you're pretty good at this. You must watch a lot of schmaltzy movies."

"I do."

"Who would have believed a week ago," I continued, "that we three strangers would be sitting here holding hands while being overcome by how blessed we are. I wish more people could have this experience."

The middle-aged waitress appeared suddenly and smiled. "I would have lit a few more candles if I thought you were going to have a séance."

"We're just new friends celebrating some good luck," I explained. "And we're hungry."

Stuart had beer, while Susan sipped red wine as we waited

for salmon and filet. But there was no wine for me. I was having coffee. I sent a brief email to my family members, who likely were about ready to go to bed. I told them that I would be filmed for later release on TV. I was hoping not to make a fool of myself.

Stuart and I had a little technical discussion while we ate. The next level, level twenty-nine, had blinds of fifty thousand and one hundred thousand with an ante of ten thousand, so I actually only had twenty big blinds. I might as well take some risks quickly and try to get more chips. But if I could chip up a little, then I should try to survive nine more eliminations because the payout for twenty-seventh place jumped to $262,574.

Stuart insisted on picking up the bill, and we thanked him profusely. My friends understood that I wanted to retreat to my room for twenty minutes to let my nerves settle, and then I had to get right back to the TV table to have them help me put on a microphone. No makeup though, I assured Susan.

Day Six Continues at the TV Table

The young male technician snaked the wire inside the front of my shirt. With the microphone firmly clipped on my collar, the wire to the electronic box clipped to my belt was invisible. I took seat two at the big table as the last seconds of break ticked down on the computer screen. I extended my hand to Daniel Negreanu, who was in seat four. He had a pretty big stack of chips, maybe five million. In my wildest dreams, I had not thought that I would be playing poker against Daniel Negreanu on TV.

The other familiar face at the table was Max Steinberg, who sat with me during day four. He was in seat nine. He was wearing a suit and tie and looked as sharp as ever. And he had a lot of chips, maybe six million. And the talkative man to my right, with whom I also shook hands, seemed to have about six million chips. At least two of the bigger stacks were on my right.

The lights were bright, and everyone knew that the stakes were high. We had been instructed to place our hole cards face-down within a marked space on the felt to allow the electronic chips to identify the cards. But they also told us then to lift up the edges of our cards as we looked at them so that the seat camera right at the level of the felt could get a glimpse as well, as a backup means of allowing our cards to be known to the broadcasters.

The cards were in the air. It was fun. I folded a few hands, and then I made some big bets, first with ace-ten, and then with ace-jack. I won both hands without opposition, and my chip stack was now above two million. Recall that even before the first bet, there were 240,000 chips already committed to the pot. A few hands later, I had ace of hearts–queen of clubs in early position. I bet three hundred thousand and was called by Negreanu, but everyone else folded. The flop came deuce of clubs, five of clubs, queen of diamonds. I was to bet first, and I decided to check. Daniel bet six hundred thousand. I thought for a second and then went all in with my remaining 1.8 million chips, which represented eighteen big blinds. Daniel mucked his hand immediately. I turned over my ace-queen and said, "Good fold."

Daniel, nearly always in a good mood, replied, "Good hand. At first I didn't think you were that strong."

Within the first half hour of the level, there were two elim-inations at other tables, so the screen showed that now there were just thirty-four players remaining. Ten minutes later, Mr. J. T. at my table got his remaining chips all in but lost, so he took thirty-fourth place. I folded all my hands for the next half hour, and my chips were declining due to the costs each round.

About an hour into the level, two players were eliminated at another table, so there were just thirty-one players remaining. I knew I needed to have just a few more chips to be able to coast into twenty-seventh place and the next pay jump. I took risks on a couple of medium-strength hands and made a few more chips. Then I went into folding mode again.

Since I hadn't played a hand in a while, I made a big bet from early position with four of diamonds, seven of diamonds. I was called by one player, although I was not looking for a caller. For such a bad hand, the flop was pretty favorable for me: seven of clubs, two of diamonds, three of hearts. I was first to bet, so I made a substantial bet of about a third of my chips. I was hoping for a fold because if I had been reraised, I would have had to muck my hand. By that time, I had a fairly tight table image, so my opponent, thank goodness, folded. This hand brought me to my high-water mark of 4.1 million chips. Having acquired this stack after the hours of struggle all day, at that moment I felt exhausted. Perhaps my dinnertime coffee had worn off. But I just wanted to retire for the night if I could. I decided that I should try to fold almost every hand for the rest of the evening.

Level thirty began, the last two-hour level to be played that evening. The blinds were sixty thousand and 120,000 with an ante of fifteen thousand. Very expensive poker. After paying more blinds and antes, I had about 3.5 million chips, or about twenty-nine big blinds. I continued to fold. The man on my left was also a physician. He was eliminated in thirty-first place at a few minutes before midnight.

My turn came to play the big blind again, and I set out the mandatory 120,000 chips, which was painful, but it was only about 4 percent of my stack. A strong professional from New Jersey, T. C., was in early position and opened with a two-and-a-half big blind bet of three hundred thousand. I had seen him play for several hours, so I was sure that he had a big pair or an ace with a good kicker, like ace-queen. Players folded around to me. I looked at my hole cards and saw pocket queens.

I snapped my cards down and looked straight ahead. I was a bit shocked because with thirty players remaining, I only needed three additional eliminations to occur before I was guaranteed a larger payout at twenty-seventh place. If Mr. T. C. had an ace, as I suspected, he likely would play the hand to the end in view of my small stack, and his chances of hitting an ace after five cards was about 25 percent. Should I take a one-in-four chance of losing all my chips in this hand? I was tired. And all I had to do was wait another thirty minutes or so, and my prize would increase by more than $50,000. Any typical poker player would raise or even go all in in this situation, but I thought there might be another choice, although it would look weird. I decided to fold.

Then I had another thought. I could gain a table image advantage to set me up for a steal in a few hands. I considered that if I folded the queens faceup, a questionable and highly unorthodox move, all the players would see that I was intending to fold all hands during the next few minutes just to make the jump in payouts. But I planned to play a little trick. I would make a very large opening bet a few hands from now, regardless of my hole cards. My opponents would know that I had just folded queens, so they would think, *What must he have now?* They almost certainly would fold, and I would win all the blinds and antes, which totaled 315,000 chips. And there would be minimal risk of me getting knocked out—if no one played.

So I folded my queens faceup. I learned later that hundreds of fans watching the real-time commentary online were incredulous and highly critical. But as exhausted as I was and with that pay jump coming, I thought that avoiding a big confrontation with Mr. T. C. just at that time was the best choice for me.

About four hands later, I was in relatively late position, and I thought that this might be the perfect time to try my table image ruse with a bad hand. Max Steinberg made a three big blind raise, and the action came to me. I peeked at my hole cards to find ace-king off suit, a much better hand than I was hoping for but a hand in which I still could lose all of my chips. Max knew that I was very tight because he sat next to me for hours during day four. And he had just seen me fold queens less than ten minutes ago. So I executed my plan and went all in, then sat quietly looking down at the felt. The action folded back to Max. He hesitated. I looked up at him and saw that he was very conflicted. He had just put 360,000 chips into the pot. I immediately dropped my gaze to the felt again. I tried to take slow, relaxed breaths. After another moment, he commented, "Pocket tens," although he didn't show his cards, and he tossed them into the muck. I felt very fortunate as I raked in a big pile of chips. I now had almost four million chips again.

Play continued for another thirty minutes or so, which was sufficient for three more eliminations to occur. We were down to twenty-seven players at twelve thirty in the morning, we were all tired, and the schedule called for us all to receive new seats, as there would be three tables of surviving players. To my great relief, the floor manager quickly decided that play would end for the day and would resume at noon. We would each have new seat assignments. We were now to bag our chips for the night. I had 3.5 million chips and a guaranteed prize of more than $262,000. My friends saw the excitement as well as the exhaustion in my face, and Susan gave me a huge hug.

Stuart mumbled, "You folded queens faceup and then went all in! What did you have that hand?"

I smiled and responded, "I could tell you that it was deuce-three. But it actually was ace-king. I was making a table image play."

"Very crazy." He shook his head. "Very crazy. But now you really have them all confused."

It was time for bed.

Day Seven, World Series of Poker Main Event
Start-of-day chips: 3.5 million

Iawoke feeling tired. I was excited to be playing in day seven of this famous tournament, but I was clearly dragging. It had been a long grind to this point.

Susan, Stuart, and I sat together at breakfast, all of us in high spirits, but I believe they could tell that I was fatigued. They didn't mention it though. They walked with me to the Amazon room, which was uncharacteristically quiet, as there were so few players remaining: just twenty-seven. I sat in seat five at table three. In terms of chip count, I was in twenty-third place. I had folded queens on day six, but my situation was different now. I had to play and win hands or I would be dead. I was the short stack at my table.

I noticed that Hsi Tseng Lee ranked fourth in chips, while Vladimir Komarov ranked tenth. They were at other tables and likely would win big money, whereas I would be lucky to survive two hours. My payout would be substantial, so I was not really complaining. As the dealing began, I ordered coffee and hoped that it would arrive soon. My breakfast coffee had seemed not to provide much stimulation, and I needed more energy. I needed it right now. Susan and Stuart stood a few yards from me. They knew I would do my best.

The first level of play that day, level thirty-one, had blinds of eighty thousand and 160,000 with a twenty thousand ante. So, as the first hand of the day was dealt, there already were 420,000 chips sitting in the middle. My entire stack of 3.5 million represented only twenty-one big blinds.

I folded the first dozen hands, and my stack declined to below three million. Then I was dealt pocket jacks. I had started as the short stack at my table, but I thought by then I may have been the shortest in the entire tournament. I needed to try to make a few chips rather than go all in and have all my opponents fold. I was first to bet and made a three–big blind bet, hoping to get one caller. A German two seats to my left raised me, and the remaining players folded the action back to me. I moved all in with about fifteen big blinds. The German thought for two minutes, and I hoped he would call with, perhaps, ace-queen. I would have about a 55 percent chance of winning the hand if I entered that sort of race. But he folded, and I was happy with that decision as well, since I was back up to about 3.5 million.

My coffee still did not arrive as I folded more hands. We were ninety minutes into the first level, and my chips were dwindling. And no one had yet been knocked out today, which surprised me. The current payout would be more than $262,000, but there was not a jump in the payouts until eighteenth place. It would be tough to survive those nine eliminations. I was going to have to gamble and win. I stretched my legs and looked back at Susan and Stuart. They were grim faced and knew that I was in trouble. I just couldn't get a good hand from the dealer.

I was dealt king of diamonds, ten of diamonds, the best hand I had seen in an hour since I had held those jacks. In middle position, I made a three–big blind bet using 480,000 of my remaining 2.8 million chips. Players folded to the big blind, who raised to one million, and the action folded back to me. I called the million, which left me with about 1.8 million chips still in front of me, only eleven big blinds. The flop came deuce of clubs, jack of hearts, queen of diamonds. With two cards to come, I would have a very low chance of making a diamond flush and a 32 percent chance of completing my open ended straight. Not very promising. If a king came, my pair might not be good. I decided that I would have to gamble with my remaining chips and hope for the best. It made no difference if I was eliminated now or seven or eight places from now; the payout would be the same amount. My only hope of making the next pay bump at eighteenth place was to gamble.

I committed with all in but then realized that I had bet out of turn. I really was tired. But my opponent and I then got all our chips into the middle, and I was resigned to whatever was going to happen. The dealer presented the turn and river, I failed to hit, and my opponent's ace-ten took the pot. I was out of the tournament in twenty-seventh place. I shook hands with my opponent and stepped back behind the rope to receive congratulations from Stuart, Susan, and a couple of onlookers. I had scored a major victory in this tournament, but the moment of being knocked out was a sad one. I had hoped to do even better.

Susan had just returned to the room a minute before my demise, a hot latte in hand, because she realized that I was waiting for coffee that never came. She was a trooper.

The clerk asked me to follow him to the manager's desk at the side of the room, where I was given a card showing twenty-seventh place to be used at the main cashier down the hall. I would be getting a big check. The momentary sadness of the knockout was fading. I had a lot to be thankful for.

The clerk guided me a few yards to one side of the desk where I was to stand on an x of duct tape in the bright lights and give a brief exit interview to the film crew. The reporter asked if I was disappointed. I replied that I was momentarily sad just at the moment of being knocked out but that as an amateur I was fully satisfied to have taken twenty-seventh place in this huge tournament. I explained that I had folded queens on day six to be sure that I would survive to be among the final twenty-seven. Then on day seven, I failed to get good cards quickly enough, so my chips dwindled further, and I couldn't recover. I also mentioned that young players seeing this interview should consider the importance of staying in school and getting their degrees before committing more time to poker. I advised that there would always be plenty of time for poker later. The reporter thanked me for the interview, and I stepped away wondering if my cautionary message to the young players would ever be aired. It turned out they never broadcast my interview.

Stuart shook my hand. "For an amateur, you had an amazing run."

"It was the poker experience of a lifetime, that's for sure," I responded, now over the shock of my exit and smiling again.

"When will you be flying home?"

"I have a reservation on an early-morning flight tomorrow."

"Let me say my goodbye now," Stuart said, and he put his hand on my shoulder. "I'm really glad we met, and maybe we'll see each other here for next year's Main Event."

"Well, I haven't thought about it, of course, but I suspect I'll be back."

"I'm driving now to meet a group of old friends in Reno. Good luck and see ya next year." Stuart smiled as he shook my hand once more. Then he stepped up to Susan and gave her a quick hug. He walked away, off to his next adventure.

I turned to Susan. "You wanna come with me to the cashier?"

"Sure." She grinned, and we walked out into the hallway and stood in a short line at the cashier. I sipped my latte.

Since most players had left town, there were few other games going on, so the cashier lines were the shortest I had seen in a week. A young lady waved to us. We were to sit across from her at a long table off to the side. She had a laptop in front of her. She examined my ID and prize card and offered her congratulations as one of the big prize winners.

"Okay," she started. "Your total prize is $262,574. Do you want us to withhold federal and state taxes?"

I had already thought about that a couple of days ago, so I quickly responded, "No. I'll handle those payments."

"Fine. And as you know, we are associated with the charity," she continued and pointed at the large poster behind her. "Many players make a donation at this point to be deducted in advance from their final check. This will lower your taxes."

"I understand, and I'd like to donate $3,000."

"Thank you." She typed briefly on her laptop and was ready with the next question. "Any tip for the dealers?"

"Yes, $2,000," I replied.

"Thank you." Her fingers fluttered over her keyboard again. "And we subtract from your earnings to be reported to the government the cost of your entry fee, which was $10,000. Do you agree with that?"

"Yes," I responded. I thought that I was handling this unique checkout session pretty well. But her next question stopped me cold.

"Would you like the entire amount in cash?"

"Uh …" I took a breath. "The entire amount in cash?"

"Yes, you can have the entire amount in cash, or some portion of it in cash with the remainder as a check." It was only days later that I realized that the casino really was pushing for winners to take a large portion in cash. The management rightly believed that a wad of cash in a pocket would precipitate more gambling and local shopping, whereas a paper check in a pocket would just travel home with the winner.

This fantastic proposition about taking a mountain of cash seemed not to bother the young woman one bit, but I regained my composure after a few seconds, smiled at Susan, then replied to the cashier, "Well, I didn't bring my large suitcase on this trip, so I'll just take a check this time."

"You laugh," the cashier said, smiling as she typed, "but many of our winners from overseas take the entire amount home as cash."

"Astonishing." I shook my head.

The young lady printed out two pages, set them in front of me, and pointed with her finger. "So, after the subtractions we just talked about, this will be the final amount of the check we cut for you today. And this page shows how we will report this for taxes. If your name, address, and social security number are correct, then please sign here and also here. You'll get copies."

I checked the data and signed. The woman stood and led me a dozen steps to a barred cashier window. She slid the paperwork in to the young man behind the bars. "Please cut the check," she directed him.

In about a minute, he handed me a form to sign that I actually had received the check, and then he slid the check out to me. "Congratulations," he said somewhat automatically as he turned to answer someone behind him who was calling his name. It was all very routine. For them. But it was quite a novel experience for me to fold a check for more than $250,000 into my front shirt pocket.

"Exciting!" Susan's eyes were wide.

"Very," I responded. "Now let's find a quiet place to sit for fifteen minutes. I want to send an email to my family to let them know I'm out in twenty-seventh place and I have the check for my prize in my pocket."

That quick communication accomplished, I exhaled and stretched out my legs. "It's still a bit surreal."

"Yep," Susan responded. "And I know you're really tired."

"When is your flight home? Mine is in the morning, as I think you heard."

"I have a choice for tomorrow morning as well, and there also is an Austin flight at 6:00 p.m. today. It's 2:20 now." She paused. "I want to say goodbye to you properly, but you need to know that I've taken unexpected days away from work. I really need to get back to my office." She gently bit her lower lip, and her expression indicated that she was trying to gauge my reaction.

I smiled and took her hand in mine as we sat side by side. "Well, I've taken unexpected days off from work as well. I'm sure my boss is really baffled and very curious." I smiled again. "Which story do you think he would believe? Story number one: I met a wonderful woman, and we have been having a grand and rather intimate time in Vegas. Or an alternative excuse.

Story number two: I kept winning day after day in a huge poker tournament, and I came in twenty-seventh place in the world, so they handed me a check for a quarter of a million dollars because I refused to take a suitcase home full of cash."

We laughed. Both stories were true.

"So, Susan," I continued, "I think we should say our good-bye right here and now. But we will definitely stay in close contact. You need to get yourself to the airport and get right back to work tomorrow morning. I'm exhausted, and I need a nap right now. And I'll take that morning flight home."

We stood and kissed, and the cashiers seemed to enjoy the spectacle. I was too tired to care who was watching. We walked together to the elevator and rode to eight. Then, after a final kiss, we parted in the hall as she walked right and I walked left. I kicked off my shoes and stumbled into bed fully dressed; I was asleep in ten minutes right in the middle of the afternoon.

Back Home

My flight connection in Chicago went smoothly, and I landed at Bradley Airport north of Hartford right on time. I kept the check in my shirt pocket all the way home. Susan had texted that she made it home okay, and I sent a couple of texts to keep her abreast of my progress. I dropped my suitcase at home and made it to my bank well before closing time.

My banker, a middle-aged, overweight, balding man who I knew fairly well, let out a giant belly laugh when he held the huge check from Las Vegas in his hands. "I play poker some Saturdays," he said. "And one time I won ninety dollars."

"Great," I congratulated him. "But I should tell you, a funny thing happened to me on the drive here."

"Really?"

"Yeah, it was weird. As I was driving, my mouth kept

repeating ha-ha-ha. It would stop, but then after a minute, it would start again. Ha-ha-ha."

"Very odd," he replied, not sure if I might be describing a medical problem.

"But then I relaxed because I figured out what was happening."

"What?"

I smiled, and then he could tell that I was joking. "I was laughing all the way to the bank."

The money safely deposited, I unpacked and had some soup, as there was nothing much else in the house. I had faced such a dinner dilemma more times than I would care to admit during my year as a bachelor. Susan and I spoke for more than an hour. She was fine and was busy again at work. She had spoken to her parents and had told them a few things about me. I told her that I would probably speak with my parents about her tomorrow.

It was July 14. I texted my boss that I was home and would be in the office at eight, bright and early. He replied, "Great. We missed you. But we're all very curious here, and we want details. Like, what's her name?" I didn't answer. There was no way to tell my story in a text.

I settled back into my work routine quite easily during the next two weeks. I had to tell my colleagues in the office about my poker adventure because they would likely see something about this on TV in a few weeks. I wasn't ashamed of having an interest in poker, but in recent years, I had rarely made mention of it at work. I viewed it as a private interest, and no one else at the office had ever mentioned poker. I was being analytical and just making a study of the math, tactics, and strategies in poker as a sort of exercise, analogous to my chess hobby. Now I wanted my workmates to know that I would appear in video on ESPN, likely in October as a run-up to the broadcast of the playoff among the final nine survivors in the first week of November. I also wanted my boss to know that the broadcaster,

Norman Chad, likely would mention my occupation and the name of my employer, since I had written that on the player information sheet where requested. My friends knew that I played chess, but the poker story was a surprise. They were also pleased to hear that I had met a special girl, though she lived in Texas.

The email from Stuart on July 30 was a surprise. He attached links to newspaper stories running that day in Las Vegas. The police announced that an investigation had been ongoing and that it was concluded that several major poker players had been poisoned during the World Series of Poker Main Event. Two of the sick men had been hospitalized about three days, but both recovered. During their illnesses, while absent from the poker tables, they had gradually lost all of their chips, ruining their chances for a major prize. It was believed that about ten additional players also were made ill, but they missed only a few hours of poker time and had not required hospitalization. Several suspects were going to be named soon. It was a conspiracy, and more information would be released tomorrow.

I thanked Stuart and told him that I was back at work and staying busy, and that Susan and I were in contact. Stuart promised to send a news update when available.

I didn't have to wait long. The next afternoon, Stuart sent a long email describing what had just been said by police at a locally broadcast Las Vegas news conference. Hsi Tseng Lee and six Chinese colleagues were currently back in China, but they were being charged for masterminding a conspiracy to sicken certain poker opponents. Several hotel maids who were US citizens also were being charged, as they were believed to be part of the plot. The maids had been hired months earlier and basically were agents who had infiltrated the hotel service staff. They could gain access to the rooms of players. They had available to them carefully manufactured dummy pills with all of the correct colors and markings of dozens of genuine drugs. These dummy pills contained no active drugs. For selected players, as directed by the Chinese, the maids substituted dummy pills for authentic pills in the medication bottles of unsuspecting guests when they were absent from their rooms. At least six different types of dummy pills had been used, leading the investigators to suspect that many different types of medications had been counterfeited so that many choices for substitution were available. The scale and sophistication of the plan suggested that a substantial conspiracy was ongoing. The Chinese individuals would be arrested for questioning if they returned to the United States. It was noted that Hsi Tseng Lee was one of the nine finalists scheduled to play again in November in Las Vegas to finish the tournament, and it was unclear if he would reenter the United States to participate. He had already received a check for about one million dollars as payment for his accomplishment of making the final nine, but he had the potential to win much more if he could play.

It was astonishing news. And I was more astonished that my quickly formed hunch had panned out. I suspected now that if a player was hospitalized, the likely plan was for the maid to immediately enter that person's room and replace the dummy pills with authentic pills so that no one could detect that a prior substitution had been made. What messed up the plan was that one targeted player who became very ill had his medication bottles with the dummy pills in his pocket, allowing the dummy pills to fall into the hands of the police. I believed that my tip to test the available medications for authenticity might have been a key contribution to solving the case, but I really couldn't say if my role was pivotal or not. But if I had helped, I was happy to do so.

Stuart had copied Susan on these emails as well, so Susan and I talked about all of this during our regular nightly phone call. She had other exciting news for me that evening. She would be taking a few days off in August to visit me, and then we could visit her parents in New Hampshire. It was happy news, though it brought back memories of when I first met Sheila's parents. But life goes on.

Susan had other interesting news. She had arranged for two job interviews in companies near where I worked in Connecticut. She hoped that this didn't sound too pushy, she said. But she wanted to see what options were available. I stopped her cold for a moment when I told her not to bother with the job interviews. I was moving to Las Vegas to become a professional poker player. She was pretty sure that I was joking, but I could tell that she was relieved when I immediately confessed that I was only teasing.

Group at NY Pitch Conference, December 2018. Paula Munier is third from the right. The author is in back row, far left.

KNOWLEDGE IS POWER*

New England was ending its hibernation. I sauntered along the roadside in my rural neighborhood noting the many signs that springtime had finally taken a tentative hold after a cold and wet March. The aroma of damp earth was an assurance that nature was awakening after the frigid months. Sunbeams and shadows danced among the barren trunks and branches as my slow steps along the road altered my perspective into the still-slumbering woods – but millions of tiny purple-green buds gave promise. It was just before noon, and I had decided to try to get some of the ten thousand steps that my internist recommended. At 68, I had been retired for three years and had put on five pounds. My main hobbies were reading, movies, chess, and poker – all sedentary. Gratifyingly, the poker hobby had been quite successful, and I had even been written up in local periodicals about winning money at poker, but sitting for hours playing cards might have been putting cholesterol in my arteries as well as money in my wallet. I agreed with my doctor that I needed to be more physically active. Fortunately, the nearby roads through woods provided interesting sights during walks, though I was wary of traffic.

A white SUV was approaching me from behind on this

---

* Phrase from Francis Bacon (1561 – 1626)

narrow two-lane road, so I moved a little further away from the asphalt to make more space. To my surprise, the SUV screeched to a halt beside me, the rear passenger door swung open, and a large Caucasian man stepped out. "Good morning, Doctor Card Shark," he growled. "Time for you to take a little ride with us." He grabbed my left arm, and within seconds I was seated in the back between two men as the SUV sped away from my neighborhood. I glanced left and right but was so stunned that I said nothing. Another Caucasian man with short hair was driving at a brisk clip.

The man on my right who had grabbed me placed his huge hand palm up in my lap. "Cell phone, please," he requested. I removed my iPhone 6 from my shirt pocket and placed it in his hand. He powered it off and put it in a small metal box, sort of like a toolbox, but with quite thick metal walls; I guessed that the box blocked electronic signals. "Just relax. We're going to take a little ride now."

Of course, I realized that I likely was being kidnapped to be held for ransom. These guys must have read a recent newspaper article about my poker prizes. I was reasonably calm, but I watched carefully as we drove, a little surprised that they had not blindfolded me. It occurred to me that their lack of concern that I was seeing their faces and the route might be a very bad omen. Perhaps they believed that I would never live to report any of that information. It made no sense to panic, though I could hear my pulse pounding in my ears. I just sat quietly as we drove to Shelton, CT and parked in front of a modest two-storey house in a quiet neighborhood at the corner of Oak and First Streets. As they walked me briskly through the front door I noted that the house number on the mailbox and also on the door was 102. Within a minute I was locked in a small room in the basement, concrete walls on all four sides.

Alone, I sat in the one chair that was present and closed my eyes while attempting to collect my thoughts. I was here, a prisoner, and that was that. After a couple of minutes I felt a little better, since it seemed that my bizarre situation likely was stable for the time being. Better to be kidnapped by semi-rational criminals trying to execute a strategy than running into an armed, crazed drug-addict in a dark alley.

I took some deep breaths, stood, and started to inspect my cell. A small, outside window about twenty inches wide and eight inches high was located above the level of my head and faced what I presumed to be the backyard. The ten- by fourteen-foot room had a wooden chair, a small wooden table with a pitcher of water and a plastic cup, and a narrow mattress on the floor with a pillow and two blankets. A medium-sized plastic wastebasket with lid was in the corner, and the roll of toilet paper next to it hinted at its intended use.

The heavy door was metal and was quite solid, with hinges apparently on the outside. I judged that these men were serious and had planned carefully. The room looked pretty secure. I walked slowly around the room letting my fingertips drag along the cool, smooth concrete walls. No pipes were visible anywhere along the walls or ceiling. The floor was solid concrete and there was no drain, a fact that lightened my mood as I suddenly re-called the classic Jacques Futrelle short story published in 1905, "The Problem of Cell 13." In the story, the brilliant Professor Van Dusen escaped from a highly secure prison cell by lever-aging the facts that there was a small drain in the floor, he had tooth powder for hygiene, he had three small-denomination currency bills in his pocket, and his shoes had been highly pol-ished when he was locked inside.

I stood on the chair to peer out the window, which I con-firmed was clearly too small for an adult to squeeze through. A piece of white, translucent plastic was leaning up against the outside of the window, which allowed light to enter but obscured the view.

Just then I heard a sliding noise of metal against metal. It sounded like a horizontal bolt on the outside of the door. The door slowly swung open to the outside, and two muscular men in T-shirts briskly entered my small space. They were the men who had bracketed me in the backseat. I stepped down off the chair and faced them.

"Looking around?" the taller man began, and he smiled. He seemed relaxed. He had short hair and a large, blue tattoo on his right upper bicep.

"Yes," I replied as calmly as I could manage. "I don't want any trouble, and I'm sure that my family will cooperate with any requests you may have. We should be able to get through this process without anyone getting hurt."

"Sounds good," said the shorter man, who also had closely-cropped hair but no tattoos that I could see. He stepped forward and set his prominent jaw. He had a broad, square face with a small scar over his right cheek bone, an impressive muscular neck, and well-muscled chest and arms. He was wearing disposable latex gloves and was carrying a half-dozen sheets of typing paper and two pencils. He set the items on the table. "Please sit down so you can write a short note. I'll dictate. Then we'll bring you a sandwich. Just do as I say." It became clear to me immediately that within this gang of three criminals, he was the boss.

"No problem," I replied. I took a seat and picked up a pencil.

"On this sheet please write your wife's name, cell number, and email address. We may communicate sometimes using those, and sometimes by paper. Then write your cell number, email address, and the combination to unlock your phone. After we have traveled to a remote location we may sometimes communicate with your family using your phone."

I complied and handed him the sheet. The two men continued to stand just inside the door, suggesting that this might be a short visit. I was struck by how well-constructed the shorter man's sentences were, a sign of education, though both men looked very blue collar. The shorter man – the boss – spoke with confidence. It was clear that he believed that he was the smartest person in the room, and he was being a little cocky to reinforce that impression. Having treated medical patients for years, though, I knew well that when several experienced and highly competent doctors were discussing a troubling case, a cocky attitude was never adopted by anyone. The world is extremely complex; many things are puzzling and plans can go wrong. I generally exhibited a confident, professional air, but I believe I never had been cocky. In fact, the smartest medical experts often spoke softly and with great humility, while the trainees strained to hear and benefit from every word.

"Now you're going to write a note. Start Dear Jane..."

"It's actually Janet," I corrected him and tried to smile. "And can I put today's date at the top?"

He seemed a little perturbed that I had interrupted him, but he quickly replied, "Sure, put the date. Dear Janet. I have been kidnapped. I am well. Do not call the police. Please get $200,000 cash together and wait for instructions. When you have the money you can let us know by replying to this text." He paused and took a breath. "Then sign it."

I signed it "Love, Joe," and I drew a small heart under my name. I reached forward to hand the shorter man the note.

He smiled at me. "You did that well, so for your good behavior I'll explain that I will drive fifty miles or so, turn on your phone, take a photo of your note, and then text the photo to your wife. And if we ever take a photo of you in this room I will use my phone, then print it out upstairs so I can put it in my pocket when I travel remotely. After traveling, I'll take a photo of the print with your phone so I can send that along to Janet. The point: you will not be leaving this room. Do you understand?"

"Yes."

"And I guess that you also understand that if I drive fifty miles and turn on your phone, and the combination you gave me won't unlock the phone, I'll be very unhappy and I'll need to come back here to get things straight. You are sure the combination you gave me will work, right?" He was not smiling as he waited for my response.

"No games from me. The combination will work."

"Good. Now you get a ham and cheese sandwich and a Coke." Then he added with a smile, "Mustard?"

⚭

Janet sat silently in the living room as Detective Kabir, a forty-three year old, quick-witted policeman who had been born in Pakistan, walked slowly around the house looking at family photos on the walls. She was certain that her decision to contact the police immediately was right, in spite of the note's demand. Detective Kabir came to the house that very first day, and now had returned on the fourth day of the ordeal after a second text from the kidnappers had been received. Janet's eyes were swollen and red, and she had a box of tissues on her lap. After a few minutes, the policeman returned to the living room and sat directly across the coffee table from her.

"You have a comfortable home, Janet. I can see you have a nice family. Two daughters, I take it. Both married now."

"Yes," Janet sniffled. "And we have two young grandchildren now."

"One is Beverly," the detective opined, "as we saw in the photo that came today. Your husband seems very calm to have sent her birthday greetings as part of all this mess."

The detective held the print-out of the latest photo sent by the kidnappers. It was a proof-of-life photo showing the victim holding today's front page of the New York Times, and also holding a makeshift birthday greeting cartoon for Beverly drawn with pencil on a sheet of typing paper. "So is Beverly's birthday this week?"

"No, it's not, so it's a little odd that Joe wrote a birthday greeting. Her birthday is May 22."

282

Detective Kabir pondered the situation, then spoke softly, "So Joseph sent this hand-drawn birthday cartoon for some other reason than to wish her a happy birthday. I think he is trying to tell us something."

Janet nodded.

"And I surmise that Joseph must be following instructions very well and has developed some rapport with his kidnappers, since they allowed him to include the birthday greeting to Beverly. So Joseph is a very nice guy?" the detective queried.

"He's a genuinely good-hearted person, and it's so wrong that this has happened to him. He has years of experience in medicine. He's interacted with patients and families from all sorts of backgrounds, during all kinds of stressful situations. Joe has always been highly regarded as a physician. And he always remains calm and logical."

"So he is nice and smart," Detective Kabir smiled.

"Very clever. Chess. Poker. A voracious reader. When he faces problems he is extremely resourceful."

The detective's brow furrowed. "He is holding his right hand up with three fingers raised with his thumb across the palm to press on the little finger. It's a bit of an odd wave. Does that posture mean something to you, or to Beverly?"

Janet held the photo in her hand and studied it again. "It's not a military salute, right? I think maybe it's Boy Scouts?"

"I think you might be right!" exclaimed the detective. "I realize now that one photo upstairs was a picture of Joseph in his Boy Scout uniform when he was a young teenager."

"You're right. He was fourteen in that photo. That's when he got his Eagle rank. He knew all about hiking, and camping, and surviving in the woods. He was taught to use a rifle, a compass, and how to send signals. And he learned basic first aid. He has lots of stories of those days." She handed the photo back to the detective.

"Hmm," he exhaled and held the print-out closer to his face.

"The birthday card has three flowers. Does that mean anything to you?"

"Beverly likes flowers, but there's nothing special about that as far as I know."

"The birthday drawing is very small in this print-out. Do you have a magnifying glass?"

Janet's sad eyes brightened and she let out a spontaneous guffaw. "A detective is asking me for a magnifying glass!" She set the box of tissues on the table, stood, and took a few steps to the desk in the corner. As she retrieved a magnifying glass she added, "But I don't have a Sherlock Holmes hat handy."

Detective Kabir smiled and thanked her as he took hold of the magnifying glass. More detail in the birthday card became visible.

"Hmm, some of these details might be important."

I heard the bolt slide, and I looked up to watch the metal door swing outward. The short man walked into my prison room and handed me a peanut butter and jelly sandwich, and a glass of milk.

"Thanks. Any word since this morning?"

"Your wife should have received the proof-of-life photo, and she was supposed to acknowledge that she understands how to drop off the bag of money at midnight, but nothing yet." Without another word he left and closed the door behind him.

In spite of the fact that I was being well treated and fed, I was continuing to worry that these criminals had no intention of releasing me alive. I had seen them and knew too much. Surely they must realize that I suspect that I will never get out of this. Frightening, but there was no use in being overcome with panic. I kept watching for some opportunity to safely escape, but no favorable situation had yet arisen. A failed attempt to escape likely would result in a beating in spite of the relative kindness my captors had shown thus far. I was now pinning nearly all my hopes on the birthday card.

"BAM! BAM!"

Huge explosions suddenly erupted inside the house upstairs, and dust fell from the ceiling. The noise was so loud that my ears hurt. I instinctively slid off the chair and huddled under the flimsy wooden table.

"BAM! BAM! BAM!"

More explosions and I could smell gunpowder. Many men were shouting at once upstairs.

It was all over in three minutes. Two policemen wearing gas masks, helmets, and vests entered my room, helped me up on my feet, and walked me up the smoky basement stairway and out into the front yard. At least five police cars with blue and red lights flashing were parked in the street.

At the curb I was greeted by a dark-skinned, smiling face. "I am Detective Kabir. Are you okay, Joseph?"

"I'm fine, and thank you very much."

"Thank you for sending such clear directions! Let me dial Janet and you can speak with her right now."

⌒⌇⌒

The joyful conversation was brief. Janet understood that Joseph would be questioned by the police for a couple of hours to tell them everything he knew. Then they would bring him home.

Janet sat on the couch in silence and wiped away a last tear. She picked up the print-out of the photo and examined it again with the magnifying glass. She actually knew the coded letters by heart now, and would never forget them.

"Morse code in the grass blades!" she mumbled. Then she read out the message one last time before going to bed, "102 Oak St Shelton CT Basement 3 men."

SUBPLOT

"Argh," I gasped involuntarily as the pistol shot reverberated in my ears. A spray of glass fragments erupted within my car as both my rear window and windshield partially shattered. They were closer now, only thirty yards behind me. Their headlights blinded me if I raised my head to peek in the rear view mirror, so I kept my head down both to avoid glare and duck from the next shot. I was hitting 70 on the narrow, two-lane Connecticut highway that wound through thick woods, but I jammed the accelerator to the floor when it appeared that the road straightened a bit just ahead. If I ran off the road I would surely be killed, either by the crash or at the hands of my pursuers. The woods were extremely dark, and I prayed that a deer would not be standing in the road ahead. I peeked in the mirror again – yes! I had doubled my distance from them. My small sedan was lighter than their oversized SUV; I could accelerate faster and handle the curves better. But they had a much more powerful engine. I was hitting 90, probably my top speed, but my turn was coming up soon. There were few houses along this stretch, but I hoped that a particular gravel driveway might provide my path to salvation. They were gaining on me again, coming up fast.

There were my cues: a "No Passing" sign next to the trunk of an ancient oak bearing a red "No Trespassing" sign, followed immediately by a "Speed Limit 40" sign, so I slammed on my brakes. A second later I careened leftward onto the driveway, which fortunately angled off the road gradually enough to allow me to negotiate the turn. It seemed that my car tilted up on its two right wheels for a second, but within another second I was solidly on four wheels. The gravel crunched noisily as I sped up the narrow driveway. But I knew it was a dead end. My headlights illuminated the white stones, which contrasted sharply with the blackness of the woods on both sides of the road and with the sudden blackness behind me. They had missed the turn.

It was another twenty seconds before the now dimmer, more distant headlights appeared behind me. But they were like the eyes of a demon coming after me in the darkness.

I didn't have far to go. I skidded to a sudden halt in front of the small, dark farmhouse. I knew that Sam wasn't there, and the house would be empty. But my goal actually was the fenced demolition site on the other side of the driveway where an ancient and very dilapidated, small house had just been torn down. A stone fireplace with a fifteen-foot chimney that once had been in the center of the house was barely visible among the shadows. I shut off my headlights and ran to the gate in the chain-link fence that surrounded the site making an enclosure of perhaps seventy by seventy feet.

At the gate I reached high above my head to unwind the securing chain that had been placed well above the reach of any child. At just that second a glare appeared some distance behind me, and I heard the grind of gravel as my pursuers braked. I swung the gate open and raced through toward the fireplace, veering rather far to my left as a shot echoed, and a bullet whizzed past my head. In a few more seconds I was safely on the far side of the stone column. But I knew that it was safety but for a moment. The stones were cold on my fingertips as I peeked around the corner. The pursuers' headlights remained on; the silhouettes of two men were visible walking briskly toward the gate that I had just opened. I crawled inside the fireplace. I could hear my heart pounding in my ears. My hands trembled as I dialed 911. The next few minutes would be critical. As the phone rang my mind involuntarily flashed a memory of when I had first received that strange letter that started this whole mess.

I retrieved my mail from the box and started the tea kettle heating. A hot drink would be welcome on this gray, cool, late-March day. I slit open six business envelopes, but quickly tossed three sales catalogs away. Electric bill. Standard Oil bill. But when I looked at the third item, I snapped to attention. What was this? A typewritten, undated, one-page letter. "Dear Tate…" it began. I immediately knew that there was something quite strange about this letter. "Still water. Stay calm. Tag sale is Saturday. Partly cloudy. Tree rings. The grasshopper. Bat cave. Slow down. Hammer head. The diamond ring. Sleep walking. Bat boy. NAFTA is a bad deal. Stomp. Taxes too high. Saw. Old hat. Pass the test. Card trick. Play ball. Trisect. Lint remover. Ham bone. Gladiator. Make a fortune. Steam engine. Birdwatching. Bass player. Without malice. Brain. Pathway. Blue jeans. Breathless. Play along. Hip hop. Bars are fun. Shit. Illinois. Batboy. The rest is history. Ton of fun. Brake lining. Sit down. Hat trick. Tow truck. Slower speed. Tap root. Summertime. Tub of lard. Ballgame. Stuck up. Need to know. Injustice. Drain cleaner. Sack of coal. Like you a lot. Bleach. Little league. Tar and feather. The mermaid. Podcast. Part Neanderthal. Slothful. Bastard. Slenderest." At the bottom it was signed with the initials T.K.

I quickly determined that the letter's envelope was addressed to Tate Wilcox, 1201 Sherman Street, New Haven, CT whereas my name, of course, was Tate Maddox, living in Orange, CT. This had clearly been some mistake by the postal system. There was no return address. Postmark: San Francisco. I smiled as I realized that this represented a challenging and perhaps amusing puzzle to be solved. I certainly would reseal the letter in the envelope along with a note, "Opened in error at wrong address," and send it back on its way. But this could be fun. I suspected that this was a coded communication, perhaps from a sweetheart to her married love interest. There was no law saying that I couldn't play around with a photocopy of the mysterious letter to try to decipher it as part of a private game. So I made a photocopy, then sealed up the original to take to the post office later that day when I went to get groceries.

That evening, a Saturday, I was winding down for bedtime. I had a quick call with Stacy, who agreed to meet me at 9:00 am Mass and then get breakfast afterwards. She was sweet. And cute. The prettiest kindergarten teacher in Connecticut as far as I was concerned. It was clear that our relationship had advanced a lot in the last six months, and who could tell where this might lead?

I was in my pajamas at the kitchen table when I reached for the photocopy of the strange letter. I wondered if anything would make sense if most of the words were superfluous and could be excluded by a mask. But if this was a secret love letter, there didn't seem to be any useful words to make a romantic message even if most words were excluded. Critical words such as "love," "heart," "kiss," were not present. I imagined that nearly all words were excluded such that only ten words remained to be read in the order left to right and top to bottom, but I couldn't imagine a sentence of a few words that made sense. Stacy and I could play games with the letter during breakfast.

⌘

Stacy and I were perusing the menu at IHOP. She was seated across from me. I knew what I wanted, so I enjoyed looking at Stacy for a minute. She had sensuous, full lips and remarkably long eyelashes. Her dark hair was shoulder-length with a slight

290

wave on both sides, which accentuated her cheek bones. She looked up at me with soft, dark eyes, and smiled.

"Having your usual, Tate?"

"I guess I'm in a rut."

"Strawberry pancakes for me," she responded.

The waitress brought our coffee, then took our order.

"Will you have a lot of programming to do this week?" Stacy asked.

"Just the usual."

"Your job is so mysterious to me," she pouted. "I don't know the first thing about computer programming, so I can't even ask any intelligent questions about what you do."

"Well, let me be clear," I responded with a smile. "I couldn't even survive three days as a kindergarten teacher. I do like kids, I think, but not twenty at once."

She smiled, "I should learn some new kindergarten commando techniques at my conference in Hartford tomorrow. Sorry I have to pack this afternoon and drive up there for the reception this evening. I'll be back Monday night by nine."

"You should have fun. Speaking of fun, I have a puzzle for you." I withdrew the letter from my shirt pocket, unfolded it, and placed it in front of her. "What do you make of this?"

She quickly read the first few words, then looked up at me with a quizzical look. "Who could have sent you this, Tate? It doesn't make any sense."

"It is addressed to Tate, but it was delivered to me in Saturday's mail by mistake. I sent the original to the right Tate in New Haven. But I thought we could try to decode the message just for fun."

"You and your puzzles. If it's not chess or computers, you're always playing around with something."

"It's what I enjoy. So what does it say?"

Stacy turned her attention again to the letter, and I let her study it in silence.

"Well, when we sat at this table two weeks ago you educated me about using a mask placed over text to let just a few words show through. But so far I am having trouble picking out a few words that might make a meaningful message."

"Hmm," I nodded as she looked back down at the letter.

"'Tag sale is Saturday' seems like an interesting phrase. 'The diamond ring' also draws my attention." Stacy gently bit her lip as her analysis continued. She looked up at me and smiled, "For now I have excluded 'Lint remover' as being important."

I laughed and complimented her for starting a promising line of analysis, then added, "Last night I thought about use of a mask as well, but there doesn't really seem to be an interesting embedded message considering entire words. But trickier would be if a mask covered only parts of many words; then a mask would exclude all superfluous data but allow the creation of entirely new words made from the visible letters. I haven't had time to follow that idea."

Stacy frowned. "But if you eliminate 90 percent of the letters and make new words from a letter here and a letter there you could make thousands of possible short phrases."

"Exactly. A challenging puzzle. The solution would be easier if we knew the context."

"Which we don't have," Stacy added.

"But there are other ways of encoding messages. I'll work on this today while you're gone."

Just then the waitress brought our food, so I tucked the letter back into my pocket.

⁓

It was raining as I drove home from IHOP. I was more certain every day that I was falling in love with Stacy. And I was pretty sure that she felt the same about me. Too bad she had things to do today and tomorrow.

I made a cup of tea as the rain pelted the kitchen window.

A good day for playing with a puzzle. I powered up my laptop and unfolded the letter.

I noted that the first letter of each word when placed in series created the sequence swsctsspctr... and that seemed quite unpromising. It was also nonsense in reverse order. I signed into my laptop and brought up a new Word document. I decided to test other scenarios by typing each word in a single column. Then I could just read down the columns of letters, as well as read up the columns of letters, seeking a hidden message. Placing every word in a single column I soon had constructed the following:

Still
Water
Stay...

I spent ten minutes looking up and down the columns of letters, but no message was obvious. This might be harder than I had hoped. I paused to reflect, and I recalled the stories of the intrepid Bletchley Park codebreakers, including Alan Turing, as they cracked the German Enigma code during World War II. I had encouraged Stacy to watch the film, *The Imitation Game*, a few months ago. She was pleasantly surprised that she enjoyed it much more than she had expected.

I had since learned about some of the German breakthroughs of Allied codes, accomplished in large part by a particularly talented engineer, Wilhelm Tranow. He was a young whiz at math and the new radio technology in the early years of the twentieth century. His budding talents and intelligence were recognized when he served as a lowly sailor, and he was promoted to work in a German codebreaking group. He had a major impact on events years later during World War II.

My wandering thoughts were interrupted when my cell phone rang. It was Sam, my office-mate at the company. He was also a poker enthusiast and wanted to set a date to go together to Foxwoods to play poker. We chose Saturday, April 10. He suggested that we could play cards very late, then spend the night at no cost at his mother's small farmhouse that he had recently inherited; it was located a few miles from the casino. We said goodbye until we should meet at the coffee machine in the morning.

My attention returned to the letter. Rather than making a vertical listing of each word, it seemed logical next to make a vertical listing of each phrase terminated by a period. I pulled up another blank Word page and began:

Still water.
Stay calm.
Tag sale is Saturday.
Partly cloudy.
Tree rings.
The grasshopper.
Bat cave.
Slow down.
Hammer head.
The diamond ring.
Sleep walking.
Bat boy.
NAFTA is a bad deal.
Stomp...

Although the columns made up of the first letters, or of the second letters, were nonsense, my heart skipped a beat as I read the third column. There it was, an intelligible message: iagreetomeetfoxwdsrainmakerstatueapriltenattwopmbluejacketredrose

The irony of decoding a meeting appointment at Foxwoods on April 10 just twenty minutes after Sam and I had planned to go to Foxwoods on the next convenient Saturday, April 10, was not lost on me. But after a few minutes of exhilaration, I began to worry. Maybe these were not lovers meeting to share a passionate stay in a hotel. The cypher method was quite unsophisticated, so I was certain that this message was not any government's work. The message was from a private individual to another private individual, both apparently amateurs at using codes. These might be gangsters. And I had yesterday sent on the re-sealed letter, though I had not identified myself. Perhaps I could still see who showed up at Foxwoods at the Rainmaker Statue at 2 pm. Sam will love this adventure.

⊙〰〰⦾

Sam laughed for five minutes on Monday morning when I gave him the details. He was enthusiastic, but agreed that some cautionary steps might be wise in light of the small chance that these might be armed criminals who were planning to rob a bank. Sam also advised that I needed to stake out this Tate Wilcox in New Haven to see what he looked like. So late-Monday afternoon I parked near that house and saw a plumber's van pull up. A middle-aged, stocky, Caucasian man got out of the van and entered the house. He seemed entirely unremarkable. I drove home.

We were busy at work, so that was the end of my surveillance. Sam and I devised a plan. Sam made phone calls to put things in place, then we waited. Stacy and I went to dinner several times but I shared nothing more with her. I wouldn't involve her in this.

Sam and I agreed to take Friday, April 9, off from work, and by 9 am that day we were each driving our own car, Sam in the lead, convoy-style, to his inherited farmhouse near Foxwoods. We parked in the gravel driveway, and Sam led me into the house to show me where I could set my suitcase and make use of the facilities. The 80-year-old, two-bedroom, single-bathroom house had five small rooms with old furnishings and was not in very good repair.

"All the plumbing works," Sam assured me.

We walked out into the front yard to gaze at the ruin behind the chain-link fence. All that remained of the small, dilapidated house that had been there for more than a century was a stone fireplace and chimney. A red and white sign on the fence read "CONDEMNED. Do not enter."

"The state inspected these two properties and demanded that I fence and tear down that one. That cost me some money because they couldn't just bulldoze it. It was dismantled only partly using a bulldozer, and partly using sledgehammers and crow bars. Notice the deep rocky crevice under the floor."

We put our noses on the metal fence and peered through the chain-link to assess the mostly missing floor suspended over a deep natural pit in the bedrock.

"Great-grandma told her son that someone had built the house before the Civil War. They built it over the geological curiosity to take advantage of having a basement without the necessity of blasting out the hole. Connecticut basically is four inches of dirt sitting on solid rock. The basement under the back two rooms was twelve feet deep and was a cool place for storage of food items. But the basement under the front three rooms had an irregular rock floor. It was twenty to forty feet deep and was not really good for anything. I was told a glacier made the crevice. Rainwater drains away down the steep hill in the back. So it's just a dry, three-sided pit."

As Sam reached up to unwind the chain that held the gate shut, he pointed out the large sheets of plywood leaning up against the fence. "Those are the four-feet by eight-feet sheets of quarter-inch plywood that I ordered. Garza's delivered them Tuesday and charged my card. You owe me half," Sam smiled.

I followed Sam through the gate, and we stopped on the edge of the precipice. Sam continued, "You need to walk this way about ten feet, then you can get out to the fireplace by first walking on this beam, then carefully turn right onto that next beam until you can step onto the stone. Follow me and don't look down."

My pulse doubled as we balanced single-file on first the one beam, then the next. Sam showed me where some sort of weapon could be stored on a narrow ledge about two feet up inside the chimney. But we had no weapon. We made our way back out across the beams, set out the plywood as we had calculated, and chained the gate closed. It was midafternoon and we were hungry. I volunteered to drive us to Foxwoods so we could have a meal, then play some Friday evening poker.

⟆⟆⟆⟆

It was past 9 am when I heard Sam using the bathroom. We decided to take one car south to a restaurant on I-95. As we ate we made adjustments to our plan. If a man wearing a jacket with a rose met another man at the Rainmaker Statue, Sam would follow them on foot wherever they went while I would go to my car in the Foxwoods parking garage and stay in touch by cell with Sam. If they got into a vehicle, Sam would alert me to the vehicle description and direction of travel, and I would follow them. They might be criminals with guns involved with drugs. We wanted to investigate, but not confront them. If it seemed like they were criminals, we could call the police.

At 1:30 pm we sat on widely separated benches within sight of the Rainmaker Statue, a depiction of a young, male Indian who was shooting an arrow up into the clouds to try to bring rain. Throngs of Saturday visitors were meandering in the hallways around the statue.

My phone rang at 2:05.

"Middle-aged man with blue jacket and red rose is here on the north side. Walking west. Another middle-aged man is now shaking his hand. Quick come look," reported Sam. And he hung up.

297

I caught sight of the two men. Caucasian. Clean shaven. Solidly built. Each about six feet tall. Probably forty years old. Slacks and sport coats. One appeared to be the man I saw at 1201 Sherman.

Within five minutes I was in my car waiting. My phone rang. "They're sitting at a table in the food court, just talking. I'll call back soon." Sam hung up.

Minutes later Sam had another report. "My heart is still pounding. I just rode up to level four of the garage in the same elevator with them, along with other people. They got into a black SUV and have started toward the down ramp. Connecticut plate AF35692."

"Thanks, Sam. Now drive and park at destination A." I started my engine and made my way toward the down ramp.

Finally on street level I could see a black SUV about three cars ahead stopped for the red light where one either turned right to go south to I-95, or left to go north. The SUV was in the right turn lane, but I couldn't see the plate. I maneuvered to turn right.

A few minutes later I was directly behind the SUV, and the plate was correct. I dropped back fifty yards as the two-lane highway wound through the woods. We headed west on I-95, approached the Connecticut River, and took the exit. Driving north I could see that we would be going past the Naval Submarine Base, New London. I stayed well back as we drove past the entrance. A couple of miles further on the SUV pulled into a fast-food place, and I kept driving north while keeping watch in my rear view mirror. I pulled into a gas station and parked. I had a view south toward the burger place. Within seconds the SUV pulled out of the lot and headed south, so I pulled out and followed. Entering the town of Groton, the SUV pulled into a restaurant's parking lot. I drove past that and pulled into the lot next to that business. I saw the two men walk to the front door of the restaurant and enter. I dialed Sam. It was 4:15 pm.

"They drove by the Naval Submarine Base at New London. Now they're in Tommy's Seafood in Groton, east of the river and south of I-95. I'm parked a block away."

"Great. I feel like some seafood. What do you think? Shall I go in?"

"You can go into Tommy's to assess, and maybe have something to eat. I'll stay in my car and be ready for movement."

"Okay. Bye."

While Sam was driving south I kept one eye on the restaurant as I searched for information about the submarine base. I knew it was important but I had no details. I read quickly. There was a public museum, but most of the base was off-limits to the public since two major types of nuclear submarines operated there. Los Angeles-class subs are older and have propellers. Virginia-class submarines are newer, built since 2000. They have pump-jet propulsors instead of propellers. The propulsors make much less noise, yet these huge submarines, longer than a football field, can reach remarkable speeds and are believed to be faster underwater than on the surface. Of course, both classes of submarines are powered by nuclear reactors, and they carry nuclear weapons as well as many types of conventional weapons.

I saw Sam's car pull into Tommy's. He disappeared through the front door. An hour passed – no activity or message. I stepped away from my car to use the men's room, and I bought some peanuts and a diet soda.

A text arrived from Sam: "They're at a back table drinking beer. Seem to be in no hurry."

"Good," I replied.

More time passed. It was now getting dark. This long wait was clearly intentional, but I was uncertain as to its purpose.

Finally another text arrived from Sam, "They're paying the bill and standing up. I'll sit here a bit. They'll be coming out soon."

"Good," I replied.

The two men walked slowly out of the building, got into the SUV, and exited the parking lot. I started my engine to follow. They drove a short distance north, then headed east on I-95. I followed a hundred yards behind. Soon they took an exit, passed under the highway, then got back up on I-95 headed west. Very peculiar. I tried to remain well back. It seemed that they were becoming suspicious that they were being followed. As we approached the bridge over the Connecticut River they slowed from 70 to 50. I had to slow also to keep my distance. As we crossed the bridge, they slowed to 45, an unreasonable speed. I needed to pass them and just keep going west or they would catch on to me. So I passed them at 60 and kept driving. Within seconds they were coming up behind me fast; their extremely bright headlights were alarming. I knew I had been spotted, and I floored the accelerator. I realized that their car was much faster than mine, so staying on I-95 made no sense. I approached a familiar exit, took the ramp at high speed, and soon I was hurtling through the woods with the menacing SUV in hot pursuit.

*

The 911 operator said that a police car would be dispatched; she promised to stay on the line with me.

The two men apparently had stepped through the open gate, although I couldn't see them because I was stooped inside the fireplace.

"C'mon out, buddy. We wanna talk to you," one shouted.

"Why are you shooting at me? I don't want any trouble. Please leave me alone."

The reply was two pistol shots, followed by laughter.

"Were those gunshots?" the operator inquired.

"Yes, I'm in a bit of trouble here. I think someone is gonna get hurt."

Seconds passed. I heard the men talking quietly, but I couldn't make out what they said. Suddenly there was the sound of splintering wood, and two men yelled before the night again grew totally silent. I peeked around the corner but no one was visible. Headlights from the parked SUV painted the neat plywood floor, although there was now one four- by eight-foot black rectangle present – a gaping mouth. As I carefully walked east and then north away from the fireplace and back to solid ground, I stooped down to listen for what sound might emerge from below, but there was only silence. I dared not switch on my cell phone's small flashlight and bend forward to peer into the pit, fearing that someone down there might take a shot. I hoped the men were only injured and not dead, but I was going to wait a few more minutes for the police to arrive before assessing that.

I told the 911 operator to send two ambulances. I sent a quick text to Sam that I was at the farmhouse and all was well. With me, that is. "The men are in the pit," I added.

I didn't have to wait long for the police. After my one minute summary and my warning of a potential gunshot from the basement, the two policemen bravely used flashlights to look down into the pit where arms and legs were unmoving and sprawled across the rocks in odd postures. They also allowed me to stand behind them as they looked in the back of the SUV. Six pipe bombs in a brown cardboard box.

PART II
CURIOUS ESSAYS

HOW DO I POLITELY DEFEND RELIGION TO MY BEST FRIEND, AN ATHEIST?

(First published in
Today's American Catholic,
March 2019.)

That man is the product of causes which had no provision of the end they were achieving; that his origins, his growth, his hopes, his fears, his loves and beliefs are but the outcome of accidental collocations of atoms; that no fire, no heroism, no intensity of thought and feeling, can preserve an individual life beyond the grave; that all the labors of the ages, all the devotion, ... all the noonday brightness of human genius are destined to extinction ... all these things, if not quite beyond dispute, are yet so nearly certain, that no philosophy which rejects them can hope to stand. Only within the scaffolding of these truths, only

on the firm foundation of unyielding despair, can
the soul's habitation henceforth be safely built.

—Bertrand Russell

"Then you are a king!" Pilate said.
    "You say that I am a king," Jesus answered.
"For this reason I was born and have come into
the world, to testify to the truth. Everyone who
belongs to the truth listens to my voice."
    "What is truth?" Pilate asked.

—John 18:37–38

Many of my friends are atheists. This is understandable because I am a physician and scientist, and in our modern
secular society a large proportion of scientists are atheists.
They generally are very good, law-abiding people who are raising
fine families. They donate to charities. They hope for peace and
care about the underprivileged. But they are suspicious about
creeds and religions. They dismiss statements made without solid
evidence. They sometimes say to me, when the bustle of Christmas
is over, how this was a very fine time for children. And they ask
me, "Jim, how can you still seriously believe in a religion?"

I want to share an outline of a defense of a belief in God that
I find very useful when I am conversing with atheist friends. I
think it may be useful to you, but because of the need for brev-
ity, at times I must simply refer you to certain sources.

The first point to make is that a belief in God generally
goes hand-in-hand with a belief in an afterlife. Very rarely can
a thoughtful person believe in an Almighty Creator but not an
afterlife, or vice versa. The necessary conjunction of these two
concepts actually turns out to be very helpful in making my argument. I presented a favorite quote at the start from the brilliant
philosopher and atheist, Bertrand Russell, who was despairing at
humankind's mortality. Can it be true that there is no God and
that a person's short life on this planet is essentially pointless?

There is no scientifically testable evidence to support a belief in God – but what is truth, and how do we determine what is true?

A major confusion has occurred in our secular world, in part because of the influence of John Dewey and some others who abandoned Aristotle's ancient correspondence theory of truth (that an idea is true if it corresponds with the grand reality even though we cannot prove it). The pragmatic philosophers instead proposed that an idea is true only if it can be rigorously proven using tests and evidence. This latter statement actually sounds very reasonable at first, but let me paraphrase a clarifying example used by Martin Gardner in his wonderful book, *The Whys of a Philosophical Scrivener* (1999 edition).

If a deck of 52 playing cards is shuffled and spread face-down on a table, and one card is slid forward face-down, the statement, "This is the Queen of Hearts," will be demonstrated to be true if some test, such as turning over the card to reveal the face, is performed. Other less straightforward tests could be used. If it is a glass table, one need not turn over the card but instead one could use a mirror under the table. An extreme test while leaving the card unturned might be to take some sort of x-ray image of the card. But the truth can only be proven by some sort of a test. An extreme pragmatist would declare that without a test, the statement "This is the Queen of Hearts" carries no truth-value whatsoever.

If, without revealing the face of that card, the deck were reassembled and then immediately tossed into a furnace and burned to ashes, an extreme pragmatist would say that the statement, "The card selected was the Queen of Hearts" has no actual meaning or truth-value. In contrast, Aristotle and most people who you might meet on the street would revert to the classic meaning of truth rather than the pragmatic meaning of truth. One could say truly, "That card was the Queen of Hearts" if, in fact, it actually was the Queen of Hearts, although we have no way to prove it at this time. The actual, literal truth of the statement "That card was the Queen of Hearts" would be true if the identity corresponded with the broader reality of the world which is outside of the minds of people. In fact, the essential truth or falsity of a statement rests "out there" and does not rely in any way on what tests or observations people make.

Another example that Gardner mentions is that mathematicians using computers discover that a very large integer having 300 digits has just been proven to be a prime number. But that integer was a prime number even in the days of Aristotle and even before any people existed. It did not suddenly become a prime number at the moment it was carefully tested and found to be prime. Truth is already "out there." (I couldn't resist quoting Jesus and Pilate at the start of this article.)

Very important in my own thinking has been my realization that Gödel's 1931 Incompleteness Theorem proves that there are large numbers of true statements (an infinite number?) that can never actually be proven formally to be true within a given logical system of thinking. Note that these true statements are not just unproven – they are *unprovable* in a specific logical system because the system's underlying assumptions are not expansive enough. Yet when the formal assumptions are expanded to deal with those truths, an infinite number of genuine truths remain unprovable using those new limiting assumptions. A rigorously defined system, even formal mathematics, will always be incomplete. This is a vital point, but is a bit technical. Please see Douglas Hofstadter's revised edition of Nagel and Newman's wonderful book, *Gödel's Proof* (2001).

Although Thomas Aquinas and many others have made arguments about the truth of God's existence, Gardner believes that these proofs fall far short. In fact, Gardner believes that, by design, God's existence cannot be proven because then humans would be coerced to believe in God. Gardner's view is that our world is set up to force us to make a moral choice. We must choose to believe in God, or not, of our own free will.

The choice to believe in God despite lack of scientific evidence is partly justified by our tandem beliefs in goodness and justice, which are widely shared. We have an intuitive sense that people who perform evil in the world must face consequences eventually. And humans, unlike any other animal, have a sense of what is good and evil even if we subscribe to no specific religion. The life of a 12-year old girl who is raped and murdered cannot end so tragically – we feel that there must be an afterlife to provide meaning to her life. An atheist would say that these are just feelings and intuitions, not logical deductions based on data. The atheist is correct. But giving credence to such intuitions, making a choice about what the ultimate truth is without solid data, can be justified, as I will explain.

Philosopher Immanuel Kant followed his magnificent *Critique of Pure Reason* with an unusual and rather difficult to read work, *Critique of Practical Reason*, in which he reflects on the moral law that we mysteriously carry within us. And he argues that this can be a foundation for belief in God. American philosopher William James extended these ideas. His influential *The Will to Believe* could have been more accurately titled, "The Right to Believe in God even without Evidence" (my invented title). Martin Gardner explains clearly what James was driving at, and I paraphrase Gardner below.

When making an important decision (perhaps whether to marry someone, or whether to believe in God) without the benefit of compelling scientific evidence, proceeding with a choice rather than fearing to make a choice can be justified if three criteria are fulfilled:

1. The alternatives must be plausible enough so that you are capable of deciding either way.
2. The choice must be forced.
3. The alternatives must be momentous, not trivial.

To illustrate, James quotes a passage from Fitzjames Stephen. "We stand on a mountain pass in the midst of whirling snow and blinding mist, through which we get glimpses now and then of paths which may be deceptive. If we stand still we shall be frozen to death. If we take the wrong road we shall be dashed to pieces. We do not certainly know whether there is any right one. What must we do? Be strong and of a good courage. Act for the best, hope for the best, and take what comes ... If death ends all, we cannot meet death better."

I should add that my choice in favor of religion (in my specific case I have settled on Christianity) also has been bolstered by my review of objective data about the physical universe, data that admittedly are only supportive and not conclusive information. Before Darwin the complexity of biological systems was used as an argument that animals and humans had been designed by a Creator, although a modern understanding of genetics and natural selection make that way of thinking rather outdated. Even so, the physical universe really does appear to be designed, as evidenced by dimensionless physical constants vital for shaping the cosmos. If their values were only a little different, then stars could not form, or nuclear fusion processes could not occur, etc., and the universe would have been incompatible with life as we know it. You can read *The Mind of God* and *The Goldilocks Enigma: Why is the Universe Just Right for Life?* by Paul Davies for more information. Or just search "Fine-tuned universe" and please stick with reliable sources.

JESUS AT MY BACK DOOR: WHEN SCIENCE MEETS RELIGION

(First published in *Today's American Catholic*, January/February 2018. Reproduced with permission.)

Finding patterns in nature and then developing a mental framework to make sense of these patterns is a valuable human ability. A randomly generated image of shadowed geometric forms and curving lines, for example, can cause a modern viewer to visualize a snake or other animal hiding in bushes. Such rapid and seemingly effortless mental construction of meaningful images from complex patterns likely had an important survival value for millennia. Quickly seeing and reacting to a potential snake or predator was extremely useful, whereas startling to a false alarm had little downside. But since our environment and daily activities have drastically changed, there can be drawbacks today.

In the modern world, some people construct conspiracy

theories or speculate about stock market trends based on coincidences or random occurrences. They readily see an interesting pattern where there actually is none. When plotted on a map of London, for example, the sites of exploding German rockets seemed to cluster, but an expected degree of clustering is merely a confirmation of the randomness of the bombing – an alternative pattern, that a rocket fell precisely into each square block of London, would have proven that the Germans had an astoundingly accurate guidance mechanism. Seeing and then confirming the existence of a truly relevant pattern is important. When John Snow plotted cholera cases on a map of London in 1854 he visualized undeniably significant clusters of disease suggesting that the Broad Street pump likely was causing the infection. This led to the institution of safer city drinking water systems that have been implemented globally.

Humans are complex intelligent creatures and they are very intuitive and creative. The important tendency to religiosity has combined with a knack for recognition of patterns to produce a number of interesting and/or curious events. Visions of ghostly figures have been reported since ancient times, and have been retold in religious books, in myths, in Greek plays, in Shakespeare, and in countless tales to the present day. The Old Testament recounts many visions/divine messages. Arguably, the entire course of Western civilization was altered by visions of the resurrected Jesus by his apostles and followers. And very importantly for the gentile world, Paul's vision as he traveled to Damascus was responsible for very widespread preaching about Christianity. The emperor Constantine saw a vision in the clouds that allowed him to inspire troops to win a key battle, and when Constantine later converted to Christianity, the significant resources and power of the Roman Empire were shifted from opposing to supporting Christianity. The Qur'an emphasizes the importance of dreams and visions as special revelations. In Hinduism, the vision or darshan has the nuance of being a gift: that something is actively allowing you to see it, as when clouds part and allow you momentarily to see a mountaintop. Mormonism endorses the existence of visions. Indigenous peoples around the globe have many traditions of visions. In the Amazon basin ayahuasca is a brew made from a vine that brings on hallucinogenic visions, whereas other indigenous peoples make use of mushrooms or other natural substances.

In our modern era, patterns in tree bark, or shadows in a window, can become significant because they form religious shapes. In December, 1996, patterns on the glass windows of the Seminole Finance Company in Clearwater, Florida seemed to represent the Virgin Mary. More than 500,000 visitors came to see the image, according to police records. A window with a shadowy image of the Virgin also was present in Mercy Hospital in Springfield, Massachusetts in 2008.

Something occurred recently that made me think further about such phenomena: Jesus appeared at my back door. Or, to be more precise, sunlight reflecting off my kitchen window and down onto my deck formed a perfect image of the Christian fish symbol that represents Jesus.

This is an ancient symbol, which reportedly first came into use during the persecutions of the late 2nd century. At that time it was dangerous to reveal to a stranger that you were a Christian. So to initiate a communication, a person might sweep out a curved line in the dirt or using chalk. In response, if another curve was drawn but bending the opposite way then a shape of a fish was created, sometimes with the addition of a dot for an eye. This was the symbol for Jesus since the Greek word for fish, ΙΧΘΥΣ (ichthys), contained the first letters of the phrase "Ἰησοῦς Χριστός Θεοῦ Υἱός Σωτήρ," or "Jesus Christ, Son of God, Savior."

This apparition made of sunbeams appeared to me on a Saturday afternoon as I was preparing on November 11 to read a scripture passage at Mass at 4 pm. It did give me pause, but as a man of science I felt both reverence and amusement. I took three photos to show my wife, who I knew would enjoy seeing the image. Within an hour the sun had shifted position and the image was gone. We have lived in the house for 20 years but we had never before seen this light display.

Of some interest is that the passage that I was about to read at church was Wisdom 6:12-16. This Old Testament reading explains that if you are genuinely seeking wisdom, then your open mind and open heart will actually attract wisdom to seek you out. She will come to you, and she will actually be found sitting by your own gate!

The sunbeams were teasing me, but how can we believe in any sort of spiritual visions or divine messages when we live in an age of science? Simple: there is no real conflict between science and religion. Importantly, we must recognize that religion has much to say about topics on which science must remain silent.

Good science starts with "common sense" and "reasonable" (but unprovable) assumptions, and then from these few assumptions, science uses experiments to collect facts which are in turn used to deduce important things. Note: science's main method is deduction – science moves in a precise and convincing fashion from the general to the specific. Science cannot even in principle provide a solid foundation for induction: the process of discovering solid starting assumptions based on detailed observations. But scientists must have some starting assumptions. Where do they come from? What scientists do in practice is a sort of a "bootstrap process," a term that refers to the humorous notion that a cowboy might lift himself up a step by grabbing onto and pulling upwards on his own bootstraps. Scientists use life's experiences and detailed observations to guess at starting assumptions, but they are guesses. They cannot be proven. For example, to make his magnificent leap forward for science with his new mathematics and the theory of universal gravitation, Isaac Newton assumed that space exists for all eternity and stretches regularly in all directions. Then objects move in that space, and the movements are clocked by an invariant ticking of "master time" which is the same everywhere. The novel equations worked perfectly in the 18th century, and scientists could then use deduction to calculate the orbits of planets, and send men to the moon. But Einstein postulated by using more advanced mathematics that space bends due to mass and that time is not constant or the same everywhere. Modern experiments have now proven that Newton's assumptions were only approximately correct and apply only to certain situations. Light and mass could not be described more accurately without Einstein's improved assumptions. The global positioning system (GPS) in your phone or car would not deliver you to the correct location using Newton's assumptions – GPS must be corrected using Einstein's notions for it to work properly.

During the 20th century scientists came to the realization that the universe is even more mysterious than had been thought. Essentially all of the "common sense" assumptions made in the late-19th century are only correct under special circumstances. In addition to relativity discussed previously, quantum theory has revealed deep new truths that allow extremely precise calculations and predictions, but the underlying quantum concepts are only partly understood.

The man in the street believes that he sees the world as it is. He looks at a table and sees a table. "Just common sense," he may say. But our eyes do not function like a camera that simply captures images. That solid table, made of atoms, is nearly entirely empty space. In spite of what we may think, none of us sees the world as it actually is. The brain actively participates to construct "the world" from electrical signals delivered by our senses. We do not see the color "red," for example. We only have a mental experience, called a qualia, of the color "red."

Let me note that science is particularly poor at attributing ultimate meaning. Science rests on the unproven assumption that all events in nature must be fully explainable only by natural causes – there is no allowance for any sort of "supernatural" cause. This is perfectly reasonable for a working scientist, but this rigs the system such that there is no way ever to deduce ultimate meaning using a scientific process. A pure-minded scientist will always end up with the conclusion that the universe – and our lives – are absurd and have no ultimate meaning.

Perhaps without thinking carefully about it, religious persons have already figured out the right path forward. This is part of what a religious person calls the "leap of faith." They also may be scientific persons, but they are willing to go beyond science by "bootstrapping" a little higher to include a new and vital assumption. One must assume, I think, as a first principle that life and the universe are NOT absurd – life and the universe do have meaning. This is a reasonable assumption, but is a bit radical for a scientist. But this is completely justifiable as an assumption. Things that religious persons might think then follow quite logically by deduction. For example, an atheist may see a small child die from a terrible disease. He might well view the child's life as pointless. In contrast, if one believes as a necessary and reasonable assumption that life is meaningful, then the fact that the small child died of the disease demands that there must be some other way that the child's life remains meaningful in spite of death. For those of us who are Christians, this meaning is provided by the promises of Christ. It is OK that they cannot be proven. It is perfectly legitimate that we must believe them as a matter of faith. As I explained, having unprovable but reasonable assumptions is a routine and accepted aspect of science.

WAS GEORGE WASHINGTON AIDED BY MIRACLES?

(First published in *Today's American Catholic*, May 2018. Reproduced with permission.)

As Christians we believe in the possibility of miracles. But as modern and mostly scientific-minded people, the topic of miracles may make us feel a bit uncomfortable. And this topic is closely related to another topic that may raise discomfort – what actually is the likely efficacy of prayer?

These topics are much too complex to cover comprehensively in a short newspaper article. But as a physician and scientist I want to share a few thoughts and, for interest, also speculate about some historical episodes that occurred during the American Revolutionary War. If nothing else, these historical incidents are great stories.

Many Eastern religions and cultures believe that the world's history may best be described as endless cycles that repeat. This is not a crazy idea, since in nature there are many cycles that clearly repeat such as seasons during the year and the phases of the moon. Eastern peoples even developed concepts of reincarnation.

But the early Jewish people latched onto the notion of linear history. The long course of history was believed to have a purpose and to consist of events that allow progress rather than endless repetition. Moreover, there is one God who acts to intervene in history. The Bible relates how God can favor one side in a battle, or can cause plagues or floods. All of these ideas carried over into the Christian tradition, but they may sit uncomfortably with the modern mindset.

The Oxford English Dictionary defines a miracle as a marvelous event occurring within human experience which cannot have been brought about by human power or by the operation of any natural agency, and must therefore be ascribed to the special intervention of the Deity or of some supernatural being. (The word was first written in English in a manuscript in 1137). The given definition is clear, but in application there is a problem: how do we really know that a marvelous event could not have been caused naturally? A teenager from a remote wilderness might at first consider TV a miracle, although likely within a week he will have learned to fast-forward through the commercials.

As a scientist, I am familiar with applying statistical tests to see if the results of an experiment differ from what might have occurred by chance. An important caveat is that one must pre-specify the desired outcome (*a prior* prediction) before doing the experiment, rather than assessing data afterwards (*post hoc*). There is bias if one is only looking afterwards. Scientists arbitrarily set a threshold that if the prediction of an experiment occurs with less than a 1 in 20 probability of being due to chance alone (called a p-value less than 0.05), then the experiment MAY have successfully confirmed the prediction, although more experiments must be done to strengthen (but never absolutely prove) the theory. It is problematic that even quite rare events can and do occur by chance. Thus, even trying to apply statistical reasoning may not definitively help us when talking about miracles.

Catholicism allows each believer to take a flexible approach to the mystery of miracles. Personally, I subscribe to the philosophy that the miracles of Jesus were primarily actions for his immediate audience, and news of them was passed verbally in the next decades; miracle stories were not intended to convince readers centuries later with watertight proofs. How can I know the intent of Jesus? I am just taking a thoughtful approach that makes logical sense to me. A key concept is that, in the modern era, the miraculous nature of an event logically must not be plainly apparent because absolute proof of the existence and action of God would coerce people into a mandatory belief in God. Forcing people to believe in the divine would remove their free choice to do good or bad actions. Humans would essentially then be puppets, not free agents. Thus, all miraculous events must be either: (1) veiled and made indistinguishable from rare natural events, or (2) for clearly non-natural occurrences such as walking on water or raising the dead, the miraculous events must be presented as matters requiring faith. I believe that God does not want to twist our arms to believe, but instead He wants us to use our emotional intelligence and our gradually developing faith to come to trust in Him. Then we choose freely to live Christian lives. The process is a bit like gradually falling in love with another person – a thoroughly human and nonscientific process – and must be experienced to be understood. This view of miracles is a bit disappointing to the scientific materialist who wants to get out his cameras and instruments, but this is right in line with the thinking of many thoughtful educated persons, such as mathematician Martin Gardner. In Gardner's wonderful book, *The Whys of a Philosophical Scrivener*, one chapter is entitled "The Proofs: Why I Do Not Believe God's Existence Can Be Demonstrated," which is followed immediately by a chapter entitled "Faith: Why I Am Not an Atheist."

In short, it is perfectly reasonable with a modern mindset to approach miracles as being special and mysterious – and real. Some may view miracles as possible but very rare, but sophisticated scientists familiar with quantum mechanics now view even the world's common atomic and sub-atomic events as extremely mysterious and wondrous. Every particle of light (photon) is, in a way, a miracle.

Having completed the serious part of my article, I now delve into a little fun regarding speculation as to whether George Washington was ever aided by miracles. Of course, this is a *post hoc* discussion as the events are far in the past. Some of the text that follows was adapted from my book, *Free To Decide: Building a Life in Science and Medicine*. Details cited are based on the books by the writers mentioned, as well as the exhibits at the Webb House Museum in Wethersfield, CT, and discussion of the Washington-Rochambeau Revolutionary Route published on-line by the U.S. National Park Service.

A first point of importance is that George Washington was known to be a prayerful man. In late-August, 1776, Washington placed some troops within the key city of New York, but he placed a strong defensive force across the East River on Brooklyn Heights. British warships with large numbers of troops were present in the harbor, and 20,000 British troops were landed on Long Island under General Howe. They moved slowly toward Brooklyn Heights. Washington felt that he had to make a stand, and during daytime he had more and more troops moved from the city by boat to Brooklyn Heights. But if the British could send ships up the East River, the bulk of Washington's army would be surrounded with no hope of victory or retreat. The American Revolution would be over. For the moment this deadly movement of ships was blocked by a strong north wind. Not the world's most experienced general, it was only late in the afternoon that Washington began to realize how dangerous his situation had become. The small boats then were used all night to move many of the men, cannon and arms from Brooklyn Heights back to Manhattan. Astonishingly, this was done in silence and in such order that the experienced British force (who were resting until morning) did not realize that this was happening. By dawn a smaller and helpless group of colonial troops still remained at Brooklyn Heights desperately needing to be evacuated – but luckily an intensely thick fog hugged the ground making the weak position invisible. According to historian David McCullough in his essay, "What the Fog Wrought," a man standing only a few yards away could not be seen, and sounds were muffled by the dense air. During this persistent fog all of the remaining troops and their arms (except for several large cannon) were silently rowed back to Manhattan. When the fog rose later that morning, Howe was astonished to find that the entire colonial army and all of their arms had completely vanished! Military historians today marvel at this improbable series of events.

A second fortuitous episode occurred when Washington's cold and starving troops, up to 12,000 men, were encamped for the winter at Valley Forge. Desperation forced Washington to order nets to be deployed into the river to see if any fish might be obtained. A huge haul of fish was caught, so large that locals reported that nothing like it had ever been seen in the area. The army ate well and gradually recovered. Sounding almost like a biblical event, Pulitzer Prize-winning author John McPhee has researched this, and he actually found a number of conflicting accounts. The fish apparently were shad (*Alosa sapidissima*), which were known to be commercially important in the area and which sometimes ran in large schools when spawning in the early spring. Sources suggested that possibly multiple large catches occurred in 1778 to save the army. McPhee has humorously referred to shad as America's "founding fish."

Throughout the war Washington had fought and retreated, then fought again and retreated again. The rag-tag American army was fighting the most professional and powerful military in the world. He knew that at all costs he must preserve the army even if he could win few battles. British troops were massed in two places in North America: New York City, and further south in the North Carolina / Virginia area. Washington wanted to team with his new French allies, who had provided about 5,000 troops, to attack one of these two concentrations of British troops, and since he and his French allies were north of New York City, Washington strongly favored attacking there, in spite of the very solid defenses. He met with French General Rochambeau in Wethersfield, CT on May 22, 1781, and Washington strongly argued for the potentially suicidal attack on New York. Rochambeau preferred not to proceed with the attack, but agreed to move his troops from Newport, Rhode Island to a point north of New York so that they would be positioned for that attack or perhaps some other plan. Cleverly, on May 28, Rochambeau sent by ship a message to the French Admiral de Grasse (then in the West Indies) asking whether he might support by sea either an attack on New York City, or instead an attack on the British Southern force operating near Chesapeake Bay. Hoping he would hear something back from de Grasse in a few weeks, Rochambeau marched his troops out of Newport in early June, 1781, and met up with the colonial troops at a point north of New York City, as promised, on July 6.

Washington, in overall command, still felt that the dangerous attack on New York was the best hope for the revolution. But a true blessing was Washington's humility and willingness to listen to others offering advice. This crucial aspect of Washington's personality may well have been the true miracle wrought during the war. Washington's best engineer, General Duportail, on July 27 provided a detailed assessment arguing that the Americans and French did not have sufficient troops to besiege New York. On August 1 Washington wrote in his diary that he likely should give up the attack in the north, and instead consider a southern attack of some kind.

On August 14 the fast French frigate Concorde arrived carrying a message from de Grasse that his fleet had left the West Indies and would sail to Chesapeake, but could only remain there until October 15. On August 16 Washington received a letter from his best general in the south, the Marquis de Lafayette, reporting that the destructive southern British force commanded by General Cornwallis was resting in the tobacco port of Yorktown, Virginia, where the British troops could be safely and easily re-supplied by sea by the powerful British navy. Washington realized that Cornwallis would be surprised and temporarily cut off by the appearance of the large French fleet. So on August 16 Washington began rushing his American and French land forces south so that Cornwallis could be locked in both on land and sea.

For security reasons only a few top officers knew that the ultimate destination would be Virginia. The pattern of the initial march made it look to the British like Washington was simply surrounding New York City for an attack there. On September 2 many troops continued to move south through Trenton, giving the first hint of the massive southward shift in force. By the time the allied troops were marching south through Philadelphia on September 5, British General Clinton in New York was beginning to devise how he could urgently send reinforcements south. But on that same day many of de Grasse' ships arrived at the mouth of the Chesapeake and fought off the British ships gathered there in the so-called Battle of the Capes. This cut off Cornwallis from aid by sea. On September 28 the allied land forces arrived to block in Cornwallis, although he still felt relatively safe because he thought the allies had no heavy cannon. But by October 9 the available American cannon began firing, and within a few days the 100 heavy siege guns carried by the French had been put in place and began bombarding the trapped British troops. On October 14 the young Alexander Hamilton led forces in a risky night attack that captured two redoubts that guarded the outskirts of the British lines, so then the French cannon could be moved forward to fire even more directly on the British. A desperate attempt by Cornwallis to ferry many of his troops away by barge on October 16 was blocked by a powerful storm, so the next day he signaled for talks. On Oct. 19 Cornwallis surrendered his entire force of 8,000 men and also had to give up all his arms. When news of this reached England there was a firestorm of criticism, and efforts to negotiate a peace treaty were begun. The negotiations took time, but the colonies had won their independence.

The events in Brooklyn Heights, Valley Forge, and during the Yorktown campaign were remarkable and unusual, but I am not sure if they qualify as miraculous. It appeared, though, that Washington's prayers had been answered.

A POKER-PLAYING PHYSICIAN REFLECTS ON LUCK

As a biologist, physician, and amateur poker player, I have thought a lot about luck. During my medical career, I have faced numerous heartbreaking clinical issues, many apparently occurring due to bad luck. On a lighter note, I have also faced countless damaging and sometimes embarrassing poker situations. Each of us seems to be walking around daily in a virtual blizzard of random events, some seemingly less random than others. How can we properly think about and negotiate this situation?

A Blizzard of Events

Speaking of blizzards, have you ever tried to catch a snowflake on your tongue? It's actually easy as long as you are not exhaling. Think of it. A tiny snowflake falls ten thousand feet and lands exactly on my tongue. We see immediately, regarding the fate of a single snowflake, the important difference between an *a priori* hypothesis versus a *post hoc* analysis. If I had identified that single snowflake in advance, when it was still at an altitude of 9,800 feet, and predicted that it would land exactly on my tongue, and then it actually hit the target, this experiment would have proven that I had amazing and sophisticated predictive power, with a p value <0.0001. The probability of that single snowflake following that exact predicted path would be less than one in ten thousand due to chance alone. It would probably actually be less than one in a million. Yet, post hoc when billions of snowflakes are falling, certainly several of them will fall on my tongue.

During my childhood in the post–World War II years, I realized that it was a remarkable fact that the pilot of the *Enola Gay*, Paul Tibetts, who dropped the atomic bomb on Hiroshima, was born in my hometown: Quincy, Illinois. This made for an interesting point of conversation, but this *post hoc* observation actually had no significance.

As a child, I rode bicycles without wearing a helmet and rode in cars without seat belts. I was familiar with Highway 104 that ran east of Quincy. Cars whizzed at seventy miles per hour on this narrow two-lane road. A kind man, Mr. Evans, who lived across the street from us, was killed on that road about thirty miles east of town when I was thirteen years old, and the tragic event raised several questions in my young mind about how improbable that accident should have been. Mr. Evans was driving east, likely at sixty-five miles per hour, when another driver who was driving south at high speed on a small intersecting road failed to stop at a stop sign. The massive fatal collision resulted. Yet it seemed to me at my tender age that this collision was extremely unlikely to have occurred. If Mr. Evans had left his driveway three seconds earlier, or three seconds later, then the cars would have missed each other. Moreover, if the other driver had left his home three seconds earlier, or three seconds later, the cars also would have missed each other. I also considered that if both men had agreed to practice their accident for one hundred days in a row, insanely attempting to collide with each other after driving many miles, their attempts almost certainly would fail one hundred times; they could never have arrived at the intersection at precisely the same instant. Yet they did. A footnote to this tale is that my father had a high school classmate friend who was driving at high speed on a gravel road with high rows of corn on both sides, reducing peripheral visibility. She drove over a railroad crossing that had no protective gate, and she crossed at exactly the same instant as a train, which killed her. Unlikely events occur all the time—because we are in a blizzard of events.

Determined versus Truly Random Events

The modern science of chaos has found that in our complex world, slightly changing the initial conditions of an experiment or situation may greatly change the result. The classic anecdote to illustrate this is that the slight breeze from a butterfly flapping its wings in China affects the world's developing weather in a way to produce a hurricane in the Atlantic. Many processes do not result in outcomes that follow a normal distribution but instead are nonlinear. A tiny input can result in a large output.[1] Importantly, events dealt with in chaos theory are not genuinely intrinsically random; instead they are exquisitely and precisely determined by the highly detailed starting conditions and a long, complex chain of causes and effects. But because we do not have infinite knowledge to categorize and analyze all of this complexity, the events end up being unpredictable or essentially the same as random events for us. I think this applies also to poker to a large extent, as well as to most clinical events that occur in patients. (But a caveat will be mentioned in a moment.)

Thus, there is a fine distinction to be drawn between unpredictable events that occur due to the interaction of thousands or millions of causes versus truly random events that could never be predicted even if we had superhuman abilities and could categorize every environmental condition. Truly random events, such as exactly when a specific single radioactive atom will undergo nuclear decay, are intrinsically absolutely unpredictable. The quantum phenomenon of radioactive decay can be precisely described mathematically, however, for a large population of atoms. Einstein had objected to this existence of true randomness in quantum mechanics, declaring that "God does not play dice!" He felt intuitively that additional scientific knowledge would someday reveal precisely why certain quantum events occurred—that a detailed causal chain could be worked out to explain them. But as decades have passed, and many sophisticated experiments have now shown, it is clear to most experts that quantum events actually are truly random by their intrinsic character, and that the best we will ever do to understand them is to use probabilities.

Macroscopic Results of Quantum Events

Importantly, quantum events are not just affecting invisible tiny particles. They also affect macroscopic events that dramatically change our lives every day. Consider that for the nuclear reaction in the sun to occur by fusion, for example, atomic nuclei must collide in a way that brings them closer together than is realistically possible by speeding their motion using even very large amounts of energy. The nuclei will violently collide at an extremely high temperature, yet calculations done using classical methods show that because their like-charge repulsion immensely increases at tiny distances, the nuclei simply cannot get close enough to consummate the nuclear reaction—but somehow they do transiently get close enough. The necessary extra increment of proximity of the nuclei is achieved by the nonclassical phenomenon of quantum tunneling. The precise momentum and position of a nucleus is undefined and exists only as a field of probabilities. Nuclei in the heart of the sun are leaping instantly from one spot to another in space (actually following all possible paths at the same time), allowing a few of them to have suddenly achieved the energetically impossible close proximity so that the nuclear fusion reaction can proceed. Thus, although conventional calculations prove that it is impossible, the sun does shine, allowing life on earth to exist. By the way, on the receiving end, photons that strike chlorophyll use a special quantum trick to allow that molecule to wiggle in just the right way so that light energy is efficiently captured, making plant life (and animal life) possible on our planet. Such strange quantum phenomena underlie the very nature of our universe. The biologist JBS Haldane commented decades ago, "The universe is not only stranger than we imagine, it is stranger than we *can* imagine."

Returning to clinical medicine for a moment, most lung cancers are due to carcinogenic chemicals, such as from smoking, but some lung cancers are due to chronic exposure to radon gas seeping into our houses from the foundations. Radon is radioactive. But even if we attempt to avoid radon, our cells are full of potassium atoms, and a fraction of those tiny atoms, some sitting within the nuclei of our cells, are radioactive and will spontaneously decay releasing energy—perhaps near a strand of DNA, causing a somatic mutation and a cancer. Thus, lung cancer and likely many other clinical conditions can be caused by an absolutely random quantum event. Likely most clinical problems are more determined than they are truly random, however. I graduated from the Pritzker School of Medicine at the University of Chicago in 1977, and one of the smartest kids in my class, Steven Lukes, died in his sleep five years later from a cerebral aneurysm. This silent, unsuspected vascular killer was more likely present due to a long chain of caused events rather than to an uncaused quantum event, but who really knows?

Embracing Randomness

The 2015 World Series of Poker Main Event in Las Vegas was providing both fun and terror for the 6,420 entrants. With my wife's blessings, I had purchased an entry ticket for $10,000 to play poker, and as a skilled amateur, I was both entertained and challenged. I had survived into day four of this large tournament, besting by that time nearly 5,800 less fortunate players. Many remaining players were professionals. I had hoped to be among the one thousand players who would earn a $15,000 minimum prize, thus making a small profit to pay for expenses. I had achieved that goal, but like every remaining player, I hoped to substantially surpass that minimum prize and continue on to win higher amounts.

I had seen the game of Texas Hold'em on TV in about 2006, and I first played a little in 2007 when my wife, Glenda, encouraged me to play when we were visiting a casino to see a show to celebrate our thirtieth wedding anniversary. She thought my interest in chess might carry over to poker, and she hoped that my careful analytical personality might aid my poker experiences. I read a half dozen books to study the game more carefully, and I practiced a little at two casinos in Connecticut. Now at the 2015 Main Event, I would test myself against some of the best players in the world.

During the first three days of play, I had built my starting stack of chips from 30,000 to 214,000, but by about halfway through day four of the Main Event, my chips had increased only a little more to a below average number of three hundred thousand, while some other players accumulated many more chips. Becoming desperate to make further gains as the costs of the blinds and antes were rising, I made a successful bluff with a big initial bet holding ace, deuce as my hole cards, and I made two other good bluffs to get my chips up to about 450,000. But one could not bluff too often, or eventually a player would challenge me, and big losses could result.

For the next hand, I was sitting in the big blind position, so I would be last to make the initial bet. But I would be an early bettor in all subsequent rounds during that hand, an unfavorable position. I was dealt nine of diamonds, ten of diamonds as my hole cards. These suited connectors were interesting but potentially high risk to play, especially out of position as an early bettor, since there was a low probability of actually connecting with the flop (the first three community cards, shared by all players). Should I invest precious chips in these speculative cards? Because I had just increased my chip stack a little after my successful bluffs, I decided that I would gamble since I could afford a small loss.

Although I have just used the term gamble, I am not by nature a gambler. Most doctors are not. As a biologist and physician, however, I recognize that chance entered my life long before I was even conceived. Genes in my ancestors were conserved or mutated (every person has on average dozens of new germ-line mutations, as well as many family-based and ethnic-based DNA code changes). Then on top of these DNA code changes, chromosomes in the sex cells of my ancestors recombined by crossing over during meiosis to shuffle the genes. This was nature's way of more quickly potentially bringing together several separate but favorable genes into a single offspring—separate favorable mutations, such as for better eyesight, better hearing, and lactose tolerance, could appear together in a single organism after only one generation due to the fortunate shuffling of the genes. Of course, by bad luck, an unfavorable gene or pairs of alleles might also be introduced and thereby result in an organism with a dominantly inherited or recessively inherited disease.

For each of us, we must not only be genetically lucky in order to be reasonably healthy and happy, but to reach our potential, it is useful to have loving and supportive parents, be born in the right century and country, avoid serious nonhereditary mishaps, have the opportunity to receive good health care, nutrition and education, and so on. And the list goes on. Most of these factors are not really within our control. But if our supportive families have prepared us properly, we can be sensible and avoid wasting valuable opportunities. We actually will study hard in college and make the most of our education, for example. But it is easy for many to go astray.

We could reflect even farther back in time to when by chance an asteroid struck sixty-five million years ago that wiped out the dinosaurs, thereby opening environmental niches aiding the rise of large mammals. That's luck with a vengeance. And consider that Huff et al.[2] have calculated that the effective population size of human ancestors living 1.2 million years ago was only about 18,500 hominids. These unusual animals were barely making the natural selection cut. A series of challenging environmental periods subsequently stressed our ancestors further. Curtis Marean of Arizona State University calculates from genetic data that a major human population reduction occurred during a very cold and dry ice age known as the Marine Isotope Stage 6 Period, which lasted from 193,000 to 123,000 years ago.[3] Although members of other species of hominids had already departed Africa, small numbers of *Homo sapiens* managed to survive in only a few favorable African locations, such as along the coast of what is today South Africa, where there was a bountiful supply of shellfish in shallow waters. Fewer than a thousand *Homo sapiens* may have existed on the earth at this time. Cave PP13B near Mossel Bay sheltered humans for tens of thousands of years, and those few people may be the direct ancestors of all of us. It was an extraordinary stroke of good fortune that circumstances allowed the species to survive.

It is thought that such recurring population bottlenecks are responsible for the great homogeneity of the genome of humans. If the long DNA sequences of any two random humans today are compared, about 999 out of one thousand nucleotides will be precisely the same. In contrast, chimpanzees are seven to ten times more genetically diverse.

Consider as well the small intrepid band of humans that managed to migrate out of Africa about fifty thousand to one hundred thousand years ago. It is thought that the group consisted of only a dozen or a few dozen persons. This small troop went on to populate the entire world beyond Africa, picking up a few useful *Neandertal* and *Denisovan* genes along the way (those hominid groups and other ancient groups had migrated out of Africa thousands of years before *Homo sapiens*). The typical modern European today has about 2 percent *Neandertal* genes, whereas some Australians and Pacific Islanders today have genomes with more than 4 percent *Denisovan* genes.[4] Of note, it is thought that some of these retained genes benefit the immune system.

Having summarized how humans have miraculously survived through the millennia, let me return now to explain how I survived my ten-minute key poker hand. Although at the time I did not view my nine and ten of diamonds while sitting in the big blind position as analogous to some pilfered favorable *Neandertal* genes, I was determined to see what I could make of these cards. In the first round of betting, a strong player in an early position made a three–big blind sized bet, the player on the button called, and I made a speculative call. The flop was great for me, showing deuce of spades, nine of hearts, nine of spades. Hitting trips on a flop occurs only about 2 percent of the time. I disguised the strength of my hand by checking. The player to my left also checked. But the man on the button made a moderately large bet. I was thrilled that he was betting, but I concealed my excitement, and after a short pause, I just called.

Surprisingly, the man to my left then executed a check-raise, making a substantial bet of about half of his chips. I suspected that he had a good pocket pair, such as two queens, and this was a wonderful development for me, since for the moment my trips had him beat. The man on the button folded. I hesitated a bit and then just called that large bet, using about three-quarters of my chips.

The dealer set down the next card (the fourth card on the board), the jack of hearts. If my opponent had pocket jacks, I was now heavily favored to lose, since only making quad nines could save me. But he might still be holding aces, kings, or queens. I paused, took a breath, and stared at my hole cards, waving them slightly, and I did *not* look back at the shared cards.

"I have a pretty good hand here, and I am not sure that I can lay this down," I said, and I looked intently at my hole cards. I was implying that I likely held two excellent hole cards but had not connected with the board.

"Then play your hand," he replied curtly.

After another brief pause, I went all in, which would require him either to call with about half of his remaining chips or else give up the substantial number of chips in the pot. He squirmed a little while thinking.

"Can you beat kings?" he asked. "Have a flush draw?"

I remained silent and looked down at my shoes. After thirty seconds, he pushed his chips into the pot, and we both turned over our pocket cards. He did have the pair of kings, while I had trip nines. Only the very unlikely appearance of a king as the last card (river card) could save him, but that card was the two of diamonds. I had more than doubled my chip stack to about 950,000. This one hand allowed me to climb the prize ladder much higher during the next days in the tournament.

A key lesson of this hand is that it is nice to get favorable cards, but you also must play your cards well so that if you are fortunate and your opponent also has very good (but inferior) cards, then you can maximize your gain in the situation. You must be both lucky and skilled. And I believe that this formula applies in other areas of life as well.

Moral Luck?

I knew that luck affects most things (I ran into my wife-to-be by accident in a Laundromat), but I was intrigued a few years ago when I read a new term: "moral luck." Yes, Pasteur famously stated, "Chance favors the prepared mind," and numerous scientific discoveries have involved serendipity, a particular kind of luck marked by finding out something important when you are actually looking for something else. But does luck have anything to do with ethics?

Bernard Williams[5] and Thomas Nagel,[6] in their separate essays, have developed a theory of moral luck. Moral luck characterizes situations in which a person is assigned moral blame or praise for an action or its consequences even if it is clear that the person did not have full control over either the action or its consequences. Alert: some of this discussion clearly applies to medical personnel working in busy, complex health care systems. Historically, people correlate responsibility and voluntary action. Blame (or praise) is traditionally assigned for a harmful action (or a helpful action) if the action was performed voluntarily and if the person understood the full range of consequences of their decisions and actions. Conversely, blame for a harmful action is mitigated if a person was coerced to perform the action, or performed the action accidentally or without fault or negligence, or if at the time of the action the person did not know the consequences that their action would bring. A result of the logic of correlating responsibility and voluntary action is that in many countries the legal punishment for manslaughter is different from the legal punishment for murder.

But situations involving moral luck may arise, and Williams, Nagel, and others often use a traffic accident example as an illustration of the concept. Two people are driving cars, and they are alike in every way. The first driver lets his attention drift, and he runs a red light, killing a child who is crossing the street. This first driver receives a significant prison sentence. In contrast, a second driver lets his attention drift and runs the same red light, but because no one is in the intersection, there is no injury, and this driver only receives a traffic ticket and a small fine. Many people agree that the first driver is due more moral blame than the second driver, but the problem is that there is no difference in the controllable actions performed by the two drivers. The only difference is that an external uncontrollable event occurred to the first driver but not to the second. If it is held that moral responsibility should be applied only when a person voluntarily performs or fails to perform some action, then each driver should have equal blame and should be deserving of equal punishment. Most people, however, find it difficult to rationalize equal punishment for two crimes, one that has resulted in death and the other that has resulted in no significant consequence.

In medicine (as in poker), we make decisions regularly with incomplete information. An internist may see a busy fifty-five-year-old male executive who has trouble getting to clinics because of his business. The physician may find that the man smokes a few cigarettes daily, has a minimally elevated cholesterol in the past history, and today for the first time has asymptomatic hypertension of 155/94 mm Hg. The physician tells him to quit smoking, schedules for the next morning fasting blood tests, urinalysis, and EKG, and prescribes a low dose of daily hydrochlorothiazide with the instruction to return to clinic for a recheck in one week. Moral luck enters the picture as

I now will describe two scenarios. In scenario one, the requested lab tests and EKG are never done since the man did not keep that appointment, and the patient also fails to show up for the recheck visit on day seven. A phone call to the home is answered by the spouse, who reports apologetically that her husband is fine and is in Toronto on business. Scenario two is similar in that the lab tests are not done and the man fails to show up for the recheck on day seven, but the scenario is different because the physician receives a phone call from a hospital on the other side of town with a request for information about a man they have in the intensive care unit. He suffered a massive stroke six days earlier, and the family is furious because the man had gone to see an internist who apparently did little to treat his hypertension found that day. I should add that something like this happened to me. Can a well-meaning physician be turned from a routine caregiver into a villain by an unexpected course of events?

I have also been involved with hospitalized patients who received incorrect medications due to hospital pharmacy errors. Several of these pharmacy errors caused important side effects. Was I not checking sufficiently every detail of the care of my patients? As teams, we must rely on the expertise of our colleagues, but what is our responsibility to double and triple-check all details? How fastidious can we really be? For further discussion of such issues, I direct the reader to my recent book, *Free to Decide: Building a Life in Science and Medicine.*[7]

I will mention briefly here that Nagel classified moral luck as being of four types. Resultant moral luck concerns consequences. The traffic accident example given previously shows how the view of the situation changed when a pedestrian did or did not sustain injury after precisely the same actions by two drivers. A different category described by Nagel is circumstantial moral luck. He uses the example of Germans who did nothing to stop immoral actions by the Nazis, yet if these same people had moved to Iceland in 1929, they would have led completely different lives and would never have faced the choice as to whether to try to stop Nazi actions. Nagel's third category is constitutive moral luck, which concerns personal character. It is clear that a person's genetic makeup, family circumstances, education, and many other factors shape their character. A person's character influences one's decisions and actions. How much do these uncontrollable influences mitigate blame? Nagel's fourth category is causal moral luck, which raises issues of free will. Does free will exist and how does that work? If persons are restricted in their decisions by events that precede them, should persons not be held fully accountable for their bad decisions or actions?

Free Will: On the Knife-Edge between Determinism and Randomness

Space does not allow a full discussion of the problem of free will. Many accomplished scientists believe that free will does not exist. In their view, all human decisions are controlled deterministically by prior environmental and genetic factors, although they admit that humans have an illusion of free will. Metabolic brain scans show that the nervous command to muscles to move one's arm does occur a fraction of a second before the subject decides in their mind to move their arm. That is disconcerting, but clever arguments can explain even this unsettling observation in favor of true free will. I refer you to the elegant discussion of the mystery of free will in Martin Gardner's classic book, *The Whys of a Philosophical Scrivener*.[8] (Be sure to get the updated 1999 edition.) Gardner points out that it is a depressing thought that all of our decisions may be strictly determined, yet Gardner also finds it depressing if unbeknownst to us all of our decisions are actually made completely randomly, but our minds just fool us into making us believe that we have made those choices. He believes in a middle ground: that free will does exist by some mysterious means. Philosopher Bob Doyle has proposed a clever two-stage model of free will (the Cogito Model) that you can read about online if you search his name.

Conclusion: Learn to Live with Randomness and Make It Work for You

In sum, we cannot escape random events. Moreover, we need to appreciate that some events are truly random and that even deterministic processes may not produce results that follow a normal distribution, as some processes are nonlinear and can produce surprising fluctuations. To cope, hedge and be well prepared. Consider, for example, setting aside 5 percent of your investment portfolio to fund investments that likely will fail but that could pay off with huge gains if successful. Pay attention to details to avoid accidents that seem unlikely but that would prove devastating if they occurred; of course, also focus on common causes of accidents. Believe in the pursuit of excellence but watch out for little oversights that might grow into big problems. Make an effort to be lucky, as good luck really does happen along with the bad, and then be ready to capitalize if you are lucky. Note that I took up poker as an interesting hobby, and I made a careful study of the game to be able to react wisely and profitably if good luck occurred. So I had developed by study and practice a moderate baseline skill. Then, being skilled, I positioned myself to be lucky. This formula can work. In that 2015 poker tournament in Las Vegas in which 6,420 players entered, I finished in twenty-seventh place and won $262,574.

Endnotes:

1   N. Taleb, *The Black Swan: The Impact of the Highly Improbable* (New York: Random House, 2007).

2   C.D. Huff, J. Xing, A.R. Rogers, D. Witherspoon, and L.B. Jorde. "Mobile Elements Reveal Small Population Size in the Ancient Ancestors of *Homo sapiens*," *Proceedings of the National Academy of Science USA* 107, no. 5 (February 2010): 2147–52.

3   C. Marean, "When the Sea Saved Humanity," *Scientific American* 303, no. 2 (August 2010): 55–61.

4   S. Paabo, *Neanderthal Man: In Search of Lost Genomes* (New York: Basic Books, 2014).

5   B. Williams, "Moral Luck," *Moral Luck* (Cambridge UK: Cambridge University Press, 1982), 20–39.

6   T. Nagel, "Moral Luck," *Mortal Questions* (Cambridge UK: Cambridge University Press, 1979) 24–38.

7   J. Magner, *Free to Decide: Building a Life in Science and Medicine* (Milford, CT: James Magner with the assistance of Russell Enterprises, 2015).

8   M. Gardner, *The Whys of a Philosophical Scrivener* (New York: St. Martin's Griffin, 1999).

WINNING AT POKER: LUCK OR SKILL?

I held pocket kings, the second-best starting hand in No Limit Texas Hold'em poker, and during the preflop betting, I had chased everyone out with my moderately big bet except for one opponent. Perfect. I wanted a little action so I could win some chips with my powerful kings, but I didn't want too many opponents. The dealer announced, "Two players still in," then dealt out the flop (three shared cards placed faceup) which, unfortunately, contained an ace!

I stared forlornly at the ace, nine, three, each of a different suit, then looked up at my opponent while trying not to show my displeasure. The man across from me was about sixty-five, neatly dressed, had his chips in carefully arranged stacks, and wore a retired military baseball cap. He had an average-sized chip stack, about the same as mine. He had played very few hands during the last hour, so I knew that he was pretty tight. He was first to bet, so I waited for his decision.

He set out a moderate bet, about 80 percent of the pot, then calmly placed his hands in his lap. He looked pretty comfortable. Did he really hold an ace, or was he just representing an ace to get me to fold? Experienced players know very well that a first-bettor may make such a continuation bet without holding an ace since the bluff can win the hand perhaps 40 percent of the time. Both players are well aware of this poker move, and each player is aware that the other knows about this. The fact that a player has insight about what his opponent is thinking is a phenomenon known as recursion. Anthropologist Russell H. Tuttle noted in his 2014 book, *Apes and Human Evolution*, that nonhuman animals have varying abilities to perceive, feel, know, and, in a real sense, to think to some degree. But only humans have a recursive first-order theory of mind, with the ability to perceive, feel, know, and think what others are perceiving, feeling, knowing, and thinking. Dr. Tuttle illustrated this unique human ability by quoting the character Prince Geoffrey in James Goldman's play, *The Lion in Winter*, as Geoffrey discussed with the queen the actions of King Henry toward his sons: "I know. You know I know. I know you know I know. We know Henry knows, and Henry knows we know it. We're a knowledgeable family."

I folded my kings. It was fairly early in the tournament, and there was no need just now to take excessive risks. An older gentleman who was neatly dressed and who had played tightly in the past hour probably did hold an ace in this situation. Had the man played more recklessly during the prior hour, I might have called his bet.

Making these sorts of judgments correctly and losing the least possible number of chips while being aggressive enough to win the largest possible number of chips are skills needed to do well in poker. Another truly key skill is knowing how to properly size bets. But having an ace appear on the flop while holding pocket kings is part of the luck factor in poker. So having success in poker requires both skill and luck, but which factor is actually the more important?

How I Came to Play Poker

I'm a doctor and a scientist. I learned to play poker in 2007, played infrequently until 2014, and then got a bit more involved with the game in 2015.

I had seen Texas Hold'em poker on TV, and I first learned to play poker when my wife and I were celebrating our thirtieth wedding anniversary by spending a weekend in Atlantic City. Subsequently, my work caused me to drive weekly past some large casinos in Connecticut, so I began to stop for an hour now and then (about every eight weeks) to play in some No Limit Texas Hold'em cash games. I was willing to buy in for about $150 for a game, and I usually lost my money and then continued my drive. As a beginner, winning at poker seemed to me to be about 50 percent or 60 percent due to chance.

I was interested in the math—the probability of various events occurring—and the tactics and strategies one could use to win even when holding a poor hand. One also had to employ certain tactics and strategies to optimize winnings when one held a strong hand; if the opponents folded early in such a hand, then you were not getting proper value. I read a half dozen good books about Texas Hold'em poker, and I decided to specialize in that type of game rather than the dozen or so other poker variants because No Limit Texas Hold'em seemed to allow for use of the most sophisticated tactics and strategies. I want to emphasize that studying the books is just as important as getting experience playing the game, and I will explain later why that is true.

I also was enjoying the company of the diverse players, about 95 percent male, who shared my interest in poker. These players came from all social and economic backgrounds, and quite a few had extroverted personalities. They joked, shared a wide variety of personal and casino stories, and teased one another. They occasionally got in small arguments, which sometimes were loud and profane but rarely escalated. Some men seemed to spend a lot of money to play poker, but most were spending much less, and I was spending about the smallest amount at about seventy-five dollars per month. I was in effect taking poker lessons. And I gradually got better. With increased skill, I began to play now and then at a Saturday tournament. In contrast to a cash game, which one can join or leave whenever it is convenient, for a tournament one must pay to play poker beginning at a certain hour (although one can choose to start a little late, up to a cutoff time). The tournament continues for many hours, and only the last few remaining players win significant money. One cannot just cash out and leave at any time. Moreover, the chips are very precious because after the first few levels of play, one can no longer pay to replace one's chips; when your chips are gone, you are eliminated, often with no prize earned. The inability to replace chips causes additional nuanced tactics and strategies to become highly relevant, so about four years ago, I specialized further so as to rarely play cash games. I became a tournament specialist. In recent years, I have paid to enter about a dozen tournaments each year, and my poker profits are far ahead of my poker costs. I consider myself to be an above-average player, and my credentials include poker tournament winnings in excess of $400,000.

But Is Winning Due to Luck or Skill?

My goal in this article is not to explain how to play poker well. That would have required a fat book. Instead, I wanted to give a brief introduction, touching very generally on my poker experience, and then come directly to the question posed in the title. Here is my bottom line. In my view, winning at poker—defined as making a monetary profit over a three-year period—is about 30 percent due to luck and 70 percent due to skill.

Next I will briefly explain my opinion. For more detail, the interested reader could consult the memoir about my scientific and medical career, since the book includes an informative general chapter about Texas Hold'em poker. My book is entitled *Free to Decide: Building a Life in Science and Medicine*.

The variation in the winning and losing results of a poker player can be mathematically analyzed in a manner similar to the variation seen in many phenomena. Think back to your high school days and consider how you might analyze a plot of the heights of all your fourteen-year-old male classmates versus the heights of all your fourteen-year-old female classmates. Many of the boys were a little embarrassed at age fourteen. Now imagine what those graphs would look like if for those same persons one plotted the heights of the twenty-year-old boys versus the heights of the twenty-year-old girls. If your memories are like mine, you will appreciate what I am driving at. Any collection of measurements can have a mean and median value calculated, and the distribution of the measurements can be assessed. Technical quantities such as the variance of the measurements as well as the standard deviation of the measurements can be calculated. A given population of measurements may be found to have several outliers that seem to be unusual, and many other aspects of the set of measurements can be described. Are most twenty-year-old boys taller than most twenty-year-old girls just because of chance? Or is this difference in height due instead to some actual nonchance factor, such as hormones? This question of chance versus nonchance can be answered (within a designated degree of certainty) by mathematics—with the caveat that a large enough sample size is available so that the calculations will be valid.

Let me give a poker example that I used in my memoir, with arithmetic numbers adapted from the mathisfun.com website. A convenient measure of performance for poker cash game players is the amount of cash won or lost by the end of each day of play. Suppose that over five days a poker player has won money every day. He is either very lucky or very skilled, or possibly both, in view of the short time frame of this sample. His winnings on the five days are as follows: $600, $470, $170, $430 and $300. His average amount won per day is $394. But the numbers from day to day vary a bit, and the technical quantity called the variance of this sample can start to be calculated by subtracting the mean winnings from the amount won each day. This gives five positive and negative numbers, so a convention is to square each difference simply to eliminate the negative numbers. One then adds these squared numbers and divides by the number of days to determine the variance. This is the arithmetic operation: $[(206)^2 + (76)^2 + (-224)^2 + (36)^2 + (-94)^2] / 5 = 21,704$ and the unit of this number is "dollars squared."

Conveniently, the variance is the square of the standard deviation, which is a widely used and well-understood tool for assessing data that are in a so-called normal distribution. In science, at this point one must stop and ask whether the phenomenon under study is actually producing measurements in a normal distribution, but for our purposes, we will assume that this is true for this poker player. Thus, when we take the square root of 21,704 dollars squared, we have approximately $147. In a normal distribution, one then can assess each of the individual data points to determine if any of the measurements is far out of what the usual pattern might dictate. In a normal distribution, 68 percent of the data points fall within one standard deviation of the mean, while 95 percent of the data points fall within two standard deviations of the mean.

Now we must discuss a very useful concept called the coefficient of variation (COV). This is formally calculated for a set of results by dividing the standard deviation by the mean. In this case, the COV is $147 / $394 = 0.373, and notice that there is no $ sign in front of the COV. Because dollars are being divided by dollars, the units cancel out, so the COV is a dimensionless number. That is an advantage of use of the COV, since a standard deviation must always be viewed in terms of a mean with proper consideration of units, whereas the dimensionless COV can be used more easily when comparing data from different sources with different units.

Let's return to assessing the string of cash wins by our player. One should view the mean of $394 as the current best estimate of the true win rate (in this case, a win rate over the period of five days). The standard deviation of $147 is a measure of the luck factor encountered by this player during this period of five days. The standard deviation is substantially smaller than the mean, a remarkable result. Thus, for this player during these few days, it seems that skill was a more important factor than luck. A vital caveat, however, is that our sample was collected over a very limited time period, which calls into serious question the validity of our results. Analyses of players' actual results over ten days of poker (about three thousand hands of poker), or even over thirty days of poker (about nine thousand hands) show that the standard deviation remains larger than the mean in nearly all of these players. In other words, even assessing thirty days of poker, the luck factor is large. For very good players, the standard deviation usually does not diminish to become smaller than the mean until a player collects data from several months of poker, generally at least twenty thousand hands or more. That is why a famous, respected, global website (The Hendon Mob) that collects results of poker players and attempts to assign them a skill score makes use of data from the most recent thirty-six months of experience for a given player. It takes three years of play to really begin to see how well a person is playing due to skill.

But why should skill level be so difficult to pull out of poker statistics if all players over a relatively short time (three months?) get exactly the same hole cards? Should not the only difference in results over three months then be due to skill, not whether one gets certain cards? My answer is that it is true that over a few months all players get the same hole cards, but there is something else important going on. In just a few months, all players do not experience the same collisions with the same frequencies! A collision is when a player with pocket kings runs into an opponent holding pocket aces, for example. But collisions are also constructed using the five cards on the board, not just from the two hole cards, so it likely would be decades before all players saw the same collisions. My seat-of-the-pants estimate is that although all players may see exactly the same hole cards over a period of three months, it might take fifty to five hundred years for them to experience the same collisions. Late in a tournament, a couple of highly improbable favorable collisions could swing a tournament decisively to the benefit of the lucky player.

An attentive reader might take issue with the last sentence. How is it possible that a highly improbable collision will often determine the winner of a poker tournament, since that event should be rare? And herein lies a vital point about poker and about the world in general. Any given prespecified highly improbable event will occur very rarely. But because there are billions of possible highly improbable events, highly improbable events occur very commonly. It is just that we cannot predict which highly improbable event will occur in this minute or in this hour. Moreover, many natural processes are nonlinear. The activities or measurements of interest do not follow a normal distribution, but instead a very small input can result in an unexpected and large output. For further insights about this, read the marvelous book by Nassim Taleb, *The Black Swan: The Impact of the Highly Improbable*.

There are many important lessons to appreciate from the material presented thus far. Let me expand on two key thoughts.

1. Poker requires skill, but retains a sizeable component of luck. Thus, one should not overspend on this game. Only bet money that you can afford to lose. That said, if one takes $500 to a casino on a Saturday to play poker, you must play fearlessly and play according to correct fundamental principles of the game even if that seems not to be working well for you that day. An old saying is that "Scared money can't win." So you need to know well the fundamentally correct strategies and tactics and then execute on them with few mistakes. If other players take big risks but beat you anyway, that is just part of the variance of the game. Such losses are called "bad beats." Although it may not be too comforting as you pass your money to another player, if you lost because of a bad beat, then at least you know that you played correctly but happened to lose on this day.

2. You cannot learn to play poker well merely by playing at the table. Of course, practical experience is necessary, but study of books or videos is required. Discussion of poker hands with knowledgeable friends or a tutor also will help. You may have won on Saturday, but if the win was based on fundamentally faulty play, then repeating that multiple times over the next year will not reliably produce positive results.

I want to illustrate how big the luck factor is, even for some of the best poker players in the world, if one is focused only on a short period of time.

The most prestigious annual poker tournament in the world, the Main Event of the World Series of Poker, was held in July 2017 in Las Vegas. Each player paid $10,000 to enter, and most players lost their entry fee within three days. But about 15 percent of players won at least the minimum prize of $15,000, so the small profit allowed some costs of the trip to be reimbursed.

These fortunate players are said to have "cashed" in the tournament. But each of the 7,221 entrants in 2017 were not seeking to win a minimum prize; they wanted to finish higher up and potentially win hundreds of thousands of dollars, or more. Among the 7,221 entrants, there were 272 women. The average age of an entrant was 40.6 years, and they represented eighty-three countries. There were 1,084 entrants who won a cash prize. Scott Blumstein won the first place prize of $8,150,000. Scott had played poker online in New Jersey, where it is legal, and in many tournaments on the East Coast. He had cashed previously in more than forty small tournaments since 2012. He was a recent college graduate with an accounting background. He had never before played poker in Las Vegas, and this was his first time to enter the prestigious Main Event. Needless to say, no one had predicted that Scott would win this tournament. He had to be skilled to win, but also his stars had to align in just the right way for this to occur.

Notably, prior to the start of the Main Event, a panel of experts listed their consensus as to which top global players most likely would cash in the Main Event. To fulfill the prediction of the panel, these twenty-three players needed merely to finish among the top 1,084 entrants, so it had been expected that many would win a minimum prize. Below I reproduce the list of these famous players (in alphabetical order), and next to each name I note their actual performance in the 2017 WSOP Main Event.

Gaelle Baumann	Did not cash
Joe Cada	948th place, won $16,024
Johnny Chan	Did not cash
Dan Colman	Did not cash
Jonathan Duhamel	Did not cash
Antonio Esfandiari	Did not cash

Phil Hellmuth	Did not cash
Maria Ho	Did not cash
William Kassouf	Did not cash
Adrian Mateos	Did not cash
Jason Mercier	Did not cash
Greg Merson	Did not cash
Michael Mizrachi	Did not cash
Chris Moneymaker	Did not cash
Carlos Mortensen	984th place, won $15,000
Daniel Negreanu	Did not cash
Qui Nguyen	Did not cash
Michael Phelps	Did not cash
Doug Polk	Did not cash
Ryan Riess	Did not cash
Vanessa Selbst	Did not cash
Richard Seymour	Did not cash
Jason Somerville	Did not cash

Thus, only two of these twenty-three expert players (8.7 percent) managed to win at least a minimum prize. Recall that 15 percent of all entrants won at least a minimum prize, so these top experts seemed to do a little worse than a typical player. Why did these talented and experienced players do so poorly? I believe that this is just an illustration of the high variance at work in poker results. One cannot judge skill based on just a week or less of poker play.

What Can a Concerned Poker Player Do to Mitigate This High Variance in Poker?

In closing this article, let me first give a rather pithy answer to the question heading this section: "Not much!"

With that realistic response out of the way, let me add a few other thoughts. Although we can do little to change many aspects of the universe, we can change ourselves, especially our skills, attitudes, and outlook. So let me list some suggestions.

1. Accept that there will be high variance in your poker performance. Plan your financial and personal matters accordingly.
2. Have a realistic and mature attitude about winning at poker. You will lose a lot as well as win. It makes no sense to fume about a bad beat. Resolve to understand the fundamental principles about how to win at poker and then apply them even if they seem not to be working in the short term. If you know the principles better than an opponent, you should win more often.
3. Importantly, recognize that high variance can sometimes work for you as well as against you. When playing poker, find ways to put yourself in a position to get lucky. But prior to the game, be sure that you have studied ways to reap maximum profit from situations in which a good card fortuitously could show up. Then, when that happens, you can take full advantage of it. I developed this technique after reading Nassim Taleb's marvelous book, *The Black Swan: The Impact of the Highly Improbable*. Consider reading Taleb's book.
4. If you are having a losing day, you only increase the risk of more losses if you stray from the fundamental principles of good poker. You need not try to finish each day by breaking even; that will not be possible. Recognize

that "it is all one long poker session." What happens after one week or one month should not elate or depress you. You must continue to study the fundamental principles of poker using books, videos, and discussions with mentors. You can only judge your play over a period of about three years.

5. Since so many players have become well educated about No Limit Texas Hold'em, you might try to find a small edge against your competition by learning to play well one of the other poker game variants. A friend I met at Foxwoods, Joe H., has found some success by playing the variety of poker known as Razz.

6. If after three years of study and table experience you find that you have lost money, you should consider quitting poker. But don't forget the humorous and pleasant experiences you have had along the way, even if in the end they cost you some money.

THE GERMAN-AMERICAN AND THE GERMAN

The past is gone, yet long chains of actions and consequences tumble forward into our present day and beyond. My father, Louis, a full-blooded Irish-American, died in 2018 at age 92 when the flu shot failed to give adequate protection, and the flu turned into pneumonia. He had married a full-blooded German-American. After we buried dad, the family strolled through the old, small-town cemetery in Illinois to find graves of other relatives. We found many, including a new one I had never before visited. Robert A. Steinbrecher (1895-1923) was my maternal grandmother's older brother who had died young from wounds sustained in World War I.

Tombstone of Robert Steinbrecher, Calvary Cemetery, Quincy, IL

I decided that day that I would use a little spare time to find out more about what had happened to Robert. As my brother and I cleaned out dad's house, some old photos and news clippings turned up that aided my research. There was a fine photo of Robert as a handsome, muscular soldier. He was wearing a high-collared, long-sleeved Army shirt with two large front pockets, and he sported a broad-brimmed hat with a knotted cord as a hat band. The photo was dated July 2, 1918 on the back, and likely was taken at Fort Gordon in Georgia just a few weeks after he had enlisted on May 27. His honorable discharge paper and his obituary from the Quincy Herald Whig provided additional details. Robert, a machinist with no military experience, had volunteered for the Army and joined the 18th Division, the 51st Replacement Company.

After brief training, his company was shipped to France. In September, 1918, less than four months after enlisting, Robert and his fellow infantrymen charged forward through thick woods in the Argonne Forest offensive, a sweeping advance

Robert Steinbrecher, July, 1918

across a broad front that was intended to end the war. Within days he received shrapnel wounds, and his lungs were horribly burned by poison gas, leaving him barely able to breathe. He survived the incident and was shipped back to the US where he spent substantial time in several hospitals, including VA Hospital No. 30 in Chicago. Constantly coughing blood and unable to maintain his weight, he gradually became a tall skeleton of a man such that on May 17, 1922, when he attended his sister's wedding (the bride, Loretta, was my grandmother), he chose to stand in the back of group photos so that only his eyes, nose and forehead appeared. But his gaunt half-face told the tale. He died the next year of pneumonia. His parents later were buried next to him.

Of note, the Argonne-Meuse Offensive began northwest of Verdun on September 26 and continued until the Armistice was signed on November 11, 1918. It is believed to have been one of the deadliest battles in US history in which more than 26,000 Americans and 28,000 Germans were killed, and hundreds of thousands more wounded. Many French soldiers also were killed, but no estimate has ever been accepted as official.

Robert Steinbrecher's Honorable Discharge

Robert Steinbrecher on May 17, 1922. Robert, thin and ailing, is in the back row wearing a hat, his face barely visible. He attended the wedding of Arthur Metzger and Loretta Steinbrecher (my maternal grandparents), who are standing at far right.

I want to supplement this sad tale of a bright, goodhearted man with the story of a different young man who was likely born in 1891, just four years before Robert. Most of us have heard stories of the intrepid Bletchley Park codebreakers, including Alan Turing; they cracked the German Enigma code during World War II. The film, *The Imitation Game*, dramatized that feat, which blazed a technological path to modern computers. Less has been written, however, about the German breaking of Allied codes, accomplished in large part by a single, particularly talented engineer, Wilhelm Tranow. He was a young math and radio enthusiast in the early years of the twentieth century. Because so few people knew much about radio in mid-1914, the young Tranow was posted aboard the German battleship *Pommern* as a radio operator. While on watch, he picked up a coded message from the cruiser *Breslau* as that ship tried to communicate with headquarters, but the signal was weak, so Tranow forwarded the message to be certain that fleet command had received it. Tranow was surprised to receive a response from headquarters a few minutes later that they were having difficulty decoding the message. So Tranow used pen and paper to play with the message, successfully decoded it, and radioed the result to headquarters. Personnel at fleet command at first were grateful, but later Tranow received a stern warning from headquarters that he must never decode secret information. A few weeks later, someone at headquarters realized that this lowly sailor might actually be very useful to try to break British codes as well as improve German codes, and Tranow was transferred to a fledgling codebreaking group, the Nachrichten-Abteilung at Neumünster. Tranow was fortunate since the *Pommern* was subsequently sunk at the Battle of Jutland on June 1, 1916, by shells and two torpedoes, which broke the ship in half, killing the entire crew of more than 700 men.

At the end of the war, Tranow was retained in Berlin as part of a tiny, eight-member code-breaking unit. In 1919, Tranow cracked Britain's Government Telegraph Code used to transmit reports of warships. In 1927 and 1932, he and colleagues broke important French codes, and in 1932, he broke the British four-letter naval code. These impressive achievements led to an expansion of his codebreaking group, which became known as Beobachtungsdienst, often spoken about as B-Dienst. By 1935, Tranow and his assistants had broken the Royal Navy's most widely used code, the five-digit Naval Code known as München. This in part was accomplished by comparing the published routes of merchant ships (given in *Lloyds Weekly Shipping Reports*) with coded messages. Though not a Nazi, Tranow was given a major leadership role in B-Dienst. In the first days of World War II Tranow could report the locations of all the major warships around the world. Tranow also could read much of British Naval Cypher No. 1, which revealed the English and French plans to occupy Norway, prompting Germany to invade Norway first on April 9, 1940. Tranow's team then deciphered multiple additional Allied codes during World War II, including Naval Cipher 3, which allowed German submarines to know the precise routes of many Allied convoys between February, 1942, and mid-June, 1943. This resulted in the easy sinking of scores of Allied ships and the deaths of an estimated 10,000 Allied seamen during that short 16-month period.

Antiaircraft Guns on the Tower of a U-boat

At the end of the war, Tranow was questioned by Allied experts at Flensburg in May, 1945, but released. He has been viewed as a brilliant man who honorably served his country during wartime. He kept a low profile during the 1950s, and it is not known when or where he died.

Robert Steinbrecher, though born in Quincy, Illinois, was of German heritage and the family spoke some German at home. As the ancestors were from Southern Germany, they were a Catholic family. The weekly Mass in Quincy was in Latin, but the sermons always were in German – until about 1916, when the pastor announced that henceforth the sermons would be in English. Such changes and conversations in the community likely influenced the patriotic young Robert, who enlisted to serve his country.

Wilhelm Tranow was a highly intelligent young German, and the man at headquarters who recognized Tranow's talent and first moved him from his lowly position as a radio operator to a codebreaking unit probably accomplished more for Germany by that one action than on all the other days that he served.

What can one say about the ultimate meaning and utility of the lives of Robert and Wilhelm, who fought against each other in World War I? One served honorably and died young without wife or children. The other survived World War I and went on to develop astonishing codebreaking methods, and he passed on that knowledge to colleagues. Wilhelm served his nation skillfully and honorably, though in support of what turned out to be, with later revelations, an evil cause that did not deserve his talents. Wilhelm also died, as far as we know, without wife or children. Like swimmers paddling in a raging river, both men were caught up in overwhelmingly powerful historical forces that dominated their thinking and shaped their goals and actions, leading to tragic consequences. However, there is triumph for both men as well. I believe we can say that these men did what they thought was right, and performed valiantly. Today we are surrounded by different but comparably strong currents, and we can only do our best and press forward. Let us pray that a century from now, history will not have played any tricks on us such that our genuine efforts, unbeknownst to us, are misdirected. Let us hope that our honest hard work to live, and love, and make the world a better place actually will end up benefitting our families, as well as humanity.

Sources:

The obituary of Robert Steinbrecher, The Quincy Herald Whig, 1923

Kahn, David. *Hitler's Spies: German Military Intelligence in World War II*, Da Capo Press, Boston, 2000

Multiple sources online were consulted to check minor details. The U-boat image was a free download courtesy of Pixabay, and is not copyrighted.

ACKNOWLEDGMENTS

I am sincerely grateful to my wife, Glenda Pritchett, for checking my grammar and for suggestions on some of the early drafts of these pieces.

My parents lovingly supported me as I grew up and pursued my education. They provided sterling examples of what it means to love and be loved, to sacrifice, to work hard, to be thrifty, and to use common sense. They also taught me how to follow one's interests and to enjoy life.

Scores of dedicated educators have invested their time and efforts over decades to help me learn to read and write, do arithmetic, and other topics, including calculus, biochemistry, physics, internal medicine, endocrinology, clinical research, and medical affairs. My teachers were Catholic nuns, religious persons, and lay persons in Catholic elementary and high school. My first calculus teacher (at the public high school), Houston Kirk, was particularly patient and superb. An elderly man, Walter Buss, taught me much about chess and is still fondly remembered. A college biology teacher and academic advisor, Judith H. Willis, had a profound effect on my development as a competent biologist and future student of medicine. As a young adult, many mentors helped me enormously, including Bruce Weintraub and Arthur Schneider. More recently, Paula Munier suggested that I write a poker mystery when I was attending a writers' conference in New York City in 2018.

I am also grateful to have been granted permission to reproduce in this book pieces that were previously published.

"How Do I Politely Defend Religion to my Best Friend, an Atheist?" was published in *Today's American Catholic* newspaper, March 2019.

"Jesus at my Back Door: When Science Meets Religion" was published in *Today's American Catholic* newspaper, January/February 2018.

"Was George Washington Aided by Miracles?" was published in *Today's American Catholic* newspaper, May 2018.

ABOUT THE AUTHOR

James Magner, MD is an endocrinologist and scientist who spent years studying the biochemistry and physiology of the pituitary hormone, TSH, and providing medical supervision for several projects within the pharmaceutical industry. He is an avid chess player and an expert poker player who placed twenty-seventh in the World Series of Poker Main Event, Las Vegas, in 2015. Dr. Magner is married and has two adult daughters. This debut collection of fiction is his third book.